I0691902

ISBN: 9781763733930

First Edition.

This is a work of fiction, first written in 2012. Names, characters, places, and incidents are either the product of the author's imagination or used fictitiously. Any resemblance to actual events, locales, or persons, living or dead, is entirely coincidental.

Cover Design & Illustration by the author, P R Bird

Trigger warning: Explicit content, R18+ (NOT FOR YOUNGER READERS)

This book contains mature themes subject to brutal violence, domestic violence, and murder.

PART I

Brazen Knight

As the sun began to rise into the sky, casting long shadows through the dense canopy of the forest. A gentle breeze rustled the leaves, carrying with it the earthy scent of pine and the distant murmur of a stream. At the edge of the forest, where the trees gave way to a narrow dirt road, a man sat with his back against a sturdy oak, an apple in hand. He wore a weathered cloak that blended seamlessly with the forest's shadows. His eyes, sharp and vigilant, scanned the horizon as he took a bite of the crisp, red apple. The juice dripped down his chin, but he paid it no mind, his thoughts focused on the task ahead.

He had been waiting for this moment for days. Since dropping the raven that sent word of the pending arrival of a caravan from the kingdom of Athelstan. It was a hefty caravan, known to carry precious cargo—gold, spices, and plump livestock. Today, it would pass through this very road, and the man intended to intercept it.

The sound of distant wheels and the clinking of harnesses reached his ears, growing louder with each passing moment. His heart quickened, but his exterior remained calm and composed. He finished his apple, tossing the core into the underbrush, and rose to his feet, brushing off the dirt from his cloak. As the caravan came into view, he stepped out from the shadows, his presence commanding and unyielding. The lead driver, a burly man with a thick beard, pulled the reins, bringing the caravan to a halt. The horse snorted and pawed at the ground, sensing the tension in the air.

"Who goes there?" the driver called out, his voice gruff and wary.

The man raised a hand in a gesture of peace, though his eyes betrayed a steely determination. "I mean you no harm," he said, his voice steady. "But I must ask you to hand over your cargo. And your goat."

The driver glanced over his shoulder at his companions, uncertainty flickering in his eyes. "And why should we do that?" he demanded.

The man took a step closer, his hand resting on the hilt of the sword at his side. "Because if you don't," he replied, his tone leaving no room for doubt, "things will get very unpleasant for you and your men. And your rather plump goat."

For a moment, silence hung heavy in the air, the only sound the rustling of leaves and the distant call of a bird.

"The goat is intended as a gift. You cannot have it," spoke the driver, "Now move, sir. I bid you. We have affairs to attend to that are of no interest to a wanderer like you."

"What's going on up there, Gunther?" called one of the men from the behind the cart.

"Nothing to fear. We'll be past this fool in a moment," called Gunther, his voice carrying the length of the caravan.

"Fool?" asked the wanderer, raising his eyebrows, ostensibly surprised.

"Aye. What fool would attempt such a heist alone, against ten men?"

"Oh, but you are mistaken. This is no heist."

"No heist? But you demanded my goat, and my cargo. If a heist is not what you intend, then why stop us?" the driver queried, "What is this?"

The man's patience had worn thin. The caravan driver, emboldened by his numbers, refused to comply with his demands. The man took a step toward the cart, raising his hand to the chestnut steed that continued pawing at the earth, its breathing grating and rapid. The man ran his hand over its neck so as to calm the animal, trailing his touch down the horses side to its knee. He took a small blade and pressed it against the steeds leg, dragging the cold steel against the flesh in one swift movement. The steed reared in protest, blood gushing from its artery.

"This is a murder."

In another swift movement, his blade sliced through the reins of the horse, and travelled through the air, embedding itself into the throat of the driver before he could utter another word.

The horse reared again, kicking against the carriage. The man slapped its rump, sending it bolting into the forest, leaving a bloodied trail that would soon lure a pack of hungry wolves. Cries of protest and confusion erupted from the back of the caravan. Guards shouted; their voices tinged with panic as they scrambled to regain control of their own steeds. The man moved with practiced precision, his bow already in hand. He nocked an arrow and took aim, his eyes narrowing as he focused on the approaching figures.

The first guard to round the corner barely had time to register the wanderer's presence before an arrow pierced his chest. He fell to the ground with a strangled cry, clutching at the shaft protruding from his body. The man didn't hesitate, swiftly drawing and releasing another arrow. The second guard dropped; an expression of shock frozen on his face. More guards surged forward, their shouts growing louder. Arrows flew true, each one finding its mark with deadly accuracy. One by one, the guards fell, their cries silenced by the swift justice of the bow. The forest, once filled with the sounds of nature, now echoed with the grim aftermath of the skirmish.

As the last of the guard fell, the man lowered his bow, his breath coming in steady, controlled bursts. He surveyed the scene, his eyes cold and unyielding. The caravan lay abandoned, bodies scattered across the dirt road. The man swiftly prepared for his next task, moving toward the carriage that contained the most precious piece to his puzzle.

†

The morning sun filtered through the ornate windows of Princess Sintra's chamber, casting a warm glow on the delicate tapestries that adorned the walls. Sintra sat at her vanity, her reflection a picture of serene beauty, though her eyes betrayed a hint of unease. Her handmaiden, Elara, stood behind her, gently brushing the princess's long, raven-black hair.

"Your Highness," Elara said, her voice soft and reassuring. "The wedding gown will truly be a masterpiece. I have a vision; the finest silks and the most intricate lacework."

Sintra sighed, her fingers tracing the edge of the vanity. "It sounds beautiful, Elara. But I can't help but feel... trapped."

Elara paused, meeting Sintra's gaze in the mirror. "It's natural to feel this way, Princess. A wedding is a significant change, especially to someone like Aleron Elowen."

Sintra's lips tightened into a thin line. "Aleron is not just anyone. I wish I could escape this royal decree."

Elara resumed brushing, her strokes gentle and rhythmic, trying to offer some comfort. "I wish I could ease your fears. But know that you are not alone in this. We will face whatever comes together."

Sintra closed her eyes, imagining the gown. "Thank you, Elara. Your presence is my only solace in this."

Elara smiled warmly, though her eyes were filled with concern. "That's what I'm here for. Together, we'll make this day as bearable as it can be."

"Maybe I could drive a blade through his heart on our wedding night."

"Oh, you mustn't say such atrocious things," growled the maid, "What if somebody heard you?"

"Yes, I suppose you're right," teased the girl smiling devilishly, knowing that her maid could not see the expression across her face, "But why do I need a new gown, wont the one I'm wearing suffice?"

Her silver gown draped loosely around her bare shoulders, revealing her pale amber skin that gleamed under the moon's gentle light. The silver satin cascaded from her shoulders, gathered at her breast and waist, flowing over her petite frame and flaring out far beyond her dainty, bare feet. Elara, her personal maid, had always tailored her gowns and eveningwear much too long for any occasion. Yet, she was also the one who ran the most glorious baths from time to time.

"My lady, you are not a child anymore. You must look presentable if you are to rule the throne as your father has for many years, and without quarrel."

"I am eighteen years, still a child."

"Not a child," protested Elara, gathering and twisting the girl's hair into a lengthy braid.

"Child at heart, maybe."

"Well, as free-spirited and juvenile as you think you may be, you are still a princess, and you will reign."

"I wish I was an ordinary girl," she scoffed.

"No more ordinary than a slave's mistress that lies with dogs?"

The princess stiffened, knowing quite well that her maid had caught her sneaking back into her bedchamber, the hem of her gown ruined and soiled with matter and grime. The filth was no wonder; it was far too long for the princess; even when she clutched it with her left hand, it dragged along the ground.

"Ah, my lady remembers," teased the maid. "I don't doubt the wash-maid does as well. You stank to high heaven," laughed Elara.

"Elara, I love you like a mother but if you speak another word of this, I will see to it that my father has your head," snapped the princess.

"Oh, Sintra, your false words wound me."

Elara placed a silver ribbon in the princess's braided mane and left the bedchamber in silence, closing the heavy wooden door behind her. Sintra sighed, deeply repentant of her words. Shame filled her heart as the hurt expression on Elara's face beleaguered her mind. She loved the dear old woman as if she were her own kin, but Sintra's secret could not escape the walls of the citadel. Her own head would be put on a stake and paraded through the streets of Crevark.

She sat at her window, looking out at the wide-open land that was soon to be hers; her kingdom that she would one day rule as Queen. She looked to the moon and sighed again. It was almost full, which only meant that she would wed Aleron in a short few days' time.

Her beloved wolf now by her side, Nyom rested her head on the princess's lap. A low whine escaped its throat as her large golden eyes peered up at Sintra.

"Oh Nyom," said Princess Sintra, taking a long, slender finger and scratching behind the animal's ear. "What am I to do?"

Tears began to fall from the princess's emerald, green eyes, landing in infinitesimal drops on the thick white fur of the wolf's snout. Nyom had been a gift from her father, King Alaric, on her seventeenth birthday. Aleron despised the animal, spitting and striking at it every chance he could. But this was the least of Sintra's worries, as she felt that the minute

Lord Aleron Elowen took her hand, her wolf would be sent away to the dungeons.

"That beast shall not see daylight again," Lord Elowen had said once after Nyom snapped at his leg.

"She fears for my safety," Sintra had replied. "She senses your malice and strives to protect me."

But this remark had only been met with the back of Aleron's hand against the princess's cheek. Sintra never understood why her father would let such an imbecile have his daughter's hand. But he was the king. A king who grew ignorant with the passing of his wife.

Queen Caprice, Princess Serena and Princess Serillah, along with the young Prince Soren, were all murdered while playing in the fields beyond the king's guard, away from safety. Aleron claimed to have been an innocent passerby when he evidently slaughtered the perpetrators and brought Soren' lifeless body before the King, attempting to appear heroic and gallant.

"I could not save them, my lord," he had said, weeping fraudulently before King Alaric. "Not Serena, not Serillah, not Soren, not the Queen; there were too many against me alone. Oh, how I wasn't able to save Your Majesty, Queen Caprice."

He clutched Soren's dead body in a back-and-forth sway as the king entered the field on horseback, his eldest daughter by his side.

The King did not know and would never know of the treachery within Aleron. No ambush occurred, that murdered the Queen and her children.

"I don't believe him," said the princess, "I'd rather give him my hand *in a wooden box*," she had stated from that day, "I would soon learn to cope with the other."

"No matter your quarrel, young Sintra, *both* your hands will be his once you wed him and you *will* take the throne in my honour."

Sintra knew she could not protest to her father; no matter the strength of kinship, he would have her head if she dared refuse his wishes. She pitied her father's ignorance.

She often casts her mind back to that day they found Aleron alongside her slaughtered family, and beguiled her mind, is the oddity of the strange cleanliness of him when he claimed to have just slaughtered a small army. No scratch, no cut, no bruise was in sight. From that moment, the princess questioned the presence of an ambush. But she dared not speak of such things before the King; she had no proof, no evidence that Aleron was truly the enemy.

At times, the princess harboured a profound fear for her own life, dreading the day she would wed Lord Elowen. His desire for knighthood was swiftly fulfilled, yet it was promptly overshadowed the moment he beheld Sintra. He coveted Sintra, and she was bestowed upon him, but what fate awaited her once he savoured the taste of power? The princess was acutely aware that if she were to wed Aleron, she would not love him as a wife ought to love her husband. Instead, she would despise him, lying awake at night, scheming his demise until he departed from her side the following day. She will lay silent and stiff beneath him while he uses her to pleasure himself, grunting and sweating like a deranged boar until he empties his defiled seeds inside her. She will bear and raise his children and grow old and hag-like, while Aleron empties his ghastly seeds into whores, stuffing his face with meat and gulping down wine until he dies a pathetic excuse for a King.

Her cheeks flushed a delicate pink, glistening with tears, she endeavoured to avoid thoughts of the grim future that awaited her. Even the sight of the nearly full moon from her window churned her stomach. A sigh escaped her lips as she rose and stepped onto the balcony, leaning against the cold stone railing, gazing out over the darkened landscape cloaked by the night sky. Her reverie was abruptly interrupted by a movement in the gardens below.

Sintra strained her eyes, peering into the dense shrubs that lined the stone pathway, which wound and twisted through short pygmy plum trees. She cast her eye over the marble statues of young, naked children, and the pond at the garden's centre, home to beautiful golden carp and delicate lime green lily pads floating on the water's surface. Her gaze drifted through the slender pine trees standing tall like Crevark guards against the citadel's stone wall, but she saw nothing. She traced the stone path with her eyes, following it through the courtyard below, but again, nothing came into view.

"Princess," came a whisper.

Nyom was at her side in an instant, a deep growl rumbling from her throat as she peered over the balcony into the courtyard below. Her thick white fur stood tall and stiff; her hackles raised in warning.

"Silence," whispered Sintra, gently pushing the white wolf aside and straining her own ears to listen.

"Sintra," the voice called again.

Without hesitation, she leapt back into her bedchamber, striding across to the other side and closing the door behind her before Nyom could barge past. The wolf whined and scratched at the door, longing to be with the princess.

"Hush, Nyom, I won't be long," she whispered, standing to check if the hallway was clear.

Gathering the lengthy hem of her silver gown, Sintra slowly made her way toward the great marble staircase, taking each step cautiously to avoid making a sound or stumbling on her garment. The hallways were dark and silent, the marble floors achingly cold beneath her bare feet. The princess slowed as she reached the end of the stairs, peering around the corner before briskly walking into the darkness when she was sure the hallway was empty. Up ahead was the dimly lit bedchamber of her father, King Alaric, which appeared unoccupied as she peered around the door. The warmth of the fireplace greeted her, softening her lips that had grown cold and stiff.

The next dimly lit chamber was the library, filled with wonderful books that mostly belonged to her mother, Queen Caprice. Fond of reading, her collection had grown over the years. Sintra often feigned illness to spend a day in the library, preferring it to sitting by her father's side on the throne in the great hall of the Citadel. There, the people and slaves of Crevark tested the King's patience, begging for wealth, land, and sufficient animals and food.

What troubled Sintra most was the haggling of sacrifices and the surrender of slaves and townsfolk. Slaves would lose a finger or two to secure scarce food for their families for a month. Others were forced to sacrifice a child to a life of slavery to pay off debts owed to the King. A child of nine years was bargained for the price of a single sheep so his family would not starve for a month. The slaves of Crevark were accumulated through such bargains, with more children being sold so their families wouldn't starve to death. Sintra was once punished for crying after witnessing a child of five years being swapped for a small cow, condemning the child to a life of slavery.

"Cease the tears and childish sobbing. Small children are better suited for cleaning grime and mud from horses' saddles and headstalls; their fingers are smaller," the King had once laughed. "They make for better stable slaves than grown men."

Sintra's heart sank to hear her father speak such words.

"You are a cruel man. What have you done with my father? The father I know would shed tears for such malice. You sadden me, you disgust me," she spat at his feet. "The Queen would have your head if she knew."

But Sintra had been struck down by the back of his hand when she dared to test his anger upon such a reply. She coward and hid for three weeks after that, not daring to open her mouth.

A warm, friendly face greeted the princess as she peered around the door into the library.

"Princess, what a pleasant surprise. To what do I owe the pleasure?" asked Cornelius, taking her hand in his.

"I was just roaming around the citadel, my friend. On my way to wish my father a good night."

Cornelius was a gentle old man, her favourite person in the citadel aside from Elara. White tufts of hair sprouted over his head, thin and feather-like with age. Crow's feet pinched at the corners of his eyes, accompanied by many other friendly wrinkles that greeted Sintra as the old man smiled fondly at her. The breast pocket of his green button-down vest bulged with his half-moon spectacles. His kind blue eyes appeared small and beady without them perched on his round nose.

"Oh, you're not staying?" asked Cornelius, a note of disappointment in his voice.

"Oh, Cornelius, my friend. I shall be back tomorrow if not sooner. You know how I enjoy your company and the company of these wonderful books," smiled the princess. "Especially the ones that belonged to my mother."

"Yes, Queen Caprice loved to read."

Sintra smiled once more, rested her small hands on the old man's shoulders before sweeping out through the doorway and into the cold darkness of the long hallway.

As she approached the hallway leading to the courtyard, a shiver ran down her spine at the sound of her name in Aleron's mouth.

"Sintra will make a fine Queen, my lord. *My* Queen," Aleron's voice boomed from the great hall of the Citadel.

The princess stiffened against the stone wall, hidden by the darkness as she crept toward the dimly lit chamber.

"Yes, but my daughter is a handful."

"My hands are empty, sir, and strong. Capable of restraining her if needed."

"She believes you killed the Queen. Are your hands more than empty, Lord Elowen? Dirty, perhaps?"

"My hands are cleaner than a newborn child's, my lord. They are merely stained with regret and disappointment, as I could not save the Queen. Not Serillah, not Serena, not Soren."

Stained with the blood of my brother and sisters, stained with the blood and innocence of my mother, Sintra thought to herself, spitting in distaste at Aleron. How she longed to interrupt their quarrel, to barge through the heavy wooden doors, but she had to reach the courtyard unseen and unheard before the night was through.

"I am aware of this, but how could you let thirty men slaughter my family?"

"There were too many, my lord. Thirty men against me alone is not a fair battle."

"Tell me then, knight of knights, were my wife and children slaughtered before you unsheathed your sword? Was their blood spilled long before you entered the fields?"

"Yes, my lord," Elowen whispered.

"Then why bother slaughter the assassins when they had already accomplished what they came forth to do?"

"Vengeance, sir? To punish them by death?"

"Vengeance?" asked the King, his voice rising in anger, "Why did you feel the need to avenge my wife and children when you knew not who they were?"

"I-,"

"Was the price to be paid, yours?"

"Someone-,"

"Hold your tongue or I will have it in my hand," snapped the King.

Sintra stifled a laugh, clutching her mouth in the darkness.

"If the price to be paid was none other than my own, then why not bring the men to *me* so that *I* may avenge my family and choose a punishment that would suffice?"

"I feared they would not follow, my lord."

"You feared they would not follow, so you took the matter into your own hands?"

"Yes, my lord."

"Why not send for the King's Guard? I have ample men, Aleron Elowen, double thirty."

"I suppose, my lord."

"No, you do not *suppose*," said King Alaric in a low voice.

Sintra knew he was as furious as ten crazed men, yet she did not care much for Aleron.

"If you would let me explain-,"

"Explain!" snapped the King, impatient.

"On the day I wandered into the fields and came across the Queen and her children surrounded by thirty men. I unsheathed my sword. By the time I had slaughtered half the men in that field, the Queen and her children were dead. Their blood spilled and their garments stained. What was I to do but slaughter the rest of the men? I could not let them escape with this act on their hands. I had to avenge my Queen, for you, for Crevark."

Lies, all lies, thought Sintra.

Hearing footsteps approaching, the princess quickly scurried past the great hall, and out into the courtyard. The cold night air greeted her face and bare shoulders, the stone path beneath her feet achingly cold and hard, but she did not care. Indignation boiled within her as her father's conversation with Aleron replayed in her mind.

"How could he be so foolish, so blind?" she muttered to herself as she ran through the courtyard toward the furthest line of trees, her hands clutching her long silver gown above her ankles.

She glanced behind her, ensuring she had not been followed. Looking up toward her bedchamber window, she smiled; never had she been more grateful to have the only bedchamber with a window overlooking the courtyard. The candle in her room still flickered, casting dancing shadows upon the walls as the dim flame swayed in the light evening breeze. The coast was clear; she knew the only being aware of her whereabouts was Nyom.

"Excuse me, madam, but I hope you are not referring to me when you talk of foolishness. I had to see you, my love. I could not bear to be away from you any longer."

Sintra's heart thudded violently in her chest, her blood rushing as she embraced the tall boy standing amongst the trees, wrapping her arms tightly around him. He pressed his lips against hers, kissing her passionately; her loins burning.

"I've missed you, Riven," she whispered, "I cannot bear to be away from you either."

"So, you do not think I am foolish for meeting you tonight?" he teased.

"No," laughed the princess, "I heard my father and Aleron quarrel in the great hall."

"Oh?"

"They talked of the day my mother was no more, the day my brother and sisters were slaughtered in the fields."

"Why? That was many moons ago. Two years."

"I'm not sure why they quarrel; I hope my father is beginning to question Lord Elowen's innocence. Tonight, Aleron's story changed. He is lying right beneath my father's nose, but he is too foolish and blind to see."

She walked toward the pond and seated on the stone wall, trailing her fingertips along the surface of the water. The moonlight bathed her face in a soft, ethereal glow, highlighting the delicate contours of her features. It cast a silvery sheen over her skin, making her look almost otherworldly. Her eyes sparkled with a mixture of determination and sorrow, reflecting the pale luminescence of the moon. The gentle light accentuated the tear tracks on her cheeks, giving her an appearance of fragile beauty amidst the turmoil within her heart.

"Do you question me?" she said in a soft voice, saddened.

"I do not," said Riven, kneeling before her as he surrendered to her sorrow, "How do you know if Aleron speaks the truth before the King?"

"I do not know. It is a feeling that stirs within me."

Sintra paused, looking down at her hands.

"The bodies, Riven. They were all stripped of their sigil and meticulously placed. There was no way of knowing where they came from, or why. There were few scuff marks; no signs of struggle. It is nothing but nonsense."

"Have you told this to your father?"

"No," sighed the princess.

"Tell him. Or I will be forced to."

"No one would believe you."

"They would believe you."

"And then what? My father takes Aleron Elowen's head?"

"It's likely."

"Even if that becomes Aleron's fate, my father will find a new knight to take my hand."

"Then I shall slaughter him."

"Or I will refuse his hand," interrupted Sintra.

"Even if that is so and your hand is freed from wed to any other knight, it does not mean that King Alaric will call me son."

"Call you son? My father is never to find out, Riven. You cannot win his affection; you are a slave, a peasant. Not fit to wed me in the eyes of my father."

"Then come away with me, Sintra. Leave this all behind; you don't need it. I can provide you with everything you have ever wanted."

"Oh, Riven, all I want is you. But I'm afraid my father will have both our heads if he ever finds out."

"He will never find out, my princess."

"My cousin, Queen Ellayda hid her affairs from her husband, King Lansing for two decades; both Ellayda and her lover's head occupy stakes on the east wall of citadel Denton, where King Lansing resides to this day. You can see it; its displayed on the wall of the great citadel."

"No matter how strong the kin, betrayal is betrayal and must not go unpunished," had said King Lansing as he swung the sword that made Queen Ellayda's head roll. "Do not tell me my father, King Alaric will not find out I'm having an affair with a slave boy."

"It's not an affair until Aleron takes your hand, my princess. The moon is almost full, we still have time."

Sintra sighed, "I can't."

"Do you not return my love?" asked Riven, wounded.

"Riven, I love you with everything I have but take such a risk and..."

Riven sighed in defeat.

"I must retire for the night, my princess."

Sintra kissed him with a passionate embrace before swiftly running to the entrance of the courtyard and through the doorway. Riven vanished through a concealed hole in the citadel wall, hidden by the tall pine trees standing like sentinels against the stone. The courtyard returned to its empty, silent state.

Royal Decree

Sintra ran as swiftly as her elegant bare feet could carry her, ascending a flight of stairs and traversing a dark hallway, then repeating the ascent and passage through yet another shadowy corridor. Her heart pounded within her chest, the cold air within the citadel walls rushing past her face, whispering insignificant screams into her ears. In that moment, she had never felt more alive. As she hurried past the darkened chamber of books, she vowed to visit Cornelius in the library tomorrow.

The princess slid up the final two flights of stairs before turning the corner and flying down the dark hallway toward her bedchamber. No sooner had she stepped inside than she found herself lying flat on her back against the cold stone floor.

She grunted, pushing the strong animal off her chest and rising to her feet. As she walked toward her large four-poster bed, she wiped away the saliva left on her face by her beloved wolf. Standing by her bed, she grasped her gown with both hands and lifted it above her head, revealing the undergarment Elara had tailored for her ensuring she would not fall ill upon sleeping in nothing but her bed furs and woollens.

"No princess of mine will sleep naked," Sintra's mother had declared to Elara when she was still alive. "Tailor my daughter several undergarments so that she may not catch her death in the night. And fix her fire, maid," she had added upon leaving the princess's bedchamber.

"She's mean, Elara," Sintra had said, feeling pity for the old woman.

"Stern, child, the Queen is stern."

"She has raised her voice to you more than once."

"She means well, my princess," the maid had told Sintra as she fitted her with freshly sewn undergarments when she was twelve, the year the princess had first bled. "To keep you warm and from falling ill, my princess."

"Yes, Elara," the princess had replied.

"Good, now into bed. Beneath the furs and woollens, you go."

The princess had always obeyed Elara; she had trusted her like a mother since her first steps. The other children, Serena, Serillah and Soren never did bond with the handmaiden as Sintra had. She was the first born after all. The first child of royal birth, born within the walls of the citadel and within the kingdom of Crevark, the first to reign and rule as she come of age and takes the hand of the first knight the King had granted upon her.

Sintra's hand was initially promised to Prince John, son of King Kent and Queen Fabianna of Lennox. However, both the Queen and Prince were brutally murdered by an indefinite assailant who slipped in and out of the citadel without taking any gold or riches. Following Prince John's death, Sintra's hand was then promised to Cormac, son of King Tien and Queen Farrah of Ironsmead. After Cormac's death, his brothers Irwin, Roald, and Tobias were also promised to Sintra, but they too were slaughtered in their sleep. No one understood why the princess remained unharmed while her betrothed met untimely deaths.

Prince Ellumin Artiss of Athelstan vanished just days after Sintra's sixteenth birthday. Rumours whispered that his caravan had taken a wrong turn, but it never returned. The King and Queen of Athelstan, upon hearing that he had renounced the throne, assumed he had eloped with a courtesan to indulge in a life of debauchery.

King Alaric then travelled to Gabor, where King George and Queen Kaylah reigned. He sought their sons to marry his daughter, but to strengthen alliances, Morris had already wed Princess Faye of Ironsmead soon after her brothers' deaths.

"So, you have two more sons?" King Alaric inquired.

"Edgar is to wed Gisela, daughter of King Cane and Queen Lenore of Westrose," had said King George.

"And Randalph is to wed Gisela's younger sister Evelyn, it's all been arranged," had added Queen Kaylah.

"Surely you have another child?" asked King Alaric.

"We have one, a girl by the name of Briony. She is to wed Azeez, son of King Marteez and Queen Brittanie of Glennock, when they both come of age."

"Bear another child, another Prince, please," the King of Crevark pleaded.

"Why, King Lysandra, so he will be slaughtered in my wife's womb before he is born and long before he comes of age to wed Sintra?" asked King Muucav, "Your Princess does not interest me. I want safety and security for my royal families, not death before a marriage. Find some other poor unfortunate soul to wed Sintra. He'll be a fool to do so, and I am no dupe."

King Alaric returned from Gabor empty-handed, without a prince to wed his princess. Upon his arrival back to the throne, Queen Lysandra waited impatiently and anxiously in the great hall of the Citadel for his return.

"Who is to wed our Sintra?" she asked the moment King Alaric entered the great hall.

"Not John Eagleston of Lennox," he began with a huff. "Not Cormac Westergard, nor Irwin, Roald, or Tobias Westergard, all of Ironsmead. Do you know why, Caprice?"

"Because they are no longer alive," the Queen replied.

"Precisely," he snapped, pacing back and forth.

"Did you see Gabor?"

"I saw Gabor and fled faster than the wind, angrier than the storm."

Queen Lysandra looked at her hands, deep in thought for a moment, before facing her King.

"Exhaustion overcomes me, Caprice."

"I'll send for a maid, to warm your bath. Do you require a wash-maid?"

"Not if my lady joins me," said the King, smirking.

"In that case I'll send for a messenger to inform the cook that you and I will be late for supper."

"Aye, my lady."

With that the King and Queen made for the bathing chamber.

†

Sintra had never questioned why no prince would take her hand. It never dawned on her until Aleron, the cunning, lying murderer who was granted her hand, set foot in the citadel.

"Be grateful to the gods that you are no prince promised my hand," Sintra had said to Riven one night. "For if you were, you wouldn't live. You would be slaughtered like swine, just like John of Lennox and the four princes of Ironsmead. Scared for your life like the three princes of Gabor once were."

"Why do you speak of such things?" asked Riven.

"They were all to take my hand."

"Long ago, before the Queen was murdered."

"It was Aleron, what better a way to take my father's throne than wed his only living daughter, the Princess of Crevark."

"He slaughtered them all to keep my hand free to wed."

Riven continued to look at the Princess, puzzled.

"Aleron Elowen wants my father's throne. And perhaps *without* a Queen," Sintra added.

"You believe that Aleron, will slaughter you once wed?"

"Yes, so that he may then slaughter my father in his sleep and take the throne. I believe it is why he slaughtered my family, so that Soren could not come of age and so he could kneel before my father and claim heroism after attempting to save the Queen and her children, thus being granted knighthood and my hand. It has been his plan all along. I feel it within me. I cannot explain how I feel it, but I just do."

"You have too many thoughts," Riven had replied, much to her growing frustration.

Sinta sighed, "I must go. I grow tiresome."

The princess felt a wave of disappointment wash over her. Riven could not meet her needs at this time, as he wasn't sure how. Feeling too fatigued to continue expressing her thoughts and feelings, she decided to retire for the night. With a heavy heart, she left him standing alone in the courtyard, the cool night air brushing against her as she walked away.

Sintra yawned as her thoughts tired her, sliding beneath her furs and woollens, she thought of her brother and sisters.

"Oh, how I miss you all. Mother, Serena, Serillah and Soren," whispered Sintra, a single tear escaped her heavy closing eyes before she fell into the deepest of sleeps. A smile soon softened her face as she dreamt of them all.

The next morning, she sat in the great hall of the Citadel alone, apart from two knights from the King's guard, eating her boiled eggs and bread on her own. The King had not slumbered until late the previous night, drinking wine and pleasuring himself with many whores Aleron had provided.

"Where is that imbecile?" Sintra asked a knight from the King's guard.

"Who, my princess?" answered Lucas.

"The knight of knights, Aleron."

"He rose before first light, madam, riding out across the fields and into the wood."

Sintra continued eating without another word, she did not care where Aleron had gone; she was quite pleased to eat alone, without *him*. He often made her feel like a child, watching every move she made, asking questions and lingering.

After breakfast she had left the great hall as her father entered, greeting him in the large doorway.

"Good morning, my princess. You slept well, I trust," said King Alaric.

"I had a nightmare. I dreamt of my mother, two sisters, and brother. I dreamt of their slaughter," she replied.

Shocked, King Alaric asked, "Oh?"

"A single man in gallant armour strode into the citadel after slaughtering the entire King's Guard single-handedly.

With sword unsheathed, he crept into the King's bedchamber and took his head, letting it roll to the hard stone floor, leaving a bloody stain. The head looked like yours, Father. I then woke and wept until first light," she replied, walking casually down the hallway and up a flight of stairs.

Her father stood still, dumbfounded in the large entrance of the great hall, mouth agape as he stared after his daughter, unable to believe what had just escaped her lips. Sintra giggled to herself as she entered the chamber of books, knowing full well that she had a perfect night's sleep, dreaming of the day Riven would wed her and take her far away. He had never asked about a dream before, but Sintra just wanted to frighten him. After all, he was forcing her to marry a man she did not love—a man of sedition and defiance, a man she loathed and wished were dead. A man that is not worthy of being known as the *knight of knights.*

"Welcome, Your Highness," greeted Cornelius, breaking her away from her thoughts.

"Good morning, my bookkeeper," she replied, "What shall we read today?"

"Whatever story your heart desires," replied the old man.

"I was hoping you had a book in mind Cornelius," the princess replied.

Cornelius always chose the best stories to read Sintra, he had taught the princess to read when she was 4 years old, still such a young girl.

"Perhaps a new story, madam?"

"A new story? What new story, Cornelius?"

"The story of how a young slave boy became a knight," the old man replied softly, glaring into Sintra's green, emerald eyes.

"Never have I ever heard of such a book."

"Aye, my princess but no book exists."

"Pardon?" asked the princess, her brow narrowing.

Cornelius frowned wearily, glancing behind him before turning back to Sintra. Without a word, he walked to the heavy wooden door of the book chamber and swung it closed, locking it with a large key. He then gestured for Sintra to follow him, his old, wrinkled finger pointing the way. Deep into the library they went, Cornelius glancing over his shoulder a few times before stopping at a smaller wooden door.

"Where are you taking me?" asked the princess, glancing behind her and then back at the old man.

"This chamber is soundproof, madam. We must speak in private at once."

Sintra frowned, feeling a mix of confusion and fear. Cornelius was an old friend, but the idea of stepping into a dark, silent chamber with him alone was unsettling.

"Do not be frightened, my dear," he said, pulling a ring of iron keys from his breeches. He fumbled through them until he found the right one, then inserted it into the lock beneath the iron door handle and turned the key. The door creaked open, dislodging dust and spider webs as if it hadn't been opened in years.

"Stay put, I'll return in a moment," said Cornelius, leaving Sintra to stand alone, staring into the dark empty space beyond the door.

The private room exuded an air of mystery and age. The flickering candlelight cast long, dancing shadows on the stone walls, revealing the room's hidden corners and ancient secrets. The air was thick with the scent of old parchment and dust, mingling with the faint aroma of melted wax. The silence was profound, broken only by the occasional crackle of the candle flames. The room felt timeless, a forgotten sanctuary where secrets were kept and whispers of the past lingered. The dim light revealed shelves lined with ancient tomes and scrolls, their spines worn and titles barely legible, hinting at the wealth of knowledge contained within this hidden chamber.

She had never been behind this door, nor had she known it existed. She had spent countless days in this library as a child, lost in the pages of books, but had never stumbled across this hidden chamber. Cornelius soon returned with a small candlestick in hand, the flame flickering in the light breeze as he walked into the dark, secluded room. Sintra watched as the blackness swallowed her old friend. She held her breath, unable to hear a sound. One by one, candles flickered to life as Cornelius shared the flame from his candle, illuminating the chamber.

"Come," he said from within the growing light.

Sintra hesitated, then took a cautious step forward, letting one bare foot enter the chamber. The stone floor was cold beneath her foot, though not as achingly cold as the night before. She stood in awe, taking in the surroundings of the chamber. Shelves lined with jars containing various oddities— roots, leaves, small animals, and insects—caught her eye. One jar, in particular, piqued her interest.

"Is that a—"

"Dragon? Yes," Cornelius finished her sentence.

"I thought they didn't —"

"Exist? Long ago they lived, my princess, but not anymore. Not here, at least."

Sintra stared at the small, undeveloped creature in the jar. Two small, rounded horns protruded from each side of its skull, similar to those lining its back and tail. She admired the profound ugliness yet beauty of the elegant creature. Its scales were small and almost transparent, flaky and delicate in their immaturity. The creature was as black as a raven's wings with a tinge of blue that glimmered in the candlelight. Its back arched, its tail curled as it rested in the foetal position inside its glass prison. Its tiny hands and feet were curled, just open enough to reveal a small sharp talon on each finger. The flesh on its hands, feet, stomach, and face was so undeveloped it was almost transparent, revealing the bone structure beneath. A shiver raced down Sintra's spine as she looked closely along the jawline of the infant beast, noting a row of tiny razor-sharp teeth clenched shut. On either side of its mouth, a fang protruded from beneath its scaled lips.

"It's magnificent, Cornelius," boasted the princess. "Why have you not shown me this before?"

"To keep you and this kingdom safe from knowing such a creature existed."

"Why? You know I love every tale you tell me that contains dragons."

"Aye, which is why it is an important secret to keep. However, I did not bring you here to speak of beasts. Now sit, we have much to discuss."

When Sintra turned to face Cornelius, she noticed he was already seated at a small wooden table in the centre of the secret chamber, with a wooden chair on either side. The princess lifted her gown and seated herself comfortably; the old wooden chair groaned beneath her weight.

"Forgive me, for what I am about to speak of, but it is in my best interest to keep you safe."

"Safe?"

"Aye, my princess, safe and very much alive. Forgive Elara, for she has spoken…"

As those words left Cornelius's mouth, Sintra knew her handmaiden had informed the bookkeeper of her affair with the slave boy.

"That wretched woman," Sintra interrupted, her temper rising.

"Now, now. You mustn't worry; Elara and I share many secrets between ourselves. This one is safe with me."

"She gave me her word," the princess fumed.

"Sintra, hush, please," said the old man, holding up his frail, wrinkled hands to silence her.

The princess sighed in defeat and let her arms drop to her lap in silence.

"Your maid spoke to me of a young lad who wishes your hand, my princess, but is aptly refused beyond questionable doubt if the King should find out, for the boy is a slave. Yes?"

Sinta nodded.

"Do you love this boy?"

Sintra looked up at Cornelius with saddened eyes. "With all my heart."

"I see."

Sintra dampened her sleeve with the tears that now flowed from her eyes.

"I cannot share it with him, ever. If the King should find out, he will have both our heads, as well as yours and my handmaidens for keeping it from him. All displayed side by side on stakes on the east wall of the citadel."

"I am aware of this, but it does not have to be that way."

"It cannot be *any* way; it is wrong, and I curse my heart for falling for that boy two years ago."

"Do not curse your heart, for it knows nothing but to love."

"Then what am I to do? I cannot flee."

"What is the name of the boy?"

"Riven," she sniffled.

"Can this Riven fight?"

"Fight?"

"With sword and axe? With spear and shield? With hammer, and bow and arrow?"

"Yes, he fights well. I've seen it with my own eyes, he slain a boar once, twice the size of yourself."

"Do you believe he is worthy of knighthood?"

"I suppose, Cornelius, he speaks fair and true but how can Riven be granted knighthood if he is a slave?"

"Aye, but what was Aleron before he was granted knighthood? A wanderer? A slave? A Squire?"

"I don't know."

"You speak of Lord Elowen in ill manner almost every day. Why, Sintra?"

"Aleron is unworthy of knighthood; he is a liar, a coward, and a schemer. He orchestrated heinous deaths and slaughtered noble princes who sought my hand, ensuring I remained unwed. It was he who murdered Queen Caprice, my sisters, and my brother, not the alleged army of men. Why? So that I might remain the sole surviving princess—the princess whose hand he was unjustly granted by my father. If a murderer like the acclaimed Aleron is deemed worthy of knighthood and my hand, then any boy of age is worthy."

"Then it is settled."

"What is settled?"

"If you believe Riven is worthy of knighthood and your hand, he is eligible to fight for it if he so wishes."

"How? It's impossible."

"Riven must wield his sword and let the heads of his opponents roll until he faces Aleron and rolls his head too."

Sintra was speechless. As much as she relished the thought of seeing Aleron's head roll, she could not bear the idea of her beloved slave boy in any battle, not even in single combat. She had seen him fight, but never against a man.

"All we must do is let King Alaric agree to a tournament."

"Simple, Cornelius, my father loves bloodshed. But it is three days until full moon, three days before Aleron takes my hand."

"Then we must work quickly, the tournament must be before full moon."

"How?"

"You are the princess, work your magic with your father. You are the closest to him; you know how to test him."

"I do," whispered the princess.

Tournament

That evening, Sintra sent a raven to summon Riven to the courtyard at dusk to discuss their future. The princess waited patiently behind the tall row of pine trees lining the citadel wall. A loose stone brick squeezed its way through the wall as the slave boy pushed it from the other side, landing with a muffled thud on the thick grass. The bricks were large, creating a hole big enough for a grown man to squeeze through comfortably.

"That brick is easier to remove than to replace," laughed the slave.

"We must talk, Riven," said Sintra, facing the pond with her back to him.

"Aye, about our future, my princess? Tell me, have you agreed to run away with me after all?"

"I have not," she replied, turning to face him. "I have a far better plan, but you must trust me. You may be hurt."

"Of course I trust you, but why am I to be hurt?"

"There is no time for questions. You must do as I say if you wish to take my hand. You must accompany me to the knight's instructor so that you may learn to swing a sword."

"Is there a war upon us?"

"Yes. But Riven, please, you must listen. I haven't much time; the King waits for his supper as we speak."

The boy bowed his head in silence, allowing Sintra to continue.

"Tonight, at supper in the great hall, my father will agree to a tournament on the day before I am to wed Lord Elowen. You must battle great knights for my hand. You must defeat them."

"I'll die!"

"Nonsense, you will do as I say. You are a kind; fair man and you can fight; my own eyes have seen it."

"Stags and swine, not men, not great knights," he replied.

"You must fight, and you must win!"

"As you wish." His words were barely a whisper. He felt the enormous pressure to please her, although losing would cost him his life.

"Meet me at the Iron Gate at first light. I will tell the King I am to collect silk and satin for new window drapes for my bedchamber. Elara will accompany me. We will go on horseback."

"The King will ask why the third horse."

"No more than two horses will be taken from the stables; you will ride on horseback with me."

Riven nodded, turning toward the hole in the great citadel wall.

"Riven?" said Sintra, making him stop and turn toward her.

"Yes?"

"I love you, slave boy. You will make a splendid knight," she smiled, placing her hand at her heart and waving him goodbye.

The slave lifted the loose brick from the wall and pushed it through the hole until it landed with a thud on the other side. He slipped through the gap, replaced the brick, and ensured it was secure. This tedious task, performed twice daily for two years, had strengthened his arms and hands. Now, he was grateful for this strength, for soon he would wield a heavy sword and fight to the death. His heart pounded with a mix of fear and resolve, knowing that every muscle he had honed would be tested in the brutal clash ahead. The weight of his destiny pressed upon him, but he steeled himself, ready to face whatever came with unwavering determination.

"Pleasant evening, Sintra," said King Lysandra, raising a goblet of wine toward his daughter. "Drink with me on this fine night."

Sintra sighed, bracing herself to ask the King for a tournament. She accepted a small goblet of wine from the servant beside her. As she sipped, she considered various ways to broach the subject. *Hold a tournament, for I love to watch bloodshed,* she mused in thought.

Hold a tournament, my King, as a gift to the knight I will wed upon the coming full moon.

Hold a tournament, Father, so I can watch Aleron's blood spill when he is defeated by my lover, the slave boy Riven, who will then be granted knighthood and my hand.

She took another sip, hiding a smile behind her goblet, pleased with her last thought. She knew how to persuade her father; she knew exactly what to say.

Placing the goblet beside her supper, she sighed, catching her father's attention.

"Sintra, what is it? You've hardly touched your pork and beans."

"Forgive my ill manner, but I am bored," she sighed again, stabbing a bean with her knife.

"Bored? How might you be bored? You have ample things to do among this citadel, but you are no child, you should be practising your wedding waltz."

"Ah yes, the wedding looms," she sighed, "How dim-witted of me to forget *that*."

"Forget? Oh no child, I know you better than that, you pushed it from your mind for you do not want him to have your hand. Why is it that you do not wish to wed Lord Aleron Elowen?"

"It doesn't seem fair to the King's Guard."

"The King's Guard?" Alaric raised his eyebrows in surprise.

"They are all of knighthood, are they not?"

"*Are*!" replied King Lysandra, eyeing her suspiciously, "I granted them knighthood myself; you know this."

"But isn't a guard of knights supposed to battle one another for the princess's hand?"

"Indeed, but no knight came forth to battle the knight of knights for they not only worship him, but they are also afraid of him; they know he slaughtered thirty armed men single handedly. Don't you remember?"

"Yes," the princess sighed, slumping in her chair.

"Would bloodshed satisfy your boredom?"

"Perhaps, sir," Sintra answered, expressionless. She knew her plan was working.

"But not a single knight will step forward, how are we to hold a tournament if the battle has only one knight? Who is he to slay? Himself?"

Indeed, thought Sintra, "Slaves?" she asked, "You have-,"

"*We!*" corrected the King, impatient.

"We have fifty slaves, surely a small few of them will suffice."

"You wish Lord Elowen to battle slaves?" he laughed, "Why that is simple victory."

"Give them armour, surely that will make for good competition."

"Aye, but what slaves?" the king laughed again, "Fifteen are small children; I will not hold a tournament to watch infants be slain."

"Certainly not."

"The rest are women and men, but no woman is to enter such a tournament. That leaves me with thirty men; far too many."

"Too many, sir?"

"If my thirty slaves are not victorious, what slaves do I have for tasks that women and children cannot succeed?"

"Enter half, to battle on the fields and the other to continue to their duties."

"Perhaps, we could always find more slaves. It is done; we will hold a tournament for you after the full moon."

"After? Why not before? We may then celebrate Aleron's victory upon our wedding night. Such a celebration and feast that will be, guests will come for miles."

"Certainly, this is true. We will hold the tournament the day ahead of your wedding," finalized the King, "Messenger!" he called.

As the King informed the messenger of the upcoming tournament, Sintra was overcome with guilt. Lives would be lost—fathers, brothers, sons, and cousins—all for one slave boy. The messenger left the great hall of the Citadel and returned moments later with a scroll.

"Summon our twelve associate monarchies. Forget Gabor," said King Alaric, as the scroll recorded each name. "Inform them of the tournament and the celebration of Aleron's victory and marriage to my daughter, the heir of Crevark."

"Will they make it in time?" asked the Sintra.

"It is half a day's ride from the far south, we can expect them, but no more. If they do not arrive on time, the tournament will still commence, as you have wished."

"If they don't make the tournament, they will make the wedding."

"Undeniably, my princess, and you will be showered with many favours on that day," smiled the King.

Sintra forced a smile and stabbed at her pork, nibbling away at the pale pink meat.

"Knight of knights?" called the King, pieces of chewed pork and bean flying past his lips, "Messenger, send for the knight of knights, I wish to speak with him."

The messenger left the great hall as Aleron strode in, his hand at the neck of a young slave boy of eleven years.

"No need, messenger," he bellowed.

Aleron threw the young boy to the ground before the King, his hands slapping hard against the cold stone pave. Sintra lifted her head toward the boy but soon looked back at her supper as she felt Aleron's eyes upon her.

"What is the meaning of this?" the King hissed.

"I caught this boy stealing bread from the cookery, my lord; he deserves punishment."

"Stand!" ordered the King.

The small boy, trembling, slowly rose to his feet and lifted his head toward the King. His heart pounded in his chest, and his legs felt like they might give way beneath him. The grandeur of the throne room, with its towering pillars and opulent decorations, only made him feel smaller and more insignificant.

"Does this knight speak the truth, boy? Do you dare steal from your King?"

The King's voice boomed through the hall, making the boy flinch. The stern faces of the courtiers and the cold, unyielding gaze of the knights added to his growing sense of dread.

"I'm sorry, my lord, my baby sister starves," whimpered the boy, his voice barely above a whisper. Tears welled up in his eyes, and he could feel the weight of his desperation pressing down on him. His hands shook as he clasped them together, pleading for mercy. He could feel the eyes of everyone in the room boring into him, judging him.

He glanced around, hoping to find a sympathetic face. The boy's mind raced, thinking of his sister's frail form and the gnawing hunger that had driven him to such a desperate act. He felt a lump in his throat and struggled to hold back the sobs that threatened to escape.

"Of what age is she?"

"Four, Your Highness."

The King paused, deep in thought. Sintra gazed at the young boy with profound pity, her heart aching for him. She wished she could help, to ease his suffering.

Sintra had never genuinely intended to take the throne; she felt no connection to it since the passing of her mother and siblings. But something sparked within her now. This cruelty, this injustice, would not do. If she were Queen, she would be fairer, kinder, and more generous. She would ensure no child starved; no family suffered needlessly. The weight of this realization settled heavily on her, igniting a fierce determination to change the kingdom for the better.

"Do you know what punishments thieves attain?"

The boy slowly shook his head.

"They're either hung or beheaded. Which is it?"

The small boy whimpered and fell to his knees, his small shoulders shaking as he sobbed deeply.

"Crying does not solve a thing," said Alaric, "Stand!" he bellowed.

Aleron yanked the slave to his feet by his collar, tearing his ratted garment.

"Now," started the King, looking to Sintra, "You, my dear, will soon reign. You decide his punishment."

"Father?" she asked, shocked.

"You said you were bored."

The small boy looked to the princess; his deep blue eyes glistened wet in the candlelight of the great hall. He was far too young to be hung or beheaded for such a small crime.

"Lock him away in the dungeons," she said sternly.

"Pardon?" asked the King.

"I'll sharpen my blade, sir," said Aleron, turning to leave.

"You will not!" said King Alaric, his voice rising, "You will stay put."

Sintra looked closely at Aleron Elowen, his strong jaw clenching as he fought back objection. Being the knight of knights and granted Sintra's hand, Aleron roamed the citadel and kingdom as he pleased. When the King agreed, he dined in the great hall of the Citadel with Alaric and Sintra, just as he would if he were already King.

"Sintra Lysandra," said the King, interrupting her thoughts, "Explain to me, why the dungeons? The crime is aptly for beheading or hanging."

"This boy is not even of age; I believe he is young enough to be taught a lesson. If he learns quickly, you could add him to the serfdom."

The King scratched his chin, deep in thought as he considered the princess's order.

"Guards," spoke the King.

As two men from the King's Guard entered the hall, Aleron looked at them in disgust, "Am I not worthy?"

"Guards, take this slave to the dungeons, lock him away with no food or water. He is to stay put until I order otherwise."

The guards took the boy by his arms, one on each side and dragged him along the floor and out the hall.

"Lord Elowen, sit, we have much to discuss," said the King, turning back to his supper and lifting a charred leg to his greasy lips.

Aleron took a seat across from the princess, his eyes not leaving the King.

"Your Highness?"

"You've defeated many men by single hand," started Alaric.

Aleron nodded.

"How simple did you find it?"

"Extremely," boasted Lord Elowen.

"Splendid, then you shall do it again the day before you are to wed my daughter."

"My lord? Are we at war?"

"Nonsense, a tournament is to be held in honour of the royal decree. You will bear new victory as you wed. A mark of your strengthen and heroism."

Aleron looked to Sintra, an eyebrow raised. His pale blue eyes looked deeply into hers, angelic against his amber skin and thick tussled black hair. He was quite handsome. He would make a charming King if it weren't for his malice and cold heart.

"Tournament against whom?" he asked, turning away from the princess and back at the King.

"Slaves," laughed the King upon taking another large bite of his meal.

"And whose idea was this?" he pushed.

"Mine," said Sintra, glaring at him across the table.

"The princess is bored," laughed the King, chewing loudly.

"Play with a doll, my princess," suggested Aleron, mocking the princess' youth.

"I haven't any," she replied.

"I'll find one for you," he said, "In fact, I know of a small girl in the village that has one. Shall I fetch it?" he beamed sarcastically.

Sintra rather not know how the knight of knights knew this.

"No need, I'd much rather play with you, my lord," she teased beneath her breath.

"Pardon?" he asked taken aback, curious at the vulgarity of the princess's remark.

"Oh yes, my lord, I simply cannot wait to see you lose the tournament, blood gushing from your jugular once your head rolls," she spat.

"Pity we haven't any lions or wolves," he replied in mockery, leaning against the table in intimidation.

"I have a wolf."

"Silence, both of you!" the King demanded, "Sintra finish your supper and go off to bed."

Sintra sat quietly, picking at her food so as to take longer; she wanted to hear what the King and Aleron would discuss.

"The tournament will be held in three days' time; you have a day or two to prepare."

"Prepare?" scoffed Aleron, "They're slaves, I needn't prepare."

"Do as you wish," replied the King, "Now, we must choose how the game will commence. Sintra, would you rather a dozen slaves against Aleron at once?"

"As opposed to what?"

"Having each slave battle by single hand until there is a victory."

"You mean until Aleron stands alone in the field, father, surrounded by slaughtered slaves?"

"Certainly!"

Not likely, she thought to herself upon answering, "Or perhaps slave fight slave until the last man stands," *Riven*, "He who stands alone fights Lord Elowen until there is victory."

"Until the victory is mine," added Aleron.

The King thought about Sintra's suggestion for a moment, sipping wine and scratching his chin.

"Aye, it is done!" he answered.

"What slaves will you choose?"

"Hmm, yes, *that*," said the King.

"Perhaps those with families, my lord, they would fight better for they have something to fight for. It would make for a better fight; a competition, it's not fair if the game is too easy."

You wouldn't know of fairness, Sintra felt like saying but she bit her tongue.

"I have many slaves in mind," grunted the King, ignoring Aleron's immorality.

"Who?" asked the princess, eager to know if her slave boy was amongst them.

"Let's see," started King Alaric, "Terrence and Fernando the gold thieves who are confined to scrubbing the sewer. Goodwin and Monoghan, the rotten scoundrels from Denton who set fire to King Lansing's stables. Those boys are confined to the King's Guard's weaponry, better watch out for them, Lord Elowen."

As Sintra listened to the names, she was surprised to hear that her father knew all their names and crimes. If only he knew that Aleron belonged on the list for his treason.

"Peter the spy whom I myself found in the bathing chamber, he is confined to sweeping dung from the stables along with Wenzel and Mark, though it seems I have forgotten why those men are slaves," he frowned.

"Perhaps the garden slave?"

Sintra's ears pricked. *Riven*. She listened carefully so as not to miss a word they might say.

"Aye, the Queen's beloved roses have died this year. I should punish him nevertheless."

"Let me, my King."

"As you wish, along with any other slave you wish."

"Leary, Dennis," started Aleron, "Especially Pedro," he snickered.

"Why so fond of Pedro?" asked Sintra, "The only crimes he has committed are stealing bread from the cookery and straw from the stables for his bed. Do you hold a secret with the slave?"

"I d*o not*!" he snapped, "Pedro is a menace of thirty years, he lingers in the shadows and flicks stones toward my own head."

"He is the same age as you." Sintra interjected.

"Right then," started the King, "I am tiresome, enough chatter. Choose whomever you wish. We will discuss the rest tomorrow," said the King, brushing his hand as if to wave Aleron out of sight.

Aleron did not hesitate; he stood from the table and strode out.

"Are you satisfied? You have yourself a tournament," King Alaric said, holding his empty goblet for a servant to fill with more wine.

Sintra beamed in false delight, "Must I ask a favour?"

"You should know by now that you can make your own orders, permission is not required."

At first Sintra was speechless, taken aback as her father always ordered her and demanded that she asked for permission on request of something.

"May you draw the Iron Gate, my lord? My maid Elara and I will travel to the village on horseback at first light."

"Oh?"

"I have asked for my maid's guidance as she is required to help me in choosing fine silk and satin to sew new window drapes for my bedchamber, and perhaps more to sew a new gown for the tournament…and another for the wedding if not my mother's."

"As you wish," he replied, reaching into the pocket of his breeches and pulling out a small bulging sack and dumping it on the table before her.

She smiled, gazing from the sack of gold and back to the King.

"Perhaps you might find new silk and satin for me too, Sintra, as I might like some new window drapes sewn for my bedchamber as well," he smiled.

Sintra sighed as she departed the great hall of the Citadel, her thoughts lingering on her father, the loving man he had been before the brutal murder of her mother, sisters, and brother. She pondered whether their slaughter had hardened the King. She could already see Aleron's insolence influencing him. Despite the bitterness and malice, he unjustly commanded, Sintra recognized her father as a sorrowful, lonely man.

"Perhaps I should marry Lord Elowen and bear children," she mused, *"so that my father might have grandchildren and retire from the throne. Grandchildren would surely bring him joy."* Yet, this thought quickly dissipated as she considered the looming treason. She suspected that Aleron would slit her throat on their wedding night and place the King's head on a stake by dawn. This only reinforced the necessity of the tournament, giving Riven a chance at knighthood, her hand, and the throne.

As the princess traversed half the hallway, a sudden thought made her pause. She turned and made her way to the dungeons, blending into the shadows as two knights from the King's Guard passed by. Stealthily, she approached the cell that held the small boy who had stood before the King in the Citadel hall just an hour earlier. Sintra fumbled through the keys until she found the correct one. Unlocking the cell door, she silently took the young boy by the hand and turned to leave.

"Have you been sent to kill me?" asked the boy.

"Nonsense," said Sintra, peering around the corner to the hallway, "Have faith in your princess, boy, I am here to save you. Now hush or you'll get us both killed."

The boy remained silent as they passed through the great hall, her father oblivious, having fallen asleep at the great table where she had left him moments earlier. They continued down the hallway until the princess halted before the cookery. Peeking inside, she saw that the cooks had departed, leaving the cookery empty.

"Perfect," she whispered, filling a satchel with bread rolls, apples, and plums. "Here, take this," she instructed the boy, thrusting the satchel into his arms and guiding him toward a back entrance.

"Leave this place and do not look back," she commanded. "Take this food to your family, feed your sister, and never speak of my generosity. Do you understand?"

The small boy nodded and ran off with a gentle shove from the princess. As she turned, she was met with the head cook's wide grin.

"You saw nothing, Prunella," Sintra said, walking past the cook and plucking an apple from the basket. "I was simply peckish for an apple after my supper," she added, leaving the cookery and strolling casually down the hallway, though her heart pounded in her chest.

Steel Knight of Sidon

"How could I be so selfish?" Sintra exclaimed, pacing back and forth in the secret chamber that night, her voice trembling with guilt and frustration.

"Selfish, my princess?" Cornelius inquired gently.

"Just now, in the great hall, I discussed the slaughter of over two dozen men—slaves who have families. I sentenced them all to death, and all for one slave boy," she said, her eyes welling with tears.

"It is not for just one slave boy, my princess. It is for your freedom and your life. For the kingdom," Cornelius reassured her.

Sintra slowed her frantic pacing, coming to a stop by the table where the old man sat, fumbling through ancient pieces of parchment that seemed ready to disintegrate at a touch.

"I suppose you're right," she sighed, her voice heavy with resignation. "If I do not do this, my head will be on a stake before first light on my wedding night, my father's head will roll, and the kingdom of Crevark will be in peril."

"My princess, the slave boy will be victorious, and we will prevail," Cornelius said with conviction.

"If the knight of knights is victorious and Riven is defeated, I will flee. I know not what else to do," she confessed, her voice breaking.

"If you flee, you will be hunted," Cornelius warned.

"I could promise the King's Guard their weight in gold and jewels if they murder Lord Elowen," she suggested desperately.

"Yes, but Lord Elowen is mighty strong," Cornelius replied, his tone grave, "And if they fail, he will soon discover your treachery."

Sintra hadn't a word to say as she was deep in thought. Images of spilled blood and carnage passed through her mind as the death of Lord Elowen was put to plot.

"Risks is all you speak of," said Cornelius, hesitating to glare at the princess before continuing, "Risks that may result in your own death."

"I must do something."

"Do as you have planned, Sintra, it is too late to change orders now. After all, the ravens fly tonight."

Sintra sighed in defeat, "I suppose you're right, Cornelius."

"Very well. Off to your bedchamber, before the King sends out a search party."

"The King is asleep at the grand table in the hall, his pillow a succulent pork belly," laughed the princess.

"All the same, Sintra, it is late, and you ride to the village at first light."

Turning to walk out of the secret chamber, "You speak with my handmaiden too often," she teased upon her leave.

At first light the next day, Sintra stepped into the icy cold hallway of the citadel, leaving the warmth of her bedchamber's wood fire behind. She moved silently down the dark corridor, descending each staircase with care until she reached the floor where her father's chambers were located. Holding her breath, she passed her father's bedchamber, peering through the slightly ajar door. The King was still fast asleep, his thunderous snores almost making the stone walls tremble.

Sintra continued with stealth until she reached the cookery, where she found Elara packing a satchel with apples, bread, and a cask of ale.

"It's still dark," whispered Sintra as she stood in the doorway, the cookery on one side and cold night air on the other.

"Once we set off, first light will appear, we need the dark blanket to conceal your friend on the short journey over the fields."

"I see," began the princess, "Who is attending the horses for our journey?"

"Wenzel. Lucas and Angus will draw the bridge upon our arrival at the citadel entrance. They will not notice the garden slave," replied the maid.

"You plan well, Elara," the princess smiled.

"The bookkeeper is the one to thank, my dear."

"I don't doubt that" Sintra murmured under her breath as she stepped into the cold air.

She strode toward the stables, lifting her violet gown above her ankles to reveal the soft cream slippers her maid had tailored for her when she turned seventeen. Elara followed closely behind, clutching the satchel of food supplies and the bulging sack of gold the King had given Sintra the previous night.

"The horses are ready," said the Squire, bowing his head and avoiding eye contact with the princess.

"Thank you," Sintra replied. "Elara, tip him."

Elara reached into the satchel, pulled out a single apple, and tossed it to the young man.

"An apple?" he questioned, puzzled.

"What would you like to tip the young man?" the maid asked, retrieving the apple from the squire's hand.

Sintra frowned at Elara, then took the apple and the bulging sack of riches. She handed the apple back to the squire and reached inside the sack. She drew out a handful of silver coins but paused, her eyes fixed on the contents of the sack.

"Do you have a wife?" she asked, not looking up.

"Yes, my lady," the squire answered, his head still bowed. "She is with child."

"Do you have ample food?"

"Not always."

Elara watched suspiciously as Sintra pulled out a single gold coin and handed it to the squire.

"For your kindness," she said softly.

She reached into the sack once more and pulled out a thick string of gold and jewels, handing it to the squire.

"For your wife," Sintra added.

The handmaiden's eyes widened in disbelief. The princess put the sack away, stuffing it back into the satchel. The squire, now holding the gold coin and the magnificent necklace, helped the princess climb onto her steed.

"Do help my maid," said Sintra as she was seated high upon her horse.

"I'll manage," grunted Elara, her stomach laying across the horse's back, her legs kicking to one side.

The you man pushed the woman's behind until she too was seated on her horse.

They trod toward the Iron Gate, leaving the Squire standing alone.

"Why so generous?" asked Elara as she continued to peer behind her shoulder toward the boy.

"He won't have a head come the full moon, he has been chosen to compete in the tournament," said the princess.

"And the necklace, it is worth more than the contents of the whole sack."

"It is," started Sintra, "But as I said, it's for his wife."

"No peasant can be seen wearing gold like *that*, not if they want to live."

"Elara, it's the least I could do, I sentenced him to death. How is his wife to live and take care of herself and her child without him? It is to be sold for riches to buy food and supplies."

"Very well, my princess, you will make a generous and fair queen one day."

A loud moan sent shivers down Sintra's spine as the Iron Gate groaned to life, slowly rising as Lucas and Angus wound its chains tight. As the gate ascended, the princess and Elara could see out over the fields toward the dark wood. A low fog blanketed the landscape, hugging the frosted ground beneath. The soft click-clack of the horses' hooves against the stone road echoed in Sintra's ears as they trotted down the path toward the fields. Wisps of white cloud escaped the horses' nostrils as they snorted, their breath visible in the cold, dim light.

"Where is he?" Sintra asked, her voice tinged with anxiety and frustration.

"He is most likely waiting beyond the field, my lady; he probably caught a glimpse of the guards. That's what I would do," Elara replied.

Sintra held her head high, stiffening her neck and straightening her back as she scanned the horizon for him. As they reached the open field, the blanket of fog began to lift, and the sun started to rise, casting rays of pink and gold across the sky.

"Beautiful, I love first light," Elara said, craning her head to admire the magnificent morning sky.

Moments passed until they finally reached the first row of trees at the wood's edge. Sintra glanced back toward the citadel; the Iron Gate had closed, and there was no sign of Riven.

"My princess," came a voice.

Sintra spun in her saddle to face a tall, handsome man emerging from behind a tree. His dark brown hair was messy, his deep blue eyes piercing, and his smile revealed immaculate white teeth. His strong jawline was dappled with rough black stubble. He wore tattered dark grey breeches and a black overcoat with a stiff collar.

"Riven," she cried, stumbling from her horse and wrapping her arms around him.

"Quite an embrace," he laughed.

"Why are you hiding out here? I thought we agreed you'd meet me at the Iron Gate?"

"I couldn't risk being seen. You had only made it halfway across the field when first light appeared. If I had waited by the Iron Gate, I would have been seen at sunrise."

"I suppose you're right," she sighed. "Come on, we must be hasty; it's a big day for you."

The forest was eerily silent as Sintra rode along the familiar path, her horse's hooves barely making a sound on the soft, moss-covered ground. The trees, tall and ancient, seemed to whisper secrets of the past, their branches swaying gently in the breeze. Her heart pounded in her chest, each step of her steed bringing her closer to the place she had avoided for so long.

She reined in her horse at the edge of the clearing, her breath catching in her throat. This was where it had happened. The memories flooded back, vivid and painful. She could almost hear their screams, see the blood-stained earth, and feel the crushing weight of loss. Her family had been everything to her, and in one brutal moment, they had been taken away. Sintra cast her eyes over the ground where her mother had fallen. Tears welled up, but she blinked them away, refusing to let them fall. She had cried enough tears.

Her gaze hardened as she looked around the clearing, her eyes resting on Wraithveil Glade. In the opening of the forest stood a grim cluster of tall, pointed stakes, their tips sharpened to pierce through flesh. A dozen stakes, each bearing the gruesome remnants of the assailants who had allegedly murdered the royal family, loomed like silent sentinels. Twelve bodies, or what was left of them, dangled from the spikes, their bones and tattered cloth swaying gently in the breeze. The sight was a cadaverous testament to the vengeance that had already been exacted, but for Sintra, it felt wrong.

The air was thick with the stench of decay, a constant reminder of the brutality that had taken place here. Sintra's heart pounded with a cold, unrelenting fury. The stakes were a warning, but they also fuelled her resolve. The man who had orchestrated this massacre would face a fate far worse than those who hung before her.

With a final, steely glance at the gruesome display, Sintra turned away, her mind set on the path of vengeance. The tournament. The forest seemed to close in around her, the shadows deepening as she rode away, the image of the stakes burned into her memory.

Two hours later, they arrived at the bustling village, where the markets were springing to life with villagers, stall vendors, merchants, and wanderers. Muffled voices reverberated through Sintra's ears. Stalls displayed an array of carpets and mats, wooden bowls and goblets, iron baskets brimming with live spider crabs, troughs teeming with live eels, and strings of fish in every conceivable shape and size. Other stalls offered caskets of red wine and ginger ale, wooden kegs of fermented grapes and bitter lemon, and finely crafted weaponry. Shields adorned with jewels, swords and daggers with leather-wrapped hilts, and furs of bear, tiger, wolf, boar, and bull were also on display. Nearly every stall was crowded with customers, their voices rising in a cacophony of haggling and shouts.

"This is where I leave you," said Sintra, jerking her head toward the stall that held fine cloths of satin, and silk lined with gold trim.

"I will see you upon your return," replied the old woman, dismounting from her horse and gathering the reins in her hand. She turned her back and walked toward a post to tie her steed.

"See you on nightfall!" the princess called after her.

Riven dismounted the steed, leaving Sintra to sit alone.

"What are you doing?" she hissed.

"People are casting looks, my princess; it's better I walk beside you."

Sintra nodded, raising a brow as she noticed the slave was right; people were indeed casting curious glances from every angle.

"Maybe I should have dressed in rags to blend in," she whispered to Riven.

"The sooner we are out of here, the better," Riven replied. "Do you know where we are to meet this trainer?"

"I sent him a raven, asking him to meet us at Dolores's House of Fine Wine and Swine. We will discuss everything there."

"He will question why a rag-dressed man accompanies the princess."

"In my letter, I said you are a knight in training. If he presses further, I will offer him a great deal of gold."

"Aye," Riven replied, saying no more.

The crowds thinned as the princess and the slave reached the far edge of the village, heading towards Dolores's House of Fine Wine and Swine. Upon arrival, Sintra dismounted her horse while Riven tied its rein to a post beside a trough, which was occupied by a drunken man and overflowing with water. The horse snorted at the drunk and sidestepped as far as it could.

Riven was well-acquainted with Dolores's House, having often dined there on roast pork and sipped the finest red wine. As a slave, he earned a mere dime every full moon from the king. Without any means to supplement his income, as one dime a month was woefully insufficient, Sintra often smuggled food to him.

"You are lucky to make a dime at all. That was entirely my daughter's decision. She is fairer than I, hmmph," the knight had sneered when Riven dared to protest his meagre pay.

A warm, enticing aroma greeted them as they stepped onto the doorstep of Dolores's House. The air was rich with the scents of peppers, salts, ginger, and garlic, mingling with other exotic fragrances. The soft melody of a wooden windpipe played from a corner, harmonizing with the light chatter of customers feasting on roast hog and sipping wine from wooden goblets.

Sintra strode toward a woman standing behind a wooden bench, wiping it down with a woollen rag. The bar maid towered over most patrons, her impressive height and broad shoulders making her a formidable presence in the bustling tavern. Her large frame was accentuated by her strong, well-defined bone structure, giving her an almost statuesque appearance. Her hands, capable of carrying multiple tankards with ease, were as sturdy as the oak tables she served. Despite her size, there was a grace to her movements, a testimony to years of navigating the crowded bar with practiced ease. Her face, framed by a cascade of auburn hair, bore high cheekbones and a strong jawline, adding to her commanding yet approachable demeanour. She moved with a confidence that spoke of both strength and kindness, her hearty laugh often ringing out above the din of the tavern, inviting patrons to relax and enjoy their time.

"How may I be of assistance?" the woman asked in a dull, dismal tone as she raised her head. "Your highness," she added, swallowing loudly as she recognized Sintra.

"Alewife, I have come for the Steel Knight, Cedric Edith of Sidon," Sintra declared. "I wish to speak with him."

"If you will wait one moment," the woman replied, stepping out from behind the bench and approaching one of her customers.

The imposing woman interrupted a man's breakfast by tapping him on the shoulder. She then bent down to his level and whispered in his ear, prompting the man to rise abruptly, as if startled. He hastened towards Sintra and bowed deeply. The princess glanced around the tavern, noting that the other patrons remained undisturbed, continuing to eat, drink, and converse as if oblivious to her presence in Dolores's House. Sintra turned her attention to the man bowing before her.

"Please, sir, rise. I wish not to cause a disturbance," she said, gently lifting his chin with a slender finger.

The man's face bore the scars of war and the wrinkles of age, a combination that suited him well. Crow's feet etched deeply at the corners of his eyes as he squinted, a half-smile forming on his lips. He wore black satin breeches tucked into high black leather boots lined with fur. His long-sleeved chemise draped lightly over his shoulders and torso, with the neck string untied and dangling, revealing a hairy chest beneath. Sintra's gaze fell upon a black overcoat hanging from his chair, its sleeves and hem edged with silver trim.

"Are you the one they call the Steel Knight?" inquired the princess.

"Aye, Cedric Edith of Sidon, the Steel Knight, at your service," the man replied.

"Very good," said Sintra.

"I have been expecting you. I received your raven. Where is he then?" Cedric asked.

"Riven?"

The slave stepped forward; his head held high as Cedric inspected him from head to toe.

"Hold out your arms, please," commanded the Steel Knight, beginning to feel Riven's arms as he extended them in front of him.

"Splendid muscle tone," Cedric remarked, placing his hands firmly on Riven's back and shoulder blades. "Swung a sword before?" he asked.

"Once, sir," Riven answered, frowning as the stranger tugged and pulled at him. "I stuck a hog."

"Stuck a hog?" Cedric's voice rose slightly. "No, no, no, one does not stick a hog with a sword. Daggers are for sticking; swords behead and slaughter. Do you not know your weaponry?"

"I think he meant slaughter," interjected Sintra.

"Right, Dolores, we need a field or an empty chamber. This boy needs training."

The woman nodded towards the knight and vanished through a doorway behind the wooden bench. She soon returned.

"If you will kindly follow me," said Dolores.

Sintra and Riven followed, with Cedric close behind. They traversed a hallway. As Dolores led the way, Sintra's mind was a whirl of thoughts. She observed the dimly lit hallways and the scent of candle wax, which evoked memories of her childhood in the citadel. The anticipation of what was to come made her heart race slightly, but she maintained her composed exterior.

When they reached the large wooden door, Sintra couldn't help but feel a twinge of curiosity about the field beyond.

"This is the back entrance to the tavern; outside is a small field where my husband's horses are usually kept. Today, it is empty, so use it as you will. It is all that I can offer you," she said, turning the door handle and propping the door open with her arm until Cedric, Riven, and Sintra had passed through. She then vanished back inside.

Sintra wondered if this humble setting would be sufficient for the training Riven needed. As they stepped outside, the cool air and the sight of the small, enclosed field brought a sense of calm over her. She noted the horse trough and the stack of straw, simple yet practical elements that reminded her of the rustic life outside the palace walls.

"This will do splendidly," said the knight.

Watching Cedric pace the field, marking out steps with his long strides, Sintra's thoughts turned to the knight's reputation. She had heard tales of his prowess and discipline, and now she would witness it firsthand. Her gaze shifted to Riven, who stood tall and resolute despite the unfamiliar surroundings. She admired his courage and determination, qualities that had brought him to this moment.

"I see that you are without armour," said the knight. "Not to worry, I'll send for my squire, Benjin."

The knight disappeared into the tavern, muttering under his breath as he pondered. He returned later, a sword in each hand, followed by a large, portly boy carrying two suits of armour. Cedric entered the small field and placed one sword on the ground, positioning it so the hilt pointed away from him. He took a few wide steps before stopping and placing the other sword on the ground, this time with the hilt facing towards him.

As Cedric and Benjin prepared the armour, Sintra's thoughts wandered to the significance of this training. She knew that Riven's success would not only reflect on him but also on her judgment and leadership. The weight of responsibility pressed lightly on her shoulders, but she welcomed it as part of her duty.

"Benjin!" he called, and the portly boy came running, his face red and beaded with sweat.

The boy placed one suit of armour and mail on the ground and proceeded to dress the knight in the other.

"Help the boy! Not me. I can do this on my own."

Riven stood stiff and still while Benjin dressed him in the suit of armour until his entire body gleamed with silver.

"It pinches," Riven said to Sintra.

Sintra felt a pang of empathy. She understood the discomfort of new experiences and the challenges they brought.

"Aye, I hear you have not worn armour before," said Cedric.

"Yes," said Riven, circling his arms and shoulders to relax his muscles.

"The armour does pinch, but there's an easy fix for that."

"What might that be, my lord?" asked Sintra.

"Jack, as it is referred to, quite peculiar as I once met a man with the same name," he laughed. "So, I prefer to call it a doublet—thick woollens in place of fine satins, several layers of quilted leather, linen, or thick wool, reinforced with metal studs and small plates. It makes for a thicker coat beneath any suit of armour."

"I see," said Sintra.

Seating herself by the straw stack, Sintra allowed herself a moment of relaxation, kicking off her satin slippers. She watched the interaction between Cedric and Riven with keen interest, knowing that this was just the beginning of a journey that would test their resolve and strength.

"Right, now we commence," said Cedric. "What is your name?"

"Riven."

"Aye, Riven," began the knight. "Stand before the hilt of your sword, please."

Riven did as he was ordered, Cedric mirroring his position once standing still.

"Now, when I instruct you, pick up your sword and hold your guard—one foot before the other, knee slightly bent. Understood?"

The slave nodded before taking his sword upon instruction, mirroring the knight's stance. They stood facing each other, swords outstretched, one foot forward, knee slightly bent. Riven extended his free arm behind him for balance, just as he had seen knights do when he was a child.

"Splendid," said Cedric. "You have done this before. Now, as I attempt to strike your armour with my sword, you must block me. Block or dodge my sword as you would if you were unarmoured. We will practice without armour later to improve focus."

As Cedric finished speaking, he lunged forward, his front foot stepping decisively, followed by his back foot, maintaining their distance. Riven mirrored the knight's movements, their swords clashing as they eagerly attempted to strike each other's armour. Sintra, seated in the straw, watched in awe. *Riven is quite splendid at this*, she thought, a smile forming as she envisioned his potential victory in the tournament.

Back and forth they went, training for hours, the sound of clashing swords and the occasional strike against armour filling the air. Sintra's thoughts drifted as she observed the intense training. She marvelled at Riven's natural aptitude and Cedric's disciplined instruction. The rhythmic exchange of blows was almost hypnotic, and she found herself contemplating the significance of this moment. Riven's success would not only reflect his own growth but also her ability to recognize and nurture potential.

As the training continued, Sintra's eyelids grew heavy. The comfort of the straw stack and the steady cadence of the clashing swords lulled her into a peaceful slumber. Her last conscious thought was one of hope and determination, believing that with Cedric's guidance, Riven would indeed become a formidable contender.

†

Another hour had passed when Sintra awoke to the sound of Cedric's voice.

"Splendid, magnificent, superb," praised the Steel Knight as Riven blocked his every strike. "Now, place your sword on the ground before you, just as I did when we started."

Riven followed the order, and both swords now lay facing each other on the ground.

"Now, upon my instruction, you will go for your sword again. This time, you will toss your sword toward me as I toss mine toward you. This will improve your sight and reflexes. If you catch the sword, we will then duel as before," said Cedric, positioning himself to pick up the sword.

Simultaneously, they both lifted their swords from the ground and tossed them. The pieces of steel flew through the air, missing each other by no more than an inch. Riven was the first to catch his sword. He then lunged toward Cedric, who fumbled and missed his own sword, which fell to the ground. The Steel Knight raised his arms in defence and defeat, staring at Riven, stunned and speechless. A grin spread from ear to ear as Sintra's face lit up; it was the most thrilling thing she had ever seen. She clapped and squealed like a small child. Sweating and out of breath, Riven smiled toward her, his eyes full of love and adoration for the princess.

"My, my, young lad," breathed Cedric, "I commend you on your efforts. You are the fastest, most able knight I have ever trained."

"Aye, but he is no knight," said Dolores, who stood leaning in the doorway of the tavern.

"Pardon?" said Cedric, frowning and looking from the woman to Sintra and back to Riven.

"She speaks the truth," said Riven. "I am no knight," he sighed, dropping his sword in defeat.

"Pick up your sword at once!" snapped the Steel Knight. "Knight or not, you do not drop your sword before your opponent. It means forfeit. If you were on the battlefield, young man, your head would roll the instant you let go of your hilt. It is dishonour to your King and to your kingdom. Do you understand?"

Riven picked up his sword once more. Sintra bit her bottom lip, concerned and anxious, unsure of how Cedric would react.

"Ah, do you take me for a fool? What knight comes to battle wearing rags?"

"I am no knight."

"Oh, but you certainly will be," said Cedric. "Now kneel before me before I choose to roll your head."

Riven knelt before Cedric, confused and a little frightened. Sintra's eyes widened in horror.

"Lord Edith, as princess of Crevark, I command you to put down your weapon or I will have my father strip you of your knighthood," she demanded, standing within two feet of him.

"On what grounds, my princess? For granting knighthood to a slave?"

"Knighthood?" asked Sintra, frowning. "You are not going to kill him?"

"I most certainly am not!" spat the knight. "Unless my princess wishes me to do so."

"I wish you not," she answered, still confused. "Who informed you of this man's duties?"

"Not informed, my princess. I see with my own eyes the grime beneath his fingernails and behind his ears, the cuts on his hands, the stubble upon his face. His strength is like no other. It does not take great brilliance to see that this man is no knight, but a slave. His combat has awed me here this day, and we haven't yet finished. If it pleases you, I would like to knight this young man."

"Why?"

"His training, his combat—I have seen it before. Only a boy of noble blood can fight like that."

"Noble blood, sir?"

"Aye, Princess Lysandra, noble blood runs through his veins. I feel it."

"How can you make such an assumption based on what you feel and what you see, my lord?"

"I possess a great gift, madam, a rare power. For I am Cedric Edith, Steel Knight of Sidon, but also Cedric Edith, son of Geraldine Edith, the Foreteller of the West."

"Geraldine Edith, Foreteller and Prophesier of the West? The Great Foreseer of the Future?"

"The very same."

"If I am not mistaken, Lady Geraldine Edith was burned at the stake for possessing great witchery."

"Not witchery, my princess, prophecy and great wisdom and knowledge of things to come. She was not a witch, but a Foreteller and a great one at that. The gift she was given by the great gods has been passed on to me; I see the noble blood that passes through this young man's veins. No son of a nobleman should be living a life of slavery," said Cedric, turning to Riven. "Young man, I feel your worth. What was your father's name?"

"I never knew him, sir; he died in battle when I was a young boy. Both my mother and I were captured and sold as slaves."

"I see," said Cedric, scratching his chin while deep in thought. "What is your second name?"

Sintra listened closely, realizing she had never thought to ask Riven's last name.

"Valahn, sir."

"Aye, noble blood indeed. Every Valahn from North, East, South, and West were all noblemen or lords, crusaders, and knights."

If King Lysandra knew of his slave's noble blood, he would have his own head on a stake, thought Sintra.

"Before the moon is at its highest tonight, you will be granted and dubbed knighthood. You will take an oath under the midnight moon to obey orders from your Princess, the coming Queen. You possess great bravery, courtesy, honour, and gallantry. You will be dubbed knight before your Princess, and you will not defy my orders, young man, or by my falchion, your head will roll."

I will not be Queen for him to obey, thought Sintra, her mind racing with the implications of Cedric's words. She felt a mix of pride and fear for Riven, knowing that his life was about to change irrevocably. The revelation of his noble blood added a layer of complexity to their relationship, and she wondered how this newfound status would affect their future.

Riven bowed his head in silence as Sintra returned to her place among the straw. She then turned to Dolores and said, "You speak not a word of this to a single soul, and you'll find your weight in gold."

The woman was shocked by the princess's generosity, her eyes wide in awe, knowing that such an amount of riches would be considerable given her height and stature.

"Squire!" called Cedric. "Bring me the Black Sword."

Benjin rummaged through a large box of weaponry Sintra hadn't noticed before. From this box, he drew a black sheath and took it to Cedric.

"Do you carry a sword by your side, boy?" asked Lord Edith, holding the black-sheathed sword in his hands, eyes on Riven.

"I do not, sir."

"This black sword," began the knight, unsheathing the blade, "is of no use to me…"

Lord Edith paused, his brow furrowing as his face stiffened. Through timid eyes, Cedric stared at the black sword in his hands as it grew red hot. Riven's face turned horror-stricken as the blade began to smoke, blistering and burning Cedric's flesh.

"Let go, Cedric, let go of that thing," said Riven. "It's damned."

But Cedric's trance-like state made him deaf to Riven's voice. He did not move a muscle or bat an eyelid, nor did he flinch or cower as the blade began to melt his flesh. It was as if he felt nothing. Riven hesitantly reached for the blade, wincing as he grasped the steel, expecting to feel its overpowering sear but feeling only the hard, strong metal. Taking the sword from Cedric's burning grasp, he laid it on the ground and tended to the knight's scorched hands.

"Benjin, fetch some water," Riven instructed.

As Benjin filled a casket from the water trough, Riven slapped Cedric's cheeks with the back of his hand to wake him from his trance. Blinking rapidly, Cedric frowned at Riven in confusion, tilting his head.

"You slap me, why? I bid you."

But Riven needn't answer as Cedric looked at his burnt, blistered hands and winced, the scorching pain hitting him all at once as he realized what had happened.

"The sword is cursed," said Riven.

"Nay," snapped the knight, taking the casket of water from Benjin and soaking his hands. "It is not cursed; it simply chooses its vessel," began Lord Edith. "I now remember why I never unsheathed that sword—it was never meant for me."

"What do you mean it was never meant for you, Lord Edith? It is an ordinary sword. And what's this rubbish about it choosing its own vessel?" asked Sintra, who had risen again and now stood behind Riven.

"That sword is of steel stronger than any other. It is made from the scorched bone of Thalor, the steel dragon, turning it from bone to Thalor steel," said the knight.

"Pardon, Lord Edith? I do not understand how pure bone can be transformed into steel," said the princess.

"The bones of a Thalor dragon contain properties similar to actual steel, hence why the beast possesses that name. A bone scorched by its own dragon becomes the strongest of all materials, freezing those properties solid and unbreakable, becoming Thalor steel, the strongest of all. When Thalor burnt the blade carved from its own tail-thorn, it became the strongest, most unbreakable sword of all."

Hesitantly, Riven grasped the hilt of the sword and lifted it into the air. Admiring its fuller, the centre of the blade, Riven lifted the scorched blade close to his eye. The fuller was covered in tiny, detailed carvings, spread and flared out as if to mimic the thorns and twigs of a rose bush or the spider-web effect of a lightning bolt. With his right hand, Riven swung the sword around freely, his wrist unrestrained by the weapon's weight.

"It is deceiving. It appears heavy, yet it is the lightest and strongest sword in existence."

"My lord, this sword was in your possession. Where did you find it? It is a beautiful piece of weaponry," said Riven.

"That sword belonged to this princess's uncle, King Thaddeus of the kingdom of Thane."

Sintra froze. "Pardon? King Thaddeus is dead. How did this sword come to be in your possession?"

"Aye, he is dead, madam. Slaughtered by the very Thalor dragon that once grew that bone."

"That is impossible."

"It is the tail thorn of the Thalor dragon. Some say he conquered Thane in vengeance. Did you not know that that very sword was made by your uncle after he severed the thorn from the beast's tail?"

"I did not, sir. But how did this sword come to be in your possession?" she asked again.

"The sword was in my possession as I woke to the cry of a raven at first light one morning. I do not know who sent it."

"Someone sent you my dead uncle's sword?"

"Yes!"

A fallen winter whisper

The land grew dim as the sun began to retire, yet Sintra could not wrap her head around who would wish to send the Steel Knight, Cedric Edith of Sidon, her dead uncle's sword, carved from the tail thorn of the Thalor dragon—the very beast that ended Thane. And why. King Thaddeus was slaughtered by the same creature following his kingdom's fall nearly a decade ago, yet the bloodstained bone-blade had managed to survive the scorching pits of the Kingdom Hell and return to the heir of its origin and creator.

"King Thaddeus, my father's brother, is dead, his kingdom Thane, ruins. And yet the presence of the beast turns in my stomach and stabs at my heart. I know it still lives; I feel its blaze and turmoil inside me as if it lives and clutches to my womb like an infant yet to be born. With all my fear, I feel it, Riven, it's coming," said the princess.

"My princess, what you feel is hunger; we have not eaten; I trained as you took slumber. Now come, we will dine at Dolores's before we set off home."

Sintra knew what hunger felt like, and hunger was not what stirred in her stomach. She walked beside Riven, his armour clattering and clanking as they made their way to the diner tavern. Once inside, Sintra's eyes widened in disbelief as she saw at least thirty men had filled the tavern—knights and guards in armour, stuffing their faces with salted roast, pork belly and gulping red wine. Peasants and slaves in rags begged for scraps at the front entrance like filthy rats. Dolores's face glowed red, speckled with beads of sweat as she tried to keep up with the hungry patrons.

"It's as if they're all heading to war," said Riven, having seen such a busy tavern once before.

In times of war, knights and guards would swarm the tavern diners across the land to feast on great banquets until their breeches burst at the seams. They ate until their bellies swelled and drank until they could not see beyond their noses. Many a fight would break out in a packed tavern, men complaining about their empty goblets or arguing about which way the wind would blow the next day. Drunken fights and arguments about petty nothings deemed important regarding the amount of wine one had consumed.

"I can hurl an axe further than any man," boasted one very large, drunken man. With that, he took his axe above his head and swung it around. Letting go of the shaft, the axe spun across the diner, faster and faster until it came to an abrupt stop against the great brick wall on the other side of the tavern, embedding its blade deep. Small crumbs of rubble fell from the wall as it began to crack and chip. Dolores's face glowed redder than before, this time with anger building inside her.

"REMOVE THAT AXE FROM MY WALL BEFORE I REMOVE YOUR HEAD WITH IT," roared the tall woman.

The tavern fell completely silent and still as every man stopped to watch. The large, muscular man stood from his seat and silently strode toward the axe in the wall. Taking its shaft, he pulled it from the stone and turned to look at Dolores with remorseful eyes.

"Out, Tuppence!" she said loudly, pointing to the door.

The large man hung his head and waddled toward the door like a hound with its tail between its legs, his expression full of trepidation as he dared not look up at the woman behind the wooden bench. Once outside, the chatter within the diner resumed, growing louder and louder as every man tried to talk over the next.

"I suggest we find somewhere else, my princess; it is too dangerous for a lady in here," said Riven, taking her hand and striding across the tavern and out the door. Sintra turned to wave toward the large woman behind the wooden bench, but she had vanished out the back door.

The air grew cold as Sintra sat mounted on her steed, the chill biting at her now red nose. Elara had joined them once more, three rolls of satin and silk hanging over the horse's shoulders. One of black satin trimmed with gold fringe for the

King's window drapes, crimson silk also trimmed with gold fringe, and one other that appeared to be for a new gown, its dainty floral pattern of both white satin and silk fused together with golden strands of thread.

"My handmaiden has chosen such fine silk and satins," said Sintra, eyeing Elara's purchase. "I am proud, as the King will be."

As they trotted towards the citadel, leaving the lively village behind them, the fog began to drift over the land. The clattering of Riven's armour made Elara curious.

"Why does the slave wear silver armour, my princess?"

"I am a slave no more, madam," said Riven.

Elara eyed him suspiciously as he sat behind Sintra, his arms clutching her waist and the steed's reins. "Pardon?"

"At this very moment, he is a slave with noble blood, but come the midnight moon, he will be granted and dubbed knighthood."

Elara was speechless; she knew not what to say, though many words clutched the tip of her tongue at once. She sat with her mouth agape; her eyes widened in shock.

"Now, now," laughed the princess. "If the conceited Aleron can be dubbed the Knight of Knights upon a lie, why can Riven not be granted knighthood for his bravery, fairness, and compliance to fight for his kingdom? He is of noble blood, after all."

"But the King…" hesitated the old woman.

"Will hold his tongue; it was he who informed me that I am of age, and of royal stature and blood, to make my own orders."

"You are, madam, but it takes several hours, days even, for a nobleman to be dubbed a knight properly. You also need—"

"A knight, a princess, a priest, and a nobleman. We have all four."

"As long as I take an oath under the midnight moon in the presence of Cedric Edith, Steel Knight of Sidon, Princess Sintra Lysandra of Crevark, and Priest William Pyst of the old church of Thane, I will be granted knighthood."

"Thane? Do not bring Thane into your affairs, Sintra, or you will be damned by the creature that dwells within its ruins."

"Hush now. We are not to set foot in Thane, and we will not. But we must fetch Priest William Pyst from the church, and the best way to accomplish such a task is in the dead of night so the dark blanketed land conceals our pale flesh from the beast itself."

"You're going tonight?" asked the old woman, flustered and shocked.

"Yes! Now not another word."

The three of them sat silent as they neared the great wood that lay before the fields. A great darkness swept over the land, a blanket of cloud that concealed the stars and moon. It wasn't long before the clouds excreted rain, and lots of it.

"I must leave you now," Riven said, raising his voice to be heard above the pounding rain.

"I'll see you soon!" Sintra shouted.

He dismounted from the steed and stood beneath a tree on the wood's edge as Sintra and Elara rode off toward the citadel. The princess turned once, making half the field, but saw that Riven had already gone. A flash of white caught her eye as something raced toward her, pounding across the field with large heavy pads, claws digging into the softened ground. Thunder grew loud, rumbling around them as lightning grew brighter and nearer with each flare; rain fell vertically, casting fat raindrops over the land.

Frostbite, thought Sintra, glaring at the animal that raced toward her. As the white wolf neared her, a dead rabbit hung limp from its jaws.

"Nyom?" said the princess as the wolf now strode beside her on the horse.

The rain died down for the time being, falling lightly around them. A few clouds separated in the sky above, revealing a layer of black speckled with tiny white spots—the stars.

Sintra looked to her wolf without a word; Nyom's feet were blackened from the thick mud, her mouth stained red with the blood of her kill.

"She is my Frostbite," the princess replied, staring at the beautiful creature with so much love and admiration. *But why have you fled the citadel?* thought Sintra.

"She limps, Your Highness," said Elara, full of concern.

Sintra watched closely as Nyom strode beside them, her brow furrowing as she observed the animal limp with every few steps.

"Her hind leg?" asked the maid.

"No, it looks to be her front and side, her ribs," said the princess.

"Perhaps she fought off a hog, madam, or a bear."

"No, Elara, she knows not to chase animals larger than herself," said the princess. "She dislikes hog, would never set foot near a bear; hare is her favourite."

"Perhaps it was while fighting the hare."

"Hares do not fight, Elara, they cower. I have my doubts. Her side does not bleed, nor does her leg. No scratch, no graze, no cut—it dwells inside, beneath the skin. What other than a blunt object could do such sightless harm?"

Such a blind injury with no wound to show could not come from any kind of animal, for flesh bleeds at their claw. The wolf was injured by a blunt object, and Sintra knew where to find it. *Aleron*!

The princess dismounted her steed once inside the citadel walls, handing the reins to the squire as Elara did the same. Crouching toward the ground, Sintra knelt by her white wolf, examining her fur to find the wound. The animal whined and dropped its kill, licking the princess's hand as Sintra touched the animal's ribs.

"A broken rib," said the handmaid, standing by the princess with the drenched rolls of satin and silk in hand.

"Elara, hang those to dry and meet me in my chamber with hot water and a clean rag."

"Kitchen hand?" she called. "Drain the blood, skin that dead animal, and bring it to my chamber, once sliced and diced."

Sintra lifted the white wolf into the air, clutching the heavy creature in her arms and making for the entrance to the Citadel. Her drenched gown slapped against her legs as she walked briskly inside.

"Lucas," she called.

The guard came toward her with arms outstretched, taking the injured animal from her grasp. "Take her to my chamber; my maid waits with hot water and a clean rag. I am too wet to carry her; I fear slipping on the stairs and worsening this poor creature's injury."

Nyom whined and tried eagerly to get closer to Sintra as she approached her father, who glared at her in horror upon her arrival.

"Forgive me for my interruption, Father; I am drenched from the heavy rains that came upon us on our voyage home. But that is not why I stand before you," said the princess, turning and glaring at a very smug Aleron who sat beside the King, stuffing his face with turkey.

"You strike my animal, you strike me," she said sternly to the Knight. "Is that how you are to treat your lady in waiting?"

"What?" asked the King.

"My poor Nyom, Father. She is wounded on the rib by something blunt and heavy, for there is no scratch or cut. The only blood that stains her fur is from her kill tonight."

"Her kill?"

"I found her beyond the citadel walls, Father. She came to me running. I am surprised she can run at all; I am surprised she does not lie in the woods upon her cold death."

"What on earth was she doing wandering beyond the citadel walls?" asked the King.

"It is my belief that someone let her out, as she does not wander without me by her side. Someone unhinged the small wall gate, striking her upon leave, leaving her wounded and weak so that she may suffer and most likely become a greater animal's kill."

"And you think I have part in this?" said Aleron, standing to his feet.

"I know you do," snapped the princess across the table.

"You do?" pushed the King.

"He is forever striking at her, kicking and thumping any chance he gets."

"Is this true?"

"I have struck the animal only once, for it made at my leg, tore the flesh."

"She protects me; she is not violent."

"Has the animal made for another on occasion?"

"On no other account. She only makes for this imbecile, as she fears for my life when in his presence."

"I see," said Alaric.

"That does not prove me guilty, Your Highness," said Aleron Elowen, pleadingly toward the King.

"This is true," said Alaric, facing the princess.

Sintra glared at Aleron now, peering at him through squinted eyelids, her lips stiffened in a grim line.

"If I may ask, my lord, when was the last time you had your boots polished?"

Aleron frowned in confusion, raising his eyebrow. "A week ago, what relevance—"

"What foot do you lead with in battle?" interrupted Sintra.

"The right, but I don't—"

"May I see your right boot?" she interrupted again.

Aleron frowned and looked toward the King, who nodded his head in agreement to the princess's request.

"As you wish," he sighed, lifting his wet boot atop the grand table.

Sintra eyed it suspiciously; she strode around the table and stood before Aleron, leaning toward the boot to have a closer look.

"May I have a cloth?" she asked her father, her eyes not leaving the rounded toe of the boot.

As King Alaric handed the princess a mouth cloth, Sintra picked at something that had wedged itself between the toe and flat of the boot. Pinching and pulling it with her index finger and thumb, out came a small tuft of white fur. Sintra placed it in the cloth and handed it to the King, who frowned toward Aleron, waving his hand so that the knight's foot would leave the table. As the King studied the fur in the cloth, Aleron swallowed loudly, beads of sweat forming at his brow as he became quite nervous. Alaric folded the cloth in half and placed it before his plate on the grand table.

"How do you wish to punish him?" asked the King, his eyes not leaving Aleron's as he spoke to his daughter.

If only you could hang him for petty crimes, she thought to herself.

"Tie him naked to a post for one night. That should do it."

"A tuft of white fur does not prove me guilty; my boot could have picked that up from the stables, or perhaps the village. You cannot condemn me from a measly piece of fur," growled Aleron.

"I'm sorry, Lord Elowen, but I'll believe my daughter. That wolf was a gift for my Sintra's seventeenth birthday; carefully selected by myself and plucked from its siblings, the strongest of the four. I left the runt to its mother."

"But—"

"But nothing. I have grown tired of quarrel with you."

"My apologies," said Aleron, his eyes full of remorse. "The animal gets beneath my skin as Gabor gets beneath yours."

"Do not compare the arrogance of Gabor to an animal my princess has considerable admiration for. King George is worse than a water-lapping beast, slyer than a fox, and conceited as a vulture. As for your confession, you will stand tied to a post in the night wearing nothing but your wretched, animal-thumping boots. There you will stay until first light. Guards!"

Four knights from the King's Guard strode into the great hall and stood before the King.

"Take this imbecile and strip him of his clothes. Tie him to a post in the centre of the quad. He is to remain there until first light."

One of the guards stifled a laugh before heading toward Aleron and taking his arm.

"Do not touch me!" he roared. "I can take myself," he snapped, standing to his feet and making for the door in haste.

"One more thing," said King Alaric Lysandra as Aleron paused and turned to listen. "You'd better pray it doesn't snow tonight, Lord Elowen. You might catch your death."

Elowen stormed out of the great hall of the Citadel, the four guards following close behind. The King looked to his daughter with kind eyes.

"Go; tend to your pet," he said kindly. "If that animal dies during the night, I'll hold my word and strip that buffoon of his knighthood."

"She won't die tonight, Father. She is strong."

"Pity," he laughed, grumbling something under his breath.

The princess knew the King's remark was not toward her beloved wolf; he loved the creature just as she did. Perhaps he was beginning to see right through Aleron. Sintra kissed the King on the forehead and made for the door, walking briskly down the hallway. She paused for a moment and glanced out the window into the quad. She giggled to herself as she watched Aleron stripping off his clothes, ready to have his ankles and wrists bound and tied to the post. Sintra turned and strode up the hallway with such haste, skipping two steps at a time as she climbed each staircase.

"How is my Winter Whisper?" the princess asked as she entered the dimly lit bedchamber, candles casting dancing shadows on the walls.

Nyom lay on a soft fur rug in front of a blazing fire that roared in the fireplace, Lucas feeding the flames with chips of dry wood. The bowl of hot water was now lukewarm and brown as Elara had wiped away the black mud from the wolf's pads. The animal lifted its head, sniffing the air and wagging its long fluffy tail as it caught Sintra's scent. The princess stroked the animal's fur as she sat down beside her, scratching behind one of Nyom's ears with a long slender finger.

"I believe her run to catch up to the horses worsened her wound, my princess. She barely walks at all now," said Elara.

"Aleron is tied naked to a post in the quad; he will remain there until first light."

Lucas grunted to stifle a laugh, for even he despised the knight.

"How did you manage to find him guilty in the presence of the King?" asked Elara.

"I found a white tuft of fur that clung to his boot; he kicked Nyom in the ribs."

"And broke at least two," said the maid. "I hope it rains heavily tonight."

"I hope we have a blizzard," the princess added. "I will find much comfort and satisfaction sitting by my fire, absorbing its warmth while he trembles in the dark cold night, frost forming at his nose, fog forming at his breath."

The chamber was silent for a moment as the maid and guard looked at each other on Sintra's remark.

"If I may speak, never have I known a woman to loathe a man as you do," said Lucas.

"I wish he were dead," said Sintra. "I hope the cold darkness takes his life tonight; it would make me the happiest princess in the entire world to not have to wed the imbecile."

Lucas stifled another laugh, clenching his jaw to stiffen his face so his incongruous delight would not be seen.

"Lucas, it would please me very much to know why you try so eagerly to stifle a laugh when I speak of the knight in such a manner?" asked Sintra.

"I wish not to offend you, as Aleron is your husband-to-be."

"Lucas, I know you loathe him as I do."

But the guard did not laugh.

"It is late, I must be getting back to the King's Guard," he said, leaving the chamber.

"I'll fetch fresh water to clean her snout, and then we will bandage her side," said the handmaiden, standing and leaving Sintra alone in her bedchamber.

The white wolf began to whine as the princess strode toward her bed and grasped two cushions.

"Hush, my Winter Whisper," she said as she walked back to Nyom and carefully placed the cushions beneath the animal's ribcage and head to soften the harsh hardness of the stone floor beneath her.

A single animal fur rug was not enough to make the wolf comfortable for the entire night. Sintra sat beside the fire, the warmth of the flames drying her gown, warming her flesh, and making her tired. She found herself entranced as she stared into the blazing flames, her eyes ceasing to blink.

"Why do you stare into the fire?" asked Elara, setting down a new bowl of clean, steaming hot water.

"I mean not to stare; a great tiredness has overcome me just now."

"Aye, but we've had a big day, two long journeys on horseback to and from the village."

Elara dipped a clean rag into the steaming water, making her fingers grow red, but she did not flinch. She then proceeded to wash away the blood from the animal's white snout.

"She's thirsty," said the princess as she watched Nyom take to licking the wet rag.

"Aye, my princess, I did send for Prunella in the kitchen to bring the wolf's kill diced in a bowl along with a bowl of clean water."

But just as the princess went to stand, there was a knock on the door.

"Enter!" said Sintra, and to her amazement, it was Prunella herself, two bowls in either hand.

"Forgive me, I took my time to drain the blood and dice the meat, but the bones were too small to break as they splintered beneath the cleaver."

"Very well," said the princess, taking the bowls from the kitchen hand and setting them down in front of Nyom.

The second the wolf smelt the meat, she began to eat, devouring the meat until there was nothing left. She then proceeded to lap up the water, not satisfied until she licked the last drop.

"That is all for the night," said Sintra as the kitchen hand left the chamber.

The princess helped Elara to wrap the wolf's side in rag and bandage until Nyom could lie on her side more at ease. Elara stroked the wolf's fur, calming her as she whined the second Sintra left her side. The animal lifted its head, craning its neck to watch as Sintra stripped out of her filthy mud and blood-stained gown and slipped into an undergarment the maid had tailored for her bed. The princess then pulled every fur, woollen, and cushion from her giant bed and dragged them in front of the fire, doubling them over and laying them out so that she could sprawl out next to her wolf.

"If I sleep in my bed, she will only struggle to join me and worsen her wound," said the princess, answering the maid's inquisition.

"Very well, my lady, but if I check on you in a few hours and your hands and feet are ice cold, I'll be putting you both into that bed," replied Elara.

I won't be here by the time you get back, thought Sintra.

The princess said nothing and continued making a floor bed for herself until she finished and sprawled out alongside Nyom.

"This is warmer than my bed," said the princess, smiling.

Elara rolled her eyes and smiled. "Will that be all, my princess?" she asked. "I'd much like to get out of these wet clothes myself."

Sintra nodded and rested her head upon a cushion as the maid left the chamber in silence. As she lay beside the wolf, she thought of a way to escape so that Nyom wouldn't know she had left, or try following her into the night, only worsen her injury. On the other hand, she was grateful that Elara hadn't mentioned a single thing about the princess's plans this evening.

Sword of Thalor

As Sintra Lysandra raced down the cold, dark hallway on the citadel's top floor, the soft padding of her slippered feet was the only sound. She occasionally ducked behind thick pillars or melted into the shadows to avoid the guards, staying clear of the silver light cast by the nearly full moon. The icy air pricked at her nose and lips, and her nipples stiffened beneath her gown as she stepped into the moonlit courtyard. The stone ground was painfully cold beneath her feet, even through her silk slippers. She glanced over her shoulder to ensure no one had seen her leave the citadel. Everyone was in deep slumber, including Nyom, who lay by the fire with a fresh log smouldering.

As she turned the iron handle of a stable door, a creak echoed through the quad. She looked back again, but there was no movement. Inside the stable, she gathered a headstall and fitted it onto one of the knights' horses, the fastest steed. The horses rested silently, apart from an occasional straw-muffled snort.

"Hey Soul," she whispered to calm the horse, "Hush now, beautiful steed."

Sintra led the giant white horse into the courtyard, wincing at the clatter of its hooves on the stone. She paused, dropped the reins, and hurried back to the stable, returning with armfuls of straw. She laid the straw in piles leading to the side gate, muffling the sound of Soul's hooves. Quickly, she guided the sleepy animal over the straw and toward the gate. With a loud creak, she swung open the door and began to lead the steed through when she suddenly heard a voice.

"And where do you think you're off to?"

Sintra's body stiffened in horror as Lord Elowen's voice rang through her ears. She turned, dropping the reins and walked slowly out into the centre of the quad.

"So, I'm not dreaming," said Aleron, "Wait until the King finds out about *this*, he will have your head."

"You're dreaming Lord Elowen," Sintra whispered.

"You lie!" he hissed, glaring at her from the post he had been tied to earlier, "Coldness is never felt during a slumber, one wakes at the touch of cold, brisk air."

Sintra knew not what to do, at any moment Aleron could yell out to one of the guards and she would then have to explain her behaviour.

I was sleepwalking, father, she thought. *On a steed?* She knew he would question. The princess looked to the moon; it was almost at its highest. She needed to escape silently before Lord Elowen could say a word. *Every dream proves desire,* she thought, *I'll pretend it's a dream, one of Aleron's dreams, and then he will have to believe.*

Sintra walked slowly toward the naked knight, placing her warm hands against his chest.

"What are you doing?" he snapped.

"You're dreaming Aleron, it is our wedding night so take me to bed," said the princess, disgusted in the words that just escaped her mouth.

"Lies, all lies!" he said, confusion rising in his voice.

Its working, Sintra thought to herself moving her hands down his bare hairy chest toward his stomach.

"What does my King wish me to do?" she asked, her voice soft and slow, seducing even.

Lord Elowen was silent; he was stunned in disbelief. The princess moved her hands past his naval and toward his now erect length. Immediately disgusted in herself, Sintra grasped hold of it with both hands, closing her eyes tight in distaste.

"Kiss me!" said Lord Elowen.

"As you wish, my King," said the princess.

She took her hands away from Aleron's length and wrapped them around his neck, running her fingers through his hair and tugging lightly.

Pretend it's Riven. Pretend its Riven. chanted in her mind.

Sintra closed her eyes tight and pressed her lips against Aleron's, making fists with her hands at the unbearable thought and horrible taste that was now in her mouth. She thrust her hips against his; Lord Elowen gave a moan of pleasure. She pulled away from him, letting her hands drop to his waist again.

Only this would happen in a dream, she thought, *and certainly not one of mine.*

"Untie me so I can take you, my Queen," he whispered.

Sintra ran her hands along his bare arms, grasping his hands with hers. She then brushed past him, not moving her hands until she was behind him.

If I had a dagger or a baselard, I could kill him right now and nobody would ever suspect it was me, she thought. *But no, I must get to Riven and Cedric.*

"My Queen?" he whispered.

The princess grasped the shackles that bound his wrists together, searching around the quad for a blunt object before spotting a small wooden pole by a trough. Quickly she ran toward the trough, took the pole and returned by Aleron's side.

"In a moment, my King," she whispered in his ear, nibbling at his earlobe and making him shiver with excitement.

She then took a large step backward and raised the wooden pole high above her head, gripping it tightly.

"Are you ready?" she asked, but before Aleron could reply she swung the pole as hard as she could, a loud clout filling the quad.

She dropped the wooden pole to the stone pave with a clatter and ran toward Soul who had made his way through the side door of the citadel wall himself. Sintra glanced over her shoulder and looked back at the limp naked body that now drooped from the post. A small gash on the side of Lord Elowen's head will be cause of query in the morning, along with an excruciating headache. Sintra mounted her steed, which sprang to life and jolted forward into a gallop as soon as it felt her presence. The princess laughed to herself, not looking back. She felt no remorse for what she had just done; in fact, she felt liberated.

"That was for my family," she yelled aloud to herself, knowing that the racing wind that passed her couldn't carry her voice beyond the citadel wall, "For Nyom, for my father and for Crevark," she yelled, "You're lucky I hadn't a sword, you pig."

The wind soared past her ears, stiffening her cheeks as the steed galloped as fast as it could through the fields. Sintra slowed him to a canter as she came to the edge of the wood.

"Riven?" she called, "Riven, show yourself."

She trotted through the trees, ears straining for a reply, but only the rustling leaves answered as the wind whispered through the branches. She urged her horse onward, its hooves pounding the earth with a relentless rhythm. Sintra clung tightly, the steed's mane whipping her face like stinging needles, testing her focus. Soul's breath came in rapid, heavy bursts as he galloped on; the moon hung motionless in the sky, unchanged since they had left the citadel.

"What do they feed you, Soul?" she laughed, marvelling at the horse's incredible speed.

As Sintra approached the village, the scent of burning wood filled her nostrils. She scanned the horizon for the source, her eyes locking onto a blazing fire. Pulling the reins sharply, she brought Soul to an abrupt halt. A dark silhouette stood a few yards ahead, blocking the path. Soul snorted in displeasure; his ears twitching as he sensed the stranger. The figure's right side glowed with the reflected flames, casting an eerie orange and red light.

"Who goes there?" said the voice.

The princess sighed in relief at the sound of Cedric Edith's voice, her racing heart slowing.

"Lord Edith, it is Princess Lysandra," she said, now dismounting from the steed and leading Soul to a post by a trough.

"Ah, splendid, we were about to fetch you," he replied.

Sintra walked toward Lord Edith, his face now visible in the light of the fire; his flesh a pale orange. The shadow of his nose danced on his face as the flames of the fire flickered in the breeze. His glassy eyes burned crimson as the reflection of the fire danced within his pupils.

"You frightened me, Lord Edith," said the princess.

"Aye and you frightened me, my lady."

"A gallant knight frightened of a girl and steed?" she laughed.

"Do you mock me, my princess?"

"No, Your Grace," Sintra laughed again, "How are your palms?"

"Pardon?"

"Your Palms, from the Thalor sword my lord. It burnt your flesh."

"Aye, but the most peculiar thing happened; the scars vanished," said Cedric, showing the princess his hands free from burns.

"Quite peculiar indeed," Sintra agreed, following Lord Edith as he led the princess to the fire.

"Shall we get on with this then?" grunted a man in white robes that were trimmed with gold fringe and tassels, "An old man values his slumber, you know."

"Priest William Pyst of Thane?" asked Sintra.

"Yes?" answered the old man, "Well, come on what is it? Out with it."

Why are you here already, she thought to herself.

"I sent him a raven," said Cedric, answering her thoughts and facial expression.

"I am Princess Sintra Lysandra of Crevark, my father is-,"

"Yes, your father is the brother of late King Thaddeus Lysandra of Thane, I know," grunted the old man, "S'pose he was a wicked man too?"

"Since the death of Queen Caprice, my mother, kind priest. The slaughter of my sisters and only brother, he has grown wicked."

"Aye, but a hard man will become of a gentle one, my lady. The widowed man aches for his Queen, and his family."

The princess sat silently on a great log, her head bowed in sorrow, not uttering a word. *I ache for them too,* she thought, *every single day I miss them and curse that wretched Lord Elowen. I should have killed him just now; there would be no need for a tournament.*

Sintra's spirits lifted as she looked up to see a tall, and handsome man approaching. He looked different with his hair trimmed short and his face clean-shaven. He wore a white vesture symbolizing purity, overlaid with a red robe denoting nobility.

"My love, you look like an angel," said the princess, standing to her feet to embrace the man before her.

"Nay, my princess, you are the angel," he whispered to her lips before kissing her deeply, each hand planted softly on either side of her face.

There were no words to describe how much Sintra loved this man and even more so now that he is of noble blood.

"Will the King protest now if I stand before him, son of a noblemen, and ask for the hand of the heir of Crevark?" he whispered against her lips.

Sintra sighed.

"How did you manage to escape, my princess?"

"I crept from my bedchamber to the stables, my lord," she answered, giggling like a small child having never addressed Riven as 'lord' before.

"He's not a lord yet," said Cedric, smirking to the two of them.

"Were the guards in a deep slumber?" asked Riven, ignoring Cedric's remark.

"One or two, but it was slipping past Lord Elowen that proved difficult."

"How so?"

"He is tied naked to the post in the centre of the quad, a punishment for striking Nyom," Sintra started, intentionally leaving out 'the dream' aspect, "She has two broken ribs and rests by my fire in my bedchamber, she is very weak."

"How did he get his hands on Nyom?"

"Something tells me he crept into my bedchamber early that day, heaven knows why but Nyom only stays in my chambers upon my orders. I told her to stay once I had left for the village. Elara and I found her beyond the citadel walls upon our arrival, feet caked with mud, her snout stained with blood and still she limped."

"Bastard would do such a thing," scoffed Riven, his vibrant beauty glowing as his anger rose.

"Right then," called Cedric, "Sir Valahn, Princess Lysandra and Priest Pyst please make your way to the chapel. Squire, with me."

As Sintra walked with Riven toward the chapel, she didn't notice Benjin sitting alone in the darkness, his cheeks bouncing as he trotted behind Lord Edith. The land was dark but not pitch black, as the moon cast a silver blanket over everything in sight. Each blade of grass on the surrounding lawns was tipped in silver light, along with the water that glistened in every nearby trough. Soul's white rump and hind legs were painted silver by the moonlight as the steed rested once more, his head hung in slumber as he faced the shadowy darkness of the post. The chapel rooftop gleamed silver and white under the light of the almost midnight moon.

Sintra lifted her grey sequined gown above her ankles, clutching it with one hand while the other rested softly in Riven's. They walked up the front steps of the chapel, the silver trim flowing gently against the ground. Once inside, the warmth of a blazing fire welcomed their cold, stiff faces, reddening Sintra's cheeks. The chapel was small but no less holy than any other; it was one of the lord's houses. Dark oak pews sat in rows, lining each side of the small chapel from the entrance to the marble altar that held a black-sheathed sword, a silver hanop filled with red wine, and a wooden herce of candles that flickered in the outside breeze until Lord Edith closed the front doors behind them.

"Riven Valahn, please kneel before the altar and before Priest Pyst to take an oath," said Cedric.

As Sintra took a seat on a front pew to the right of Riven, who knelt silently before the altar, there was a loud knock on the chapel entrance door.

"Who disturbs this ceremony?" yelled Priest William from the altar, his hands placed on either side of the marble bench in a frustrated lean.

The doors swung open to reveal the Squire of the Steel Knight, Benjin, along with what appeared to be the village people of Crevark.

"We have come to bear witness, noble Priest; a gathering has formed to witness this ceremony in the name of the new Queen Sintra for she will reign true this kingdom and our village," said a middle-aged woman, pushing her way past Benjin.

"How did you come to know this?" asked Cedric, glaring at his Squire.

"A crow's whisper," said the woman.

"And what is your reason for wanting to bear witness to this ceremony?" asked Sintra, now standing from her pew.

"The crow's whisper, my lady, told us of your marriage to Lord Elowen under the coming full moon. The village people cannot let this be as we feel your detest for the knight of falsehood."

"How so?" frowned Sintra.

"On more than one occasion Aleron has rode into the village, throwing back and forth his weight, stealing from venders and taking stallage tax. He dines and drinks at Dolores's, becoming blind of his nose and groping our women. He strikes our animals and roars at our children like a great bear, my princess; those are not the manners of a King in waiting…"

Sintra raised her hand to silence the woman, "By your own free will you are more than welcome to join this ceremony. Bear witness to the dubbing of a new knight, a knight that will one day be your King."

"King, my lady?"

"Aye, there will be a tournament held tomorrow as this knight to be, fights Lord Elowen on the battlefields behind the great citadel of Crevark. I bid your presence village people; to witness this knight's victory," said Sintra, holding out her hand toward Riven.

The Priest raised his eyebrows as at least fifty village people passed through the entrance, filling the small chapel.

"Very well," sighed Cedric, closing the entrance doors and squeezing his way through the crowded pews. Even the isle was packed with village people.

Sintra stood four feet before Riven to one side right of the altar, Cedric joined her, taking the other side left to the altar. The village people fell silent and kept still in their seats as Priest Pyst held his arms into the air above his head, raising his hands to the heavens while whispering a silent prayer. He then lowered his hands before Riven and spoke.

"I, Priest William Jonathon Pyst, priest of Thane the fallen; stand here in the village chapel of Crevark before Riven Valahn as he takes oath before the Holy Lord. Witness of noble blood, say *Aye*."

"Aye!" said Lord Edith.

"Witness of royal blood, say *Aye*."

"Aye!" said Sintra.

"Witness of any other blood that seats in this chapel, say *Aye*," said the priest.

"Aye!" said the crowd of village people, their heads' remaining bowed.

"I, Priest William Jonathon Pyst, proclaim that the Holy Lord witnesses this ceremony from the heavens. Lord Cedric Edith, Steel Knight of Sidon, and Princess Sintra

Lysandra, daughter of King Alaric and the late Queen Caprice of Crevark, stand as witnesses. I, Priest William Jonathon Pyst of Thane the fallen, also witness this knighting ceremony of Riven Valahn, as he takes an oath of allegiance to the Holy Lord."

With this, the priest raised the hanop of wine above his head, whispered a silent prayer, took a sip, and lowered it. Sintra and Cedric each took a sip from the hanop before placing it on the altar and bowing. Priest Pyst nodded to Riven.

"I, Riven Valahn of noble blood, take an oath of allegiance to the Holy Lord and to Princess Sintra Lysandra of Crevark. I swear before Priest William Jonathon Pyst of Thane the fallen, and before the Steel Knight of Sidon, Lord Cedric Edith. I vow to never traffic with traitors, give evil counsel, or strike anyone without orders from the kingdom. I vow to obey all commands from Crevark, never forfeit my role as knight, and never surrender to the enemy. I solemnly swear to serve and protect my kingdom in honour as a knight of Crevark. This I oath!"

Riven bowed to the priest, lifted the hanop, whispered a prayer, and took a sip of the wine. He then joined Sintra before the altar while Cedric bowed and kneeled before the priest, who held the black-sheathed sword above his head in silent prayer.

Take my hand right here, right now, thought Sintra as she looked lovingly toward Riven, *we have a priest and a chapel.*

"As we do not have a King among us tonight, I ask Lord Cedric Edith of Sidon, Steel Knight, to dub thee Riven Valahn, Knight of Midnight Moon, Knight of the Thalor Sword," said the priest, lowering the sword and handing it to Cedric who rose slowly to his feet.

Sintra took a few steps backward as Riven knelt before Cedric, and before the Thalor sword. Lord Edith took the hilt and unsheathed the sword, ensuring he did not touch the blade this time, and lowered it to one of Riven's shoulders.

"Before holy, noble and royal blood I grant thee the honour of knighthood. Shall you be gallant, victorious and fair."

Cedric lifted the sword from Riven's shoulder and proceeded to lower it onto the other.

"With this sword I, Lord Cedric Edith, Steel Knight of Sidon, dub thee Lord Riven Valahn, Sir Knight of the Thalor Sword."

With that Riven rose to his feet and bowed before the priest, turned and bowed before the princess before turning back to Cedric who now knelt before Riven. He quickly bowed his head and took the sword from Lord Edith.

That was close, thought Sintra; *we would surely face eternal damnation if the priest were to know we brought a damned sword into the house of the lord.*

"Now for the celebrations," said Cedric cheerfully, a grin from ear to ear as he pushed his way through the crowd toward the entrance of the chapel.

Lord Edith pushed the doors open and walked out into early morning darkness, the moon still casting silver light over the land. Sintra turned to the altar in time to see the priest vanish behind a curtain, holding a hand to his mouth as he yawned greatly. She turned back to Riven who hadn't taken his eyes off her since Cedric had left.

"Is something wrong Lord Valahn?" she asked, grinning before wrapping her arms around his neck.

"Not at all, my princess, I just had a thought."

"Enlighten me, Sir Knight of the Thalor sword."

"Without quarrel of your father, Sintra, I can take your hand," he smiled, raising her hand to his lips to kiss it.

Sintra's heart fluttered like a thousand butterflies, her loins burning for his love. Her blood coursed through her body, her breath quickening. She leant in to kiss Riven, but the moment was interrupted.

"Excuse me, my princess, but Lord Valahn is wanted outside," said Cedric, clearing his throat and jerking his head toward the entrance of the chapel.

The last remaining hours of the night, the village people held a celebration in the new knight's name, dancing and feasting around the fire, drinking and singing until everyone grew tired. Sintra danced with Riven until she felt drained, resting her head on his shoulder as he swayed from side to side to the soft sound of the music.

"I must get going," whispered the princess, not lifting her head at all as she spoke.

"Soon, my love," he whispered back.

"Is the princess in love with the new knight?" came a small voice.

Sleepily, Sintra lifted her head and frowned when she saw a small child standing not two feet away from where they danced.

"Pardon?" she asked.

"Is the princess in love with the new knight?" the child repeated.

Sintra looked to Riven with sleepy eyes, "Am I dreaming?" she asked.

"No, my love," he laughed.

Sintra then turned to the child, girl or boy she did not know, and replied, "Very much, sweet child. Now off you go, its way past your bedtime."

"Oh, my princess," laughed the child, "But I've been to bed and had my slumber, it's almost first light."

Sintra's eyed widened in disbelief, her heart almost pounding out of her chest in angst. She looked to the moon, but it had almost vanished, the child spoke the truth, first light was almost here.

"I must be going," she said, kissing Riven before turning and rushing to find her steed.

Soul was surrounded by small children who gathered to pet him; his mane and tail were braided magnificently, intertwined with flowers and leaves.

"Excuse me children," she said, mounting the steed.

Just as she gathered her reins for a fast ride back to the citadel, she heard a voice say something she never expected.

"He is not worthy of knighthood, madam," the voice said. "Aleron Elowen committed the greatest betrayal almost three years ago. I saw it with my own eyes, my princess. The Queen took her last breath at the hand of him."

Sintra paused, her breath catching. *I knew it,* she thought. *I could feel it tugging at my heart.*

She turned to see a young boy, a few years younger than herself, with ragged clothes, knotted hair, and a dirt-stained face.

"You there," the princess began, "I ask you to speak before the King today before noon. You will tell him what you just told me."

"What if I don't, my lady?"

"You will find your weight in gold if you do," she said, eyeing the thin boy. "Twice your weight."

"Four times my weight and you'll see me at noon," the boy replied.

Sintra had no time to bargain. "Four times," she agreed, nodding.

She dug her heels into Soul's side, breaking into a full gallop and leaving the village behind.

Within twenty minutes, Sintra was back on royal territory, riding for her life as Soul galloped toward the citadel wall. She slid off the steed, her legs like jelly, and quietly opened the side gate. Listening for any guards, she only heard the snorting and hoof-digging of the restless steeds in the stable. Confident the quad was clear, she led Soul back to his stable, hung the headstall, and scattered the straw with her feet to make it look natural.

Sintra glanced at Lord Elowen, still slumped as she had left him, and walked briskly to the citadel entrance. Just as she was about to grasp the door handle, it turned. Four guards emerged, heading toward the naked man on the post. Sintra slipped inside the hallway before they could see her.

They've come to untie the murderer; she thought as she ran down the hallway and up the staircase. If the princess weren't so exhausted, anger might've burned inside of her for she now knew the truth, and it will only be a matter of hours until the King was informed by a witness at noon.

Before heading down the next hallway, Sintra peered around the corner to ensure the King had already gone to the great hall for breakfast. The hallway was silent and dim as the sun began to rise. She ran as fast as she could, up flights of stairs and down hallways, her breathing hoarse by the time she reached the top chambers of the citadel.

Entering her bedchamber, she found Nyom still resting by the burnt-out fire, with only warm coals smouldering. Sintra curled up beside her Winter whisper and closed her eyes as the first light streamed through her window.

The Dawn of Change

Sintra woke to the friendly greeting of Nyom licking her face and neck. The princess yawned and turned over, exhausted from having slept only a few hours.

"Time to rise, my princess. Your father requests your presence, and it's almost noon," said Elara, entering the bedchamber.

"Almost noon?" groaned the princess, rolling over.

"Yes, and we have much to do today, so free yourself of those furs and woollens before I do."

"Don't bother yourself," said Sintra, sitting up and looking around her bedchamber. "Why are my maid's tailoring tools in my bedchamber?" she asked, eyeing the dress-making tools now occupying the wooden bench in one corner of the chamber.

"For tailoring your new gown, madam. Did you forget?"

No, how could I forget that I am supposed to wed a murder? she thought. *Tis not likely to happen anyway, so what's the need for a new gown?*

"I will be tailoring two new gowns for you today: one of crimson silk trimmed with gold and the other of white satin and silk lined with gold thread," said the maid.

"Crimson? I believe the crimson silk is for my window drapes."

"Yes, my princess, though it seems I have more than I bargained for."

Sintra rose to her feet, stretching her arms above her head as she yawned and groaned. She made for her oak closet and pulled out a pale blue day-gown, which sat perfectly above her ankles as she slipped it over her head and smoothed out the wrinkles with her hands.

"My dear, I hope you will be wearing something a little more elegant after noon," said the maid.

"And why do you hope that Elara?"

"The tournament and the feast, my lady. Where is your head this morning?"

"In the clouds, it seems," yawned the princess, passing the maid and heading for the door. "Please tend to Nyom; it seems my Winter whisper has made a mess during the night," she added upon leaving.

Elara frowned as she noticed wolf droppings in one of the corners of the bedchamber, "Oh Nyom," she sighed.

As Sintra made her way down the hallway to the great hall she overheard her father talking to one of the other maids.

"Blasted owls in search for stable mice have made a mess of the quad, scattered straw from here to there, wretched night birds. See to it that it is cleaned at once."

Greta, one of the King's maids passed the princess as she walked through the entrance to the great hall. Sintra held her hand to her mouth so as to hide a yawn, but no yawn came for she meant to stifle a laugh upon seeing the great gash in the side the Lord Elowen's head.

"Sleep well, my princess?" asked the King.

"Like an infant, father, as I hope to sleep tonight. No Queen to be shall have darkened rings beneath the eye on her wedding day," she lied.

"Aye," said the King, smiling.

Lord Elowen stared at Sintra with desire; his eyes had not left hers since she arrived at the grand table.

"Sleep well, Lord Elowen?" she asked him, but no reply came.

"Our knight of knights seems to be a little out of sorts this morning, I'm yet to discover who gave him that nasty gash upon the side of his head," said King Lysandra, "Most likely one of the guards took pity on his bound wrists and saw to pick a fight knowing damn well he couldn't budge an inch. I've asked him, but he does not remember."

Good!

"I see," said Sintra, "Did the guards hear anything in the night or in the morning? Or whenever you suspect this happened?"

"Not a thing, Sintra," he replied, "I was just telling Greta of the blasted night owls that scattered stable straw from here to there in search of mice."

"Oh?"

"Cornelius informed me a few hours ago, said he went for a light morning walk to wake his spirit for the day. Those wretched birds must've been up all night."

"I see," said the princess, biting her lip.

"Aye, you should see the mess for yourself."

With no reply, she frowned and looked off into the distance as if deep in thought before changing the topic of conversation.

"What time shall we expect the first guests?" she asked.

"Hmm, after midday I believe. Why?"

"Oh nothing, father, I just wanted ample time for Elara to tailor my gowns."

"Gowns?"

"One for the tournament and the other for the feast, and perhaps for the wedding."

"I see. A new gown for the wedding? I was under the assumption that you would be wearing your mother's."

"I wanted something...new."

Sintra felt a pang of pity for her father, knowing she would never wear her mother's wedding gown to wed Aleron. She also felt a twinge of shame, for it was a magnificent garment. The gown featured white silk sleeves that extended from puffed shoulders to slim wrists, a white sequined corset with a golden pearl-trimmed square neckline that sat just above the bust, revealing only a hint of cleavage. From the corset flowed exquisite white silk and satin, culminating in a fine train that stretched ten feet long, all adorned with thousands of small white pearls and tiny gold-studded diamonds. It was the most beautiful gown she had ever seen; she never understood why her mother hadn't displayed it proudly in a tall ambry.

Maybe I could try it on just once, she thought. *My mother's dead, so it wouldn't worry her, and nobody would find it odd given the upcoming decree.*

The bell chimed noon, interrupting Sintra's thoughts.

"Ah, a late breakfast feast," said the King as bowls of soup and black manger were placed on the grand table before them, along with golden goblets and hanops of fine wine and mead.

"We haven't dined on black-manger or tasted mead in a good while," said the princess. "Why the sudden change?"

"Ah, but a change," he laughed. "Change is upon us," he added, not saying another word as he scooped a spoonful of soup into his mouth, the liquid dribbling down his chin.

"I do hope you will shave before the tournament," said Sintra. "Or is that another change?"

The King felt his face. "Ayyeee," he replied, drawing out the word as if deep in thought.

"Perhaps another change, my lady," said Lord Elowen, speaking strangely kind for once.

Change is upon us indeed, she thought. *Just you wait and see.*

Sintra's appetite waned; she suddenly wasn't hungry at all as her mind replayed the incidents from the previous night. She snickered toward Lord Elowen; he had seemed different since his 'dream,' which disgusted her; she knew he would be reminiscing it whenever he gazed at her.

"My sincere apologies father, but I'm suddenly not hungry."

With that she stood and left in haste, she wanted to be so far away from Aleron as possible.

I hope his 'dream' did not give him any ideas, or I will have to carry my baselard, she thought as she hurried down the hallway.

"Cornelius," she greeted as she saw the old man dusting books among the shelves as she entered the book chamber, "Or should I say 'hoot, hoot'."

The old man smiled warmly, stifling a laugh with a small grunt as he pretended to cough. He jerked his head toward a woman in the 'Horticulture' aisle and turned toward the secret chamber, with Sintra following. Once inside, Cornelius immediately began lighting candles, each wax stick neatly placed on a wooden herce instead of scattered around the small chamber.

"My princess," he finally greeted, bowing his head. "I was informed of your escape to the village in the night," he said, rubbing the glass of his moon-shaped spectacles with his royal green button-down vest.

"Elara?"

"She told me of a young man who was to be knighted beneath the midnight moon."

"I rode to the village in the night as I was needed."

"Needed?"

"To attend a knighting ceremony, as I am of royal blood."

"Ah, I see. Were there holy men and noblemen present too?"

"Aye, Cornelius. Priest William Pyst and Sir Cedric Edith of Sidon."

"Cedric Edith?" the old man gushed in disbelief.

"Yes, you know of this knight?"

"I do, my princess. He is a great knight known throughout the land. A true gallant, victorious, noble knight who has fought and won many battles, served, and survived war upon war. Lord Edith is a great man and a great friend of mine, as was his mother, may the gods rest her soul."

"I hadn't the slightest idea, Cornelius," said Sintra, stunned.

"Yes…hmmm, back to the topic," he grunted, clearing his throat. "Tell me, what happened? How did this ceremony come to be?"

"Riven trained with Cedric yesterday, and as the blood of the great Prophesier runs within his veins, he proclaimed Riven was of noble blood. He said he had seen it, felt it in his veins, and heard it on the wind by a great spirit."

"Ah, I see. Cedric felt Riven's worth and granted him knighthood because he truly deserved it?"

"Yes, Cornelius."

"Aye, the King will be furious once he discovers he bought a nobleman as a slave," laughed the bookkeeper.

Sintra frowned and continued. "Cedric Edith dubbed Riven Sir Knight of the Thalor Sword, which was blessed by Priest Pyst. When the ceremony ended, the village people celebrated and feasted until it was time for me to return…"

Sintra paused, her mind drifting back to the witness who promised to show at noon. She blinked rapidly before looking at a concerned Cornelius.

"What is it, Sintra? What's wrong? Tell me."

"Before I left the village…" she hesitated, "a young boy told me something. He witnessed the death of the Queen…and my sisters and brother…by the hand of Lord Elowen."

Cornelius froze, his eyes widening in horror and disbelief. "Inform the King at once, bring this witness forward," he said, his voice shaky with fear.

"The boy has not arrived yet. He promised to speak before the King at noon. He swore as I promised him riches."

"Did you give him any riches before he was to speak before the King?"

"Never, I know better than that," she snapped.

"Then he's just late. He may still arrive. In good time, my princess, in good time."

"And when he does, Cornelius, he will inform the King of Lord Elowen's treachery. My father will have no option but to torture the truth out of him. Once the truth is spoken, Aleron's head will roll at the Falchion by my father's hand."

"That it will, my lady."

"I will not be forced to wed that wretched traitor. He will be dead, and I will pray to the Holy Gods that I may wed Lord Valahn, Sir Knight of the Thalor Sword," said Sintra.

"Change is upon us, Cornelius."

"Aye, my princess, change is indeed upon us."

†

As Sintra stood in her bedchamber with her arms outstretched, she anxiously awaited news of her witness's arrival. Time dragged on, but no word came.

"Ouch, Elara, that one drew blood," snapped the princess, wincing.

"Hush now, stop moving," ordered the maid, carefully lining the fabric with pins. "This is the last before I darn, my princess."

"Good, I've been standing for an hour. My arms feel like cast iron, heavy yet weak; I feel they begin to shake."

The gown was a masterpiece in the making. The crimson satin, rich and lustrous, flowed over Sintra's body, its gold trim catching the light with every movement. The gathered corset cinched her waist tightly, accentuating her slender figure and pressing her breasts against her chest. The squared neckline, adorned with delicate gold fringe, revealed a generous cleavage, the fringe tickling the top of her breasts like tiny, playful fingers.

The sleeves were a marvel of design, starting long and slender from the shoulder to the elbow, then flaring out gracefully and cascading over her wrists in an elegant waterfall of fabric. Each edge of the sleeves was meticulously trimmed with the same gold fringe, adding a touch of opulence. The hem of the gown, also adorned with gold fringe, flowed past Sintra's feet, pooling on the floor in a luxurious train.

"You always make them too long, Elara. I almost trip, you know. I could break my neck yet."

But the maid ignored the princess's complaint and continued to pin and darn the garment together, threading gold fibre along the seams. A golden tasselled robe tie belt hung from Sintra's hips, trailing down between her legs at the front of the gown, resting against the crimson silk. From Sintra's hips, the gown flowed delicately over her legs, the crimson fabric lined with golden thread and adorned with small pearls dipped in gold paint.

Elara had tailored a pair of matching padded slippers while Sintra slept that morning. She had risen at first light to tailor the window drapes that now hung from the citadel window of the princess's bedchamber.

"It is complete, Your Highness," said the maid, smiling as she stepped back to admire her work.

"Now I match the drapes," laughed Sintra. "I could stand by them unseen. My new slippers would never give me away."

"Yes, yes, very good," said the maid. "Now out of that so I can start your other gown. We have two hours before the tournament commences."

Sintra sighed and ever so gently lifted the gown over her head, revealing her undergarments. She placed the new gown on her bed furs and stood with her arms outstretched as Elara draped white silk and satin along her arms, midsection, and legs, measuring it for size.

"When I am Queen, gowns will only be fitted and tailored once a month. No lady should grow arms of steel like men; it's unbearably ugly."

"Aye, my princess, no woman should be as masculine as a man," agreed the maid. "But a Queen should have more than one gown tailored a week, madam. A Queen's wardrobe must be abundant."

"Yes, but change is upon us, my maid."

"If you say so."

An hour passed as Sintra stood straight and stiff, her arms outstretched while Elara tailored her gown for the feast. Nyom lay by the window among fresh furs and woollens, her bandages freshly renewed, watching silently as the maid sewed seam after seam. This gown was more elegant than the last, revealing Sintra's bare shoulders with its sleeveless design. The white satin corset was laced with gold silk thread that wove from the waistline to the breasts, flowing like the stems and leaves of a rose bush. The thread spiralled upward, the floral embroidery overlapping the satin beneath.

From the waistline, the silk and satin gold-threaded cloth flowed elegantly down the princess's legs, flaring at her feet. More floral embroidery trailed down the centre of the gown, meeting the gold trim that ran around the edge of the bottom of the garment.

"It's magnificent, Elara. I adore your craftsmanship," said the princess.

The handmaiden stood back and admired her newest creation, smiling to herself before racing out of the princess's bedchamber.

"Where are you going in such haste?" asked Sintra, striding out the door after the maid.

Sintra started to make for the staircase, frowning and confused, but she soon stopped and turned as Elara called out to her from behind, out of breath from climbing the stairs so quickly.

"Come madam, I have something for you," said the maid, vanishing into the bedchamber.

"You force me to run around like a child. This is no game, Elara. You must tell me where you are going; you gave me a fright," Sintra said, turning back into her bedchamber. But as she paused in front of the maid, her mouth gaped open as her eyes rested on the most beautiful jewel choker she had ever seen.

"It was your mother's, my lady; perhaps you can wear it tomorrow."

"Perhaps," said Sintra, stunned.

The neck choker was made of the finest white silk-threaded satin ribbon, neatly placed around the neck and joined at the very centre where a bright red ruby sat. The ruby was surrounded by small white gold-studded diamonds, all firmly attached to a small golden plate. The plate's edges were etched and carved with tiny golden roses and leaves. The brooch-like pendant was heavy in Sintra's hand, the silk-threaded satin ribbon soft and delicate against her flesh as she caressed it with her thumb.

I'll wear this tonight, she thought, for Riven's victory feast.

But as that thought passed through her mind, she was interrupted by a messenger at her bedchamber door.

"My princess, a raven has been sent for you," said the messenger, handing the princess a small piece of parchment fastened with the wax seal of Golorah.

Taking the parchment from the messenger's hand, the choker still clutched in her grip, she pulled on the wax seal and unfolded the parchment.

Princess Sintra Lysandra of Crevark,

I, Edmund Artec, the third King of Golorah, extend my heartfelt congratulations to you on the occasion of the coming full moon as you wed the honourable Knight of Knights, Lord Aleron Elowen. It deeply saddens me to inform you that I will not be able to attend this evening's tournament or feast due to pressing matters that I cannot disclose in writing. My deepest regrets and sincere apologies also extend to the morrow, as I will be unable to witness Lord Elowen take your hand in marriage. In my absence, I send many gifts and riches as a token of my goodwill.

Yours sincerely, E. W. Artec Third King of Golorah

"Shame," said the princess, saddened, "I wonder what business Edmund has."

Sintra strode to her oak bench in one of the far corners of her bedchamber and placed the parchment beneath a gold paperweight.

"There is more, Your Highness," said the messenger, striding toward the princess and handing her another parchment, this one rolled and tied with hemp-thread.

Madam Princess Lysandra of Crevark,

Have you seen my son? He left before noon this morn to speak before the King as you had requested before first light. Regarding Lord Elowen, which was to be kept secret, he has not returned home since. If you see him, please send him home. Many thanks.

Yours, L. P. Moth

Sintra frowned as she read the parchment; she now understood why her witness had not yet come to speak before the King.

"What is it?" asked the maid.

"My witness is missing, Elara. I received a letter from his mother," said the princess, her voice trembling. "He left before noon this morning and has not yet returned home. But what's more peculiar is… he never arrived here."

"Perhaps he wandered. Perhaps it slipped his mind," suggested the maid.

"Great wealth in exchange for a secret does not slip one's mind, Elara. This seems all a little strange to me."

Sintra turned to the messenger, her eyes narrowing. "Out!" she demanded; her voice sharp. "Messengers do not linger in the quarters of a princess unless otherwise ordered."

The messenger hastily exited the bedchamber, closing the door behind him.

"I may be terribly wrong, Elara, but I fear that this boy will not be found unharmed, if found alive," Sintra said, her voice dropping to a whisper.

"Whatever do you mean, madam?" Elara asked, her eyes wide with concern.

"As Cornelius would say, a crow's whisper is untrustworthy more so than not, my maid. I fear the intention of my witness has entered the ears of Lord Elowen."

"If this has come to be, why would Lord Elowen wish to harm an innocent child?"

"To protect his own flesh, Elara. Upon leaving the village in the ungodly hours of the morning, before first light, this boy came to me and spoke of witnessing the Queen's death at the hand of Aleron Elowen, my sisters and brother too."

"Good heavens," gasped Elara, her hand flying to her mouth.

Sintra took two pieces of parchment and began scribbling a reply to each letter she had received, fastening them both with a wax seal before standing and striding toward the door.

"Your gown, madam," interrupted Elara.

Sintra slipped the gown over her head and handed it to the maid. She then reached for her blue day-gown she had taken from her cupboard earlier that day. Elara remained silent, standing in the centre of the bedchamber, unsure of what to do with herself.

"Father?" Sintra called as she entered the great hall, heading straight for the throne where the King sat. "May I have a word, Your Majesty?"

"Certainly. What seems to be the problem?" he asked, frowning at a patron as he waved him away.

"There's been a murder, my lord."

"A murder?" he gasped, "Great heavens, who?"

"A young boy from the village."

"My princess, there are many young boys in the village."

Sintra frowned as she didn't know the name of the boy; he never told her; she gazed at the parchment within her hand, grateful to see the last word scribbled was in fact the boy's last name.

"Moth," she replied shortly, "The young Moth boy."

"*Aye!*" the King replied, pushing her to continue.

Sintra paused; she couldn't tell her father how she came by this boy, for he would have her head for travelling beyond the citadel walls after dark. She had no choice but to tell a partial lie, so she continued.

"As Elara and I journeyed to the village, a young boy came to me and told me the gravest thing, father. He spoke of the day my mother was killed for he witnessed the horrendous happening with his own eyes. The Moth boy promised to come forward and kneel before you, but I hear he is missing, I fear that he is dead. Dead by the same hand that murdered the Queen."

As the words escaped the princess' mouth, the King's eyes widened in shock and disbelief.

"Who?" he bellowed, anger rising within him.

Sintra paused for a moment, a little frightened to answer.

"Lord Aleron Elowen," she breathed, wincing as if expecting to be struck down.

The King fell silent for a moment, deep in thought, his temper rising silently. He scratched his hairless chin, having shaved and groomed for the afternoon's events.

"GUARDS!" he yelled, to which four guards came running, "Find Lord Elowen and cease him, bring him to me in chains. Send four of my fastest men and steeds to the village on the outskirts of Crevark. Find me the young Moth boy and do not dare return until you have him. He is a witness; I want him unharmed…if you shall find him alive."

With that the guards fled the great hall of the Citadel, two returned moments later with a very agitated Aleron.

I could get used to seeing him bound so often, thought Sintra.

"What is the meaning of this?" demanded Aleron, the guards pushing him to his knees before the King, "Too often I have been bound and struck for no apparent reason. What is the meaning of this? Tell me!" he spat.

"It seems a witness saw with his own eyes the events that occurred when my dear Queen Caprice and children were slaughtered," started King Lysandra.

Aleron's eyes widened in utter disbelief; shocked at the words that were falling from the King's mouth.

"It has been said that *you*, took the life of my dearest Caprice. Does the witness speak the truth?"

"No," he snapped, "I, I…the witness mistakes me for someone else," he stammered, "One of the many men…in the field, my lord."

"We will soon be accompanied by the witness, Lord Elowen, if they should find him. Then he may inform me if he is mistaken or not," the King spat, "If the witness is not mistaken, I will send for my Falchion, Lord Elowen, and your pretty little head will roll. Do you understand?"

Lord Elowen did not reply; he slumped forward with his head hung to his chest not daring say another word. Sintra swore she saw the corner of his mouth twitch and turn upright as if to grin with delight.

"Take him over there, I do not want to look at him," King Alaric said to the guards, "And send in more patrons," he grunted, "That line keeps growing the longer I put them off, it will stand from here to bloody Thane the next time I get around to it."

Sintra stood by her father's side as patron after patron knelt before him, begging for riches or land, trying to bargain a slave for a sheep. The twenty-second patron to kneel before the King was a short thin man, his cheeks hollow as starvation had overcome him.

"What can I do to please you if he were to grant me a sheep? I am starving."

"I see that patron, what is your name?"

"Jose Hinkley."

"Aye, I knew you looked familiar," snapped the King, "You often come before me asking for a sheep or a cow and not once have you returned a favour. Why should I grant you one more sheep?"

"I starve, my lord, I am weak and unable to do much labour for myself. Forgive me, I will try harder I promise you."

"What good is a promise if you can't keep it? Not once have you kept your word Jose Hinkley, now out!"

"Please sir, please, I starve."

"Plead to a farmer, Jose Hinkley. I do not help men that do not keep their word."

The guards dragged the thin man out of the great hall, struggling once or twice as the man made for the grand table which was occupied by half a roast turkey that had gone cold and covered in flies, stale bread and thin wine that had weakened. Jose's pleas were then heard all the way out into the quad.

"Starvation has made the man crazed; he begs for food and then tries to steal it from his King upon refusal," spat King Alaric.

"Surely he could have the cold remains of the turkey, father," said the princess, "At least give him the stale bread."

The King rolled his eyes before waving over a guard, "Throw that turkey out in the quad to that old starving fool, along with the stale bread. Keep the wine."

"The princess is kind," mumbled Aleron who knelt in the corner.

Oh, shut up you, thought Sintra, *I'm the reason you're in chains in the first place.*

Moments had passed as Sintra waited for her witness, her father tending to the many patrons that seemed to have more petty problems by the minute. Suddenly there was a loud knock on the door and in came three guards, one of them clutching the witness.

He's alive; thought the princess, *thank heavens!*

"Ah, just in time, let us see if we'll have a tournament or not, my princess."

The witness knelt before the King, confused and shaken.

"Are you the young Moth boy?"

"Aye, sir."

"Your parents are Newton and Liza Moth?"

"Yes sir."

"Very good young lad," said King Alaric, waving the guards over with the prisoner.

"Do you know this man? Have you seen him before?"

"Aye, he rides through the village often. He is Lord Elowen, the Knight of Knights, sir," said the young boy.

"Aye, did you or did you not see this man slaughter the Queen of Crevark along with the two princesses and young prince?"

Finally, the truth is revealed, thought Sintra, *I can almost taste the vengeance.*

"I did not, sir!" said the boy, frowning.

Sintra's heart sank; she looked at the boy in shock, feeling fooled.

"You dare betray me?" she said, her voice rising, "You told me of this man's treason, and I requested you speak of it again before my father, I promised you riches and now you defy your princess."

"I'm sorry, my lady, I know not what you speak," stammered the young boy, fear in his eyes.

Sintra did not understand; she shook her head, feeling a deep sense of betrayal and disappointment. How could this boy lie before her in the presence of the King, denying his word when she had promised him riches? Her heart pounded with a mix of anger and hurt; her trust shattered.

What boy would lie before me in the presence of the King, denying his word when I promised him riches? she thought, her mind racing. She felt taken for a fool, her face flushing with a mix of rage and humiliation. The betrayal stung deeply, and she clenched her fists, her nails digging into her palms.

"OUT!" she yelled, "All of you out! Leave me with my father."

The guards led the young boy out into the quad while the others set Aleron free; a smug expression crossed his face.

"What is the meaning of this? I demand you tell me child," said King Alaric.

"I don't understand father; that boy told me what he saw, and he now defies me in your presence when I promised him four times his weight in gold. I've been taken for a fool."

The King paused for a moment before replying, "Indeed, you have been taken for a fool, but you will soon learn. Now let's get on with this tournament, I am eager to see some bloodshed."

Sintra said not another word as she walked out into the quad. Jose Hinkley caught her eye as he devoured the remains of the turkey and stuffed the stale bread down his breeches.

"Do you want to be locked up for stealing?" asked the princess.

"I stole nothing, my lady," he stammered, getting to his feet.

"Empty your breeches."

The man did what he was told and out fell the stale bread.

"It was given to me, my lady, I stole nothing," he whimpered.

"Hush now, Jose Hinkley, I know you did not steal a thing for *I* was the one that granted you the remains of my father's lunch. Now carry that bread by your side and be on your way."

The thin man clutched the bread and made his way toward the Iron Gate, occasionally looking back at the princess. Sintra clutched the parchment reply she had scribbled for the Moth boy's mother and searched for the boy herself.

"You there," she called as she spotted the young boy petting a horse in the stables while deep in conversation with Wenzel, the stable boy and slave.

The boy walked toward the princess; his head lowered as if he was about to receive a great punishment.

"Yes, madam."

"Go straight home and give this to your mother, I wish to never see your face in this quad again. You're lucky I don't punish you for your betrayal."

The boy took the parchment from her grasp and turned to flee the quad, his confused expression taunting her every time he turned over his shoulder to glance at her.

A Sword's Origin

As the trumpets blared across the battlefield, guests arrived from every direction. Horses and carts, wooden boxes on wheels covered in fine silk and satin, Kings and Queens on horseback surrounded by their guard knights, flags of House Sigils flapping in the wind. Sintra watched as various royals approached, their flags waving, but no offspring in sight.

The stands filled with Kings, Queens, and knights, but no Princes or Princesses. Sintra sat centred by her father, with other royals to her left and right, their flags standing tall. There was no sign of King Edmund Artec, as he had mentioned in his letter. But where was Lorenna, his Queen? To her right sat another King and Queen, along with Theodore, who sat alone, head down and eyes to the ground, their House Sigil the great Eagle.

He still mourns for my sister, Serillah, Sintra thought to herself, as do I.

"Greetings and welcome, all. I give much thanks to you for coming here today. From near and far, I thank you," said King Alaric in a loud, stern voice, bowing his head to each kingdom as he spoke their name.

"I, King Alaric Lysandra of Crevark, have brought you here on this splendid afternoon for a tournament. I thank you kindly as I see no offspring in sight. My reason being no child should witness the slaughter of fifteen men. Additionally, I ask you all to bear witness tomorrow as my princess, Sintra Lysandra, weds the knight of knights, Sir Aleron Elowen, upon his victory here today. It is upon Sintra's wishes to hold a tournament, for she finds herself bored," said the King, facing the princess as he finished his sentence.

Sintra's face grew scarlet as muffled laughter was heard from the stands.

"It is upon her request that the knight of knights, Sir Aleron Elowen, takes battle in the fields before us, facing fifteen slaves as no knight would come forward. As Aleron has declared, no other knight should stand in the running to take the princess's hand."

More laughter echoed from the stands as the King continued.

"However, if a slave should become victorious, his head will reside on a stake. What slave could ever be eligible to wed my princess?" the King laughed.

"Why not hold a melee with blunted swords, Alaric? Then our children would not have been forced to stay at home," interrupted another King, but his question was ignored.

"Furthermore, once victory is achieved, I invite you all to dine with us in the great hall of the Citadel on fine wine, roast pork, and salted lamb. We shall feast until our stomachs bulge and drink until we're unable to stand. Enjoy the tournament, in honour of Princess Sintra and her future King, the knight of knights, Lord Aleron Elowen."

Sintra grew cross, knowing nothing of a victorious slave being beheaded. However, Riven was no longer a slave but a gallant knight, though her father was not aware.

"This is supposed to be fair," she whispered when the King had seated beside her.

"What on earth are you babbling about? Of course it's fair. I wouldn't have it any other way."

"Then why roll the head of a slave if he is to become victorious?"

The King laughed long and hard. "If a slave is to become victorious, he is to be beheaded, for no princess wants to wed a slave," he said between breaths, laughing so hard tears streamed from his eyes. "Does my princess wish to marry a victorious slave?"

"A victorious slave having slaughtered a knight is worthy of knighthood, am I mistaken?"

At that the King's laughter halted. He stared at Sintra with a blank expression before his brow narrowed.

"Bullocks," he answered, "If the knight of knights dies here tonight, we shall find you a prince to marry, perhaps Harry Courtendaen of Dunlaw when he comes of age. No princess will wed a slave and make a fool of her father, especially not you. Now stop your whining for you have yourself a tournament. Not another bloody word."

Her blood boiled at the insolence of her father, but Sintra not dare say another word for she knew the truth of Riven's knighthood would slip from her tongue. Her father would kill him immediately if he knew.

The battlefield lay within a circular arena, its raised stone walls lined with rows of short iron spears protruding every few feet from the base to the top, ensuring no escape unscathed. On opposite sides of the arena stood two grand wooden stands; one filled with royalty, the other vacant, a few hundred feet away. Flanking the arena were pits, typically housing lions and tigers released upon gladiators for sport. Today, however, only one pit was used to contain the slaves, preventing their escape.

Sintra waited patiently as the King's Guard corralled the fifteen slaves, locking them behind the iron bars of the pit. She observed as Lucas Deer and Rodney Horn, two of her closest allies in the King's Guard, distributed armour and swords to the slaves. Yet not every slave received armour, meaning they would likely have to claim it from the fallen if they hoped to stand a chance against Aleron.

"What is this?" the King demanded, breaking Sintra's thoughts.

She followed his gaze to the hills, where a large swarm of villagers—families and friends of the soon-to-be-slaughtered slaves—approached.

"I invited them, my lord," she replied.

"Why? For heaven's sake, are you daft? There are children among them."

Sintra was surprised her father even cared about the children, but she doubted his concern was genuine. He simply didn't want peasants at his tournament.

"I sentenced their families to death, father. What more could I do for them?"

"So, you invited the maidens to watch their husbands be slaughtered? You invited small children to witness their fathers' throats being slit? You're a mad woman, Sintra Lysandra."

"I invited them to say goodbye. Every slave in those pits will be dead by tomorrow. Their families deserve to bid them farewell, do they not?"

"Very well, have them seated at once," he ordered three men of the King's Guard.

The villagers crowded into the stand a few hundred feet across from where Sintra sat with her father. The benches overflowed as they took their seats.

"Open the pit, father," Sintra commanded. "Open the pit so they may say their farewells before Lord Elowen becomes victorious."

The King grunted to Lucas and Rodney, who swung open the heavy iron gates of the pits. The arena teemed with armoured slaves rushing to their families and friends to bid farewell. Yet, there was no embrace, as the stand was mounted too high for the men on the ground to even touch fingertips with their wives or children. The women wept, the older children sobbed, but the infants had no clue what was happening.

I'll let you all live in peace someday, thought Sintra as she watched, *freedom I promise you.*

"That's enough," ordered the King, "Put them away, put them away."

Every slave was ordered back into the pit; some fought desperately to be with their families but were only struck down and dragged away. All was silent for a few moments, apart from the low murmur of talking that echoed through the stands of the kingdom's reign. The trumpets sounded once more as Lord Elowen stepped out onto the field in a silver suit of armour and mail that gleamed in the afternoon sun. The slaves waited behind the gates like small pups preparing themselves to hunt and kill for the first time, tails metaphorically between their legs as a few cowered and whined.

Sintra stood at the edge of the field, her heart heavy with regret. She had invited the families, hoping to give them a moment of reunion, but now she felt overwhelmed by the weight of her decision. The sight of the slaves being torn from their loved ones filled her with a deep sadness. Tears welled up in her eyes as she realized the cruelty of the spectacle, she had unwittingly orchestrated. Her afterthought made her feel a profound sorrow, and she wished she could take it all back.

"Ah, just in time," said a familiar voice as Cedric sat down beside Sintra. Her eyes widened in disbelief.

"Where did you come from?"

"Aye, I'll tell you later," he said, jerking his head toward the King, who suddenly turned his head and frowned at Cedric.

"You, sir. Are you a guest here?" asked King Alaric.

"Aye, I am Lord Cedric Edith of Sidon. The princess invited me."

"Oh?"

"Yes, I don't mind a good tournament myself, King Alaric. In fact, I prefer bloodshed to the ridiculous melee with blunted swords."

The King grunted in reply, stunned at the presence of a great knight. Sintra was grateful her father hadn't asked how she and Cedric had met. The King watched as Lord Elowen placed his sword on the ground before him, hilt facing his toe.

"State the rules, father," said Sintra.

"Rules?"

"Yes, every tournament has rules. Now state them, or I will."

The King grunted and stood once more. "Before this tournament begins, I must state the rules," he started, clearing his throat. "No other weaponry is to be used other than a sword. The hilt does not count as a different weapon. Every opponent must be dead and stripped of their armour before they are dragged to the fire or the dogs. The knight will fight one on one against his opponent unless otherwise ordered by me, the King. The knight will not throw any disembodied remains toward the audience, or he will be disqualified. Disqualification is punishable by death, as is any broken rule by the knight or his opponent. Now, let this tournament begin."

He's changed the game, thought Sintra as she remembered agreeing to a slightly different match. She looked on, keeping her mouth shut as the game of bloodshed began. King Alaric seated himself once more and took out a scroll of parchment, from which he read.

Sintra's heart sank as the tournament began. She had hoped for a display of skill and honour, but the reality was far more brutal. The sight of knights fighting to the death, their bodies stripped and dragged away, filled her with a deep sense of guilt. She glanced at Cedric, who seemed unfazed, and wondered if she had made a terrible mistake by inviting him. The weight of her decisions pressed heavily on her, and she felt a profound melancholy wash over her. She wished she could turn back time and change the course of events that had led to this moment.

"Terrance Lyonn," the King called.

The iron gates of the pit opened as the first armoured slave stepped out, trembling in his iron boots. Terrance walked toward Aleron, his sword shaking vigorously as he held it in two hands.

"Don't be afraid," yelled a man from the villager's stand, "Kill the bastard."

Aleron picked up his sword slowly and stood still, not moving a foot. Terrance made his way toward him, thrashing the sword around as he stepped closer. The clash of metal on metal filled the arena as Aleron blocked every blow Terrance made. Clash after clash came until Lord Elowen became impatient and thrust his sword into Terrance's stomach as if it were no effort at all, twisting his blade and ripping through the flesh. A woman screamed as Terrance's insides fell to the ground, followed by his body. Sintra watched as her father took his quill and scratched out Terrance's name. Lord Elowen wiped his blade clean of blood while two guards collected Terrance's remains and took them away.

"Feed him to the dogs," barked one of the King's men who sat further alongside King Alaric.

"Fernando Gabe," called the princess' father.

The iron gates of the pit opened again and out shot Fernando Gabe, running with his sword in hand and shield in the other. Fernando swung and missed, swung and missed until Aleron casually slit his throat with one swing of his sword. The next in line was Goodwin Trollope, who too shot out of the pit, his sword pointed toward Aleron as he ran. Stumbling as he neared the knight, Goodwin tumbled over his feet and landed headfirst beneath Lord Elowen's chin. With one hack of Aleron's sword, Goodwin's head rolled.

"Ah, this is too easy, let two in," snapped the King, reading two names from the list.

Monoghan O'Malley and Mark Griffin walked out into the arena. Monoghan ran straight for the bloody armour that was still on Goodwin's back while Mark made for Aleron. As Monoghan stumbled to take off the blood-covered armour, Lord Elowen swung his sword and let his head roll too. He then turned and gutted Mark, who ran screaming up behind him with his sword pointed. The King scratched off two names at once and proceeded to read another.

"Wenzel Grace," he called.

Wenzel hesitated as he stood in the gateway of the pit. Sintra's heart sank as she knew the man well; he had tacked her steed many times and always spoke kindly to her. *What have I done*? she thought to herself as she watched Wenzel walk out into the arena. I'm just as monstrous as Lord Elowen.

Wenzel lowered the visor on his armour, held his shield in front of his face, and made his way toward Aleron, who let out a roar of laughter. Wenzel swung his sword blindly, thrashing the blade until it struck Aleron's arm and split open the armour. Blood gushed, infuriating Lord Elowen. The knight of knights charged Wenzel, slashing his legs followed by his stomach, then took his head in his hand and lifted it above his shoulders.

"No one can defeat me!" he shouted, throwing Wenzel's head. "Not even with a blade as sharp as that."

A loud cry came from a woman, followed by words of disgust and great hissing. Aleron threw the sharp blade as far away as possible, ensuring it landed behind him, out of reach to his opponents.

"Your knight finds this simple, my lord, perhaps let the rest out?" said King Lansing Bronn of Denton.

"Aye," said the King, scratching off Wenzel's name before calling four names this time. "Peter Glade, Christophe Drone, Benedict Rolland, and Richard John."

The four slaves walked cautiously from the pit, huddled together as they planned to attack Aleron together.

Peter, Christophe, Benedict, and Richard spread out and walked toward the knight.

"They have him surrounded," laughed Cedric.

"As a noble knight, Lord Edith, one would think you would cheer for one of your own," said the King.

"Lord Elowen is not one of my own," Cedric said under his breath, just loud enough for Sintra to hear.

One of the slaves in the arena shouted a command to which all four followed, charging toward Aleron with their swords outstretched. Lord Elowen's sword clashed with Peter's before kicking him to the ground. Then came Christophe, his sword clashing with Aleron's blow after blow. Benedict came from behind, but just as he swung his sword at Aleron's legs, Aleron leapt into the air. The blade missed him and hit Christophe, cutting through his flesh and severing his knees from his shins. Christophe lay in agony while Benedict came to his side, apologizing and trying to stop the bleeding. Lord Elowen went for Richard, dismembering his arms and knocking him to the ground. He then plunged his sword deep inside Richard's chest, twisting and turning his blade until he pulled out the heart of the slave.

"I am the knight of knights," roared Aleron. "You cannot defeat me."

With that, he threw the blood-soaked heart toward the iron gates of the pit and then made for Benedict, who was still crouching by Christophe's side.

"Fight me, cowards!" yelled Aleron, swinging his sword and rolling Benedict's head.

The guards took the bodies out of the arena, dragging limbs and tossing heads, their hands soon becoming bloodstained.

"Splendid!" said the King, satisfied with the tournament so far. "Leary Lunde and Anton Ruiss."

Anton was just a boy; he could barely carry his sword with one arm. He followed Leary out onto the battlefield, his large shield almost concealing his entire body. Aleron stood silent, casually looking around as if he were bored. Leary swung his sword, but Aleron jolted backward, blocking the blade with his shield. Anton wandered around the arena, waiting for the perfect opportunity to strike. Leary ran toward Aleron, their swords clashed once and then twice, and the slave's sword was knocked to the ground. Lord Elowen struck the slave with the hilt of his sword, knocking him unconscious. Just as Aleron lifted his sword to plunge it into Leary's chest, he was knocked to the ground by a charging Anton; his sword sent flying through the air. Aleron grasped the boy by the throat and threw him across the arena, where he landed hard against the ground. The knight lifted his sword and plunged it into Leary, lifting it out and plunging it in again.

"I think he's dead," called King Tien of Ironsmead.

Lord Elowen lifted his sword and wiped it free of blood as he walked toward the boy, slow and fierce like a lion hunting its prey.

"Stand and fight me, boy."

"I don't want to, sir," replied Anton, shaking in his iron boots.

"Coward!" spat Aleron, but just as he lifted his sword to swing, he was knocked to the ground by Pedro Finnegan, who had pushed past the guards and squeezed through the iron gates of the pit.

Lord Elowen climbed to his feet and roared in anger as he charged for Pedro, but the slave was ready. With his shield, Pedro struck Aleron over the head and swung his sword at his thigh, cutting the armour deep enough for the sword to graze the flesh. Blood trickled from his leg where Pedro had struck him.

"Your jack isn't thick enough," teased Pedro, but he was met with another roaring outburst as Aleron charged him again, this time knocking him to the ground.

Lord Elowen sat on top of the slave's chest, weighing him down so he couldn't escape. He lifted his sword to plunge it into Pedro's chest just as he did to Leary, but the sword was knocked from his grip by Anton. Lord Elowen roared with rage, taking Pedro's sword and slashing the boy's legs open with one blow. As Anton fell to the ground, Aleron swung the sword again and severed the boy's jugular, spraying both him and Pedro with blood. The slave beneath Lord Elowen began to stir, trying to free his arms, but Aleron was too heavy.

"Fight me, scrawny peasant."

"I can't, you fat fool," spat Pedro. "A pig has me pinned."

Lord Elowen raged like a bull. Lifting his sword blade toward the sky, he positioned the hilt of the sword toward the slave's chest. With a great thrust, Aleron pounded Pedro's skull with the pommel of his sword, again and again. Blood sprayed Aleron's armour as he disfigured the slave's face until all that was left was splintered bone and blood.

"BROTHER!" yelled Dennis, who was let out of the pit.

Dennis Finnegan charged the knight and swung his sword, splitting open Aleron's side. Lord Elowen rose to his feet; spitting blood from his mouth, he swung his sword hard against Dennis'. Their swords clashed, Dennis taking an occasional blow to the arm and leg until Lord Elowen slit his throat, the fine tip of the sword just severing his windpipe. Aleron swung his sword again, splitting his throat further before thrusting his sword deep into the slave's stomach, pushing and plunging it further until Dennis dropped dead to the ground. Lord Elowen then turned and grasped young Anton, strode toward the arena wall, and hung his body on a sharp spike that protruded from the cold stone, pushing the body until the spike now protruded from the boy's chest.

The village people roared in protest, throwing whatever they could find into the arena. Cries of anger and sorrow filled the air.

"SILENCE!" ordered the King. "We have one more contestant."

The arena silenced, Sintra's heart almost thumping out of her chest as she watched Riven walk out onto the battlefield. Once the village people recognized Riven, they cheered and roared in praise.

"Take his heart in your hand," said a woman.

"Roll his head," said another.

But Riven's eyes did not leave Lord Elowen for a second. He stared him down like a boar about to charge, his suit gleaming silver in the sunlight. Lord Valahn's suit of armour was as black as his sword, made from Thalor steel. The armour was etched with lightning bolt-like patterns matching the sword. The armour fit snug as it was tailored for him hours before the tournament, setting comfortably with the structure of Riven's body.

"Good boy, concentrate just like we practiced," whispered Lord Edith.

As Riven walked toward Lord Elowen, Aleron let out a shrill squeal, grunting and snorting like a small piglet as the slave stopped before him. A great cheer was heard from King Courtendaen of Dumbrell, whose House Sigil was a Boar.

"Ready to die, slave?"

Riven hesitated before answering Lord Elowen. "Do you know the origin of your sword?" asked Riven, glaring at Aleron. "I know mine, as does your King," he added, unsheathing his weapon to reveal the Thalor sword, the sword King Alaric's brother had carved from the tail thorn of the very beast that ended Thane and his life soon after. Lord Elowen's eyes widened in disbelief; he knew the sword Riven held; he knew the sword from the beast that conquered Thane. Lord Elowen did not answer, and for the first time in a long time, Sintra saw real fear blaze within his eyes.

"I am no slave. I am Lord Riven Valahn, Sir Knight of the Thalor Sword, and this I ask you, Aleron Elowen…are you ready to die?"

With that, Riven leapt forward on one foot, sword outstretched, his other arm behind him to keep his balance.

"A slave that knows how to fight?" said one of the knights on a bench.

Lord Elowen leapt backward, his expression twisted in confusion and rage. Riven swung his sword, its tip cutting open the chest plate of Aleron's armour with ease.

You will die today, coward, thought Sintra, glaring at Aleron. *I will never let you take my hand.*

"Just like we practiced on the Pell," murmured Cedric, gazing at Lord Valahn through squinted eyes.

Riven thrust his sword, hitting Aleron's shield with a loud clash. He thrust again, the tip of the sword grazing the iron beneath Lord Elowen's armpit.

"That's it, boy, aim for the weakest part," murmured Lord Edith.

Riven thrust his sword again, hitting the same mark he had just made. This time it cut open the armour as if it were a tapestry. Lord Elowen's eyes lit open in shock at the strength of his opponent's sword.

The crowd erupted in a mix of cheer and gasps; the tension rising as they watched the duel unfold. Cries of encouragement and shouts of anger filled the air, creating a cacophony of emotions that mirrored the intensity of the battle.

"Aye, Elowen, it is the sword from Thalor the steel dragon, the strongest steel to come by," teased Riven, thrashing his sword and hitting Aleron's shield again.

"Coward!" Sintra yelled toward Aleron. He frowned toward the princess upon hearing her bark.

"Ah, yes," started Riven as he inched closer to Aleron, "That."

Lord Elowen's eyes flicked to Riven's; his brow narrowed in confusion for the slave knew something he did not.

"Oh my," laughed Riven, "The coward doesn't know."

"Know what?" snapped Aleron.

"That the princess," he said, turning his head to glance lovingly at Sintra before turning back to Aleron, "is indeed my lover."

"You lie!" snapped Lord Elowen, striking his sword through the air.

"It will be our anniversary soon, almost three long years together."

Lord Elowen grew furious. He swung his sword again and again, but each blow was blocked by Riven's sword.

"Kill him, knight!" ordered the King.

"Is he talking to you or I?" asked Lord Valahn, teasing.

"You are a slave, not a knight, you fool."

"Oh, but I am indeed a knight, Lord Elowen. You see, if I were still a slave and became victorious with your head in my hand, my head would roll, and the hand of the princess would be granted to somebody else. But I am no longer a slave, for I told you before, Lord Elowen, I am Lord Riven Valahn, Knight of the Thalor Sword, and once I roll your head with my delicate little sword, I will take the hand of the princess, and she shall be *my* Queen."

"Abomination is what you are, a slave cannot be a true knight," spat Aleron.

"But I am of noble blood, Sir. And I believe that you are not, for you are truly a thief, an assassin; a murderer. Do I speak the truth, Aleron?"

"Whether you speak the truth or not, fool, it matters none as I will roll your head as I have these other cowards. I will then place your head upon a stake within the Citadel so that you may watch as I take the princess's hand and slaughter the King before taking his throne. Sintra will be locked away in the dungeons as a pretty little whore should stay, and I will reign as King of Crevark."

"Why do you converse? KILL HIM!" bellowed the King.

"Take his head, Lord Valahn, take it for our Queen," shouted a man who sat among the villagers.

King Alaric frowned at the remark, glancing toward his daughter.

Aleron swung his sword in fury. "Your head is mine," he yelled, stepping toward Riven while thrashing his sword.

The crowd erupted in a mix of jeer, their emotions a whirlwind of anticipation and dread. Cries of encouragement for Riven and shouts of anger at Aleron filled the air, creating a discord that echoed through the arena. The tension was palpable, every eye fixed on the two combatants as they prepared for the final clash.

The blades collided as Riven blocked every blow, occasionally slashing at Lord Elowen's armour. Aleron thrashed his sword toward Riven's legs, knocking him to the ground without so much as a scratch to his Thalor steel armour. Riven rolled as Aleron plunged his sword, stabbing the earth in an attempt to hit him. Lord Valahn picked up a shield and held it above him just as Aleron plunged his sword through it, splitting the shield in two. Riven yelped as the very tip of the sword pierced his armour and pricked his flesh like a penknife. Aleron roared as he pushed against the blade with all of his strength, but the sword wouldn't travel any further through the armour.

Sintra tried her hardest not to speak a word, knowing it would give her away. She sat back in her seat, clutching the wooden armrest and clawing at it with her nails in suspense.

Riven twisted the shield with his arm, freeing the blade from Aleron's grasp. He then climbed to his feet and slashed his sword toward Lord Elowen. The former slave boy swung his sword again, oscillating the length of steel above his head. He moved toward the angered knight with haste, the blade brushing past his opponents face again and again. Aleron inched backward but his steps were not fast enough. The tip of

Riven's sword swept toward Aleron's upper face. In one swift motion it missed one eye, sliced through the bridge of his nose and proceeded to slice through the rest of his upper face.

Aleron screamed in agony, holding his hands up to his face. But he readied himself as Riven continued the blow, slicing through the Gauntlet and Vambrace iron plates on Aleron's armour, revealing the bare flesh of his hand and lower arm. Blood gushed from his veins.

"Hot blade," he called to one of the guards, who came running with a hot iron rod glowing white and orange, having been used to turn over the burning bodies beyond the arena walls.

Aleron held out his arm as the entire arena fell silent and watched. He groaned in anguish as the guard placed the blazing rod against his bloody flesh, burning it and cauterizing the wound. The flesh sizzled and melted beneath the rod, closing the wound. A new smell of burnt flesh and hair filled Sintra's nostrils, more potent than the burning bodies smouldering in a pile outside the arena.

The angered knight put his fingers to his bloodied eye and swiftly pulled his severed eye from its socket, exploding in a guttural rage that reverberated through the arena.

"I will have victory!" he shouted, putting his black and red blood-stained arm behind his back to hide it from the Thalor sword.

Riven stood patiently, ready to strike again as he bent his knees and held his sword outstretched. Lord Elowen charged with his sword outstretched in front. Aleron missed Riven, who leapt to one side to avoid the charge. Aleron was belted across the back with the hilt of Riven's sword, knocking him to the ground. Lord Elowen lay flat against the ground, belly down. Riven hovered over him, leaning down to slit his throat while Aleron reached for his sword, but it was too far away.

"You will not have my head," Aleron grunted, taking a small baselard from his hip.

"Princess," interrupted the messenger, "You have a letter, my lady."

"Later," waved the princess, sitting on the edge of her seat as the suspense within the arena built.

"It's urgent, my lady, it's about your witness."

Sintra took the letter from the messenger and skimmed over it with her eyes, her heart almost stopping in her chest as she looked up. Laying lifeless and still in the arena was Riven, Aleron hovering over him now with the Thalor sword in hand, raising it above his head to plunge it into Riven's chest. Sintra gasped in disbelief. She straggled over the benches before her, barging past the Kings and Queens and knights that were seated on the stand, knocking and pushing them.

"Sintra, stop!" ordered the King. "Someone cease her!" he commanded.

But the princess did not stop. She scrambled to the edge of the wall and looked down. It was steep, but she had to jump, she had to save Riven. Swinging her legs over the edge, Sintra slipped from the wall before any guards could grasp her. Into the arena she fell, clutching her ankles as they strained to hold her weight after such a large impact. Panic surged through her veins as she watched Aleron hold the sword over Riven's body, seconds away from plunging it into his chest.

I can't lose him, not now, not like this! Her mind raced with fear and determination. Every second felt like an eternity as she pushed herself forward, her heart pounding in her chest. *Please, let me reach him in time. I have to save him. I have to!*

"That sword does not belong to you," she called to him.

As the words escaped her mouth, Lord Elowen frowned, freezing in a stupor as the sword began to burn the flesh on his hands. Smoke rose from the sword as it glowed red hot. Sintra watched as Aleron couldn't move, fixated just like Cedric had been the previous day when he too clutched the sword. The air was thick with tension, every second stretching into an eternity.

The princess knelt down beside Riven, who barely clung to life. Her hands trembled as she gently pulled a silver bloodstained baselard from his neck. Ripping her crimson garment sleeve, she wrapped his neck to cease the bleeding, but it kept coming, though slower than before. Desperation clawed at her as she reached for the hot iron rod that was still red hot on one end. She pressed it against Riven's neck, the smell of burning flesh mingling with the acrid smoke from Aleron's hands.

Guards swarmed the princess, their faces a mix of confusion and fear as they watched Aleron stand stiff and mindless, engrossed in the sword that burned away in his palms. The crowd held its breath, the suspense unbearable as they waited to see what would happen next. Sintra's heart pounded in her chest, each beat echoing the urgency of the moment. She glanced at Riven, praying that her efforts would be enough to save him.

"Cease him!" Sintra ordered.

"What is the meaning of this?" the King bellowed, his voice echoing through the arena. "Lord Elowen is victorious."

Sintra rose and walked over to her father, glaring up at him from the arena below, two items clutched in her hands.

"Lord Aleron Elowen cheated!" Sintra said sternly, anger rising within her. "The rules stated no weaponry other than a single sword, am I mistaken?"

"Not mistaken, princess, but—"

"Lord Elowen brought a baselard onto the arena," she interrupted, holding Aleron's bloodied baselard into the air.

"This act was premeditated despite the rules you stated. This baselard was lodged in Riven's neck," she spat.

The King was momentarily speechless, his face contorting with a mix of shock and anger as he frowned at the weapon in his daughter's hand. Sintra threw it to the ground before her feet and pulled out the parchment the messenger had just given her.

"A raven was sent to me just now," she started, her voice trembling with urgency. "From the Moth boy's mother."

The King raised an eyebrow, his confusion evident. "That matter has been resolved, my princess. The boy was found alive and well. And he had not witnessed any crimes you spoke of—"

"Liza Moth gave birth to two boys, King Alaric, twins of the same face. The Moth boy I spoke to in the village was returned to his family… DEAD! You can read it yourself if you wish," she said, holding the parchment into the air. "A wound, similar to that one on that man's neck that lies before you, was found on the boy's throat."

"The work of a baselard, princess?" asked Queen Farrah of Ironsmead, standing to attention.

The King's face turned pale as the realization sank in. His eyes darted from the bloodied baselard to the parchment in Sintra's hand, then to the lifeless body of Riven. His voice, usually so commanding, wavered with a mix of disbelief and fury. "This... this cannot be," he stammered. "Lord Elowen, a cheat and a murderer?"

The crowd murmured in shock, the weight of the revelation settling over them like a dark cloud. Sintra's heart pounded as she awaited her father's next words, the tension in the arena rising.

"Aye, indeed, a baselard, Your Majesty," replied Sintra.

"I know that wound, King Alaric," started Queen Farrah, "I saw it within the neck of my son Cormac the night he died."

King Alaric shifted within his seat, looking profoundly confused and angered.

"Lord Elowen murdered the Moth boy, murdered my witness so that he may not speak before you, of Aleron's treachery. He murdered your Queen and children."

"SILENCE!" bellowed the King, louder and angrier than ever before. "Guards, seize that man and put him in chains. Take him to the torture chamber and torture him until he confesses his crimes."

The guards surrounded Aleron, who was still in a trance, and tried one by one to take the burning blade from his hands but they couldn't. Sintra strode toward Aleron and grasped the sword without thinking, breaking the trance. Lord Elowen looked to her in horror as she turned the Thalor sword and thumped him fair in the side of the head with its hilt, knocking him to the ground.

"Take him, before he escapes!"

Sintra knelt by Riven's side, one hand clutching the sword as the other clutched his hand. Cedric was by her side in an instant.

"You fought well, brave knight," said Cedric, "and you will live."

"What happened?" Riven whispered.

"He cheated, Lord Valahn, with a baselard. He is to be tortured for the confessions of his crimes of treason."

The princess looked to her hand and frowned' the blade had ceased burning; it did not feel warm against her flesh. She blinked rapidly in disbelief before looking to Lord Edith, who was also stunned at the sight.

"It chooses you too, my princess."

"What's the hold up? Throw that body on the fire before it begins to stench," snapped the King.

"He's still alive!" said Sintra through gritted teeth.

"Guards! Kill that slave and then throw his body on the fire."

Sintra stood and unsheathed the Thalor sword as guards surrounded her.

"This man is no slave; he is Lord Riven Valahn, Knight of the Thalor Sword. The sword carved from the tail thorn of the Thalor dragon that ended Thane and killed your beloved brother, Thaddeus," snapped Sintra, glaring at her father. "No further harm will come to this man!"

"Send for the nurse," called Queen Farrah. "Save that knight. He is victorious."

"Nonsense," barked the King. "This man's knighthood cannot be proven; besides...he is an abomination, for he is not of noble blood."

"I, Lord Cedric Edith of Sidon, dubbed this knight, King Alaric. He is a Valahn; he is of noble blood."

The King roared with fury, standing to his feet. "That man will die, noble blood, slave, or knight. No nurse will attend him, for no soul of the damned can be saved. King Thaddeus of Thane was damned upon creating that sword, and he is long dead. Leave that man where he lies until the darkness of death takes him, and when it does, he will burn as a slave with his brothers," the King demanded. "Ladies and Lords of kingdom reign, please follow me as we dine on feasts and drink until we no longer see our noses. If you wish not to stay upon such the ill manner of my princess, then return to your reign, I bid you well."

The King vanished from the stand. To dine or take leave, the spectators disappeared out of sight. Sintra and Cedric were still surrounded by guards. Lord Elowen was dragged in chains to the dungeons and torture chambers, his cries muffled by a bloodied rag in his mouth as he passed the princess, cursing and kicking toward her with every ounce of energy he had left.

The Price of Treason

"Fetch me a nurse, Lord Edith, we must save him. I must return to the citadel at once. Wait for my return," said Sintra as she mounted Soul and rode vigorously into the early night.

First darkness had come soon after the arena had cleared, the full moon casting silver light over the land, lighting up the dark thick smoke that rose from the pile of charred dead bodies that lay beyond the citadel, the stench stale on the air. The wind howled past Sintra's ears as her steed galloped out of the village and through the dark wood, the citadel looming closer with every few hundred feet. Soul's feet thumped hard against the ground, his breathing hoarse and ragged as he pelted across the fields.

"Open the gate," Sintra yelled as she neared the citadel.

The loud clanking and screeching of the iron chains and cogs sounded in the night as the Iron Gate opened, letting the princess into the quad. She dismounted Soul and tied his lead to the centre post of the quad where Aleron was tied the night before. The princess stormed into the entrance of the citadel, her feet padding loudly against the stone ground as she ventured down the hallway, passing the great hall that was filled with laughter and music. She greeted the guards at the dungeon doors who thought not twice upon letting her pass. The torture chambers were accessed through winding passages which served to muffle the agonizing cries of prisoners, but silence is all she heard as she ventured deeper into the dungeons.

"Where is he?" she spat, her voice dripping with vehemence as she searched for the prisoner.

"The prisoner is being tortured at the well as we speak," said the executioner who strode alongside the princess.

"Torture by water? That's not good enough; chain him to the stretcher at once."

A half-naked Lord Elowen was brought out of the well chamber and tied to a large wooden table that stood upright, the shackles in each corner were immediately bound around his ankles and wrists. Each shackle was chained to its own iron cog that would be wound, pulling and stretching the prisoner's limbs until a confession was heard. The executioner strapped Aleron's midsection to the wooden table, buckling it tight so that he could not move upon the stretching of a limb. The table was lowered horizontally; Lord Elowen's arms and legs were outstretched, positioned at every corner of the wooden table.

Sintra stormed into the chamber, her eyes blazing. "You will pay for your treachery, Aleron," she spat, her voice trembling with rage. "You thought you could deceive us all, but your time has come."

Aleron sneered, his defiance still evident despite his predicament. "Ah, Sintra, my princess," he said slyly, "Care to join me?"

Sintra's anger flared even hotter. "You dare mock me?" she hissed, stepping closer. "You murdered innocent people, betrayed your king, and now you will suffer the consequences."

She turned to the executioner, her voice cold and commanding. "Begin the torture. I want to hear his screams echo through these halls until he confesses every vile act he has committed."

The executioner nodded and began to turn the iron cogs, the chains tightening and pulling at Aleron's limbs. His face grimaced, but Sintra's expression remained hard, her wrath unyielding.

"You will confess," she said, her voice low and menacing. "And when you do, you will beg for the mercy you never showed to others."

Sintra stood over him, her eyes blazing. The executioner continued to turn the iron cogs, stretching limbs to the brink. His face was contorted in pain, sweat dripping from his brow.

Suddenly, Sintra raised her hand. "Stop," she commanded, her voice echoing through the chamber. The executioner halted, looking at her in confusion.

Aleron gasped for breath, his eyes filled with a mixture of pain and hope. "Have you come to your senses, princess?" he croaked.

Sintra took a deep breath, her expression softening. She stepped closer to Aleron, her eyes locking onto his. "Perhaps I have," she said quietly. "Perhaps there is a part of me that believes in mercy, even for someone like you."

Aleron's eyes widened in disbelief. "You… you would show me mercy?"

Sintra nodded slowly. "Yes, Aleron. I will show you mercy. But only if you confess your crimes and beg for forgiveness. The sooner you confess, the sooner you will be out of those chains and out of this chamber."

"And locked in a dungeon for all eternity," he added slyly.

"Perhaps not, Aleron. We can bargain if you wish," she lied.

"Bargain for what?" he spat.

"Your life, your freedom," she lied again, "Confess to your crimes and I'll make this all disappear."

"I don't trust you and I don't believe you."

Sintra looked to the executioner who wound the cog again, stretching Lord Elowen's arms and straining on his waist. The gash on his side was taught, threatening to burst open at any moment.

"You will rot in the scorching pits of hell, princess, along with your damned lover."

Sintra's eyes burned with a mix of fury and determination as she glanced once more at the executioner, who was now winding the cog that pulled on Aleron's ankles. The sound of the mechanism tightening echoed through the chamber, heightening the tension.

With a deliberate stride, Sintra approached the table laden with an array of sinister instruments. Her gaze swept over the needle-thin knives, the hooks, the double-ended prongs, and the cleavers. Each tool seemed to call out to her, promising pain and retribution. Hammers and thick hooks lay alongside sharp chisels of varying thickness, while smaller blades, reminiscent of penknives, were meticulously arranged in a row. These were the tools of her vengeance, designed to inflict precise and excruciating agony.

Sintra's fingers hovered over the selection before she picked up a slender blade, its edge glinting menacingly in the dim light. She turned towards Aleron, her eyes locking onto the burnt wound on his forearm. The sight of his injury only fuelled her anger, a reminder of his betrayal and the justice she was about to deliver.

"Watch you don't slice off your pretty little fingers," teased the mad man, but Sintra ignored his taunts.

The princess slowly walked toward him, positioning herself beside his forearm that was injured in the tournament. With deliberate slowness, she pressed the small, razor-sharp blade against the hard, burnt flesh. Blood flowed immediately, but he uttered not a word.

"Did you slaughter my mother?" Sintra demanded, her voice cold and unyielding. Still, there was nothing.

She dug the blade into Lord Elowen's flesh and dragged the wound open. Blood oozed down his arm and welled in the nape of his neck, but he remained silent.

"You broke the rules when fighting in the tournament, Lord Elowen; you will also be punished for cheating once you confess to your treachery. It's going to be a slow, painful death for you, traitor."

Thick beads of sweat formed at his brow as he slowly bled from his arm, blood pooling on the chamber floor beneath the table. Sintra pulled the blade from his flesh. Gently she picked at the edges of the charred skin of his wound, lifting the scab with the fine edge of her blade.

Aleron winced.

She slowly pulled at the flesh, tearing it from the arm. Strands of blood and pus filled the space between Lord Elowen's arm and the flap of charred skin. He grunted beneath his breath. Tears pricked at the corners of his eyes. But still not a word.

Sintra walked to his feet. As she slowly sat the blade between two of his toes, he waved his feet around in protest.

"Executioner, restrain his foot please."

The executioner grasped Aleron's foot, holding firmly in his grip as the prisoner tried to free it.

Resistance, good, thought Sintra, *torture will soon break him.*

Sintra placed the blade between his toes and cut deep, slowly dragging the sharp metal through his flesh. One by one she slit between his toes until both feet wore blood-red sandals. Aleron cringed in pain but remained silent. The princess then proceeded to do the same with his fingers, starting at the flesh between his thumb and index finger of his right hand, the hand he uses to swing his sword.

"I'll confess!" Aleron shouted, growing tumultuous.

Finally!

"There were no men," he started.

"And?" pushed Sintra.

She sat the small blade back on the table and chose a different tool of torture, a chisel and hammer which she then handed to the executioner.

"I can no longer do it for it is making me ill."

The executioner took the chisel and looked to the princess for direction.

"Shin!" she ordered, and as the word sounded through his ears, the executioner placed the chisel against Aleron's shin.

Aleron began to laugh. "Do it!" he urged the executioner.

The princess nodded toward the executioner who positioned the chisel in the centre of the shin and held the hammer high before slamming it hard against the chisel. Aleron screamed from the pain, his bone crunching beneath the chisel. His screams were a mixture of agony and humour, as laughter echoed through the chamber.

"I slaughtered the fucking Queen!" he yelled, followed by a cackle.

"Speak her name!"

"Caprice," he spat, "Your mother."

"My sisters and brother?" pushed Sintra, "Serena, Serillah and Soren?" but Aleron said not another word.

The executioner tugged on the chisel hard, but it wouldn't move; it was lodged deep into the bone. The executioner waved over one of the guards who grasped the chisel and wrenched it from the shin. Aleron screamed. The veins in his neck pulsating as his cries escaped his throat.

He began to laugh once more.

Sintra raised her eyebrows in surprise, yet confusion overcame her.

What the fuck? Is he enjoying this?

"Caprice, Serena, Serillah and Soren...I killed them all!" spat Aleron, tears of laughter streaming down his face.

"Lock him in the dun..." Sintra's order was cut short.

"Oh, the Queen Caprice. My half-sister."

Sintra's interest was ignited.

"It should have been mine. All of it. Not hers."

"What are you playing at? Is this a game to you?"

"She didn't recognise me, in the field that day. She'd have seen the resemblance if she had anything to do with our father, but that wasn't her fault. It made it all the simpler when she chose not to offer me solace with open arms."

Sintra's breath hitched, her mind reeling from the unexpected revelation. She stared at Aleron, her expression a mix of confusion and disbelief.

"Our father," Aleron continued, his voice steady but laced with resentment, "died just days before I entered the field. Pestilence. It was only upon his death that I learned of my royal sister."

He paused, his gaze hardening as he recalled the hardships he had endured. "He left me with nothing but the clothes on my back," Lord Elowen spat in disgust.

Aleron's voice grew colder, his eyes narrowing. "He said I was promised riches and royalty, just like Caprice. But while she was born into royalty, I was not. I was left to fend for myself, to scrape by in the shadows of her grandeur. How I curse him for not telling me sooner."

He clenched his fists, the bitterness in his voice rising. "I asked Caprice for help, for a chance to claim what was rightfully mine. But she refused. She turned her back on me."

Aleron's voice cracked slightly, a rare glimpse of vulnerability breaking through his hardened exterior. "Do you know what it's like, Sintra? To be so close to everything you ever wanted, only to have it snatched away? To be denied something by your own family?"

Sintra's mind went to Riven. His lifeless, bloodied body came to mind. She felt a surge of conflicting emotions— anger, confusion, and a deepening sorrow. The weight of Aleron's words pressed down on her. She took a deep breath, trying to process the revelation.

Sintra's heart ached with the weight of this new knowledge. She didn't want to believe his words. She refused to believe that she was his kin.

"Lock him away. I'll inform the King of his confession," said Sintra.

"No!" he shouted, "There's more. Don't you wish to know the truth in its entirety?"

"What else is there?" the princess queried.

"What else is there? What else is there?" the crazed man repeated her words in jest, as if hoarding more truths than he could hold. "Serillah…your sister," he started, spitting at Sintra's feet.

"What of my sister?"

There was a silence that fell over the torture chamber, a heavy, oppressive stillness that seemed to amplify every heartbeat. Sintra's heart pounded rapidly within her chest, each thud echoing in her ears as the anticipation climbed. She glared into Aleron's eyes, her gaze piercing, studying his facial expression for any flicker of emotion, any hint of morality that might betray his cold exterior.

Aleron cleared his throat, the sound sharp and jarring in the quiet room. His demeanour shifted, becoming unnervingly calm and composed. He met Sintra's glare with a steady gaze, his eyes devoid of remorse or compassion. The corners of his mouth twitched slightly, as if he were about to smile, but the gesture never fully formed.

"She was with child. *My* child. *My bastard.*"

"You were…"

"What? In love?" Aleron roared in laughter, "Of course not. She wouldn't let me have her. Kept kicking and screaming. But I accomplished it anyway. Quite a few times, if you must know. It went on for months."

Sintra's breath caught in her throat, her fury simmering just beneath the surface. She could feel the weight of her sister's death pressing down on her, fuelling her resolve. She would not let Lord Elowen see her break. She would not give him the satisfaction.

But bile rose to Sintra's mouth, a bitter taste of dread and despair. Her hands and feet began to sweat, cold and clammy against the sudden rush of heat that surged through her veins. Her body trembled uncontrollably, a violent mix of fury, disgust, and grief. She closed her eyes, trying to block out the horrific imagery that flooded her mind.

But the vision of her younger sister, lifeless and broken at the hands of a cruel man, was relentless. It clawed at her consciousness, refusing to be cast away. Sintra shook her head vigorously, as if the physical act could dislodge the tormenting thoughts. Her heart pounded, each beat a painful reminder of her sister's suffering and the brutal end she had met. The brutal end of her unborn child.

She clenched her fists, nails digging into her palms, grounding herself in the physical pain to distract from the emotional agony. Tears welled up in her eyes, blurring her vision, but she refused to let them fall. She had to be strong. For her sister. For herself. Sintra took a deep breath, forcing herself to focus. She left the torture chamber in haste.

As she entered the passage leading to the great hall of the Citadel, she clutched a windowpane and stuck her head out into the fresh air to stop herself from throwing up. Dizziness overcame her as she rested her head on the windowpane. The cool night breeze greeted her face, soothing her ill manner. She stumbled into the hall where loud music and laughter filled her ears.

"Father," she called, clutching her stomach, "Father he confessed."

The King stood to his feet at once, concerned and frightened. Queen Rachel Artec held her arms as King Alaric took the other and seated her on a chair at the grand table.

"My dear, are you ill?" asked the King.

"Do we need a nurse?" asked Queen Rachel.

"No," Sintra gasped, "Father, I've come from the torture chamber...he confessed, Lord Elowen killed my mother. He raped my sister. He...he..."

The princess slipped unconscious, falling limply in Queen Rachel's arms. Her sweaty brow dampening her hair. The weight of Aleron's confession overwhelmed Sintra so much, she collapsed, her body unable to bear the emotional burden. Queen Rachel, her face a mask of concern, gently lowered Sintra to the ground, calling for the royal physician. The King stormed out of the great hall and made for the torture chamber, raging like a mad bull, a group of guards behind him. His fury was palpable, each step echoing his wrath as he vowed to uncover every hidden truth.

"Executioner!" he called, barging through the passageways like a great hungry bear, "Executioner!"

Through the torture chamber door he burst, guards on either side of him. He gasped in shock as his eyes lay on the dead executioner, a cleaver lodged in his forehead. The surrounding guards all bled out from stab wounds to the neck.

"Ah, Your Highness," came an alarmingly familiar voice.

The hair on the back of the King's neck stood on end as goosebumps prickled down his spine in fear. His surrounding guards stood stiff, their swords at the ready.

"Cease that murderer," growled the King sternly, his voice low and grim, "And fetch my Falchion."

PART II

Arrow of Despair

The rhythmic clatter of horse hooves and the screech of rusted iron wheels jolted Sintra awake. Dizziness washed over her as the cart swayed from side to side. Nothing around her was familiar: a silver suit of armour, a box of weaponry, cabinets with unknown contents, and unopened casks of wine surrounded her. Empty jars and bottles clinked in a crate, their glassy chimes mingling with the other sounds. The cabin-cart plunged into darkness as the full moon hid behind a cloud. Soft furs and woollens cushioned her, offering comfort, but the princess had no idea where she was headed or why. Beneath her head cushion, she found a piece of parchment. As she pulled it out, she recognized her own wax seal. Sintra unfastened the seal and unfolded the parchment.

Sintra,

It saddens me to inform you of the death of King Alaric, your father. The madman Aleron Elowen escaped the dungeons and slaughtered everyone who tried to stop him. He set the stables ablaze, killing the steeds within, and now he comes for you. As the rightful heir to the throne, he cannot take reign until you are dead, along with the wounded knight. Thus,

I sent you away. When you reach the village, find Lord Edith and flee as far as possible. It is not safe for you here. Aleron is a madman! Your maid and I have locked ourselves in the secret chamber, and your Winter whisper is safe with us. Send a raven when you are safe, but do not reveal your whereabouts, as a crow's whisper is often untrustworthy. I bid you well, princess. Stay safe!

Cornelius

The flickering light from a nearby lantern cast eerie shadows on the paper, making the words seem to dance before her eyes. She read the letter once, then again, her mind struggling to process the dire news. King Alaric, her father, was dead. Aleron Elowen, the madman, was coming for her. The weight of the shock pressed down on her, making it hard to breathe.

Sintra's thoughts raced. She had to find Lord Edith and flee, just as Cornelius had instructed. But where was this village? How far had she travelled while unconscious? She peered out of the cart, trying to get her bearings. The dense forest around her was unfamiliar, the towering trees casting long, menacing shadows in the moonlight.

The cart hit a bump, jolting her back to the present. She needed to stay focused. She tucked the letter into her cloak and took a deep breath, trying to steady her nerves. The sound of the horse's hooves and the creaking wheels became a steady rhythm, a reminder that she was still moving forward, still alive.

As the cart emerged from the forest, the landscape began to change. The trees thinned out, giving way to rolling hills and distant lights that marked the edge of a village. Relief washed over her, but it was quickly replaced by a sense of urgency. She had to find Lord Edith and warn him of the impending danger.

The cart slowed as it approached the village, the horse's pace becoming more measured. Sintra gathered her courage and prepared to leap out as soon as they stopped. She had no time to lose. Every second counted in this desperate race for survival.

Sintra opened the drapes at the back of the cart. She gasped in horror, tears pricking her eyes as she looked over the treetops of the great wood and saw a number of sections of the citadel ablaze. Climbing through the cabin, she looked out the front drapes to see a single white steed pulling the cart as they entered the village. She climbed through the front, pulled on the horse's reins, stopping the steed abruptly before leaping out into the darkness.

"Soul," she breathed, greeting the horse, grateful that he wasn't among his burning brothers and sisters.

"Sintra!" called Lord Edith, rushing out of one of the small village huts. "I feared the worst but thank the Holy Lord you're okay."

"Thank Cornelius, Lord Edith," said the princess, rushing past him and into the hut. "How is he?"

Lord Edith froze as Sintra's eyes fell upon the cold, lifeless body before her. Riven had been stripped of his armour and reclothed in fresh garments, prepared as the dead are for burial or burning.

"No, no, no…" Sintra whispered, "No, this can't be."

She knelt beside Riven's body, brushing the hair away from his closed eyes as tears welled in hers.

"I'm sorry, my lady. He lost too much blood," said the nurse, leaving the hut in silence.

"You were supposed to live… you were supposed to take my hand," she whispered.

Tears streamed down her face as she cried like never before. Her heart felt like it was being torn apart, her mind a chaotic storm, for her beloved knight had passed. No more would she feel his comforting warmth, kiss his tender lips, or hear the soothing voice of the only man she ever loved.

"It's all my fault. It was all for nothing," she whimpered, her voice breaking. "All those men died for me, for nothing. Their families are left with wounded hearts, just as I am tonight. I've lost my mother, my sisters and brother, my father, and now my lover, my knight, my Riven. All to the hand of one man, that monster," she growled, her sorrow transforming into a fierce, burning rage.

Cedric entered the hut with a parchment in his hand, a stern expression on his face.

"Sintra, you must flee. Lord Elowen hunts you, my lady; I must come with you, to protect you."

"I am not leaving here. Give me the Thalor sword and I will take Aleron's head myself!" she snapped between hard sobs.

"He is very strong alone, Sintra, but I fear he is building an army," replied Lord Edith.

"A phantom army, just like the one he claimed to have killed my mother. Who would follow him after all his done?"

"A very real one, my lady. King Edmund Artec took Lennox this night. I dare say a few fleeing knights and guards may join Aleron in vengeance. His strength is growing."

"King Edmund Artec of Golorah took Lennox?" she repeated, stunned and confused.

"Aye, my princess. Edmund took King Kent's head in his hand with no struggle at all. It was as if the widower wanted to die, my lady."

Sintra's eyes widened in disbelief, her face wet with tears. "Does King Edmund take the throne?"

"Aye, he took it, with ten dozen men at his wing. He reigns Lennox as King, his Queen beside him, madam."

That is why he couldn't attend, she thought. *The business he could not speak of was the ambush of Lennox. This explains King Kent's absence too.*

As Sintra connected the dots in her thoughts, there was an interruption at the door of the hut as Cedric's squire barged in unannounced.

"Forgive me for the intrusion, madam," started Benjin, his cheeks glowing red, "But this... *person*... wishes to speak with you right away."

Sintra frowned at the black-hooded figure that now stood in the hut before her. The hood hung so low that the princess couldn't see a face. It was no wonder the boy found it difficult to address this being as man or woman, though "person" seemed appropriate enough... for the time being.

"Who are you and what do you want?"

"Do you wish to save your beloved?" asked the hooded being, its voice gruff and raspy.

Sintra raised an eyebrow before replying, "This man is dead, what is there to save?"

"His soul," said the being.

The princess frowned and looked to Cedric, who shrugged and also frowned in confusion.

"Do you wish to save your beloved?" repeated the being.

"Is it possible?"

"Indeed, it is."

"Do you speak of dark magic?"

"Dark magic is for fools," hissed the hooded being. "I speak of reincarnation, resurrection of the dead. But it comes at a price."

"What price? Tell me, I bid you. I will match it twice."

"Not riches, foolish child, a sacrifice. An eye for an eye," said the being, dragging out its words. "I believe you must hurry as I hear thumping hearts and pounding feet on the horizon. They come for you, princess."

Cedric peeped his head outside of the hut and pricked his ears for any sounds coming their way, but he heard nothing.

"What's the sacrifice?" asked Sintra.

"This body," said the being, spreading its hands over Riven's dead body, "for another."

"I want to save *him*—"

"Oh, but you will!" snapped the being, interrupting the princess mid-sentence. "Beating hearts get closer, princess."

Sintra looked to Cedric, her eyes pleading for help, but Lord Edith shrugged his shoulders. This was her decision and hers alone.

"Okay, I'll do it!"

"Very well," said the being slyly, turning toward the door.

"Where are you going? I said I will do it," said the princess.

"My child, it cannot be done where you stand; it must be done beyond the land," said the being.

Both Sintra and Cedric frowned as the being lifted an arm, its black cloak slipping backward to reveal green scaled flesh. It raised a wooden staff in the air, grasping it with two green scaly hands as it stood in the doorway.

"You must hold on," it said, as the staff was raised higher.

The princess placed a hand on Riven's body and grasped the being's black cloak, feeling a shiver of unease at touching the odd creature now that she had seen its flesh. As the staff rushed downward through the air, Lord Edith grasped the black cloak before the end of the staff slammed into the ground, and the four of them were gone. Benjin stood in shock, left inside the hut with nothing but a wisp of black smoke circling in the air where three people and a body had just been.

The squire ran outside upon hearing the whinnying of horses. Through the great wood, he saw fire torches approaching. Three men on horseback; one of them was Lord Elowen, the madman who slaughtered the King. Benjin climbed a nearby tree to conceal himself within the darkness of the leaves. The sound of a steed's snort made the hair on the back of his neck stand on end as they drew closer.

"Search every hut," commanded Aleron to his men. "Set your torches to the rooftops. If they hide, we will find them."

"What about the families, King Aleron? The men, women, and children," asked one of them, his voice trembling.

"Take the women and children to the dungeons; I slaughtered all the old slaves. Offer the men allegiance alongside me; if they refuse… kill them."

"Yes, sir," said both men, riding into the village and dismounting their horses with haste.

Gordon Leoss and Francis Gregory, once loyal members of the King's Guard before King Alaric was slaughtered, now found themselves under Aleron's command. Gordon, a ragged-looking man with long dark hair and thick stubble on his broad jaw, had no family. He always needed a leader, someone to give him orders. It was no wonder he joined Lord Elowen after the King's death. Francis, on the other hand, was well-presented, clean and sharp-looking, with a jaw always free from stubble and hair slicked back with oil. He fought not for the sake of fighting but to honour his kingdom. He had a wife and two small children, whom Aleron threatened to kill if Francis did not join his allegiance.

"It is life or death, Francis Gregory," Lord Elowen had said. "Not just yours, but your family's too."

Francis had no choice but to fight alongside the madman. Both men obeyed their orders differently. Gordon barged down doors, dragging women and children out by whatever he could grasp, kicking the men into the dirt before ransacking the huts and setting them alight. Francis had a very different approach, calmly pulling the women and children from the houses and ordering the men to stand in groups. He would then search the house and walk back out upon finding nothing, leaving the torching to Gordon, who seemed not to care about destroying the lives of innocent people.

"You're too sensitive, Francis," grunted Gordon. "That damned morality of yours will be the death of both of us."

"The only thing damned in this entire affair is the madman making orders," Francis snapped, his voice tinged with frustration.

The groups of men, women, and children soon grew into large crowds as every hut in the village was raided and burnt to the ground. The women and children were bound and escorted back to the citadel, where they would remain in the dungeons until further orders. The men were given a choice: allegiance or death.

"Peasants of Crevark," greeted the madman, "Your wives and children will find humbleness within the cold stone walls of the dungeons. You, on the other hand, will be given a choice: bargain for your life. You will either join my allegiance, where you will fight like a knight and live and eat like a king, or you may refuse and simply walk away."

The village men stirred and chatted as they made their decision, forming groups and separating into two groups.

"Let me guess," started Aleron, looking toward the larger group of men, "You all wish to walk away. How very disappointing."

Lord Elowen dismounted his steed, struggling as his ruptured shin gave him agony. He limped a few feet before giving up and standing on the spot.

"You boy, come to me," he said, holding out his hand.

The boy came forward and stopped two feet before Aleron. He was a young man, still considered a boy as he was not yet of age.

"Do you wish to walk away, young man?" Aleron asked.

"Please, sir," mumbled the boy.

Lord Elowen pushed the young man and pointed out into the open fields beyond the village. The boy started walking, looking back every now and then. The village square was filled with a tense silence, broken only by the crackling of the fires that consumed their homes. The villagers stood in a tight cluster, their eyes wide with fear and desperation as they watched the young boy walk away, his steps hesitant and trembling.

"You see, gentlemen," Aleron started again, "You may walk away…"

He paused and took a large bow from his steed's saddle before taking an arrow from the scabbard on his back. Lining the arrow with the boy.

"Please, sir, let him go," an older man cried out, his voice choked with sobs. "He's just a boy!"

Aleron ignored him, his cold eyes fixed on the boy's retreating figure. The villagers dared not move, their bodies rigid with terror. They knew that any attempt to help the boy would be met with swift and brutal retribution.

"RUN!" called the old man.

The boy glanced back, his face pale and streaked with tears. "Please," he whispered, his voice barely audible over the crackling flames. "I don't want to die."

Aleron raised his bow, the string taut and ready. The villagers gasped, their hearts pounding in their chests. "No!" another man shouted, falling to his knees. "Please, spare him!"

Aleron continued to ignore the pleas. He lined up his shot and let the fletching slip from his fingers. The arrow flew through the air with a deadly hiss, striking the boy squarely in the back. He crumpled to the ground, a small, broken figure against the dark earth. A collective wail rose from the villagers, their cries of anguish echoing through the night.

"I can't guarantee that your life will be spared," he finished.

"Why?" one screamed, his voice raw with grief. He fell to his knees, his hands reaching out toward the boy's lifeless body. "Why did it have to be him?"

The villagers' pleas grew louder, their desperation climbing. They wanted to run to the boy, to cradle him in their arms and offer some small comfort in his final moments, but fear held them in place. Aleron's presence was a dark shadow over them, a constant reminder of the danger they faced.

Tears streamed down their faces as they watched the boy's still form, their hearts breaking with each passing second. The weight of their helplessness pressed down on them, a heavy, suffocating force. They had lost one of their own, and there was nothing they could do to change it. They too would lose their lives if they disobeyed.

Aleron looked to one of the guards, "Who spoke up against me?" he said softly.

The guard pointed to two men. The older man had remained where he had sunk to his knees on the earth. He sobbed uncontrollably into his hands. "He was my grandson. My…grandson. Oh, Tommin. I'm sorry."

Lord Elowen strolled over to the old man and bent down so that he was closer to his face before speaking, "Go to him."

The old man took no chances. He climbed to his feet as quickly as his frail body would allow. The villagers watched on in silent query.

"No, Thomas. He cannot be trusted," one of them called after him, but he was too far away to hear, too desperate to get to his grandson.

Aleron drew an arrow again from his scabbard. He walked to one of the guards that held a torch of flame, and proceeded to lit the arrow, placing its tip into the fire. With his burning arrow, he lined it up with the old man who had almost reached the boy's side. With a clearing of his throat, Aleron let the arrow fly. The old man was struck down, the blaze igniting his clothes. He fell right beside his grandson and drew his final breath.

"This is what happens why you defy my orders. I will not ask you again. Walk. Or join me."

A low murmur came from the villagers as both groups formed into one.

"That's what I thought," said Aleron, climbing back onto his steed, wincing as the pain in his shin surged through the rest of his body.

The villagers huddled together, their grief a shared burden. They whispered prayers and promises of vengeance, their voices a quiet murmur in the darkness. They had been broken, but their spirit remained unyielding. They would remember the boy and his grandfather, and they would fight for a future where such cruelty would never again befall their children.

Benjin, who had witnessed the whole ordeal, scrambled from the tree he hid in and ran into the field beyond the village, escaping into the night before he was forced to join Lord Elowen's allegiance.

†

As Sintra blinked rapidly, an overwhelming realization hit her: she was no longer inside the hut. The cool breeze of the night air greeted her face as she took a deep breath and looked around. She was riding on the front of the very same cart she had woken in not an hour ago. She peered through the drapes; Riven's body lay still on the furs and woollens that occupied the cabin-cart floor, the tinkling of glass-on-glass chiming in her ears as the cart swayed.

I don't understand, she thought to herself. *I was just standing inside the hut with Lord Edith and that thing. I blinked and now I'm here.*

"Lord Edith?" she gasped, looking around the cart.

"Here, Your Highness," said Cedric.

Sintra looked above her head to find Lord Edith seated on the roof of the swaying cart. But as the princess searched, there was no sign of the hooded being.

"It's gone," said Cedric. "That black oddly creature. It vanished upon our arrival."

"How did we get here, exactly?" asked the princess.

"I cannot say, my princess. I don't really know myself," he frowned, climbing down from the roof and sitting beside Sintra. "I blinked and found myself here."

"Where is here?" she asked, taking in the dark, mysterious landscape, but nothing looked familiar.

"Not sure of that either, my lady," he grunted, looking around for himself. "But I do not doubt for a moment that that thing will return."

"What was that thing, Lord Edith?"

"Aye," he said, "Good question, though if I'm not mistaken, I do believe it deals with some form of dark magic."

"It believes dark magic is for fools, Lord Edith, you heard it."

"Aye, Sintra, but beings like that are hard to trust."

The princess swallowed loudly, hoping with every fibre that she had not made another mistake when she agreed to the hooded being's proposal, for she had made enough foolish errors over the last few days. As Soul pulled them across the countryside, there was not a village or kingdom citadel in sight. The princess felt tired but fought her heavy eyelids to stay awake.

"Rest in the cab, princess, you've had a long day," said Cedric, grasping the reins.

But Sintra ignored the suggestion; she did not want to rest within the cabin alongside the dead body of her lover. She knew she would not sleep but weep all night long as she mourned for him. She could not stare at his loving face or brush her fingers through his hair; it would feel wrong. Even though a part of her craved to feel his soft, warm flesh, the other part knew it was cold, and dead. She longed to hear his voice again, to feel a whisper against her lips, but her broken, empty heart taunted her as she knew she would never kiss him again. Sintra reached an arm inside the cabin and pulled out a woollen blanket. Wrapping herself in its immediate warmth, she felt a small measure of comfort. She folded her arms, clutching the woollen blanket tightly around her, concealing her bare chest, and rested her head on Lord Edith's shoulder. She closed her eyes and let reality slip away as sweet dreams found her peaceful mind, engulfing her saddened thoughts and replacing them with the sweetest, richest of dreams. She was soon fast asleep.

The Infinite Forest

Sintra woke to the beaming rays of the sun in her eyes and the sweet sound of chirping birds greeting one another in the morning's first light. She sat up to find herself by a campfire, wrapped in furs and woollens that had kept the harsh cold night air off her chest as she slept. The screeching of iron cogs and wheels was gone; the cart was parked beneath a tree, the reins hanging unoccupied as Soul grazed on green grass, basking in the warmth of the morning sun.

"Good morning, princess," said Lord Edith, sitting before her, leaning against a large rock. "Sleep well?"

"Fine! Where are we?" she frowned, gazing at her surroundings.

Every tree and rock in sight looked strangely identical; same colour, same shape, same size. It was like a wood of unseen mirrors mimicking its surroundings with the intention to confuse.

"The Infinite Forest, Sintra," answered Lord Edith. "Have you not heard of the legends?"

"I have not," she replied, letting the furs and woollens fall away from her body as she stood.

She wondered why Cornelius had never read her any stories or legends of The Infinite Forest, though she had heard its name in conversation. Maybe it was one of those legends that remained untold for a very good reason, she thought, a reason to protect and stop anyone from entering it, as they may never return.

"Take note of how all the trees look the same, as do all the rocks and blades of grass. Every stick and every stone too."

"Yes, but why?" the princess queried, plucking a leaf from a thin twigged branch.

"Magic."

"Magic does not exist, Cedric."

"Aye, but it does, my lady. Every kind of magic lives in this forest."

"I cannot see it."

"Ah, but it is unseen and unheard."

"Then how do you know of this so-called magic?"

Cedric stood from the ground and lifted his head high into the air, taking a deep breath as the wind swept a great breeze past his nose.

"I feel it, my lady, it is very real."

The wind blew beneath his nostrils once more, sending his eyes into a frenzy as they searched the forest.

"What is it?"

"Boarschvine, I smell it on the wind. It is strong... and near."

Lord Edith narrowed his eyes, took a bow from beside the campfire, and slung a scabbard full of arrows onto his back. He handed Sintra the Thalor sword and held a finger to his lips to silence her query. She stood stiff and silent as Cedric disappeared into the forest. Sintra was frightened. She did not know what a Boarschvine was, nor did she want to know, as Lord Edith had handed her the sword and vanished through the trees.

She slowly unsheathed her blade, clutching the hilt with both hands, holding the edge out in front of her. She waited patiently, though she had no idea what she was waiting for. A rustle in the bushes made her jump to attention, outstretching her arms. Her breathing became rapid, her eyes flicking from tree to shrub, until a loud snort came from behind her. Sintra slowly turned, her eyes widening as she saw a great beast before her, though its attention was focused on the cabin-cart that held their supplies.

The beast resembled an enormous black boar, its flesh was scaled like armour. Two large black tusks protruded from each side of its jaw, each tipped with a silver blade. Sintra studied the creature. It looked like a boar but also something else entirely. Its wrists displayed silver bangles, each holding a row of tiny razor-sharp blades that circled in a complete loop. The princess gasped silently, holding her hand to her mouth as the beast rose onto its back legs, standing at least eight feet tall. It rummaged through the cabin-cart, punching its large fist through the satin cloth that hung neatly over the cart and pulling out a casket of wine. With its tusk blade, the hideous creature punctured the casket and tipped the liquid down its throat until there was no more.

It took another casket and set it down on the ground beside its large leg, continuing to rummage through the cart.

"Hey," shouted Sintra, wishing the word hadn't escaped her mouth as the beast turned its head and snorted at her.

The behemoth stepped away from the cart and lowered itself onto all fours, slowly making its way toward the princess, baring its razor-sharp teeth and fangs, drooling from its ugly hog snout. Sintra held her arms outstretched, the blade shaking in her hands as she trembled.

"Cedric?" she called, "Lord Edith, help!"

The large creature took slow, deliberate steps, inching toward her. She swiped her sword through the air wildly, missing the beast with every blow. It glared at her. Its lengthy, dirt-caked ears flapped away the flies that lingered.

"Behemoth!" yelled Cedric as he appeared by the cart.

The animal turned to the knight, rising on its hind legs. It snorted and scraped one of its hooves against the ground, preparing to charge. A deep growl rumbled from its throat as it hastily paced toward him. Cedric reached into his scabbard and pulled an arrow, aimed for his target, and let go of the fletching in one swift movement. The arrow pierced the beast's leg, infuriating it. Cedric cast another arrow; the bodkin hit its armour scaled torso and fell to the ground. Arrow after arrow was cast until the scabbard was empty. The Boarschvine strode toward Cedric, arrows protruding from its legs like insignificant twigs.

"Use your sword," yelled Cedric in a panic, "I'll distract it… I think."

Sintra froze, too frightened to move. She wanted to help Cedric, but her legs betrayed her. Desperately, she grabbed a rock from the ground and hurled it at the creature's back, but it did not turn. The Boarschvine inched closer to the knight, pausing and standing within a foot of him. It raised its massive hand and struck Cedric, sending him flying through the air. He crashed into a tree and fell to the ground, blood trickling from his grazed forehead.

The behemoth lowered its head, standing on all fours, its hooves scraping the ground one by one. With a loud grunt, it charged. Sintra, holding her sword high in the air, charged as well. Cedric closed his eyes, welcoming the darkness of death as the beast neared within a meter of him. The princess let out a great roar as she struck down the Thalor sword with all her force, the blade slicing through the beast's neck, severing its head.

Dust settled as Lord Edith let out a gasp, having held his breath in suspense. Sintra stood stiff and pale-faced, the sword hanging limp from her grip as she stared at the headless creature that lay before her, dark blood pooling in the dirt. Stunned and silent, the knight swallowed loudly as he rose from the ground. He took the sword from Sintra's hand and dropped it to the ground before it started smoking and glowing upon his touch.

"Never have I slaughtered any living thing… in my life," the princess said softly, her eyes still fixed on the lifeless behemoth, her white gown sprayed with dark blood.

"You saved me," Cedric sighed. "If it had killed me, it would have gone for you. It also would have found Riven's body."

"Riven's body?" she breathed. "Where would it have taken him?"

"I do not know. Back to its civilization, I suppose."

"Civilization?"

"You think any ordinary hog fixes blades to its tusks, did you?"

"And its armour?"

"Ah, not armour, Sintra. Scales. That is what makes a Boarschvine, and they get a lot bigger than that."

"Bigger? That thing stood as tall as a village hut."

"Quite. It was only a young creature. Probably wandered from its pack."

"They have packs, as well?"

"Yes. They hunt in packs. Hunt for prey or stalk carts for ambush. We are blessed with luck to have not run into another."

"Don't speak yet, Lord Edith. I doubt that Boarschvine wandered on its own."

"Aye, we should keep going. I'll tidy the cart; you find our steed."

Sintra slid the Thalor sword into its sheath that now hung strapped to her waist. Cedric lifted the heavy casket of wine and placed it back inside the cabin-cart as the princess vanished through the trees. Soul grazed peacefully on a patch of luscious green grass; a trickling stream heard not too far from where she now stood.

"Soul," she called softly so as not to startle the horse. "Click-click-click," sounded her tongue alongside her teeth as she called the horse over.

The magnificent white steed lifted his head to the princess and gave her a snort before turning his flank toward her and continuing to graze.

Stubborn mule, she thought to herself, knowing quite well that if she had said it aloud, the horse would have most likely run away, offended. Soul was an intelligent horse, one of the smartest among the stables, as well as the fastest. As the thought crossed Sintra's mind, sadness welled in her stomach as she remembered a particular line in Cornelius's letter.

"He set alight the stables and the steeds within."

Anger burned inside her now. She was glad to have Soul. He was her favourite steed, but she mourned for the others. She slipped the headstall over Soul's ears and led him to the camp. Cedric was pulling arrows from the boar's legs, the bodkins bloodied and blunted.

"Why not make some more?" asked Sintra, tying the steed to the cart.

"I am no arrow-smith, and I haven't one, besides we don't have the time," he answered, wiping the small blade against his breeches to remove the dark blood. "I'll wash them, sharpen them, and place them back within my scabbard.

You should wipe down your blade as well, princess. Blood rusts too, even on steel like that."

"Yes. I heard running water just past that patch of green."

"Very well, we had better stock up too, I suppose."

As Sintra finished filling the last leather flagon with water, a wisp of light caught her eye as it flashed by beneath her nose. The princess suddenly glanced up to find herself looking at a distorted mirror version of herself. She slowly rose from the stream, not shifting her eyes from her mirrored version. Sintra raised her arm slowly; the movement was followed by the mirror. She turned her head from side to side at a snail's pace, her eyes not shifting once. Just as she expected, the mirror mimicked her movement. She bent down toward the stream once more, cupping her hands beneath the water as they filled with the cool, clear liquid. She watched as the distorted mirror imitated her every move. The princess drank from the water cupped in her hands, as did the reflection. She stared in awe, slowly reaching out a hand to touch the silent echo before her. As her arm gradually outstretched, she began to lean over the stream, her long dark hair floating along the top of the water as the small currents pulled it under. Inch by inch, she neared closer to the reflection, straining her arm and hand to touch her mimic.

"Stop!" called Cedric, taking his bow and an arrow from his scabbard and casting an arrow into Sintra's reflection.

The distorted mirror broke into a million pieces, each piece flying into the air like a single butterfly until not one piece remained in sight. Sintra rose from the stream, her hair and shoulders drenched in water as she had fallen upon being frightened by Cedric's arrow.

"What's the meaning of this? I bid you," she snapped, twisting the water from her long dark hair.

"If you had fallen into that stream any earlier, should I come by those blasted things would have drowned you."

"What blasted things?" she asked, looking around. "There's nothing here."

"Do you suppose a mirror like that just appears in thin air? Those were Fairies of the Silent Echo, my lady, evil little devils that have been the death of many folk that have tried to pass through this forest."

"Nonsense, how could an insignificant creature like a fairy kill a human?"

"In great numbers they lure their prey. If it weren't for me, you'd be dead."

"If it weren't for me, you'd be dead."

Cedric rolled his eyes. "From now on, you stay with me; don't ever leave my sight again. You hear?"

You should be taking orders from me; she thought to herself. But Sintra dared not make the situation any worse, for it was kind of Lord Edith to offer to help her. He did know this forest a little better than she did, after all.

†

"Gordon! Francis!" ordered Lord Elowen as he stood in the centre of the quad. "Bring to me the kingdom's finest maidens. Seeing as my whore of a Queen wishes to defy me, I need someone else to warm my bed in the meantime. Make sure they're pretty and inform them of their King's requests. Any quarrel will be dealt with by my Falchion."

"Every maiden in the kingdom is in the dungeons, my lord," said Gordon.

Aleron's expression turned cold as he glared into the eyes of the guard, raising an eyebrow in scorn before turning and walking away. Gordon and Francis disappeared into the dungeons while Lord Elowen watched as slaves piled the dead bodies of King Alaric's knights and guards into one gigantic heap, along with the dead knights and guards from the many other kingdoms that stayed to fight after the tournament, before setting it alight. Thick black smoke swallowed the quad, stinging the eyes of any man who came within twenty feet of the blaze.

"Fan the smoke, peasants. I do not wish to have dead traitors in my eye," ordered the madman.

Overwhelming expressions of sadness beamed across every slave's face as the headless body of King Alaric was pushed onto the heap. His head resided on a stake that had been bound to the post in the centre of the quad, the crown sitting erroneously on top of Aleron's head.

"If there be a traitor here amongst all men, 'tis that madman who wrongfully claimed the throne," said one slave to another as they watched him from a distance, cautious he would not hear a word.

"Lord Valahn will rise, as will the Queen," the other slave replied.

As Aleron admired the sight of King Alaric's body in flames, a group of slaves dragged logs of timber from the great wood beyond the citadel's Iron Gate. One by one, they laid the logs by the burnt-out stables and proceeded to cut and bind them, replacing the blackened and weakened beams that once held the straw roof of the stable. Only three steeds would reside here, those taken from the associate monarchies as they fled in the darkest hours of the night.

King Elmore had stayed with his men to fight, as his wife Queen Rachel, alongside Queen Farrah, had stayed to tend to Sintra when she fell unconscious at the sight of blood. They too fled when their numbers had weakened. King Lansing Bronn had fled with Queen Fleur Rithe after they stated Aleron had become strong with a crazed soul as he battled almost fifty men single-handedly. Others saw minor truth within Lord Elowen's claims to have slaughtered that many men before slaughtering the Queen and her children, but soon fled for fear of becoming as doomed and blood crazed as him. Not a single guard or knight that hadn't already fallen, fled, as they saw no hope left for King Alaric's reign.

Aleron looked to the sky as a black raven caught his eye. As it started to slowly descend, Lord Elowen noticed that it clutched a piece of parchment.

"Bow!" he ordered from a slave, reaching into the scabbard full of arrows that was still slung over his shoulder.

The slave fumbled the bow as he handed it to the knight. Lord Elowen lined the arrow with the raven, aimed, and released the fletching. The raven let out a loud squawk before it fell from the sky, tumbling through the air as its feathers slowed its fall. Aleron walked toward the dead bird and reached for the parchment. He opened it hastily with one hand, pushing the fold open with his thumb and index finger.

Cornelius

I am grateful my maid and my Winter whisper are safe; I send many thanks. Though I am disappointed that The Legend of the Infinite Forest slipped your mind when telling me a great story, for its myths may have come in great use to me. I travel safe and well, my friend, I will write again upon arrival. I wish you well!

Sintra

Lord Elowen crushed the parchment in his hand, making a tight fist as rage swelled within him. He turned to the slave boy who had handed him his bow, waving him over.

"Point your nose to the sky and close your eyes," said Aleron, taking another arrow from his scabbard and lining it with his bow.

Aiming for the slave's foot, he pulled on the arrow and let the fletching pass through his grip. The boy screamed, bending down to clutch his foot as he tried to pull the arrow free.

"You see this?" snapped Aleron, waving the parchment before the boy's face. "This is a letter containing

vital information about the whereabouts of my whore Queen.
And I almost missed it. The next time I send for my bow, you
come in haste, slave boy, or that arrow will protrude from your
chest cavity," he finished, handing the slave the dead raven
before pushing him away.

The slave boy was soon accompanied by an older man,
a slave who ran from the stable. Aleron raised an eyebrow in
his direction before rolling his eyes in distaste. He may object
to the old man's kindness and send him to resume his duties,
but at this point in time, he had far better things to deal with.

"Guards!" he called. "Gordon! Francis! What is taking
so long?"

Gordon and Francis escorted four of the prettiest
maidens from the dungeons and ordered them to form a line in
the quad before Aleron, who eyed the women carefully.

The first grew long golden locks that spiralled
alongside the young girl's grimy face. Her eyes were pale blue,
her lips pink and plump.

"Why are you not as thin as the others?" asked Lord
Elowen, "Do you feel your King request's *fat* whores?" he
asked, glaring at the women's swollen belly.

"Not sir, I am with child," said the girl, bowing toward
him and clutching her full stomach.

"And how did this come to be? Who owns the bastard
child? Am I to send for a tax? A fine perhaps?"

"No, my lord, there is no need for tax or fine for the baby belongs to my husband," said the girl softly.

"And who is your husband?"

"Sam Stifle, Your Grace."

"And where might I find this Sam Stifle?"

"On your burning heap."

"Ah yes, *that* boy," spat Lord Elowen, "Gordon, take this one back to the dungeons. She is to stay there for as long as I command; she will take punishment for her husband's crimes."

"But sir, I cannot raise this child in a dungeon. It's cold and wet…"

"So, maiden," interrupted Aleron, taking his hand and stroking the woman's soft cheek, "You wish for something a little warmer…and somewhat dry?"

The pregnant maiden nodded her little blonde head.

"Very well, maiden, you will have warmer and drier for I am no monster."

With that Lord Elowen jerked the girl away from the line, pulling her hard by the arm and pushing her to her knees against the hard cold stone floor of the quad. He then returned to Gordon and handed him his Falchion.

"Send the woman to her husband, the child to its father," he whispered coldly, "Give the woman warmth and a dry bed," he finished, his voice a little louder so that the pregnant woman could hear, "And do not forget that it is a great honour to swing that rapier, Sir Leoss."

Lord Elowen returned to the line of women who now wept and cowered for their own lives as they watched Gordon line the heavy sword with the blonde maiden's neck.

The second maiden had hair as red as fire, her eyes as brown as leather, her thin face was spotted with freckles, and her lips plump and perky as were her breasts. Aleron raised an eyebrow in admiration as he grasped a breast of the weeping girl, feeling its firmness and weight in his hand. Satisfied he moved on to the third maiden, this girl was thin, and pale skinned. Her eyes emerald against her long dark hair that reminded him of the princess.

"I don't care much for long dark hair, maiden; it reminds me of a whore I was to once wed."

He snickered, took his baselard from his waist and raised it against the girl's hair. With one swift motion the blade cut through the hair, the large bundle of darkness falling to the ground. Simultaneously Gordon swung the Falchion, slicing through the blonde maiden's flesh and bone with one swing, severing the head and letting it drop to the stone floor with a hard thud, beside it fell the swollen headless body it once occupied.

"I will not let the unborn suffer for I am no monster," started Aleron, "Burn it!" he ordered, turning to face the fourth and final maiden who stood before him, tears streaming down her soft cheeks.

Aleron admired this maiden's beauty. She was much older than the others. Her hair was black and thick, tussled much like his own along with her pale blue eyes that sat angelic against her wrinkled amber skin. This woman looked strikingly familiar to Lord Elowen as he noticed a long scar across her old, wrinkled neck. His eyes narrowed as he glared at this woman, the familiarity building within him like bile rising to his throat. He could not stop it as it came; it was there, and it there it would stay.

"I had wondered where you had got to," he spat, "I should have ended you when I had the chance."

The woman wiped the tears from her face and stood tall against the mad man, looking deep into his pale blue eyes as if hers were mirrored.

"I guess the mother of the devil cannot be killed so easily," spat the woman, "Not even by her own son."

Aleron looked at her in disgust, glaring at the woman who had given birth to him, the woman he once loved.

"I am no devil, woman, I am King of this kingdom, and you will bow before your supremacy," he spat.

"I will do no such thing; I will not bow before you for *you* are no King," said the woman sternly, staying upright,

"You're nothing but a glorified abomination, a fool, a bastard-
,"

Aleron stopped the woman midsentence with the back of his hand hard against her old cheek as he struck her down. Blood dribbled from her mouth as she stood upright once more.

"You make me sick, *mother*," he spat, "Francis, take this old hag back to the dungeons and lock her away in the deepest cell, I never want to see her face again. And when you get back take these wenches to the bathing chamber and have the wash-maid clean them. I want them dressed in fine silk. They will accompany me for a grand feast in the great hall. And later in my bedchamber."

The woman spat blood at Aleron's feet as she was dragged away toward the dungeons, the hurt in her eyes was soon replaced with hatred for the man she once called son.

Two slaves dragged the body of the dead maiden onto the fire along with her golden head as two others scrubbed the dark blood from the pave. The fire roared, casting more and more thick black smoke into the air and high above the citadel.

"Gordon!" called Aleron, turning toward the guard who handed back the Falchion, "Find the princess's maid and bring her to me along with the one they call Cornelius."

Gordon scurried off into the citadel entrance and out of sight, leaving Lord Elowen standing alone in the quad while he watched the dead bodies smoulder before him. The smell of boiling blood, burning flesh and charred bone and hair violated the nostrils of every man that occupied the quad.

The Legend of Braegor and Brencis

The sun shone brightly over the fields of Crevark, casting a warm, golden glow over the landscape. Queen Caprice and her children were lazing in the grass, the soft blades tickling their skin as they read books and talked together. The citadel loomed in the background, its tall spires reaching toward the sky, a silent guardian over the kingdom. On either side of the open field, dense forests framed the scene, their ancient trees standing like sentries, their leaves whispering secrets in the gentle breeze.

Birds chirped merrily from the treetops, their songs a harmonious backdrop to the peaceful morning. Wildflowers dotted the meadow, their vibrant colours painting a picturesque scene. The children laughed and played, their carefree voices mingling with the rustling leaves and the distant murmur of a brook that wound its way through the forest.

Caprice watched her children with a serene smile, her heart full of contentment. She lay back on the soft grass, feeling the warmth of the sun on her face, and closed her eyes, savouring the tranquillity of the moment. It was a rare respite from the duties of the crown, a chance to simply be a mother and enjoy the simple pleasures of life.

But the peace was abruptly shattered by the arrival of a stranger. His imposing figure cast a long shadow as he approached, his eyes dark and filled with a simmering rage. The birds fell silent, and the children's laughter faded as they sensed the tension in the air.

Caprice looked up, her serene expression turning to one of confusion and concern. "Who are you?" she asked, rising to her feet and shielding her children behind her.

Aleron stopped a few paces away, his gaze locking onto the Queen. "You don't recognize me, do you?" he growled, his voice low and menacing. "I am Aleron Elowen, your brother."

Caprice's eyes widened in shock. "My brother? How can that be?"

"Our father kept many secrets," Aleron spat, his voice dripping with bitterness. "I was born in squalor, left to fend for myself while you lived in luxury. I came seeking aid, riches to rebuild what was taken from me."

Caprice was taken aback, struggling to process the admission. "Aleron, I… I didn't know any of this. But even so, our kingdom's resources are stretched thin. We cannot afford to—" she lied.

"Cannot afford?" Aleron interrupted, his voice rising with fury. "You sit here in the sun, surrounded by comfort, while I am left to rot in poverty! You dare speak to me of struggles?"

He took a step forward, his fists clenched at his sides. "I have fought for this kingdom, bled for it, and this is the thanks I get? You turn your back on your own blood in my time of need?"

Caprice's children clung to her, sensing the danger in Aleron's tone. She placed a protective arm around them, her own fear barely contained. "Sir, please, understand—"

"Understand?" he roared; his face contorted with rage. "I understand that you are a coward, hiding behind your wealth and titles while others suffer. You will regret this, Caprice. Mark my words."

With a final, furious glare, Aleron turned on his heel and stormed away, leaving a trail of tension and fear in his wake. Caprice watched him go, her heart pounding in her chest, knowing that this confrontation was only the beginning of a much darker storm.

†

The princess sat beside Cedric at the front of the cabin-cart as Soul effortlessly guided them through the Infinite

Forest, occasionally grazing on grass. She loosened the reins slightly, giving him more freedom.

"I swear I've seen that rock before, my lord," Sintra said, frowning.

"The ways of the forest, my lady. Everything looks the same," Cedric replied.

"Tis the same rock," came a voice from nowhere.

Lord Edith and the princess looked up towards the roof of the cabin-cart where a dark hooded figure had suddenly appeared.

"How long have you been up there?" the princess asked, frowning.

"Not long!" it replied.

"Show us the way, great hooded one!" Lord Edith said, bowing his head towards the figure.

"Stop that, fool. You do not worship me," it spat, suddenly appearing before Lord Edith with a sharp blade at his throat. "My kind are not to be worshipped."

Cedric swallowed loudly, not daring to move an inch. Sintra, however, held the Thalor sword to the creature's heart, its sharp tip almost piercing the dark, leather-like cloak.

"Do it," hissed the being. "You will be doing me a favour!" it said to the princess.

"Let him go," she spat. But just as she began to push the sword into the being's flesh, it vanished into thin air, leaving behind a wisp of black smoke.

Cedric sighed in relief, grasping his throat. He frowned, meaning no harm with his mockery.

"You will get nowhere without my help," came the voice again. But as the princess searched around, there was no face or body to match it. "You do not worship my kind."

"We are very sorry. It will not happen again," Sintra said, looking around the forest, confused by the creature's sudden change in character.

"Princess is forgiven. Knight is not," said the being.

Lord Edith rolled his eyes and apologized, retreating inside the cabin-cart to escape in case the being returned.

"What is your kind?" Sintra asked softly, her eyes wandering through the trees.

"Death!" it spat, reappearing beside the princess.

Sintra jumped, her eyes widening as the creature startled her once more. She caught a glimpse of its green, scaled flesh as it repositioned itself on the bench.

"You stare, princess."

"My apologies, sir, but I have never seen such flesh as yours," she said, startled.

"You lie," hissed the being. "Your thoughts tell me of a jar, an infant Blackwing that dwells within its glass prison."

Sintra frowned at the words. She remembered seeing the jar in the secret chamber and what it held, but she had never told anyone.

"How do you know this?" she frowned.

"It is in your thoughts, princess; your eyes have seen Blackwing."

"Blackwing?"

"Aye, Blackwing. A great dragon species that lived centuries ago before it was wiped out by its most feared predator."

"Dragons fear predators?" the princess asked, confused.

Dragons are the largest, fiercest creatures to have ever roamed the earth, she thought to herself. *And they now fear predators?*

"Have always roamed the earth, have always feared predators," it said.

The princess froze, her eyes widening in disbelief.

"You read my mind?"

"I do, my princess."

"Why?"

"To see if you lie."

Sintra's brow furrowed. *I do not lie,* she thought.

"But you do, my lady, on several occasions. You lie to your father, you lie to the madman, and you lie to your lover. Liar, liar, liar."

"I lie to protect them from the truth."

"So, you confess…"

Sintra rolled her eyes, growing fed up with the childish games.

"So, what is your kind?"

"I am afraid that I cannot inform my princess of my kind."

"And why is that?" she snapped, becoming frustrated.

"You fear the truth," it replied.

Sintra slumped in her seat, her gaze fixed on the dirt track ahead as her mind wandered. The princess did not quarrel or press further; part of her feared the truth, but another part demanded answers, screaming for clarity. *Why did the creature have green, scaled flesh? Why did it refer to itself as Death? Would she ever hold Riven in her arms again, hear his sweet voice, or feel his whisper against her lips? Could the creature truly save her lover by bringing him back from the dead? What if it couldn't, and the whole journey was a waste of time? Would the being betray her, delivering her into the jaws of the malevolent Aleron? Was her father really dead? Was she truly the last of Lysandra's royal blood? Was Aleron really her kin? Was Serillah at peace?* As each thought passed through her mind, a tear trickled down Sintra's cheek. She needed to know the truth, but she feared it more than death.

"I am Brencis," the hooded creature began, sighing with a hint of sorrow for the girl. "I don't expect you've heard the Legend of Braegor and Brencis, but I will enlighten you all the same. For a young princess who has lost her entire family and lover to one madman, it is the least I can do. After all, you must know what is to come of your dead knight when he awakes."

"What do you mean?" the princess asked, sniffling. "What will become of my dead knight…*when he awakes*?"

"Dear lady Lysandra, I will tell you what is to come of your knight soon after I explain myself. Is that not what you requested?"

"Yes but—"

Brencis raised a green, scaled finger to silence her before laying his hands in his lap and resuming his story.

"You may not believe all that I am about to tell you, Sintra, but you must keep an open mind and believe that anything is indeed possible."

The princess nodded slowly; trepidation etched on her face as she stared at the creature.

"I am Brencis Laiceps, once a glorious and gallant knight who served in allegiance with the great King Lyndon Baster of Krad Serutaef. I was the most dedicated knight and guard among all his men, close enough to King Baster and trustworthy enough to the kingdom and village people to almost be pronounced the King's Hand. But it wasn't until the great battle of Orhtaed Muucav that I became wounded and weakened, too weak to serve as the true knight I had aspired to be for many years. I was severely injured by one of Muucav's men, took three arrows to the chest, and watched as my own blood spewed from my open lung as I pulled each arrow free. I was near death; it surrounded me like an icy blanket, taking away all light and leaving me in darkness.

"Braegor, my brother who fought alongside me, took me to a nurse, but she was no ordinary nurse; she was a witch. The Queen of the darkest magic to ever exist in this world, Tuantuem. She offered my brother a bargain to save my life. At first, he was hesitant but soon changed his mind as death clawed its sharpened talons into my soul.

"Tuantuem escorted my brother and me to the edge of the earth, to where the devil resides in his black, empty fortress of hell. Where fire-like water bubbles, boils, and spits from beneath. I grew too weak and slipped under; I don't remember much after that."

"What do you remember?" asked Cedric, who now had his head poking between the drapes from the cabin within.

"I remember waking in a daze; it was hard to see, though everything looked different. I could see, hear, and smell *everything*; it drove me mad. But the one thing I could not fathom was seeing my own lifeless body lying before me, wounded and bleeding with a gaping hole in my chest. But I couldn't feel it. All I felt was great weight and hunger, hunger for flesh and blood. Braegor tried to calm me, but my blood-crazed mind overpowered even me. I had no control over what I did…to anything and anyone."

Brencis fell silent for a moment, as if reliving the precise moment he turned. The memory haunted him.

"My brother told me what the witch had done. I then watched through eyes that weren't my own as my human body rose before me, just as crazed as I was. As I glared into its soul, I knew it was no longer me in that body, not even my spirit. It just looked like me. Its veins thickened. Black blood coursing beneath the skin. Its eyes grew red and wild, twitching as it eyed its surroundings. Fangs grew from its mouth, and coarse, steam-like breath pulsed thickly with every raspy pant the beast exhaled. I watched in horror as sharp talons sprouted from its fingertips, splitting the skin. Standing before me was my body, yet beneath it dwelled something far more sinister.

"Braegor ordered me to kill the beast that had taken over my body, but it escaped before I knew I was strong enough to destroy it. My brother hunted it for years, following a trail of blood and gore as it massacred and fed its ravenous self from village to village. Splintered bone, and carnage were all that was left in a village, along with the distorted, disembodied remains of men who were once great knights, left for the crows to pick at. When Braegor finally came face to face with the beast, he saw that it had grown green, scaled flesh over its entire body. He tried bargaining for my life, pleading for my body, but the beast refused. Braegor formed an army. They hunted the beast for a year, another year to Braegor that seemed like another lifetime.

"Tuantuem lured the beast out of my body and into its own, which was burned the moment my heart was placed back inside my body where it belonged. My body was never the same; it never grew back entirely human. The scales never faded, my eyes remained red, and I was forever known as the *beast that wandered the earth*, the immortal dragon-possessed human that butchered its way from village to village. Since then, I have lived beneath this cloak, concealing myself from the world as I wished not to be hunted anymore. For centuries, I have not aged, I have not suffered, and I have not felt pain."

"What happened to your brother and the beast dragon's body?" Sintra asked.

Brencis sighed.

"The dragon turned to stone, but Braegor...my brother, I killed him; took his head with my bare hands while I slept through the night," Brencis breathed in sorrow. "You see, child, the beast still dwells within a part of my soul. At times,

I cannot control the sudden outbursts. I have harmed many people and many loved ones. It has forced me to live a life of recluse."

Brencis then turned to Lord Edith, his eyes narrowing. "Do you understand why you must not worship me or my kind?" he snapped.

"I'm not sure I want that for Riven. He won't be Riven anymore. I would rather just give him the send-off he deserves."

"Ahh, but timing is everything. Your dear Riven will not grow to malice if the exchange is done correctly and swiftly."

"What brought you to me?" Sintra queried, her voice trembling slightly.

"I do not know. The soul of the knight, perhaps? My legend, perhaps? Who knows, but I am here as you request my guidance."

"That is if you still request it," Cedric added.

The princess sat silently on the bench, deep in thought, her mind far away from the Infinite Forest. Lord Edith raised his eyebrows at her ignorance of his remark.

"Princess, think about what you are doing; you may never hold, or love Riven again. No human can love a dragon."

"How does it work?" she asked, ignoring Lord Edith.

"A dragon must be defeated and the heart of another must beat in its place, Sintra. The heart of your love must be placed inside the body of a dragon."

"What is to be done with Riven's body?"

"It must be set alight and burned to ash once the dragon's heart beats within it. Exchanging the hearts seals the bond; your lover will then live on as a dragon until the end of time. But I am afraid Lord Edith speaks the truth, my princess. It means you will never love him as you have before."

Regardless of my decision, I lose Riven anyway, she thought.

"No, princess, Riven will live and thrive as a dragon. He will protect you and your kingdom," said Brencis, replying to her thoughts.

"Are you certain you wish to do this, Sintra?" asked Cedric.

"I must, Lord Edith, for my kingdom. I cannot let Aleron Elowen destroy everything my mother and father built. I cannot let him slaughter anymore. He will die by my sword or by my dragon. It's the only way we are to stop him. I promised the families of those slaves who died on the battlefield in the arena; I promised that they will have freedom. This is the only way."

"Very well, then you must follow your sword and slaughter the dragon. Do as I have said, and your dragon will give you vengeance."

With that, Brencis vanished into thin air once again, leaving behind a wisp of black smoke that soon faded to nothing.

"What does he mean, follow my sword?" asked Sintra, frustrated at Brencis's departure. "I don't understand. How are we supposed to get out of this damned forest?"

As Sintra complained and queried, the Thalor sword began to smoulder at her side, burning a hole through her white gown as it grew red hot within its sheath. The princess took it out in haste, holding it away from her singed garment. As she held the sword in the air, it forced Sintra to lower her arm as it suddenly grew quite heavy. Cedric eyed the weapon suspiciously, peering at it through narrowed eyes, following the direction in which it now pointed.

"Sintra," he said, "Sintra, look at your sword."

The princess stopped fumbling with her garment and glanced at her sword, raising an eyebrow.

"Lord Edith?" she asked, finding nothing suspicious about the sword whatsoever.

Lord Edith stood on the bench and leapt to a low branch. He climbed the tree, reaching for limb after limb as Sintra pulled on the steed's reins to halt the cabin-cart.

"What is the meaning of this? I demand to know," she snapped, tilting her head back as she watched Cedric climb to the very top of the tree.

"Raise up your sword," he called from a distance, "So I can see it."

"Well, of course, you won't see it, you fool; you're all the way up there."

"Just do it, Sintra."

The princess sighed and raised the sword high into the air, clutching it with two hands as it grew heavier and heavier.

"Do be hasty, Lord Edith, my arms tire at the weight of this steel."

Cedric descended from the treetop, swinging from branch to branch until he landed on the bench of the cabin-cart once again.

"Finished playing childish games?"

"Oh, princess, open your eyes," he replied, catching his breath.

"I do believe they're open, Lord Edith."

"Then open your damned mind, Sintra. That sword is our map; it just pointed us in the direction we must go."

The princess frowned, glancing at the sword in confusion before turning to Cedric in query.

"While you were fumbling with your gown, you should have been following the direction in which the sword points, my lady, for it points to our destination…according to my calculation."

"And you came to know this, how?"

"I feel it, princess, and I happen to know that that sword was not growing heavy in your arms but showing you which path to take."

"If your little calculation is correct, then its pointing toward the ground. Am I to dig to our destination?"

"Not likely, madam, but that attitude will get you to that destination quicker than you think if you keep it up. That treetop was able to show me that our destination is, in fact, downhill from here, if it pleases your impertinent remark."

"Then where are we going?" asked Sintra. "Where does this piece of steel want to take us, my lord?"

"Thane."

Sintra's heart sank, for she knew what resided in Thane. She knew Thalor still searched for its tail-thorn, which sat smouldering within her clutches. She knew the Thalor sword had chosen its very own dragon to slaughter; the only question that remained was whether she had the strength and ability to swing it.

†

"Where is she?" Aleron asked coldly.

"She did not say," answered a frightened Cornelius, quivering in his soft leather boots.

"I know that you fool. I read your letter. But you know a little more than you let on, old man."

"I don't know where she is, I swear," trembled Cornelius. "I'm sorry, I can't help you."

"You will help me, Cornelius. If you will not tell me where she is or where she is going, I will find the maid and I will torture her until she confesses."

"The maid knows nothing," spat Cornelius, cowering as he spoke.

"Tell me where I can find the Infinite Forest."

Cornelius glared into Aleron's eyes for a moment before scurrying off into the many aisles of books within the library. On the other side of the secret chamber door, Elara held Nyom's snout as the wolf fought to bark and growl at the sound of Aleron's voice.

"Hush, pet, you will give us away," whispered the maid.

Cornelius pulled out a large book titled *Legends of the Infinite Forest*, with a detailed carving of a map on the brown leather cover.

"Why is it that you never told the princess of this forest?" asked Lord Elowen, taking the book from the old man's grip.

"For its dangers. The creatures that dwell inside are far too dangerous for any man to go wandering into the forest," the old man replied, his hand shaking with fear as he dabbed a white rag to his sweaty brow.

Lord Elowen opened the large book, landing on a page titled *Fairies of the Silent Echo*. His fingers traced the words as he read, frowning in mockery as he found the creature more amusing than dangerous.

"Let's not venture into the Infinite Forest, Gordon," he said to the guard at his right shoulder. "I'm afraid we might be killed by a tiny fairy."

The both of them roared with laughter as Aleron slammed the book shut, dust escaping from its spine as it was near old enough to rupture upon minor force.

"There are far more dangerous creatures in that forest than fairies, my lord; great giant beasts of all kinds," said Cornelius, though he wasn't generally concerned about the safety of Aleron as he was the life of the princess.

Lord Elowen and Gordon left the book chamber, leaving Cornelius standing alone in the silence of the book aisles. He waited a few moments until he was certain he was alone and rushed back to the secret chamber.

"What news?" asked Elara, freeing the white wolf from her grasp.

"Sintra passes through the Infinite Forest alive and well. She requests you and Nyom stay hidden until she returns," he replied, closing and locking the door behind him.

"What about food? We must eat, Cornelius, especially this wolf before its instincts kick in and she eats me."

"Hush now, Elara. I believe Aleron is ordering his men to saddle the horses as we speak. But first, I must send a warning to the princess," the old man replied, taking a piece of parchment and scribbling a message before folding it and handing it to Elara.

"What are you doing? Are you leaving me again?"

"I'm afraid so, Elara. Aleron will be back for me soon, I know it. I must be out of here before I give you both away," he finished, jerking his head toward Nyom.

"What about this?" asked Elara, holding up the letter. "I need a raven."

"Aleron shot down our last raven with an arrow, tis how he got his hands on my letter. You'll have to coax another, my dear maid, and it will not be easy."

"My word, it will not be easy, Cornelius. How am I to summon a raven when I am trapped within this chamber? I'll die in here before that happens."

Cornelius pointed to the ceiling where a single square-shaped groove was carved neatly into the stone.

"That, my dear friend, is how the raven gets in and out. Tis an old air vent. I carved it myself many years ago when I was a young man. You simply push the square and slide it to one side; it reveals a tiny passageway big enough for a bird to squeeze through. More like a decoy for those who hunt parchment birds, as the opening lies at the mouth of the septic passage. Many letters have been lost in that tiny passageway, holding decades of secrets that never reached their destination."

Elara stared at the square groove in the ceiling for a moment before looking back to the old man.

"Cornelius Thatcher, I hope you do not take me for an old fool," she spat, but the bookkeeper frowned to stifle a laugh as he unlocked the secret chamber door and disappeared onto the other side once more.

Elara glanced around the small chamber in search of something she could use to lift the square and open the vent. She cleared the small table before climbing on top and reaching for the ceiling, but it was too high. As the old woman stretched her arms out, her tiptoes danced on the weak surface of the table, its legs groaning beneath her weight. Nyom stood to attention as a sudden crack echoed through the small chamber, one of the legs giving way. Elara came crashing down on top of the table, broken shards of old wood snapping beneath her. She was suddenly in total darkness as the gust of wind from her fall blew every candle out.

"Old fool," Elara cursed herself, resurrecting a small flare from a candlestick as she held it against a rag she had accidentally ripped from her apron upon her fall.

She waited a few moments, catching her breath as she listened for any movement on the other side of the door. All was clear. She then resurrected each and every candle, filling the chamber with light once again. Elara gathered each table leg and laid them on the ground in a straight line. She then took the rags from Nyom's bandaged ribs and used them to bind the table legs together. The old maid stood on her tiptoes once more, stretching out her arms as far as she could manage while prodding the ceiling with her makeshift pole. Elara held the pole directly over the square before prodding it hard against the stone, freeing the flap and letting it fall to the ground. Along with the stone square came the dried-up remains of a dead crow, a parchment tied to its feet with faint scribbles too faded to read.

The old woman laughed in triumph as an idea crossed her mind. She looked at the floor of the chamber with her hands on her hips in disgust. The floor was covered in shards and splinters of wood, along with some empty broken glass jars she had not noticed before. Naturally, the old woman started to clean, humming to herself until all the broken, sharp pieces of wood and glass wreckage occupied one single corner of the chamber. Elara sat on the cold, dusty stone floor, peering at her surroundings in search of something she could use to lure in a raven.

Jars of roots and leaves occupied the shelves along with bottles of oddly coloured liquids. Dried worms and grubs covered in dust, a dried-up inkwell, and a frail feather quill sat distorted from years of solitude and confinement in this small space. As candlelight flickered from a slight breeze sent down through the now open vent, the orange shimmer of light against a glass jar caught the maid's eye as she glanced at one of the shelves.

A gasp escaped her mouth as she hadn't noticed this particular jar before. Her eyes widened in disbelief, the realization overwhelming as the creature within became too familiar to her. Elara rose to her feet and stepped toward the Blackwing creature inside the jar. Fear and admiration both flooded her thoughts as she gazed at the tiny, black-scaled beast. And then suddenly it came to her.

"What luck," she said to herself, placing both her hands on either side of the dusty jar and taking it in her grasp.

She held it above her head for a moment, pausing to turn to the uncertain white wolf that stood behind her.

"Now look out, this could be dangerous," she said, throwing the jar hard against the stone floor.

Shattered glass and yellow liquid consumed the stone pavement; the wet, limp, disembodied remains of the Blackwing creature lay in pieces, having been seceded due to the force of the glass against it. Nyom cowered behind Elara, eyeing the creature.

"At least I know you won't eat it," laughed the old maid.

She took a large piece of sharp broken glass and sliced it through the dark transparent flesh of the infant beast, revealing white meat and muscle beneath. She then reached into her apron and pulled out a small bobbin of thread.

"I shall catch us a raven."

She tied a piece of dragon meat securely to her thread before placing it upon the end of her large pole. She raised the pole into the air and inside the vent; carefully, she laid the bait on the edge of the passage opening and sat the pole aside.

"Now we wait," she said, looking at the white wolf that still cowered behind her. "You are a fool, Nyom. That creature is dead; it cannot harm you."

But even that did not reassure the animal.

Satan's Bastard Child

Heavy boots echoed through the great hall of the Citadel as Aleron strode toward the grand table, clutching a large book. Gordon followed a few paces behind, struggling to pull along the stubborn old bookkeeper. The walls of the hall were lined with guards, once slaves and villagers, now standing to attention in silver armour, clutching their chosen weapons.

"I trust that you will all obey me," Aleron began. "You will be granted knighthood if your duties serve me well. Every man in this Citadel will accompany me through the Infinite Forest. Disobey my orders, and you will be punished by death. Any man who brings the princess forward will be rewarded with his weight in gold and the freedom of his family. Now leave before I change my mind."

"How do we get there, my lord? We haven't any steeds," asked one of the guards, hesitating at the entrance.

"Then I suggest you start walking. The steeds I have are being re-shod for Sir Leoss, Sir Gregory, and myself. If you wish to acquire your own mount, search the nearest village or forest. Perhaps you will find a mule or a rather large goat to satisfy your needs."

Lord Elowen waved the men away, frowning as he raised a golden goblet to his lips and sipped the red liquid. He stabbed a chicken breast with a fork.

"Do you wish for your guests now?" asked a servant.

"Guests?"

"Your young companions, my lord; the two you handpicked yourself."

"Ah, yes," he started, "No, I'm suddenly not in the *fucking* mood. Send them back to the dungeons."

"Perhaps you would like something to torture for your amusement? Perhaps a slave?" asked Gordon, still clutching Cornelius's arm.

Lord Elowen's eyes widened, malice filling his twisted mind. A grin of sadist joy spread from ear to ear. He suddenly had a thirst for a game of death, and he knew exactly who to play with.

"Francis," he called, to which the young guard strode in, "Bring me my mother."

Francis disappeared through the entrance to the great hall, the sound of his feet hitting the stone floor echoing through the hallway until it was heard no more. The great hall was silent, now free of guards, apart from Gordon who snickered and frowned at the old bookkeeper who refused to kneel.

"Keep still or I'll bind you," Gordon whispered angrily.

"No need to whisper, Sir Leoss, the great hall is empty and sound travels within empty spaces," said Aleron, his nose deep in lines of ink and illuminated parchment.

Lord Elowen admired the golden strokes and fillings that lined the ink-patterned borders of each page. Ornamental leaves and flowers were hugged by winding green vines and royal blue flowing water. He frowned as he came to a page titled "Trolls."

"Old man, tell me, are there really trolls that wander throughout the Infinite Forest?" he asked Cornelius.

"Yes, and they are great, ugly beasts with such a stench it makes your eyes water," the bookkeeper replied.

Lord Elowen lowered his head to the book, no reply intended. He carried on reading, turning page after page until he reached the centre of the book where a map of the forest spread out over two pages.

"Ah ha," said the madman, "This is what I'm after."

His fingers traced the perimeter of the Infinite Forest, following tree lines and great mountains scattered throughout the forest terrain. Aleron lifted the book in his hands, stood from his seat, and walked toward the old man.

"You will find out where she is going, or your head will roll by my falchion. You have one hour," said Aleron, placing the open book before Cornelius.

The sound of Francis' footsteps carried up the citadel hallway and into the great hall. Lord Elowen turned to welcome the guard, who was accompanied by the old woman that had spat at his feet earlier in the day.

"Good evening, Mother Elowen, I've been expecting you."

"Expecting me for what?" she spat, "And how dare you call me that. I never wed your father. You are a bastard!"

"Come," said Aleron, holding his arm out to embrace her, but she refused. "Dine with me."

"Why on earth would I want to dine with you? You'll have my head afterward no doubt, so go on and get on with it."

"Always were an ungrateful cow," he growled.

"I was a mother, and I tried to protect you-,"

"Protect me? You threw me out into the cold with so much as rags on my back."

"You were twenty-seven years, Aleron, time to fly the coop. It was no business of mine; your dealing and trading on the black market, until you brought death into my home. Your father and I never did understand why you had not yet found a fine girl to wed or raise a family. It would have been nice to have grandchildren, but instead we had death threats and farm animals poisoned. Murderers lurking in the darkness as they waited for your arrival."

"Stop your whining you old bat, you could have so much more…here with me."

"You never earned that crown on your head," spat the woman, "The only crown ever given to you was from me. And *that* was when giving birth to you," she finished, spitting at his feet once again.

"I apologise for tearing your insides on my arrival into this world, *mother dear*, perhaps you should have bled to death to avoid having to have raised such a disappointment."

"Mark my words, Aleron, if I knew what was to come, I would have thrown myself from a cliff long ago, your festering foetus still attached to my womb."

"I'm *that* much of a disappointment?" he mocked.

"You're an abomination, a thief and a murderer. But most of all Aleron Elowen, you are a coward."

Aleron raised his eyebrows at the woman's final choice of words.

"A coward?" he roared, "I am King of Crevark, supremacy of this kingdom and-,"

"You murdered your father before trying for me; you slaughtered the entire Lysandra family just so you could rule erroneously as King. You cheated your way to reign," said the woman, the words flying out of her mouth at such a speed, "You're a traitor. You betrayed your kingdom; you betrayed your land, and you betrayed your people. The only thing that comes for you, Aleron Elowen…is *death,* for you are Satan's bastard child. Not mine!"

As the last word rang through his ears, Lord Elowen raised his falchion as Francis held the woman down, Gordon grasping her other arm as he left Cornelius standing to watch.

"If I am Satan's bastard child then you are Satan's fucking whore. Now mother, *death* comes for you," spat Aleron, swinging his sword and severing the woman's head.

"My father succumbed to the pestilence!" he added.

A dark red pool of blood grew larger as the old woman's headless body lay on the cold stone floor, her head rolling to a stop.

"Put her head on a stake and burn her body, I would have had much pleasure in hearing her scream as she burned alive, but her mouth ran too wild for my liking," said Aleron, catching his breath as anger pulsated through his blood, "Send for a maid to clean this before it stains; I'd much rather *not* have to inform guests that the old hag was indeed my mother."

Cornelius quivered in his soft leather boots, kneeling to the stone floor and proceeding to study the map. As much as he wished not to help the mad man find the princess, he valued his life and feared for what was to come at the end of that very hour.

†

Sintra and Lord Edith had travelled for hours, slowly venturing down the mountain toward the edge of the Infinite Forest. Soul, their white steed, groaned in exhaustion as his hooves began to give him grief.

"He's been trudging down this mountain for hours; he deserves a break," Sintra argued with Cedric.

"It's too dangerous, princess; the steep mountainside leaves us out in the open for any predator."

"You mean the dragon," she added, but Cedric did not reply.

As the steep slope started to curve to their advantage, Sintra halted the cabin-cart, concealing it behind a thick grove of trees.

"Very well, my lady, but do not leave my side this time, or I will be burying you alongside him," said Cedric, pointing an arrow toward the cabin-cart.

"As you wish, but I'm more than capable of looking after myself," she answered, pointing the Thalor sword toward him.

She freed the white steed of his reins and let him wander close by while Lord Edith set up a small camp. The princess wandered over to the cabin-cart, frowning as she heard a peculiar sound coming from inside. As she peered into the cabin, her eyes rested on a large, green-scaled creature that looked too human to be a wild beast. Its long taloned toes scraped the wooden floor of the cabin as its hands fumbled across the pale, dead flesh on the body before it. As the afternoon rays of sunlight beamed in through the drapes, the beast glared back at her with red, raging eyes. Sintra screamed as it leapt at her, knocking her to the ground and holding a sharp blade to her throat.

"What do you want?" it growled, baring its razor-sharp teeth, its long-forked tongue vibrating as it hissed.

Lord Edith leapt to attention, lining three arrows in his bow as he aimed for the creature. The beast looked toward Cedric, a deep growl escaping its throat before it suddenly vanished into thin air, leaving behind a wisp of black smoke. The Steel Knight slightly lowered his bow, frowning in confusion as he still stood to attention. Sintra rose to her feet and dusted herself. She cautiously moved toward the cabin, wary of the beast's return.

"Was that in there?" asked Lord Edith, his three arrows pointed to the ground.

"Aye, but for how long? And what was it doing?"

The princess climbed into the cabin to examine the strange markings that covered Riven's pale flesh. Various odd symbols were carved into the skin, surrounding the heart and chest.

"Brencis," whispered Sintra, "It must have been Brencis."

Lord Edith stood at the entrance to the cabin-cart, his face still tainted with confusion; he hadn't heard nor seen Brencis enter the cabin. Sintra climbed out of the cabin-cart and searched around the forest for any sign of the creature.

"Brencis," she called, "Brencis, come back. I demand to see you," but there came no answer.

Why wasn't he wearing his cloak? She thought, *and what was he doing to Riven's body?* The princess knew that the dark creature could not resist when it came to reading her mind; it felt the need to answer her thoughts. *Is the demon inside Brencis, taking over his body?* She thought, *was it trying to take over Riven's body?* Sintra knew it was only a matter of time before the creature would answer her.

"I was doing no such thing," said the voice she craved to hear, "But clever girl, I commend you."

"Commend the princess?" asked Lord Edith, "For what?"

"Sintra knows to summon a beast by thought and thought alone," said Brencis, still not appearing before them, "This is good, very good."

"Why is it-,"

"She now knows how to summon her dragon," he interrupted, appearing before Lord Edith, glaring at him within a foot from his face, their noses almost touching.

Cedric's eyes widened in horror as he caught a glimpse of Brencis' face beneath the hood. His red, rage-filled eyes glared back at him like discoloured cat eyes, the pupil nothing more than a vertical black slit. Lord Edith cowered from Brencis, hunching and leaning away from the green-scaled creature.

"Ah, you fear my true form," said Brencis.

He raised both scaled hands to his black hood and lifted it over his head, but as he did so, his body vanished, leaving the black cloak to fall to the ground in a heap. He then reappeared beside it, a green metallic scaled creature that resembled both lizard and man. The princess was grateful he reappeared with short breeches to conceal his manhood. Dark tufts of hair still grew from his scalp, his arms and legs like a man's though much thicker in muscle tone. His long toes were each tipped with a sharp talon that curled toward the ground. His facial features were still very much human, apart from his eyes, scaled flesh, talons, and razor-sharp teeth. Sintra cringed as she noticed two large, distorted lumps protruding just above his shoulder blades.

Wings, she thought.

"Aye, my princess, they were indeed wings," he replied, turning toward her slowly.

"Were?"

"I had Braegor hack them off to my flesh when I took back my body. The beast had begun a full transformation over the years he possessed my body. He grew wings but hadn't learned to use them. It was something that angered it. A part of me grew enraged at the idea of hacking them off, but I no longer wanted to be a beast. I wanted to be the man my mother gave birth to, not the monster that was born within the fire. I hated the damned things."

Lord Edith and Sintra stared in astonishment at the scaled creature before them. It was unlike anything they had ever seen. Brencis robed himself, hiding his reptilian body beneath the dark cloak, his face disappearing into the darkness of the hood.

"Seems my appearance has frightened you," he said, now standing as the black hooded creature they had first laid eyes on.

"So, what were you doing to Riven's body just now?" asked Sintra.

"I was preparing his body for the exchange; those carvings upon his chest are to ensure that once the beast is inside his body it will not escape. It will dwell inside the human chest cavity for all eternity, a dark, silent, empty prison surrounded by bone. And all of it *must* be burnt to a crisp, ash blown away on the wind."

"Why did you feel the need to lay a blade at my throat in such haste?" Sintra frowned.

"I apologize, my princess, I apologize deeply for that was not I," said a repentant Brencis, lowering his hooded head in shame.

"I'm off to hunt," interrupted Cedric, hesitating and raising an eyebrow as he glanced at Brencis.

The princess waved him on as she made her way to the cabin-cart, pulling out furs and woollens to make a bed for the night.

"Perhaps you should sleep within the cabin tonight," said Brencis, watching her intently.

"And why would that be, Brencis?"

"Tis extremely cold on this part of the mountain at night, madam, you will freeze."

"I have a fire to warm me."

"I'm afraid you will have no fire tonight. The blaze will attract the great Thalor dragon, and that is something I do not wish anyone to face. Especially not you, my princess. Not yet."

Sintra frowned; she couldn't do anything without being ordered around by others. She found it impeccably frustrating as she was of royal blood yet hadn't given a single order, not that Lord Edith or Brencis would take any notice of her demands anyway. As the princess made her bed, a raven landed on a nearby rock, a parchment bird carrying a letter at its feet.

"Seems you have a courier," said Brencis, retrieving the letter from the crow and handing it to Sintra.

"It's from Cornelius," she said, opening the folds of the parchment before reading the ink scribe.

Sintra,

I did not receive your latest parchment as the mad man plucked it from the sky. I hear word that you have reached the Infinite Forest. I must warn you, princess, you must flee. Lord Elowen sends many guards as he rides himself to the Infinite Forest in order to capture you. Bloodshed and pleas for life is all that goes on within the citadel walls, so if you journey for reason, please hurry. If not, flee princess, and never come back for I fear that as you near the end of this parchment, my head rolls at Aleron's hand by your father's Falchion, as will your maid's soon after. I wish you well Sintra, I wish you haste!

Cornelius Thatcher

Tears swelled in the princess' eyes at the thought of losing both Cornelius and Elara to the mad man. She scrunched the letter within her hand, the parchment crumbling beneath her fist. She had never hated Aleron more than she did at that moment.

"He won't stop until we're all dead," she said softly, her voice trembling.

"Do not weep, princess, we do not know if Cornelius is dead."

"I fear he won't be alive much longer. I need to go back, I need to stop Aleron; roll his head with my sword and take back my throne, take back my kingdom."

"You've come this far, Sintra, do not turn back now or you will perish along with the village people. Hold on a little longer, until you have your dragon by your side. Then you may take Aleron's head, throw it into the dragon's mouth so it swells within its belly. Better yet, command your dragon to swallow him whole so that you may hear him scream and beg for mercy from the inside out."

Sintra raised an eyebrow toward Brencis.

"Brencis," she started, looking toward the creature. But she needn't say more for he knew what she wanted.

Sintra felt a strange warmth envelop her body; she could feel a strange power seeping into her mind. Her body began to hum with an unfamiliar energy, a sensation that was both comforting and unsettling. Suddenly, a sharp pain pierced her head, causing her to wince. Her eyes burned as if they were on fire, and she instinctively closed them, seeking relief. But instead of darkness, she was met with a vivid vision.

Serillah pinned the note to her door with trembling hands, the words hastily scrawled: "Too ill for dinner. Will come out when ready." She hoped it would be enough to keep her absence unnoticed for a while. The citadel was quiet, the halls echoing with the distant sounds of the night. She waited until she was sure everyone was asleep before slipping out of her chambers.

The moonlight guided her steps as she made her way through the citadel grounds, her heart pounding with a mix of fear and excitement. She reached the edge of the field, where she had hidden a bundle of raggy clothes earlier that day. Quickly, she swapped her elegant gown for the coarse, worn clothes, feeling the rough fabric against her skin. It was a small price to pay for the freedom she craved.

With her identity concealed, Serillah made her way to the village. The air was crisp, and the sounds of the night surrounded her. She felt a thrill of anticipation as she approached the tavern, a place she had only heard about in whispers. It was a world away from the opulence of the citadel, and she longed to experience it for herself.

Inside, the tavern was warm and lively, filled with the chatter and laughter of villagers. Serillah felt a sense of liberation as she mingled with the crowd, enjoying the anonymity. It was here that she met Aleron, a striking figure with a confident smile and a bold demeanour. His presence was magnetic, and she found herself drawn to him.

They talked for hours, Aleron's stories of adventure captivating her. He was unlike anyone she had ever met, and she felt a connection that was both exhilarating and terrifying. When he invited her to his house, she hesitated only for a moment before agreeing. She wanted to escape her life, if only for a little while. She felt alive in a way she never had before, but as the hours went by, a sense of unease began to creep in. She knew she couldn't stay out all night.

The vision changed a little. Sintra saw her sister, Serillah, bound in ropes, her face grimaced in agony. The room around her was dimly lit, shadows dancing on the walls as if mocking her suffering. Serillah's cries echoed in Sintra's mind, each one a dagger to her heart. She could see the bruises and cuts that marred her sister's once flawless skin.

Sintra's breath caught in her throat as the vision shifted. She saw the cruel face of Serillah's captor, Aleron, his eyes cold and devoid of mercy. He laughed as he had his way with her, his groans and Serillah's muffled cried a haunting chorus that filled the room. Sintra's heart pounded in her chest, a mix of fear and rage surging through her veins.

As the vision continued, Sintra remembered a time when Serillah had been absent from their family meals for three days. She had been told that Serillah was unwell, as she left a note pinned to her door one evening. But now, seeing this vision, Sintra realized the horrifying truth. This was where her sister had been, enduring unimaginable torment as the hands of Aleron Elowen.

The vision changed once more. Sintra saw her mother and her siblings in the fields of Crevark. The Queen Caprice, Serena and Soren were lifeless on the ground. Serillah's eyes widened in shock as she saw Aleron moving toward her.

"No, spare me," she cried, clutching her newly swollen belly.

Aleron glanced at her growing waist and looked her in the eye. Serillah couldn't gauge the emotion that coursed through him, though she felt it wasn't warmth as he took long, deliberate steps toward her.

"Please," she pleaded, grasping hold of his hand that gripped her throat.

"There will be no bastard of mine to ruin my plans," he spat, "I should have known that you were royalty. With your soft, uncalloused hands, and flower-scented hair."

He slowly raised her by the throat, her toes dangling just inches from the grass. He drew a baselard from his waist and plunged it into Serillah's pregnant belly. She gasped for air, tears streaming down her cheeks. The vision grew more intense, the details sharper and more horrific. She could feel

Serillah's pain as if it were her own. Tears flowed down Sintra's face, her body trembling with the intensity of the emotions coursing through her.

Aleron thrust the blade into her again. He dropped her to the ground. She whimpered quietly, clutching her waist in attempt to stop the bleeding. Serillah cradled her body in angst, fearing the worst for her unborn child. She was soon alone, left to bleed to death beside her family.

Just when she thought she could bear no more, the vision began to fade. The pain in her head lessened, and the burning in her eyes subsided. She opened her eyes, gasping for breath, her body still humming with the remnants of Brencis' power.

†

That night, while Lord Edith and Sintra dined on roast hare, pullet, and red wine from the remaining casket, Brencis vanished into the darkness of the forest. He sought something more bloody, raw, and breathing. Perhaps hare and pullet did not suit his taste; he might prefer swine or goat to sink his razor-sharp teeth into. Cedric extinguished the fire as soon as their meal was cooked, aware of the dangers that night fires attracted. He called it a death wish, something grief-stricken men did in the depths of despair after losing everything they held dear.

Sintra resolved to wait one more night before avenging Thane and slaying the dragon. Her plan was to creep up on it as it slept, rather than risk being eaten alive while she slept within her furs and woollens on the edge of the Infinite Forest.

As Lord Edith lay beside her for warmth, both wrapped securely in furs and woollens, Sintra's eyes grew heavy, and she drifted off to sleep. She slept soundly and dreamlessly for hours until the prick of coldness deadened the tip of her nose. Something else lingered in the air, violating her nostrils. The princess wrinkled her nose as she slowly sat up to locate the source of the stench. At first, she glanced at the cabin-cart, thinking it was Riven's body, but something told her it was far worse than a rotting corpse. And much livelier. A warm breeze blew down her neck and back, sending a cold shiver down her spine. Sintra slowly turned her head, widening her eyes in the darkness as she strained to see what now stood behind her.

"TROLL!" yelled Lord Edith, leaping to his feet with a sword in one hand and a large axe in the other. His voice echoed through the night, filled with urgency and fear.

The troll growled, a deep, guttural sound that resounded through the forest. It raised its giant arm into the air before slamming its heavy fist into the ground, missing Cedric by mere inches. The impact sent a shockwave through the earth, scattering dirt and leaves.

Lord Edith ran from the campfire, his heart pounding as he led the great, ugly beast away from the cabin-cart and Sintra. His breath came in ragged gasps, but his determination to protect the princess fuelled his every step. However, his efforts soon weakened as another troll emerged from the shadows behind Sintra.

This troll was even more monstrous, its great round belly protruding from its waist, meeting Sintra's face as she stood. Through the darkness of the forest and the dim light of the night sky, the princess could see the profound ugliness of the troll's face. Its crooked yellow teeth jutted out from its wet mouth, glistening with saliva. It glared down at her through small, beady eyes, frowning as it tried to see her within the darkness.

The troll raised its fist and slammed it into the ground beside Sintra, a growl escaping deep inside its throat as it missed. The ground shook, and Sintra stumbled but quickly regained her footing.

"What do you want?" the princess asked, her voice trembling. But of course, there came no reply from the daft beast.

The troll raised its arm again, and this time, as it swung its fist toward the princess, she ducked and dodged, slashing the troll's arm with her sword on her way past it. Blood spewed from the open wound, angering the beast. It clutched its arm in agony before charging toward Sintra, who turned and ran into the forest.

The troll barrelled through the trees, snapping branches and toppling smaller trees in its path. It tried eagerly to grasp her with one enormous hand. The princess turned to face the troll, her heart racing. She swung her sword again, opening the flesh on the beast's other arm. The troll wailed in distress, clutching both gaping wounds as blood spilled from each gash.

Sintra felt a pang of remorse as the troll fled into the forest, its cries echoing through the night. She was left alone, lost in the darkness, her breath coming in short, panicked bursts. But her respite was short-lived. A great smashing and crashing came from a distance, and soon she was accompanied by a bigger, angrier troll than the last. This one was even more menacing, its eyes burning with rage. Behind it was another, clutching a blade that was curved like a claw, its eyes fixed on Sintra with deadly intent.

"I pissed off the whole family," she muttered to herself. Her snide remark was met with another charge from an enraged troll.

As the large troll neared her, three arrows suddenly sprang from the shadows, piercing through the troll's legs and embedding deep into its thick, elephant-like flesh. The beast roared in agony, collapsing to the forest floor with a thunderous thud that shook the earth around it. The troll lay writhing in pain, clutching its wounded legs, while another charged at Sintra, swinging its claw blade wildly from side to side.

She braced herself, blocking the troll's blow with her Thalor sword. The sound of clashing steel screeched through the air, a harsh, grating noise that echoed in her ears. The troll growled, its claw blade catching Sintra's sword and pushing it down with its immense weight. She struggled to stay upright, her legs trembling under the strain. Just as she was about to collapse, she squeezed through the troll's legs, slicing its calf muscles as she went. The troll roared in anguish, dropping to the forest floor and clutching its legs.

"That sword is made for killing, Lady Lysandra, not wounding," said Lord Edith, emerging from the trees and wiping blood from his own sword.

Sintra frowned, her thoughts turning to the only living being she truly desired to kill, Lord Elowen.

"I don't find a particular interest in slaughtering the innocent, my lord," she replied.

"What makes you so sure these putrid beasts are innocent?" Lord Edith challenged.

"I'm not certain, Lord Edith, but they have done no wrong by me, so I don't find them guilty," Sintra said firmly.

"Stupid girl, they're trolls. They eat whatever they kill, shit wherever they please, and don't doubt for a second that they won't hunt you down until you're dead just for wounding them. Grow a backbone, Sintra, they would have killed you," Lord Edith snapped, his voice filled with frustration.

"I am not stupid," Sintra replied, her voice steady. "I happen to have a heart."

"Oh, Lady Lysandra, right now your kingdom needs a warrior, not a righteous Queen…nor a dead one. Now slit their throats before the rest of them come. You harm a handful; you've awoken an army. Kill them."

"Rest of them?" she asked, pausing as the thought of ten more trolls barging through the forest to feast on her flesh and pick their teeth with her bones sent a shiver down her spine.

The suffering families back in her kingdom plagued her mind. She envisioned Aleron slaughtering every woman and child without hesitation, swinging her father's falchion and wearing his crown while laughing in the face of the innocent. Anger rose within her as the truth of Aleron's treachery tormented her heart. The screams of her sisters and brother echoed in the back of her mind, mingling with the trolls' moans of agony.

Slowly, one of the trolls rose and charged her. The princess snapped out of her thoughts and charged the beast with her sword pointed directly at its giant belly. She ran and leapt into the air, swinging her sword and slashing open the troll's gizzard. Its steaming insides spilled to the ground. She slashed her sword once more, severing the troll's head and letting it fall to the ground at her feet with a heavy thud.

"Now put the other out of its misery," ordered the princess, wiping blood from her face while catching her breath.

Lord Edith followed her command, plunging three arrows into the other troll's skull from close range, killing it instantly. The arrow flew straight through the creatures head and embedded itself inside a tree trunk. He then plucked his arrows from wherever they landed and wiped each bodkin clean, placing them back into his scabbard. A deafening rumble echoed through the forest as more trolls approached.

"More trolls," winced the princess, remembering the smaller troll that had fled after she wounded it.

"Aye, they must smell us," said Cedric, sniffing the air. "I smell them…nine trolls coming down the mountain. Best to say goodbye and slit our own throats."

Amid the panic, Sintra had an idea. She fled through the trees back to their camp.

"Princess?" queried the knight.

"Pack everything, rein Soul, I have an idea," she replied.

Sintra took a warm coal from the campfire and held it against a handful of straw, blowing softly until the bundle ignited. She then disappeared through the trees, returning seconds later as a great fire blazed behind her.

"What's the meaning of this?" demanded Lord Edith, sitting on the bench of the cabin-cart. The white steed stirred as the blaze neared. "The trolls will kill us, princess, you don't have to wait for the dragon."

Sintra smiled. Cedric panicked, hastily slapping the reins against Soul's flank, moving the cart forward as it started to roll down the slope.

"We have fire to our advantage, Lord Edith; it races upward as it climbs the slope while we descend. The trolls are on the other side of that blaze; it will chase them back up the mountain and away from us."

"What about the dragon, Sintra?"

The princess grinned devilishly, knowing that her main drive to light the fire was to see the dragon. As Sintra climbed onto the cart, roars of rage echoed from a distance. Yet, the princess waited for a different roar.

"You may be bright, princess, but you sure are foolish at times. Let's hope the dragon sleeps tonight; I don't fancy being charred and eaten alive," Lord Edith muttered, his eyes scanning the dark horizon.

"Calm, Lord Edith. We are well away from that blaze now. If the dragon wakes, the darkness of the night will conceal us from its prying eyes," Sintra replied, her voice steady but filled with anticipation.

"Aye, but 'tis almost first light, Sintra. We have only a few short hours left, and we'd better be off this mountain and out of this damned forest before the sun is high in the sky," Lord Edith cautioned, his tone urgent.

Sintra nodded, her mind racing. The thought of seeing the dragon both thrilled and terrified her. She knew the risks, but her desire to confront the beast was overwhelming. As the cart rolled down the slope, the fire behind them blazed higher, casting eerie shadows on the trees. The trolls' roars grew fainter, but the tension in the air was thick.

The princess kept her eyes on the horizon, waiting for the first sign of dawn. The forest around them was silent, save for the crackling of the distant fire and the occasional rustle of leaves. Every sound seemed amplified in the stillness of the night.

As they descended further, the sky began to lighten, a faint glow hinting at the approaching dawn. Sintra's heart pounded in her chest. She knew they had to move quickly, but the allure of the dragon was too strong to ignore.

"Keep moving," she urged, her voice barely above a whisper. "We must reach the valley before the sun rises."

Lord Edith nodded, urging the horse forward. The cart picked up speed, the wheels crunching over the forest floor. Sintra glanced back one last time, the fire now a distant glow. She took a deep breath, steeling herself for what lay ahead.

A Vision of Dragons

Before first light that morning, Lord Elowen set off to the Infinite Forest on his black steed, shadowed by Francis and Gordon on their own horses. Aleron's men blanketed the earth, marching in numbers along rivers and through the great wood, covering the land like a giant sheet, flattening everything in its path. The slow stampede of heavy feet and the clanking of metal armour and weapons echoed through the great wood, accompanied by the rumble of thunder and the clash of lightning as a dark storm loomed.

The slave and village men grew fierce with greed, spurred on by Lord Elowen's promise of great riches and freedom should they find the princess alive. Their hatred and defiance toward the madman turned them hard and bloodthirsty, each man craving vengeance as they were forced to fight alongside Aleron. Their abhorrence became the driving force as they marched through the forest terrain.

"I could have killed him simply, my lord," said Gordon, trotting alongside Aleron. "I could have broken his neck with my bare hands. Like a small rabbit."

"Hush, Sir Leoss. If I wanted Cornelius dead, I would have done so myself. He has been of great use to me, which is why he remains in the dungeons. It's astonishing what you can force one to do under threat," Aleron replied.

"It was a simple suggestion, my King."

"Yes…I know, Gordon. Not to worry, you will have your fun. I believe my little whore princess is not alone."

Aleron rode ahead to avoid the guard, growing tiresome of Gordon's constant thirst for blood. At one point, he was tempted to hit him over the head with the pommel of his sword just to silence him.

"You really should shut your gob before you get us both killed," said Francis, shaking his head in disgust as he trotted off among a thicket of trees.

Although Gordon couldn't get enough of Lord Elowen's slaughter, it was Lord Elowen himself who seemed never to quench his thirst for blood. Screams and pleas for help and freedom rang with satisfaction through his ears. Bloodthirsty with a taste for the throne, Aleron wouldn't stop at any slaughter of the innocent. He felt no remorse when slitting his own mother's throat. He was strong with anger and now more powerful than ever, and there was no stopping him until he laid a cold, sharp blade across the princess's throat. He felt no further need to wed her, as he wore the crown, having wrenched it from the King's bloodied, dead grasp.

An hour passed as Aleron's soldiers made their way further into the Infinite Forest, bearing shield and sword, arrow and axe as they strode. Thick smoke greeted them as they descended the mountain, stinging the eyes of every man as they strove to see through it. The black remains of fallen trees lined their path, with smouldering trees providing just enough seared foliage to conceal them from the sky. The impenetrable dense smoke lifted, carried by a sudden gust of wind, filling the lungs of every man on the mountain. Lord Elowen frowned, squinting as he tried eagerly to see through the thick haze as numerous large figures approached in the distance.

"Something's coming," he yelled, as he unsheathed his sword.

Francis and Gordon sat by him on unsteady steeds, their swords unsheathed and ready. The armoured men stood still and silent, more terrified of the unknown than of death itself. The low thumping of racing hearts echoed through the clearing as every man grew fearful, the dense smoke blinding them from what approached. An overwhelming stench lingered in the air, the smell of rotting flesh, excrement, and blood filling their throats and mouths with bile. A loud cry from one of Aleron's soldiers suddenly pierced the air, fading away as if carried off by the wind. Another cry followed from the opposite direction, accompanied by the loud crunch of a tree crashing to the ground.

"TROLLS!" cried Lord Elowen, his horse panicking and stamping its hooves against the ground, eager to escape, eager to run.

The armoured men scattered like headless poultry, swinging their swords and axes blindly as they feared the beasts picking them off one by one. One of the men cast arrows into the thick smoke, wounding whatever and whoever lay in their path. Another gust of wind lifted the smoke, revealing nine large trolls.

"KILL THEM!" ordered Aleron.

As the command escaped his mouth, his soldiers sprang into action, roaring as they charged the beasts. Axes flew through the air, striking the large, ugly creatures, followed by a shower of arrows from the many bowmen. Francis charged a troll, digging his heels into his stubborn charger while aiming his sword at the troll's throat. With a loud howl, Francis lifted his sword as he charged, driving it straight up through the troll's jaw and into its brain. The beast fell hard and heavy against the forest floor. Dismounting, Francis ran toward it, dragging his sword from its body. He turned, slicing into the flesh of another troll that had cornered Gordon. The troll's hook blade was still buried deep within Gordon's horse's throat.

The troll turned toward Francis, growling as it faced him, its yellow bloodshot eyes filled with wrath. Francis swung his sword once more as an arrow plunged into the side of the troll's head, the red fletching marking it as Lord Elowen's. The troll swayed with disorientation, looking from Francis to Aleron and back to Gordon as it stood confused and cornered.

"What are you waiting for?" yelled Gordon, impatient. He charged the creature with an outstretched blade, plunging it deep into the troll's belly and out the other side.

Cries of anger and effort soon died down as Aleron's soldiers fought and killed every troll in sight. The stench of the dead filled the air.

"Hold your positions," commanded Lord Elowen.

The men grew restless, eager to leave the forest and its many dangers, but they held their positions as ordered. Gordon wrenched the troll's hook blade from his steed's body, wiping it free of blood, claiming it as his own.

"Spread out," ordered Lord Elowen. "Slit the throat of every wounded man who cannot be saved. I will not have weak and wounded soldiers slowing me down." He turned his horse and proceeded to make his way down the mountain terrain, Gordon close by on foot.

As the madman's soldiers spread out in search of wounded men, Francis decided to make an order of his own once Lord Elowen was out of earshot. Sir Gregory made his way toward a tall, muscular man who held a large, sharp axe and carried a scabbard of arrows. He stood in confusion as Francis approached him, glaring up at him as Sir Gregory remained on horseback.

"What is your name?"

"Lionel Strippence, Sir," answered the man.

"Strippence, I demand that every wounded soldier be granted freedom. If any wounded man is slain, I will have your head," Francis commanded, his voice firm.

"But Lord El-," Lionel began to protest.

"Do not disobey me, Strippence. They are to climb the mountain and flee as Aleron journeys to Thane."

With that, Francis turned swiftly on his steed and rode down the mountain toward Lord Elowen. Lionel did as he was commanded, spreading the order silently until every wounded man was sent free and pointed in the direction of the nearest village.

"Do not journey to Thane," Lionel instructed. "Turn another direction, go to your families, and speak of nothing that has happened here."

Three wounded men hobbled up the mountain, still bearing shield and sword for protection against any dangers that might come their way. Francis Gregory knew Aleron would have his head in an instant if he knew of this treason, but the freed men climbing the mountain would speak of Francis's generosity when they reached their families. If they still lived.

Sir Gregory was not a monster and felt for any man who had a family, for he had his own. He felt no shame for disobeying Lord Elowen's orders, as the madman's commands were sinful. Francis also believed that this reign would crumble one day, if not soon. Aleron would fall with undoubted defeat and betrayal by his own men, if not by Lady Lysandra, the rightful heir to the throne.

†

The array of forest trees lessened as the mountain began to descend flat and gentle until the slope was no more. A worn stone path appeared against the dry grass and dirt on the ground, embedded and cracked as it had aged over the decades, overgrown with roots and insignificant blades of grass. The path meandered over the land, stretching and weaving out over a clearing that divided the Infinite Forest from the village of Thane. As the princess and Lord Edith started along the path, the isolated village in the distance neared them, forsaken and silent as if no being occupied it at all. Its profound eeriness and neglect hinted at the dangers that dwelled beyond the clouds in the sky above them.

"It is deserted," said Sintra.

"Aye, my princess, but it is no marvel. We must move hastily; we haven't much time."

Sintra glanced around to ensure they weren't already being followed; she then looked to the sky in search of Thalor. A part of her feared the beast, but another part deep inside beckoned it to show itself. She felt a strange connection with the creature, an attraction she could not explain. It was not love, for they ventured toward it for only one thing: to slaughter it and exchange its heart with the heart of Riven.

"I must send a raven to Elara; inform her of our arrival to Thane."

"And let it fall into the wrong hands once more, my princess? You know a crow's whisper is untrustworthy more often than not."

Sintra froze as the last sentence spilled from Cedric's mouth. She had only ever heard that expression within the walls of the citadel, from Cornelius himself, the great bookkeeper of the Crevark reign. She remembered when the bookkeeper spoke fondly of Cedric, but she never thought the men had met formally.

"What did you just say?" asked the princess, suspicion welling inside her.

"Do your ears fail you, my princess?" joked the knight.

"Lord Edith, as the princess, I demand you repeat that sentence at once."

"Lady Lysandra, I said a crow's whisper is untrustworthy more often than not. I do believe that you shouldn't—"

"That's it," she interrupted. "Where have you heard that expression, Lord Edith?"

"It is a common phrase. Whatever are you getting at?"

"There is only one place in all the kingdoms where I have heard that phrase, and hearing it spill from your mouth was not the first."

Lord Edith narrowed his brow, confused.

"From whose mouth did you first hear that expression, my lord?"

"I cannot recall, my princess. It must have slipped off the wind on my way through a village."

"You lie, Lord Edith, for the only place that phrase is ever heard is inside the walls of Crevark."

"You cannot simply state that as the truth, Sintra. You have not left that citadel or the kingdom of Crevark once. Not until now, not until embarking on this journey of which you now accompany me. You cannot state that no other being says or knows the phrase you speak of."

The princess was speechless for a moment; Lord Edith spoke the truth. She couldn't possibly know whether any other being knew the phrase or not. But that did not yield the feeling she felt deep inside. What she couldn't fathom was how Cedric Edith came to know this expression and why it was of such importance to be kept secret.

"Why do you keep the truth from me?" she asked.

"I am truthful, my lady. I have said nothing but the truth."

"Then why can you not inform me of whom you spoke with that first filled your ears with the expression I speak of?"

"I—" started Cedric.

"Do not fill my ears with lies, Lord Edith; I know you did not hear the expression while travelling through a village, for its origin lies within the stone walls of the citadel. There is one man who first spoke this phrase to me, for he was the one who coined it as he wrote *The Thesis of the Raven's Whisper: The Parchment-bird*. It seems you have either read the thesis or have spoken to Cornelius Thatcher himself. Well, which is it, Lord Edith? For both remain within the library of Crevark, a place I doubt you have ever set foot."

The Steel Knight was speechless, stunned by the princess's words. He looked to the ground in defeat before lifting his head toward her once more.

"I was young," he sighed, "when I had my first prophecy."

Sintra frowned, confused by Lord Edith's words and their irrelevance.

"I knew of you, before I had met you."

"I am the princess of Crevark, Lord Edith; it would be insolent not to know of me."

"I knew of your affairs with the slave boy."

"How is this possible?" she asked, more confused than ever.

"I saw it all, Sintra, from your first name day. I saw it all within the prophecy."

"From my first name day? Until my last?"

"I am not certain of your last name day. The vision was blurred with heat and light before it vanished into darkness, and I woke as if from a dream."

"Heat and light?" she pushed. "You mean fire?"

"Quite possibly, Sintra…" Cedric hesitated, narrowing his brow as he tried to remember the prophecy. "The prophecy ended with the vision of dragons, Lady Lysandra, three to be exact. But after that, there was nothing."

"Three dragons? Did you know of this journey before it began?"

"I did, my lady."

"Did you know of Lord Elowen's betrayal? Did you know Riven, and I would find you?"

"I knew it all, Sintra; it was just a matter of time before it all unravelled. Before the truth of the prophecy came to be."

"Then tell me, I bid you. Tell me what you saw," demanded the princess.

"I saw Aleron slaughter your family. Forgive me, I saw him slaughter Queen Caprice, Princess Serena, and Princess Serillah. I saw him slaughter your dear brother, Prince Soren, before laying his dead lifeless body before the King. I saw Aleron claim to be gallant and valiant as he clutched your brother's body. I saw him lie through his teeth before King Alaric."

Tears swelled within Sintra's eyes. She wanted to question why he did not warn them of this coming perfidy, but she knew her father never believed in superstition or prophecy alike. A stabbing pain tugged at her heart.

"Did you not come forward because you feared my father would cast you away or burn you at the stake for preaching witchery and fallacy? Did you not attempt to save my family because you feared for your own life?" pushed the princess, tears running down her cheeks.

"Forgive me, Sintra. I did not believe my own mind. I did not believe such a prophecy, as I thought it too evil to be true."

"You thought your own prophecy to be false?"

"Aye. Forgive me. I would have come forward if I thought otherwise." Cedric's eyes were full of remorse; he hung his head in sorrow for the princess.

Sintra waved her hand for Lord Edith to continue. "Did you see the tournament? Did you see the death of Riven?"

"I saw it all, my princess. Riven's death and Aleron's treason. I saw that he would escape and take over the kingdom. But it is not as if I did not act, Lady Lysandra. After I saw the dragon and your involvement, I had to see for myself if Thalor existed or not."

"You saw the death and betrayal of my family but chose to act upon the vision of dragons? Are you ill-minded, Lord Edith?"

"That I am not sure, Sintra, as my mind shows me many things whether I believe them or not. But this particular vision caught my attention after the death of your family, and not before. Because I did not believe in the brutal murder of your family when my mind showed it to me, it was proven very real many years later when Lord Elowen did in fact slaughter the Queen and her children. I thought then that I must see for myself if the dragon existed. I had to know whether I could save the kingdom and the rightful heir to the throne, my lady. I had to know whether I could save you."

"Save me, Lord Edith? I hardly need saving."

"Sintra, if it weren't for your affairs with the slave, you would be married to Lord Elowen as we speak. If it weren't for my friendship with Cornelius Thatcher, you would have never come looking for me. I would have never known Riven of noble blood, and there would not have been a tournament. Don't you see?"

Sintra's eyes widened in disbelief as she heard the words slip from his tongue, the words she was eager to hear.

"So, you admit it, you do know Cornelius, and that's where you heard the expression."

"Lady Lysandra, we have more pressing matters to discuss."

"How do you know my bookkeeper?" she pushed.

"After the vision of dragons, I sought a bookkeeper to inform me of the Thalor dragon's existence. I found Cornelius Thatcher after the fall of Thane. We ventured to Thane, I to see the dragon in flesh and blood, he to conclude the last chapter of his book. It was after that day that the Thalor sword was sent to me, and to this day, I still have no clue who sent it."

"Well, I suppose the secret's out," said a voice.

Thick black smoke appeared from nowhere, swirling before them to reveal the dark hooded creature.

"Brencis?" asked Cedric.

"Aye, I sent you that sword," started Brencis. "After reading your thoughts, I too saw the prophecy and acted upon it."

Brencis then turned to Sintra before continuing.

"But I have the decency to inform you, princess, that this prophecy was never meant to be in your favour."

"In my favour?" she asked, confused. "What does he mean, Lord Edith?" she asked, turning to Cedric.

"The prophecy ends…" he hesitated, sighing, "in your death, Sintra."

Sintra's eyes widened in dread. She couldn't believe it. Was the entire Lysandra family supposed to die? Why has fate ill-favoured her and her family?

"What exactly did you see, Lord Edith?"

"Near the end of the prophecy, I saw smoke and fire. I saw the Thalor dragon. I watched as you approached the beast, blind to its danger. And then you vanished…as if you had died," said Cedric.

"Vanished?"

"It was as if the dragon slaughtered you, Sintra. You disappeared into black smoke and bright flame. You were gone."

"Then what happened?"

"The prophecy ended with the vision of three dragons."

"Three dragons?"

"The Thalor dragon and two others. Blackwings, I assume."

"Blackwings?"

"Dragons as black as coal like Thalor."

Sintra remembered seeing the infant Blackwing in the secret chamber inside the library, though Cornelius never spoke of it in detail.

"I'm sorry, my princess, I cannot control what my mind shows me."

"Does Cedric speak the truth? Is that what you're saying, Brencis? Am I supposed to die?" she asked, her voice weak with fear.

"It is the truth, Lady Lysandra, but it is also the reason I sent Lord Edith the sword. I knew it would find you, I knew it would rest in your hands someday."

"Why?"

"To slay the dragon."

"I always assumed that it would be me to slay the beast, but I planned to hand the sword to Cedric," she whispered.

"It must be you, princess. You are the only one with the power to do so," said Brencis.

"But Lord Edith is ten times as strong as I."

"It is the power within the heart that makes you stronger, as you truly want this, more than me or Lord Edith. Don't you?"

"With all of my heart, I wish to save Riven, but I do not believe that I can slay the beast."

"Do not doubt yourself; you must believe you can do it. Faith is strength. The sword chose you."

"So…as the prophecy goes, I am meant to die. But now that I have the sword carved from the tail-thorn of Thalor in my possession, I will live?" frowned the princess, trying to make sense of it all.

"Not necessarily. You must slay the dragon. The sword is your only protection."

"Was the sword in the prophecy, Lord Edith?" she asked.

"It was not. Now that you have the sword, it changes everything," said Cedric before turning to Brencis. "Why were you at Thane?"

"I hadn't left. I felt drawn there by the dragon and couldn't bring myself to leave. But once I saw the prophecy, I knew I had to find you again, to leave the sword with you. I knew you would find Sintra. I knew the sword would be left in her possession. I know she can slay the dragon."

"But the sword chose Riven, not I," said Sintra.

"It chose you both. There is a strong bond between the two of you; even now that Riven is dead. A link, a connection stronger than any other," said Brencis.

"Love?"

"No, not love, my princess. Something far stronger, something invisible that I cannot explain. It binds the two of you together so that you are one."

"Marriage?" asked the princess.

"No, Sintra," answered Brencis, becoming frustrated. "Stop guessing! I do not know what it is."

Sintra said not another word; she was shocked at his sudden outburst of frustration.

"I apologize. I understand you were only trying to help," he said. "I must go."

Before the princess could stop Brencis, he had already started evaporating into thin air before vanishing completely, leaving behind nothing but his trademark wisp of black smoke.

Sintra and Cedric sat silently at the front of the cabin-cart as Soul strode along the path, his ears twitching and lying flat to his head every now and then as they neared the village. The worn path behind them wound its way back across the field they had just crossed. They were so engaged in conversation that they did not realize they had made it across the entire open field, alive and undetected by the dragon. Disappointment stirred within Sintra, for she had hoped to see the beast, yet she knew its slaughter by her own hand would soon come.

They pushed on toward the entrance of the village, the old stone path sinking into the dirt until all that carried them was a dusted dirt track with few pebbles and blades of grass.

"The track is still worn down," said Sintra. "The village is deserted. The track should be abundant with grass. I don't understand."

"Merchants and travellers still use this road; the village of Thane connects to the ocean side. It's one of the very few pathways that lead straight through the Infinite Forest and onward to the other kingdoms."

"I thought no man dared pass through Thane for fear of the dragon?"

"This is true, Sintra, but those who must use this path do so at the dead of night when the dragon sleeps."

"I thought this path was used during the night so that the darkness may blanket any man or woman from the beast."

"That too," added Cedric.

Their conversation was suddenly cut short as Soul came to an abrupt halt, his ears pricked forward and stiff, his stance rigid. The white steed gave a loud snort and stamped his hoof against the ground, his breathing hoarse and heavy.

"What is it, boy?" said Sintra, calming the horse.

"He senses something," said Lord Edith, stiffening his back.

"Perhaps we should go around."

"That will take another half day, princess. We haven't the time."

"What if he senses the dragon?" asked Lady Lysandra.

"Believe me, if this steed sensed that dragon, he would have left us here in a heap by now, cabin-cart still in tow."

A few moments passed before Soul returned to his lazy self, walking on casually into the village. Sintra and Lord Edith took in their surroundings. Each hut had wooden planks and bars fixed to its windows, some blackened and scorched by fire. Sheets of thin iron lay fastened tightly atop every straw roof, chimneys filled with mud and stone to seal them off. Each door was also fastened with an iron sheet, locked securely with chains. There was no sign of life in sight—not a sheep, not a cow, not even a single bird or insect.

"They've fled," said Lord Edith.

"But why barricade their windows and chain their doors if they don't plan on coming back?"

"Strange."

Cedric peered through the village, ensuring there truly was no sign of life at all. He then leapt from the cabin and landed firmly on the ground.

"Come, our steed needs to rest. We must find sufficient shelter from the sky."

Lord Edith searched for a vacant hut as he slowly made his way through the deserted village. Aside from the barricaded huts, there were burnt-out buildings that only consisted of old stone walls that would slowly erode in time. Scorched wooden beams protruded from the wreckage, sharp and splintered, fierce and dangerous. A loud crunch sounded from beneath Cedric's leather boot as he stepped further into the village. He lifted his foot to reveal a tiny black skull, scorched by fire. Lord Edith took a step backward, his heart sinking deep into his stomach as he saw blackened charred bones small enough to have once belonged to a child. As he forced back the tears that threatened to swell in his eyes, he buried the charred bones beneath the dirt, pushing earth and pebbles over the remains with his feet until they were seen no more. Cedric looked ahead, eyeing a stable that barely held its door upright, its hinges rusted and worn over time. He turned toward the princess and waved her toward him, holding his index finger to his mouth so that she would remain silent and come as quietly as she could manage.

As Sintra slapped the reins against the steed's flank, Soul moved slowly and casually toward Cedric, the large steel wheels of the cart screeching louder than ever with each turn. Lord Edith looked to the sky warily, but not even a bird flew by.

"We have a long way to go yet," started Cedric, talking softly to the princess. "And we need the body, so there is no use taking it out. Leave it put."

Sintra frowned. She loved Riven, but there was no way on earth she would touch his dead body; the thought sent shivers down her spine. Even thinking about Riven's pale, hard flesh made her cringe.

Lord Edith took Soul from the cart and led him into the vacant stable, which had, to their luck, overgrown with luscious grass for him to feed on. Insignificant rays of sunlight beamed in through the straw roof and ceiling, feeding the grass with sufficient light to keep it alive, although most of the grass was browning already due to the seasonal change.

As the princess took furs and woollens from the cabin-cart and placed them inside the stable, she frowned as something caught her eye on the way out. Cedric followed her gaze. Beneath the cart were more blackened bones, half-buried and protruding from the dark earth. As Sintra looked around, she noticed more and more of the same remains—black and broken bones scattered near and far. Splinters of bone shards and hollow skulls lay in the ruins of the huts and sprinkled over the earth sporadically. Large skulls of animals—sheep, cows, and horses. Small skulls that once belonged to smaller animals and birds. The princess tried anxiously to push the thought of children from her mind, but she knew as she glared into the hollow empty sockets of the smaller skulls that they once belonged to the small children who played by the stables. The night of Riven's knight ceremony crossed her mind as she remembered the small children fussing over Soul. Tears swelled in her eyes as hurt stabbed at her heart.

"They're scattered like breadcrumbs," she whispered, "sprinkled carelessly as if fallen from the beast's mouth."

Lord Edith rested a hand atop the princess's shoulder; slowly he turned her toward the stable and inside the door.

"A vision of dragons, my lady, is what you see," Cedric whispered back. "A vision of dragons!"

Thane, the Fallen

Sintra woke at first darkness that evening as the smell of sizzling mushrooms filled her nostrils and wet her tongue. Her empty stomach danced with hunger, aching to be filled. She licked her lips, now thirsty for the hot, melting juices of cooked mushrooms. The princess sat up, pushed her furs and woollens to one side, and rose to her feet. Two metres beside her, Soul lay comfortable and content within the stable, undisturbed from his lull. Sintra assumed Lord Edith to be the chef as he was nowhere in sight.

The princess strode out of the stable, the cold night air greeting her and biting at her hardened skin. Goosebumps rose from her flesh, the brisk breeze making each tiny hair stand on end. The frigid night air grew with warmth and the smell of mushrooms and burning wood. As she turned the corner of one barricaded hut, a small fire came into view, just big enough to heat a pan or boil an iron billy. The princess neared the fire, her nose leading her straight to the contents cooking in the pan. She was oblivious to Lord Edith and the many village people that surrounded the fire. Her hunger-crazed mind blinded her to the very real civilization that still occupied the village of Thane. Cedric watched as she walked straight toward the pan, not blinking an eyelid or lifting her head, as if she were walking in her sleep.

"Princess," started Lord Edith, taking Sintra by the elbow and swinging her around to face him.

Sintra blinked rapidly as she came to face Cedric, waking from her hunger-crazed daze. Her eyes widened as she took in her surroundings, which were much different than before. A crowd of at least one hundred people surrounded her, just as awestruck as she was in that single moment.

"They live," mumbled the princess. "They had not fled at all."

The village people gazed at Sintra like something they had never seen before. Her blood and dirt-stained gown had grown pale brown along her adventure; it was no longer pure white, nor did it gleam or shimmer with elegance. If she hadn't worn a gown so petite and silk-woven, she would have appeared a slave. The hem of the gown had grown black with grime, its fine edge lightly frayed. Amid the filthy state the princess was in, she was still very much the princess in the eyes of the village people. The Queen they so desperately needed, the Queen they had greatly craved for many years since the fall of their own King and sovereignty.

"We welcome you fondly, Queen of Crevark," said one man, bowing his head.

A woman lowered to her knees, bowing her head. "We have waited for your arrival for many years, my Queen. Please free us from the reign of the dragon so that we may live in peace once again."

Sintra frowned, her brow narrowed as she looked to Cedric in bemusement. Lord Edith nodded before turning to the crowd.

"Forgive our Queen, for she has just woken. Let her eat and gain her strength. Then you may speak with Her Grace."

The crowd of village people lessened, descending back from wherever they had appeared. Lord Edith took a small bowl, filled it with warm mushrooms, and handed it to the princess.

Her mouth filled with hot juicy liquid as she pushed the food into her mouth. She took another and another, pushing them into her mouth until the bowl was mushroom free. She held the wooden bowl to her lips and emptied the warm juices into her mouth, gulping back the liquid that warmed her belly. Cedric took the empty bowl from the princess and refilled it with more mushrooms.

"I've had quite enough, Lord Edith; the ache in my stomach is no more."

"You need your strength, Sintra; you need to eat as much as you can. You need to be strong and fit to slay the dragon; it is not just Crevark that is counting on you now."

"Whatever do you mean?" she asked between mouthfuls of mushroom.

"The Kingdom of Thane needs a Queen, my lady; the village people need a leader once again. They tire of hiding in the shadows from the great beast, they wish for freedom and peace. Man wish to grow crops and have many sheep; woman wish to have children. Children that have grown old in the shadows wish to play in the daylight with the sun warming their faces."

Sintra's heart ached with a deep, unrelenting sorrow as she recalled the haunting sight of the burnt, blackened skulls of children she had seen earlier that day. The weight of her responsibility pressed down on her, but it did nothing to diminish her fierce desire to free these people from the dragon's tyranny and reclaim her own monarchy. The lives and fates of many now rested in her hands, and only she possessed the power to bring about change. It was an immense responsibility, teetering precariously between life and death. The villagers of Thane, along with the remaining villagers and slaves of Crevark, depended solely on her.

I must save them. I want nothing more than to free them all, she thought to herself, her resolve mingled with doubt. *But I am not sure I can.*

"Do not doubt yourself, child," came a soothing voice within Sintra's mind.

The princess glanced around, knowing that Brencis was near, though he remained hidden. He had great reason to stay in the shadows, for the people of Thane lived in constant fear, and the sight of a half-man, half-dragon would not lift their spirits.

Sintra marvelled at how the villagers could maintain an open flame without being detected by Thalor. As she looked up, the answer became clear. The night sky was devoid of stars, obscured by a large black sheet made from various materials sewn together for one purpose: to conceal them from the sky. The villagers had crafted their own shadow, large enough and high enough for them to move about freely. The massive blanket of silks, satins, and cottons hung from tree branches, the peaks of huts, and tall wooden poles, each corner tied securely. It was vast enough to hide a small army from the sky.

"I admire their skilled minds and craftsmanship," Sintra said to Lord Edith, her voice filled with genuine admiration as she gazed at the ingenious creation.

"Aye," he replied, his voice filled with a mix of admiration and disbelief. "I too, my lady, never in my life would I have thought to do something like that. And it works."

"If I may," started an elderly man from across the campfire, his voice raspy yet strong, "I would like to tell you of how this blanket came to be."

"What is your name, kind sir?" asked Cedric, his tone respectful.

"Maynard Bala, my lord."

"Continue," replied the princess, her curiosity piqued.

The elderly man cleared his throat before speaking again, his eyes reflecting the flickering fire. "Many years ago, as you know, Thane was ambushed by a single dragon. Nobody knows why the slaughter of the kingdom came to be. Nobody knows how the beast found its way to our shores, but some say it followed the great King of Thane, Thaddeus Lysandra, for he loved to sail across the ocean. Great myths say the beast swam beneath the ocean in search of gold and flew across the sky in search of islands. It is said the beast crossed paths with the King of Thane, resulting in a great battle that cost the King his men and the dragon its tail-thorn. The very tip of the beast's tail was considered its one true pride and honour, as it was used as the greatest of all weapons; the only weapon that could withstand the heat and armour of any other dragon or water beast. This is why the dragon is considered the most powerful; the strongest of all dragons.

"After that day, King Thaddeus took an oath that he would hunt down the very same dragon that took his men, carving the beast's tail-thorn into a sword, a sword that would be stronger than any other yet as light as a feather. A sword that Thaddeus planned to plunge deep within the heart of the very beast that grew it. As he plotted against the great monster, King Lysandra cleared his citadel quad that overlooked his beloved ocean, knocking down pillars and walls, watching the stone crumble at his command. Thaddeus grew mad with obsession; he grew barmy with hate and craved vengeance for his men. He sold everything he could in exchange for gold and riches. The heap grew large over time, consuming the quad and spilling into the ocean that licked the cliffs and sheer drops at the edge of the citadel walls. The gold and riches sat for months, gleaming in the sunlight to lure in the dragon until one day it showed.

"Whether the dragon truly sought revenge for its tail-thorn remains a question, but Thaddeus Lysandra's plan was working. Thalor, the steel dragon, became so entranced by the gold and riches that it plunged deep within the heap and remained there for a whole day before emerging to feast. Thaddeus stood before the beast as his stable horses were scorched and devoured. The King grew with wrath and madness and vowed to the dragon that he would give him no more. But as Thaddeus drew the Thalor sword from its sheath, the dragon grew crazed and took all from the king, slaughtering the entire royal family along with every slave, guard, knight, squire, and maid in sight. Every man, woman, and child until there was nothing but charred, broken bone scattered near and far. The dragon moved toward our village, taking any being it saw fit for feasting. It sprayed its fire down upon us, forcing us out, forcing us to flee. We tried barricading our homes and sacrificing our stock, but that wasn't enough.

The dragon wanted us gone, and it wasn't going to stop until the last of us were dead.

"It wasn't until a small boy hid within a large foxhole that we decided to retire underground. We dug our way deep with stick and shovel, carving tunnels into the earth that soon became our home, our only refuge. Silence grew eerie above us as the land grew vacant and deserted. For years, we've been sleeping during the day and hunting during the night when the beast cannot see us. We've become nocturnal like the owls, but not even owls reside here anymore. No animals dare come near this place, for they fear the beast as well.

"We travel into the Infinite Forest at night in search of a good kill that could last us a few days. But sadly, our numbers weaken as disease and starvation pick us off one by one. We are the living dead, my princess; we sleep in our own graves in fear of becoming that thing's next meal."

The man paused for a moment, gulping down a wooden hanop of ale before continuing. "During the nights of the full moon, we would run around with black sheets on our backs, blending in with the dark ground. We soon tired of running around like headless pullets, thus devising a plan that would keep us all safe at once. To keep us all together. To keep us from running at all. One night, we combined every black sheet we could gather and raised this blanket, this shadow of darkness. It has been raised at sundown every single night since, and not once has it failed us."

"The beast smells your fire or the meat you cook, does it not?" asked the princess.

"It breathes fire; all it smells is the scent of its own heated flesh," said Maynard.

"I believe you're mistaken, Mr. Bala," started Cedric, a dumbfounded expression across his face. "Dragons have a higher scent than any other man or being; they can smell the sweat of man from another world away. Perhaps this beast knows you're here but chooses not to stir."

"Whether it is truth or not, I do not know, but it comforts my mind. I and the rest of us would rather believe such a theory as my own than any other," said the old man.

"You're blind is what you are, old man. That beast can track you if it desires—"

"If that thing desires to hunt us, why has it not already?" interrupted Maynard.

Cedric did not reply; he did not like being interrupted by strangers when they knew nothing of what they spoke. The old man was blind and knew nothing of dragons. Sintra thought Maynard Bala to be somewhat daft, as everything she knew of dragons, she had learned from the many books Cornelius had read to her. Dragons scorch their meals before devouring them; the beasts eat burnt flesh and bone. No carcass, no kill of a dragon is left to rot. Any dragon's kill is never left unscathed by fire; the greedy beasts leave nothing but scorched and blackened bones. Not even maggots, flies, or crows bother a dragon's kill, as there is no decaying flesh left to be picked at.

"A gift for my Queen," said a young girl as she approached Sintra.

The girl handed Sintra a bundle of fur, which appeared to be a cloak of deer, as she unravelled it from the hemp thread and held it out before her. The princess smiled warmly toward the girl and lifted the cloak over her head, resting it on her shoulders. The thickness of the fur immediately trapped in the heat from the fire, warming the princess, thawing her bones and muscles so she could move freely once again.

"Many thanks, sweet petal. What is your name?"

"My name is Saoirse, Your Majesty," replied the small girl.

Her long-braided hair was the rosiest blonde, a strawberry gold that matched the light freckles dotting her soft, pale skin. Her pink, plump lips parted as she smiled, revealing a neat row of white teeth. Her eyes were a golden brown, like the pelt of a young deer calf, speckled with flecks of pale brown. As the princess stared into the eyes of young Saoirse, she felt a sense of warmth and love, a connection with the young girl. It was as if she knew the girl, though the thought of her youngest sister Serena wouldn't leave her mind. The princess smiled warmly, recognizing the uncanny resemblance between the two. But sorrow weighed heavily on her heart as she began to miss her sister. The longing for her family was soon replaced with vexation as she remembered the madman who brutally ripped them away from her. Her purpose rushed back to her, filling her heart like a ball of fire, each ferocious lick of flame stinging her wounds as the thought of every lost soul passed through her mind.

Sintra stood from her seat in haste, taking a deep breath as she began a speech, the village people pausing to listen.

"For my mother, for my sisters and brother, for my father and the King's Guard, for every man, woman, and child that lies dead at the hand of Lord Elowen. For my father's reign, for the kingdom of Crevark and the kingdom of Thane, I will slay that dragon," stated Sintra, her voice rising sternly in anger. "I will free every one of you just as I have promised. I will grant you peace, I will grant you freedom, and I will grant you life, for not only am I your Queen, but I am also your saviour."

The crowd grew as the princess spoke, each man and woman bowing and lowering to their knees. They could not roar with gratitude toward Sintra for fear of waking the dragon.

"For those of you that are not aware, I must warn you of the dangers that are to come. You are to retire underground tonight, or you will face an unspeakable death at the hands of the erroneous King of Crevark. Do not be mistaken, village people of Thane the Fallen, he will not hesitate to torch your children or throw your wives to the warg of the Infinite Forest with their entrails on the outside. He is crazed with power and bloodthirsty for my own head, but I can assure you that the madman will not take my head today. Nor will he take my head any other day. I will feed him to the beast myself."

"Thane has fallen, and Thane will rise again," cried a man from the crowd. "Glory to our Queen, may she be victorious."

The rest of the crowd cheered, "Hurrah," raising their fists in the air for Sintra.

"Away with you all," said the princess. "Into the night you go before you return to your refuge underground."

Cedric raised an eyebrow as the villagers followed orders; Sintra was not yet a Queen, though the village people of Thane considered her theirs already. Lord Elowen was not yet dead, and the crown did not yet rest upon Sintra's head, but already the villagers sought to follow her. They were desperate for a leader; they needed supremacy; they needed a Queen.

"Perhaps you should have had me practice on the Pell, my lord," said Sintra. "Seems it was but a waste of time to train Riven, as I am the one to slay the dragon after all."

"Yes, princess, it seems wise now, but never mind," replied Cedric. "Aim for the heart and you will do just fine," he finished.

†

An hour had passed, and the moon rose high in the night sky. The villagers retired to their underground refuge as Sintra waved them farewell. Lord Edith waited with the cabin-cart on the outskirts of the village, Soul reined ready and waiting, revitalized from his lull in the stable. The heavy iron wheels of the cart creaked as they began to roll across the stone path once again. The clinking of glass on glass sounded from inside the cabin as it swayed from side to side, the steed casually pulling it along with no effort at all. The path weaved and meandered through open fields and hills of grey, rolling on and on like a seam knitted into the dark earth, luminous beneath the glowing silver moonlight that was cast over the land like a lucid blanket waiting to be lifted at first light. As eager as the night's vibrant yet delayed moon was to already elude, the sun was hours from rise, though it too would not rise with haste for all the stars in the night sky awaited the unruly darkness that was soon to augment.

"The earth is afraid, my lord, I feel it tremble," said Sintra, breaking the silence that had fallen between them. "Or is it angered, for I feel heat?"

Lord Edith frowned toward the princess, baffled at the sentence that had just passed her lips. "Are you falling ill?" he asked, pressing a hand to her forehead, which proved to be warmer than usual. "Perhaps you're nervous."

"I am not nervous, but I feel strange. I feel a tremble, a vibration that I cannot explain."

The smell of singed fur filled the air, along with a small faint stream of smoke that lifted from the princess's side. Cedric lifted her fur cloak to reveal a red-hot sword, trembling within its sheath. He grasped the hilt as fast as he could and pulled the sword from it.

"The dragon is close," he said. "I do hope that it does not sense its tail-thorn as its tail-thorn senses it."

Sintra's eyes widened as she stared at the hot blade trembling in Lord Edith's grip. She took it from him the second he ceased blinking, and his hand started burning.

"Thank you," he grunted, quite embarrassed.

The princess removed the burning sheath from her side, the scalded leather crumbling away at her touch. She held the sword in her hand, her grasp tightening as the blade repeated its actions it had made once before, pointing itself in the direction of the large rolling grey hills that waited patiently in the distance. Soul's feet clambered along the stone path, the steed moving hastily in a fast walk. The princess's mouth dropped open in awe as the ruins of the citadel came into sight.

"Thane, the Fallen," whispered Cedric.

Lord Edith swallowed hard, fear-stricken and anxious as he remembered the beast that lay beyond the ruins of the citadel walls. His eyes fixed on the looming stone wall that now faced them front on, growing tall as they approached it. The princess trembled with fear.

I can't do this, I can't do this, she chanted in her mind. *I'm going to die.*

"You will die," said Brencis, appearing beside her in an instant, "but not today."

Sintra was hauled off the seat of the cabin-cart and dragged inside the cabin. Riven's body never looked so peaceful as in that moment. Brencis shoved a chest plate toward her.

"What are you doing?"

"Put that on. You must wear a cuirass if you wish to succeed, my princess," replied Brencis, pushing more pieces of armour toward her along with a thick jacket of wool and leather. "Put that on first; it'll stop the pinching."

The princess did as she was ordered, slipping the doublet over her head before covering her body with steel armour and mail. Brencis grasped her gown and ripped it clean off just above the knees. Her dainty, thin arms gleamed silver with armour, as did her legs, bound in leather beneath to stop the pinching. Sintra looked down at her body, feeling like a princess no more. A darkness filled the cabin-cart as it swayed to a halt, and simultaneously, Brencis slapped a helmet atop the princess's head. Looking out from the cabin as she lifted the cold steel visor, her eyes rested upon the great stone wall that was no more than a hundred metres away. Soul stirred, eager to turn and run.

"End of the line, princess. This steed will go no further," said Cedric.

"Aye, it is no marvel, for Thalor is close," said Brencis, eyeing the sword still clutched in Sintra's hand.

"We need to get past that wall," said the princess, a part of her screaming on the inside, ordering her to turn and run.

Brencis outstretched his scaled arms and placed a hand on Riven's forehead. He then held his hand out to the princess. "Take my hand, my lady," he said softly.

Sintra hesitated before grasping Brencis's cold, scaled palm with her empty hand. As before, her world spun in a black spiral of thick smoke. She opened her eyes to find herself within the citadel ruins, Riven's body by her side, but Brencis had vanished once again.

Why couldn't you have done that in the first place? She thought. *Could have saved us a day.*

It drains me of energy too quickly, came a thought in her mind.

"Do not doubt yourself, princess," said his voice from a distance. "Find the dragon. Aim for its heart."

The princess grew overwhelmed as the voice disappeared; she had never felt so alone. Through the visor, she took in her surroundings, but the small slit across the helmet was not to her advantage as she could see nothing but grey stone.

"How is anyone supposed to fight with that? I may as well be blind," she spat, lifting the helmet from her head and letting it clatter to the ground.

Her body stiffened as an ice-cold shiver ran up her spine, the hair on the back of her neck standing on end. Her eyes widened as the sight before her scared her half to death. A loud, ear-splitting screech that rang through her ears only added to her terror. The dragon let out a hellish howl, and clutching her ears was useless as the loud shrill shriek deafened her in seconds.

It knows, she thought to herself, gulping down the bile that rose to her mouth. *It knows I'm here; it knows I've come for it.*

"Stay brave," said Brencis. "It merely senses the sword; it is blind to the warrior that holds it."

I am a princess, not a warrior. A girl, not a gallant knight.

"Find the dragon," said Brencis, his voice fading. "Aim for its heart."

Sintra looked around her, though the grave-like scenery that surrounded her was no comfort. Blackened, broken bones piled in every direction, the silver armour and shields blackened with soot as they too were scattered as far as the eye could see. As the princess looked on, she knew how hard and brutal Thane had fallen, for the graveyard she found herself in no longer resembled a citadel.   All   that surrounded her were crumbled stone walls and burnt and splintered wooden beams, just like she saw in the village. Blackened skulls of men, the heads of great knights and guards who fought to keep this reign, but the only reign Sintra saw before her was that of Thalor himself. Another shrill, barking howl sounded from the dragon, along with a gust of hot, gassy wind that knocked her to her feet.

"Come for me!" she cried, standing to her feet.

The princess walked along the wreckage of a balcony, which seemed to have been one of the many hallways in the citadel long ago. Its fallen stone walls had crumbled away; bricks of stone had plummeted to the ground, collecting at the floor of the citadel centre, which was once known as the first floor. Among the wreckage and rubble that lay scattered on the ground, spilling from the balconies and open hallways that were no longer sheltered by walls, was the old marble floor of the great hall of Thane. Its magnificent black and white chessboard design was now pillaged with fallen rock and stone, occupied by broken, burnt bones of the royal family that once lived here. The grand table on which supremacy dined, shattered and splintered and blackened to coal. Left to perish. Great marble spiralled pillars and poles that once stood tall and strong beneath the citadel floors now lay shattered and ruined against the cold stone ground. Its intricate gilded design now flaked and chipped, veins of cracks weaving through and through, the delicate gold wasted.

Sintra slowly made her way through the wreckage, climbing over jagged stone and leaping over large cracks in the ground, the floor threatening to break away beneath her feet at any moment. As she passed down a hallway, large gaping holes in the walls that still remained. Detailed paintings hung, their brilliance aged and worn. Sintra's heart weighed heavily as she recognized a portrait of her first cousin, Princess

Ravenna Lysandra of Thane. Little memory she had of the girl as they were banished from seeing one another due to an exhausted disagreement between both their fathers, something she never understood.

Find the dragon, find the dragon, she chanted within her mind, finding every minor detail of the remaining reign too distracting. She hadn't set foot in the citadel of Thane since she was thirteen, still only a young girl.

She clambered down the remaining stone stairs, rocks falling from the steps as her feet hit them, her armour clanking loudly. She stopped abruptly, her lungs ceasing to move as she suddenly held her breath. Her large emerald eyes fixated on a large, peculiar object that lay metres before her. It occupied the remaining stone archway that once held a great wooden door opening into the stone quad of the citadel.

The princess slowly let out a deep breath, glaring at the large black stump that lay across the entrance to the quad. She had never been so grateful to have almost run headfirst into the back of the dragon. Sintra eyed it in admiration; its once magnificently black scaled tail-thorn had truly been severed, the tip of the tail shortened into a black stump. Heatwaves wafting from the dragon's flesh formed beads of sweat at the princess's brow as she moved closer to the beast, her heart pounding beneath her ribcage as both fear and excitement surmounted her.

As she took a step toward the creature's tail, a scorched bone cracked beneath her foot. Sintra stopped still, not daring to move an inch, but it was useless for the dragon had heard her. She doubled back, ran for cover behind a stone wall, holding the sword against her front. The sound of falling coins filled her ears, a shrill and violent sound that had her grasping for her ears. Her heart pounded inside her mind as she peered around the corner of her refuge. But to her bemusement, the dragon was nowhere to be seen. She stepped out from behind the wall and made her way toward the entrance to the quad. She stood still and silent. A gigantic mountain of gold lay before her, gleaming red and orange in the light of a fire that burned to one side. Sintra froze as she noticed the cabin-cart from which she had just come not half an hour earlier. Shattered and burning black. The princess sighed, relieved that no white steed or knight occupied the wreckage. But the one thought that made her turn with haste was Riven's body. As the princess turned on hr heel, her heart almost stopped as she now found herself staring down Thalor.

A low, guttural growl rolled from deep within the beast's throat as it glared at the princess. Gassy fumes and smoke rising from its nostrils. As the moon appeared from behind a cloud, the silver light cast down over the citadel ruins. Dense diamond-shaped scales that overlapped its entire body shone in the moonlight, each metallic diamond gleaming silver and black. Stronger ridgelike scales lined its neck and stomach, surrounding the solid chest plate on the breast of the creature, and continuing to the stump of its tail. Horn-like ridges seamed along its spine, protruding thick and sharp.

The creature was deathly masculine, with defined muscular legs and feet, each finger containing a sharp hook-claw talon that effortlessly cut into the stone ground. It grew two lengthy sharp-tipped horns on either side of its elongated head, others much smaller protruded in tiny rows from the edge of its jawline. Its black scaled lips parted to reveal a row of razor-sharp teeth. Solid scaled ridges lined its deep golden-red eyes like thick eyebrows.

She eyed the monster before disappearing behind the archway, snatching a soot-covered shield from the remains of a dead body as she passed. Thalor let out a shrill, ear-piercing shriek, followed by a breath of orange flame that missed Sintra by inches as she ran for cover. Finding refuge behind a fallen pillar, she quickly sat against it to catch her breath, pushing down the steel armour that covered her legs, removing each cuisse and greave so she could run more freely in bound leather alone.

The earth shook, stone and bone trembling as they hopped along the ground, moved by the heavy steps that came for the princess. Leaning to one side of the fallen pillar, Sintra saw her opportunity and ran for her life, holding her shield in front of her body to conceal it from yet another ball of flame. She patted her leather-bound legs as they began to heat and smoke from the fire. She listened for the thundering feet but heard high-pitched howling from the sky. Looking up, Sintra saw that the dragon had taken to the air. She stiffened, her breathing rapid as the Thalor dragon soared toward her, its razor-sharp teeth bared as its mouth began to open. Another fireball was cast her way, but Sintra ran again, dodging the smouldering orb of heat that crashed into the stone wall she had once taken refuge behind. Catching her breath, she grew frustrated and tired of running.

"Come for me!" she yelled at the top of her lungs. "I am not afraid of you, Thalor!"

The dragon barked loudly, turning in the sky as it made for her again, but this time Sintra held her ground. Shield above her head and sword raised, she braced herself as the dragon cast its fire down upon her, a heated gust of wind almost knocking her off her feet. She tossed aside her burning shield and turned, running for the dragon, sprinting upward along a raised pillar that had half-fallen into a stone wall.

As her feet pounded the pavement, she miraculously caught up with the beast that now soared slowly beneath her, preparing to descend into the citadel quad. The beast flapped its wings and soared directly under the pillar off which Sintra leapt, throwing herself into the air and onto the dragon's lower back. Thalor roared in protest, and pain as she buried the sword into its flesh. Her body weight drove the blade in deep, missing its spine by three feet. Crashing to the ground, the dragon cried out in anguish as the blade trembled and burned deep within its flesh.

"Do not mar your dragon, Sintra. We need its body intact for the exchange." Brencis's words rang through her ears as if the creature sat by her side.

Sintra felt a pang of guilt; she wanted to slay this magnificent creature, but it was too late. She knew if she gave up now, it would burn her alive.

The steel dragon wailed in agony, stomping its large heavy legs and shaking its body in an attempt to free the sword. Thalor flapped his wings furiously, turning his head and snapping at the princess who clutched the sword with her life. Fireball after fireball was cast into the air as Thalor screeched and roared. Sintra tightened her grip as the dragon took flight again, climbing into the air so high the princess feared she would fall to her death.

The dragon swayed heavily from side to side, the princess rolling from left to right along its scaled back. It turned and spiralled in the air, but Sintra clung to the sword. It flapped ferociously, snapping and barking until it soared for the citadel ruins as fast as it could, making for the large pile of gold. Its refuge.

As the dragon neared the citadel ruins within an instant, the princess braced herself. She clutched the sword as tightly as ever as it was ripped from Thalor's flesh when the beast hit the mound of gold and buried itself beneath the heap. The princess was thrown from its back and into the air, landing hard against the stone pave, metres from the cliff. She lay silent and stiff against the cold stone rubble, her body motionless. Her eyes closed.

The Reign of the Dragon will
be mine

Time passed for what seemed like an eternity as the princess lay unconscious. The dragon too, exhausted from its wound, resting beneath the mound of gold. A few hundred metres on the other side of the citadel ruins, Lord Edith was still searching for a way inside, the entrance blocked by fallen, crumbled stone. The white steed raked its hoof against the ground, impatient and eager to run as an army of men approached from across the field, emerging from the Infinite Forest like an army of angered ants.

Arrows arced through the air, each bowman running on foot, loading and reloading his bow with arrow after arrow. Lord Edith turned in revulsion, lifting his shield to protect his body from the scatter of flying arrows, a few hitting his shield while others buried deep into the stone wall behind him. Cedric cast three arrows at once, striking three men as they approached from afar. The knight was a splendid aim, but there were too many men for his small scabbard of arrows. Retreating behind a fallen stone pillar, Cedric mounted Soul while he could and dug his heels into its sides. Soul jerked into a full gallop almost immediately, vanishing behind the remains of the citadel wall.

Among the army of men that loomed toward the ruins of Thane was an enraged man, thirsty for the blood of the princess and any man who tried to stop him. Aleron commanded his army forward, Francis and Gordon by his side as they awaited their orders.

"Why come here?" he spat. "Of all places across the sixteen bloody kingdoms, why come to the secluded ruins of this pathetic reign? Perhaps to hide alongside the rotted remains of her second royal family," he finished in distaste, cringing at the thought.

"A black beast reigns here," said Francis.

"Long ago," laughed Aleron. "No beast resides here. Don't be a fool!"

As Lord Elowen laughed to himself, he was soon proven wrong, for Thalor had woken. His eyes widened in disbelief as the dragon let out its hellish howl, breathing fire high into the air, lighting up the night sky and all the land beneath. Aleron's men started to retreat, fearing the sound that deafened their ears. Lord Elowen cast an arrow toward a man who began to run, striking him through the heart and killing him instantly.

"Any man that runs from the beast will be thrown into its jaws, dead or alive," he threatened. "Now find a way in. I don't care if you have to climb," he shouted. "Bring the whore to me!"

Inside the ruins, Sintra stirred, blinking her eyes open until she was conscious again. She sat up, her head dizzy and her body unbalanced.

"Thalor," she breathed, searching for the beast, but Thalor was nowhere to be seen.

Finding her sword on the ground, shooting pains travelled up her spine as she twisted her body to reach down for the blade. The princess clutched her side, clutching an open wound that felt wet against her fingertips, the harsh sting making her cringe. She raised her hand into the moonlight.

Blood. My blood, she thought to herself.

She looked to her hip, a large gash bleeding profusely. The princess swayed, disoriented and weak as blood flowed from her body.

I am going to die.

"Not today, Sintra," said Brencis within her mind. "Stop the bleeding with your blade. Find the dragon."

Stop the bleeding? she thought, stumbling in a daze. *But how?*

Sintra remembered the tournament; she remembered the sight of Aleron's open wound, blood gushing. She looked to her sword; it trembled and glowed faintly as the dragon was far from her at this moment. She knew it trembled ferociously when the dragon was near, burned scorching red when in the presence of the beast.

"Thalor!" she yelled at the top of her lungs. "Come for me!"

The princess didn't know what to say but summoning the dragon this way seemed like her only option. Thalor came into sight, a faint black speck in the sky just big enough to see in the darkness of the night. It grew fierce and fast, flying with such haste as it eyed the princess in the quad near its precious gold heap. Thalor howled and barked, baring its teeth as its jaws opened, fire growing hot within its belly.

"Come for me. I have the sword carved from your tail-thorn," shouted Sintra. "I am Princess Sintra Lysandra of Crevark, first niece of King Thaddeus Lysandra of Thane. I have come to avenge the man that took your thorn."

The beast screeched louder than ever as the words rang throughout its ears. Thalor was no dumb creature; he understood the English language, but it was the sight of the glowing sword that angered the beast more than anything. Sintra held the trembling, scorching blade to her flesh, crying out in agony as the heat cauterized her wound, ceasing the bleeding. She raised her head as Thalor soared for her, open flame pouring down upon her. The princess dropped to the ground instantly, covering her face with her armoured arms. The heat and flame burned the back of her legs, the black leather melting to her flesh. Sintra screamed in distress.

"Get up!" said a voice within her mind, but this time it wasn't Brencis. "Get up and fight, Sintra. Get up! Get up!" it screamed.

The princess lifted her head from the ground and rolled to her side, cringing as her burnt legs stung hot. Rage coursed through her body as another part of her emerged. She staggered to her feet, her legs stiff and aching, her knees refusing to bend as the pain was too much.

"Rip its belly open," the voice screamed. "Drive the sword into its heart. Avenge your family. Avenge your father; take Crevark from the madman that hunts you."

Sintra realized it was her inner being that screamed at her, her inner strength, her inner thought. All the things she bottled up inside for years were finally coming out. Fury drove her mad with the thirst for Aleron's blood. The princess eyed down the dragon that approached her fast. She stood strong and fierce, clutching the trembling sword with both her hands. Sintra took a deep breath and waited for Thalor. As the dragon opened its mouth, Sintra charged, arms outstretched in front of her, sword in hand as she charged through the flame, ignoring the heat that encased her.

"The reign of the dragon will be mine!" she screamed as she charged beneath the beast.

She leapt into the air as high as her feet would take her. She plunged the sword deep into the beast's heart, ripping open its chest as Thalor flew over the top of Sintra in a slow motion that dragged on for what seemed like forever. The sword heaved through its flesh, ripping open its belly as the princess slowly descended. The dragon crashed to the ground, its hot steamy insides spilling, its heart severed in two, but Sintra kept falling. No ground rushed toward her as she had let go of the Thalor sword. The cliff face rushed past her as the princess fell rapidly through the air, screaming as she realized she now tumbled to her death.

I missed the cliff's edge; she thought as her body collided with the raging ocean rapids that crashed against the rocks. The faint beating of her heart thudded softly in her ears as she sank beneath the black water, too stunned to move as she barely clung to life. The ice-cold water soothed her burnt legs and wounded side as she drifted into a lull, watching the moon travel further and further away as she sank deeper beneath the water. Rays of moonlight shone brightly through the rippled glass wall that separated her from reality.

I died. I'm dead. I'm gone, she thought. *I threw myself clean off a cliff; I jumped to my own death, to the sharp stone boulders of the ocean that will soon crush my skull as the tide takes my lifeless wounded body.*

The sway of the rolling ocean waves knocked her beneath the water, pushing her toward the wall of jagged stone, pushing her toward death. The last words that escaped her mouth played over in her mind like an echo that never ended.

The reign of the dragon will be mine. The reign of the dragon will be mine. The reign of the dragon will be mine.

As the words chanted in Sintra's mind, realization swamped her. She had slaughtered the dragon, left the blade to burn within its flesh as it lay lifeless at the top of the cliff. The reign of the dragon was hers, for the heart of Thalor had stopped by her hand. She sprung to life, pushing herself upward as fast as she could manage. Breaking through the surface of the water, she gasped for breath. The bitterness of the icy air scratched at her lungs, but she ignored the pain for the smell of victory empowered her.

Sintra clung to the cliff face with stiff, cold hands, climbing up the stone wall like an old, fragile spider. Her entire body ached, the burnt flesh on the back of her legs stretching and cracking, bleeding and blistered, but she pushed on. As she climbed the cliff face, she pulled herself up onto a ledge. The princess stiffened, now standing in the entrance to a dark cave that had a heated, eerie sense about it.

Sintra raised her head and discovered at least ten caves above the one she stood, pocketed over the cliff face like holes in a sponge. To her left, she saw more, at least twenty or thirty. To her right was double that, stretching out along the cliff face as far as she could see. Sintra did not like the feeling that danced within her stomach, for a beast none other than a dragon like the one she had just slaughtered would live inside a cold, dark cave overlooking the ocean. And she had just found herself more than five score. The princess only heard of great stories of caves like these. She didn't know where they led; she wished not to think of the creature that dwelled inside, so up the cliff face she continued.

The struggle lasted several minutes before Sintra reached the cliff's edge, but her hands were too tired and sore; she couldn't pull herself up.

"Take my hand, princess," said a familiar voice.

Sintra grasped hold of the outstretched hand that jutted from atop the cliff. Lord Edith hauled the princess to safety, letting her exhausted body lean against his as she fought for consciousness.

"You're victorious, my princess, the reign of the dragon is indeed yours," said Cedric, holding her upright on her feet.

Sintra sighed in awe and relief as her eyes rested on the lifeless body of Thalor, the sword still protruding from its stomach where she had left it. Metres away from the creature stirred Soul; Riven's body slumped over his back and shoulders. As the princess moved toward the dragon's body, she stumbled on her aching feet.

"You're wounded, princess," gasped Cedric. "You need medical attention at once."

But Sintra ignored the knight's fuss and glared down at Thalor. She pulled the sword from its stomach, the blade silent, still, and as cold as steel should be. The dragon truly was no more. A shower of arrows broke Sintra's gaze as they poured down over the citadel ruins.

"Aleron," she gasped. "He found me."

She knew she must hurry now, for it was only a matter of time before the madman and his army found their way into the citadel. The princess rushed toward Soul, Cedric helping as they both lifted Riven's body from the steed's back. Lord Edith took his arms as Sintra took his legs, carrying Riven toward the beast and laying him alongside its body.

Without hesitation, the princess dug the sword into Riven's body, dragging it through the hard, dead flesh, revealing the blackened heart of her lover. Lord Edith took the cold blade and climbed atop the dragon. He plunged it into Thalor's severed heart, pulling it from the body. The beast's blackened heart weighed heavily on the end of the sword, much larger than that of Riven's. Sintra carefully pulled Riven's heart from the dead body and proceeded to climb atop Thalor's chest where it gaped open, the blood still warm.

"Exchange the hearts," said Brencis, appearing before them in a wisp of black smoke. "Bind the pipes. Bury the souls within."

Lord Edith lowered the dragon's heart into Riven's body. Sintra repeated the action, placing Riven's heart into Thalor's body. Once both hearts rested, Brencis began to mumble a chant beneath his breath. A spiral of black smoke circled each of the bodies, engulfing them completely, concealing them from sight.

"Exchange the hearts. Bury the souls," shouted Brencis, his arms outstretched toward the sky, dark shadows circling him. "Exchange the hearts. Bury the souls. It is time for new life as I command you to wake, I command you to rise. Rise, Thalor dragon, rise with the soul of another. Rise with new life, rise with new meaning as I summon you from death. Hear me, Riven Valahn, I command you. Hear me, knight, as you slumber in death no more. Awake a dragon, awake a beast of the skies, for noble blood runs through your veins no more. Let the dragon be your temple, let metallic blood fill your spirit, let it consume your soul, for you are no man, but Thalor the steel dragon. You are no human, for I wake you a metallic beast. Wake, Riven Valahn, for you now have the metallic heart."

Silver rays of light shone from inside the chest of each body like lightning captured inside their ribcages. The light shone blindingly bright as the flesh of the wounds was bound, seamed together with silver gild. The scars gleamed metallic as the open wounds were sealed tight. The exchange was complete, the new prophecy fulfilled.

Time stood still as Sintra glared at the stirring dragon as it raised its head. Its eyes flickered open, searching its surroundings before landing on the princess. A deep growl escaped its throat as it glared at her, fixated. Lord Edith and Sintra both stood stiff, equally stunned; they couldn't believe their eyes. The dragon stared at them both, its eyes passing from one to the other like a frightened hound.

"Go, Sintra, you must flee atop that dragon," said Brencis, disappearing into thin air as another shower of arrows poured down upon them.

The dragon roared, casting flame over the army of men that now climbed down over the citadel ruins like ants. Aleron stood high on one side of the citadel wall, glaring in astonishment as he had just witnessed the exchange. He had just seen new creation and the legend of the metallic heart. Lord Edith and Sintra stood stiff in amazement, for the dragon had not harmed them but protected them.

"Riven," called Sintra, standing before the creature.

The dragon stopped abruptly, lowering its head toward the princess as it glared into her eyes. Sintra's heart pounded as the beast neared her, stopping within three feet of her face. She raised her hand and rested her palm on its snout. Her world spun as a word filled her mind, a name. A name she knew to be none other than her own.

"Sintra," said the beast.

A glacial shiver prickled up her spine. Thalor was no more. Standing before her was a dragon with the soul of a man. A metallic heart. The heart of a Knight.

"Go, princess," shouted Cedric, mounting Soul who stirred violently.

Sintra ran to her sword, clutching it tightly as she then scrambled up onto the dragon.

"Sintra!" said the dragon.

The ground fell away as the dragon rose high into the air; the princess squeezed her knees tight to hang on as there was nothing to grasp with her hands. As the dragon circled the citadel ruins, Sintra gasped as a white speck fled the citadel. The steed galloped across the open field and headed straight for the Infinite Forest. But before the princess could command the dragon to follow Lord Edith, her heart sank as up the cliff face now climbed dark-winged figures, emerging from the caves that lined the stone wall.

"Blackwing," she breathed, watching them climb onto the cliff and into the ruins, hunting Aleron's army as if they hadn't eaten in years.

Confusion overwhelmed her; what would have summoned them from their caves?

"The dragon's mind still holds secrets, Sintra," said Brencis within her mind.

She looked down, but he was nowhere to be seen. She thought of what he could have meant, but her mind was blank. She did not want the army harmed as they were innocent men taking command from Aleron. And then it dawned on her.

"Stop!" she shouted to the dragon. "Stop, they're innocent."

But the only reply she heard from the beast was her name. Sintra knew Riven meant well, but it was Thalor who summoned the Blackwing, for only he knew where they nested. It was Thalor who drove the Blackwing to climb the cliff face.

"Stop!" she shouted, pounding her fist against the creature's back as it hovered in the sky, its wings slowly moving up and down. "Riven," she said within her mind, "If you can hear me, please stop this madness."

But it was useless; Thalor's mind was too overpowering. More and more Blackwing emerged from their caves, taking on three men at a time as they fought sword and shield.

"Riven," whispered Sintra, but her sentence was left unfinished as sleep began to envelope her.

Her body swayed; her mind dizzy as it was all too much. Her eyes closed, and her body slumped forward as it rested against the dragon's neck. She was soon unconscious.

†

"Sintra," came a voice inside the princess's mind.

A voice that wasn't so familiar to her, though she had heard it once before. It repeated her name, but the princess did not stir as she assumed she was dreaming, a light breeze in her face resembling the breeze that swept in through her bedchamber window.

"Sintra, wake up," said the voice.

"Who?" she mumbled, her eyelids shaking as she strove to see, but her eyes would not open.

"It is Riven."

Riven, said the princess inside her mind, blinking rapidly as this time her eyes flew open. Harsh reality rushed back to her almost instantly, striking her in the face as she sat stunned and confused.

"It's not a dream," she said, glaring down at the black and silver scaled beast beneath her.

Her head spun as she peered down toward the ground but saw nothing but clouds. A mixture of colours—orange, yellow, pink, and purple—filled the sky as first light appeared. Each ray of light breaking through the white clouds.

"Where are you taking me?" she asked the beast, well aware that Thalor somewhat controlled a minority of his body, though Riven had taken over the soul completely. The knight's metallic heart pulsed inside the creature.

Sintra expected not much of a reply as the dragon's vocabulary resembled that of an infant learning to speak. The princess knew Riven would have to learn to speak again; he had a profound need for training as his new life was indeed very new to him.

"Riven, I know you can hear me. Take me home, take me to Crevark."

Almost immediately, the dragon turned, emerging through the clouds as it descended toward the land. Sintra then knew that Riven was the one in control, at least at that very moment. The earth loomed beneath them, an array of earthly colours rushing past. From high in the sky, the assortment of crops and fields made like a patchwork quilt. Shades of green, brown, yellow, and bronze.

The dragon soared toward the earth, the wind whizzing past Sintra's ears like tiny foreign whispers she couldn't understand. Her long dark hair danced and spiralled in the gust. The beautiful landscape warmed her heart as the princess stared in admiration. It was quite a view. Though something else tugged at her heart, a hurt she could not elude, for it grew with fear and longing.

I can love you no more, she thought to herself, sadness overwhelming her. *I can touch you no more, I can kiss you no more, no more can I have you for you are a beast and what princess...what woman can love a beast? What human can love an animal the way I wish to love my Knight? My Riven.* Tears swelled in her eyes. She had wished to save her beloved slave boy, but saving his soul was all that could be. Saving him in spirit was all that came to be. She could hear his voice as he spoke to her, but it was not the same familiar voice she loved. She could have conversations with him, but it wasn't always Riven she spoke to, for Thalor still dwelled within the body of the dragon. Thalor still clung to his body, living in the mind of the beast. The beast that now occupied two very different forms of spirit. Spirit of the mind and spirit of the soul. Sintra could not help but wonder if Riven would become overpowered by Thalor, just as Brencis is overpowered by the beast that lingers inside him. She knew the hurt and confusion Brencis caused when he could not control his mind. Hurt and confusion in the dragon's hand would play out very differently, catastrophically as she imagined.

What if Thalor takes over? Destroys the land and everything in its path, she thought. *What if Riven turns rogue as the exchange did not work properly? What is the use of such a legacy, such an exchange if the mind-spirit of the beast itself may still linger within, once the exchange is successful? Able to rule and overpower just as it had as if an exchange never took place.* Sintra questioned, the possibilities overwhelming her. She planned to summon Brencis once they landed. Questions need answers and she had many a query.

"Crevark," said the voice, waking the princess from her daydream, oblivious to the thoughts that rolled through her mind.

"The quad," she ordered.

The dragon soared toward the citadel, descending into the quad, slowly flapping its wings as it lowered its upright body to land. Slaves hid within the stables and cowered behind straw heaps. The princess slid off the dragon, her cuirass clattering against the beast's scaled body.

"Do not cower from me; I am your saviour," said the princess, taking off her leather armour to reveal the remains of her blackened gown.

"Princess Lysandra?" spoke a man all too familiar. "Princess, we thought you were dead, we thought all was lost and ruined."

"As did I, Jose Hinkley. But I must say, I am proud to see that you are still alive," said Sintra.

The slave smiled with few rotted teeth. The princess turned to the other slaves that hid among the stable posts.

"Do not fear the beast," she said. "He will not harm you; he takes orders from me."

"You are the Dragon Queen?" asked a small boy.

Sintra hadn't the time to think of formal names, but there was something about this one that fit just right.

"If that is who you see, that is who I am to be."

The young man grinned in excitement, having never seen a real-life dragon or a Queen who rode one. Sintra heard muffled cries coming from within the dungeons and, frowning, she strode toward the entrance without hesitation. Down the stone steps she went, ignoring the sting at the back of her legs.

The cold stone walkways were dark and eerie, but the princess had seen enough to frighten her for a lifetime. As she came to the first cell, she gasped in disbelief. It contained several small, thin children, boys and girls. The next cell contained elderly women, few able to stand, their frail bodies too weak; their fragile bones too old.

"Let them out at once," Sintra demanded, eyeing the sleeping guard further up the stone corridor.

The guard jumped to attention, snorting as he woke from his slumber.

"I take orders from King Aleron," said the guard, "Not small, puny women—"

The guard stopped mid-sentence as he neared Sintra, his eyes widening in disbelief as he realized he spoke to the princess. Fumbling with the heavy iron keyring, he pushed a slender key into the lock and turned it. A loud clink filled the dungeons, echoing throughout the corridor.

"All of them," said Sintra.

"As you wish, Your Majesty," stuttered the guard.

The princess turned toward the entrance of the dungeons and strode out, the small hands of the children clutching her legs as they stumbled in the darkness. She smiled to herself, her heart weighing heavily as two small girls on either side of her slipped their tiny, cold hands in hers. Sintra felt a sense of comfort and gratitude. She hadn't been so grateful as in that one moment for not letting herself sink to the bottom of the ocean. Sunlight filled her eyes as she emerged from the entrance, a crowd of women and children spilling into the quad, stopping abruptly as they stood in fear of the dragon.

"Fear not this beast," said Sintra, walking toward the black, curious creature. "He means no harm."

With that, the princess stroked its snout, comforting it as well as the growing crowd before her.

"Children," said the voice inside her mind.

"Yes," replied Sintra, "And they're free."

She watched as the last elderly women emerged from the dungeon entrance, followed by the guard who beamed at Sintra apologetically once he rested his eyes upon the dragon.

"My deepest apologies, my Queen, my deepest regrets," said the guard, bowing his head toward her.

The princess nodded in forgiveness before turning to the crowd. She looked upon their thin, grimy faces, sadness looming. She sighed as so many things came to mind, things she wanted to say, things she wanted to promise. But letting them down was not one, as the madman was still at large.

"I am Princess Sintra Lysandra, rightful heir to the throne. Guards and Knights obey me, for Aleron Elowen is *not* your King," she started. "For years I have waited for this day. Not only to take the throne and avenge my family, avenge my kingdom, but to free you all from this slow death. My father, King Alaric, was once a great man, but forgive him as he grew hardened and fierce before his slaughter. Forgive his judgment; forgive his spiteful humour, for it was compelled upon him by the madman himself, Lord Elowen.

"Above all, I wish for your forgiveness. I wish for your praise, I wish for your service, and I wish for your love. I wish you not to work another day of your lives and go free as I promised. Go peacefully and with haste, as it is not safe here. He will return, and he will return mightier than ever. As the princess, I pledge to you that I will take the throne. I will take the crown from Lord Elowen's head even if I have to roll it first. I will take reign, and I will be your Queen," she shouted.

"Praise the Dragon Queen," cried an elderly woman, the sentiment echoed by a chant that spread like wildfire over the crowd.

Sintra spoke no further as the crowd was so thrilled they refused to quieten, but the princess soon raised her hand as a familiar face caught her attention. In the entrance of the dungeons stood an old man with white tufts of hair sprouting upon his head, thin and feather-like due to old age. Crow's feet pinched at the corners of his eyes along with many other friendly wrinkles that greeted Sintra as the old man smiled fondly at her.

The breast pocket in his familiar green button-down vest sat bulging and full where his half-moon-shaped spectacles sat. His kind blue eyes were small without them perched on his round nose. A tear streamed down the old fellow's cheek as he softly blinked them back, gazing at the princess as if he hadn't seen her for a lifetime. Sintra grinned so hard her face began to hurt, her wind-burnt chapped lips stung as they cracked. Tears streamed from her eyes as she ran to embrace her old friend.

"Cornelius Thatcher, I am so glad you're alive."

"As am I, my princess," he replied, embracing her with a bone-crunching hug.

"Where is my Elara, where is my maid?" asked Sintra.

PART III

The Darkest of Possessions

"It's about bloody time," grumbled a voice from behind the secret chamber door, Cornelius fumbling at the key and lock.

The library was silent, the darkness eerie. Once the door of the chamber opened, out came a flash of white, knocking the princess to the ground. Sintra laughed and squealed in joy as Nyom licked her face like never before. Much needed reprieve from all the loss and grief the princess had endured.

"Oh," said Elara, forcing back tears as she saw Cornelius and Sintra outside the chamber door, "I knew you'd come for us; I just knew."

The old woman embraced the bookkeeper, showering his face with kisses. She then pushed the white wolf aside and hauled Sintra up off the floor and into her arms.

"Never have I been so happy to see you, my child. I feared the worst when your letters stopped coming."

Sintra sighed apologetically; she hadn't a word to say. Time was the reason for the abrupt silence; the princess found herself too occupied to even put quill to parchment, let alone have anything to say.

"A crow's whisper is untrustworthy more so than not," she said. "Isn't that right, Cornelius?"

"Aye, my princess, you remembered that phrase."

"I needn't remember it as it was preached to me by an old friend of yours," she replied, her hands on her hips, "And for that, he quashed any thought of mine to send a raven at all."

"An old friend?" asked Elara, confused.

"Lord Cedric Edith accompanied me the entire journey," started the princess. "He spoke of your unlikely friendship. He spoke of a prophecy," she said to Cornelius.

The old bookkeeper glared at Sintra, stunned. He blinked rapidly before any words could spill from his mouth.

"I...I...I," he stuttered, "I should have told you, Sintra, I am sorry."

"Aye, indeed, you should have, old man. Of what manner does knowing the future death of your princess slip your mind?"

Cornelius sighed in defeat, looking to his feet. A saddened expression crossed his face. The princess could see that the old man was exhausted, having not slept for days inside the dungeons. Her frustration escaped her with a sigh; she wanted not to argue anymore. She was done with arguing. Peace was all she desired. Peace and quiet, and her warm, comfortable bed with her Winter whisper by her side.

"It is alright, Cornelius. I am not mad," she said softly as she rested a hand atop his shoulder. "I'm glad to be home and in your presence again, for the prophecy was only partially fulfilled. What fallacy."

Cornelius turned away, turning his back to Elara and Sintra as he spoke.

"I should be punished; I should be thrown back into the dungeon for defying you."

"Whatever do you mean?" she asked.

"I gave you away," he replied in a huff. "Forced by the madman, I was to give you away, to read the map that led through the Infinite Forest. I showed them where you'd go…"

Cornelius turned with saddened, wet eyes, tears streaming down his cheeks.

"I had to choose, Sintra, please forgive me. I chose to protect my own life before the life of my princess."

"Then you chose wisely, Cornelius Thatcher, for I am here, and I am alive. And quite frankly, I wouldn't know what to do without you if you had chosen otherwise."

She embraced the old man, comforting him with a warm hug. She loved the man dearly; she couldn't bear to see him upset.

"I must apologize too," interrupted the maid, "I'm afraid I've made a mess of your chamber."

Cornelius frowned as he passed Elara and stepped inside the secret chamber, still dimly lit by candlelight. The old man took in his surroundings, disappointment casting over his face as he eyed the small mound of splintered wood that was once the table and chairs occupying the centre of the secret chamber. His expression changed as he noticed the broken glass jar that once contained the infant Blackwing, shattered over the floor.

"Whatever happened here, Elara?"

"My deepest apologies, Cornelius, but that small dead thing was my only source of bait."

"Please tell me you did not feed that thing to Nyom, Elara," said Sintra, jutting her head inside the chamber.

"Oh, heavens no, my lady, it was for the raven. I had no other means of capturing a new parchment-bird as Aleron killed our last," said the maid.

"You fed that creature to a raven?" laughed Cornelius, raising his eyebrows as he turned toward the maid.

"Aye, I did. Worked famously."

"Well, I must say we shall not be seeing that particular parchment-bird ever again."

"And why is that?"

"Those creatures...Blackwing...are poison," said Cornelius. "I am not the slightest bit bothered that you fed that thing to a raven, sweet Elara, though we must burn the remains immediately."

"And the table, Cornelius?"

"Oh, never mind about that old thing, dear. It was rickety and weak, sworn to fall apart if I used it any longer. Burn it too."

Sintra fell silent for a moment, her thoughts remaining with the infant Blackwing. *Blackwing are poison,* she thought to herself as Cornelius's words rolled over and over in her mind.

"Cornelius," started the princess, "Tell me about the Blackwing."

"The Blackwing? Well, they are the most feared creatures to have ever existed, the most evil beasts to have roamed the earth."

"Greater than the Thalor dragon?"

"Yes, a little smaller though deadlier in numbers. But I do not understand, princess—"

"Cornelius, if the kingdom were to come by this creature…what would become of the land and the people that dwell here?"

"Blackwing are ultimate predators. Their blood, if ever spilled, would poison the land. The gassy fumes a Blackwing breathes are not like the fire an ordinary dragon would breathe; it is not fire at all but a toxic emission that can melt the flesh of a man in seconds. Melt the flesh down to the bone before melting the bone itself. One Blackwing can be brought down by ten men, so thank the heavens this one was dead before I stumbled across it so many years ago."

Sintra's heart sank; the only thing that went through her mind at this moment was what she saw on the coastline as she flew to safety on the back of her dragon. An overwhelming sense of disbelief overcame her. Did her eyes deceive her?

"And more than one?"

"Well, catastrophic things would prevail," replied the old man, confused and a little anxious. "We would witness doomsday itself."

Sintra stiffened. A bone-chilling shiver coursed through her.

"What is it, princess? You are as white as a ghost," said Elara, but Sintra's words failed her as she stood, stunned and overwhelmed with fear.

"Sintra?" pushed Cornelius.

But neither Elara nor Cornelius were answered as the princess strode out of the small chamber and through the library. She strode down the hallway toward the flight of stairs, the maid and bookkeeper hastily catching up behind her. Sintra flew down the stairs, her feet slapping the stone floor. She did not stop until she reached the entrance to the quad.

"Lady Lysandra, I demand you tell us what is going on," said Elara, pushing the princess from the large wooden door and barricading it with her body, her arms outstretched. Sintra sighed.

"War is coming," Sintra started, then turned to Cornelius who came to a stop before her. "We are in the gravest of danger, Mr. Thatcher. I fear Lord Elowen commands an army of Blackwing as we speak."

"How on earth is this possible?" he asked in disbelief. "They have not existed for decades, not one has been seen since…"

"Since you travelled to Thane?"

"Aye."

"Oh Cornelius," sighed the princess, her eyes swelling with tears. "I jumped from the cliff, I fell into the ocean, but when I emerged, I saw them…"

"Saw what, Sintra?" asked Elara, her eyes wide in fear.

"A nest…along the coastline as far as the eye could see. Caves…four score caves, and more."

"Did you see?" pushed Cornelius. "Did you see what dwelled inside?"

The princess slowly nodded her head as tears streamed down her face; the fear in her eyes was enough for Cornelius to know that she needn't say another word.

"Move from the door, Elara," he snapped, looking to his feet, deep in thought.

The maid moved from the door as Sintra pushed it open and walked out into the quad. The old woman soon doubled back in horror as her eyes rested upon the large, black and silver scaled dragon that basked in the morning sun.

"Fear not. It is Riven," said Sintra as she strode toward it.

"Riven?" whispered the maid in disbelief, her feet glued to the ground.

As the princess stood by her dragon, the quad filled with guards and village people. But before the princess could speak, a knock upon the Iron Gate sounded loud and fierce.

"Open the Iron Gate," roared a voice all too familiar to her.

"Open the Iron Gate," Sintra repeated, and her orders were obeyed.

A loud moan sounded, echoing through the quad as the gate groaned to life, slowly rising as the remaining guards wound its chains tight. As the gate rose, the princess's eyes rested upon the Steel Knight of Sidon.

"Sintra," shouted Lord Edith as he pushed past the villagers, the white steed reined behind him. "My princess, I bring news…"

"What news, Sir Knight?" asked a guard.

"What news, Cedric?" whispered Sintra as she approached him swiftly, stopping within a foot of him.

"When you fled Thane upon that dragon, I saw with my own eyes," he started. "Blackwing on the edge of the shores, beasts…they emerge from the cliff face."

"It is true," gasped Cornelius.

"There's more…"

"Lord Edith?" pushed the princess.

"Aleron forms an army, for he witnessed the exchange, my lady."

"Impossible, no man can control a Blackwing," snapped Cornelius, his denial overwhelming him.

"I'm afraid greater things have unravelled...dark things, inhuman things. For the legend of the Metallic Heart has come to be more than once."

"Oh heavens," whispered the princess. "It is far worse than I feared."

"Aye, it is the darkest of possessions, my lady; I have seen it too," said Brencis inside Sintra's mind.

"Brencis..." whispered the princess.

"Brencis?" queried Cornelius. "Why have I heard that name before?"

"Brencis is nowhere; he refuses to reveal himself," scoffed Cedric.

"I needn't that manner at this time, Lord Edith. My people will be frightened enough when their eyes rest upon the man-beasts and Blackwing that will so wrongfully slaughter them. I need not the presence of Brencis at this time, thus why he chooses to remain hidden," said Sintra.

"My apologies, Lady Lysandra, but man-beast is a mere understatement, for they are far more deadly than one could fathom."

"Someone please...I must know what is going on," said the maid.

"Evil has awoken, Elara, and it comes for Crevark. A great war is upon us, and we know not how to stop it," said Cornelius in the softest voice so that only the small group of them could hear.

"Man-beasts of the Blackwing; dragons with the heart of men...and men with the heart of dragons," said Lord Edith. "And they come for our kingdom as they come for our blood. They will not stop at the Iron Gate of Crevark."

"Forgive me, but I do not understand. Sintra," she said, facing the princess, "When you say that dragon...when you refer to it as Riven, do you mean you did as Lord Edith has just said? Did you exchange Riven's heart with the heart of the beast?"

"I did, Elara."

"And you, Lord Edith, you speak of man-beasts as well as the Blackwing."

"Aye..."

"If beast can dwell within man and continue to roam the earth freely, then...where is Riven's body?"

Sintra looked to Lord Edith with sadness in her eyes. She did not know. She had fled the ruins of Thane before she could burn his body, before she could truly wish farewell to him.

"It lies in the ruins," said Cedric, looking to Sintra. "I could not burn it…my own eyes saw it…"

"Saw what, Cedric?"

"My princess, Riven's body turned to stone, thus I could not set it alight. Flame does not burn stone, my lady, it would not burn."

"The man-beast of the Blackwing will turn to stone?" asked Elara.

"No. Sintra's dragon is quite different from the Blackwing beast," said Cornelius. "The Thalor dragon is a huge beast, its heart much too large to beat within a tiny human body, thus turning to stone for eternity. Blackwing are smaller creatures with hearts the size of man's; an exchange is entirely different; both hosts live. The legend of the Metallic Heart can prevail with any man and any winged sky beast, though the Blackwing is deadly."

"No such legend should exist," grunted Elara.

"What will happen, Cornelius?" asked the princess.

"Such a creature will not stop until all is dead; they are greedy creatures with only the thirst for man…"

"They'll kill us all," whimpered Elara in a panic. "Princess, call upon the kingdoms, send for help. We need knights, guards, and soldiers…not villagers and slaves."

"That is why I fly to our sixteen kingdoms, to seek treaty. To seek an army."

"Fly? On that beast?"

"You need medical attention, princess, you may not last the journey."

"Nevertheless, someone must inform them," she said under her breath as she passed the knight. Sintra sat upon the dragon before speaking to the villagers. "I regret to inform you that we are all in grave danger. As your Queen, I ask for your service one last time. I ask for your allegiance as we must go to war. Gather all you know, men of young and old, that can swing a sword, throw an axe, and cast an arrow. Gather your weapons and gather your courage, for we will fight to the death. War is coming."

"War against whom?"

"I cannot speak of what we must fight, but they are led by the madman, Lord Elowen himself."

"Cannot speak of what we must fight?"

"An army approaches," said Lord Edith, raising his voice so all could hear. "An army of both man and beast, an army of a Black Death like none other."

"Winged creatures with the thirst for human blood. Sky beasts with the taste of man flesh," said Cornelius.

"You mean dragons?" asked a small boy.

"Blackwing! A creature fiercer than any other."

"A beast like that dragon there?" asked an old man, pointing to Sintra's dragon.

The quad filled with hissing and cursing as the villagers cast threats toward the dragon.

"SILENCE!" ordered Sintra. "Fear not this beast, for he is your saviour. Bow to him as you would your King; he has the soul of a nobleman."

The crowd silenced to listen to Sintra.

"As the rightful heir to the throne, I am Queen of Crevark. As your Queen, I speak nothing but the truth, and when I say this creature will not harm you...believe me, for this creature may be as tame as a hound. Fear not, for he is your saviour, and with him...Aleron will be no more."

†

Aleron's soldiers stood within the ruins of Thane, surrounded by a mass of black-winged beasts. Each man shook in his iron boots, fearing the same malicious death that had already claimed many. The black, deathly creatures howled deafening shrieks, barking calls that summoned more and more beasts scaling the cliff face. Their flesh-melting fumes filled the air, a toxic waft of death that would slowly consume a man from the inside out, eating away at the flesh and bone until nothing was left.

The villagers and slaves cowered; true soldiers they were not. One man, Lionel Strippence, became cornered against a stone wall as a Blackwing crept toward him, its head down and teeth bared. The creature loomed in. Lionel swung his sword, barely close enough to strike the beast at all. The Blackwing screeched its ear-piercing howl. Lionel dropped his sword to the ground as he clutched his ears, a move he deeply regretted. The beast stood on its hind legs before spraying its toxic seethe over his entire body. Strippence froze as he eyed the suspicious liquid that covered him from head to toe. He then screamed in agony as his flesh began to shrink and melt away, revealing the muscle and bone beneath his skin before that too melted to almost nothing.

The Blackwing screeched loudly once more, snapping at the emaciated, distorted remains of Lionel's body as it fell to the ground. Charred splinters of black bone were all that lingered of the soldier, his armour now melted into an iron mess that clung to the stone ground of the ruins.

"Hold your ground," ordered Aleron as his soldiers began to flee.

More and more Blackwing emerged from the cliff face, hunting the men like hounds. The ruins of Thane teemed with ravenous black beasts that wanted nothing more than to feast upon the charred, melted flesh of man.

"Slaughter them all," ordered the madman. "Take their hearts."

"My lord?" asked Gordon, his voice trembling with confusion and anxiety.

"I wish for you to switch them. Put the heart of every man within the body of a beast and do the same for every heart you take from a beast...put it inside a man."

"That is madness, my King. That is dark magic," said Gordon, panic rising in his voice.

"Fear not, Sir Leoss, but it is the darkest of possessions and it can be done. It will be done."

"Aye, my lord. But how am I to do such a task on my own?"

"Half the task is already done for you, Gordon," replied Aleron, jerking his head toward the ruins which now contained bodies of both beast and man.

"But...the fumes...they'll kill me."

"Then I suggest you take extra precaution, Sir Leoss. If you succeed, I shall grant you knighthood on our return to Crevark."

"My lord, you granted me knighthood...as did you every man here," replied Gordon. "Is Sir not the proper and formal title of a true knight?"

"Are you daft?" spat Aleron. "Do as I order, and I will see to it that you partake in a proper knighting ceremony, Sir Leoss. Now get on with it. Francis?"

"Yes, Aleron," said Sir Gregory as he strode toward the madman.

"Accompany this fool with the orders I gave him; it seems he cannot comprehend the task at hand. He will inform you of my wishes."

†

Five hours passed, and all that lay in the ruins of Thane were the dead, bloodied bodies of both man and beast, their chests ripped open to reveal a silent, cold heart within. But no silence spread throughout the fallen citadel as the Blackwing came like an endless rain, a flood of black-scaled creatures that emerged from the cliff face a few hundred metres before them. Blood drenched the small group of ten men that now stood to defend their King's erroneous reign, ready to slaughter the coming beasts that swelled in thousands just as before.

"There is fifty beasts to one man, my lord, there is not enough," said Gordon.

"And they keep coming," added Francis.

"Find the ringleader," spat Aleron. "Bring it to me…alive."

Francis and Gordon led the group of soldiers toward the cliff face; Aleron remained within the ruins as he studied the lifeless creatures that lay cold and silent on the stone ground before him. Blackwing took to the sky as the threat now moved inside their nest, looming toward their leader. Aleron knelt down alongside a Blackwing, admiring its black scale-armoured body that glimmered metallic in the morning sunlight. Its open chest revealed a black heart that once pumped a bloody poison through its veins.

Taking a slender silver dagger from his belt, Aleron sliced through the purple flesh of the beast, removing its heart. He then dragged the body of a soldier and placed it by the side of the heartless beast. Aleron proceeded to cut through the flesh of man before taking the heart in his palm. The madman then grasped the black heart of the beast in the other palm and glared at them both in admiration for what seemed like an hour before placing them within either host. He then waited. And waited. But nothing happened.

Aleron examined the wounds closely, for they sat, still and jagged. He waited, but no flash or rays of light emerged. Frowning, he searched the ground, picking up a splinter of blackened bone. He then pulled a leather thread from his doublet stitching and proceeded to sew the wounds of both man and beast, closing the gaping holes that revealed each heart. Aleron stood confused and frustrated. His plan was failing.

"Rise beasts," he started in a murmur, mimicking the actions and words of the black-hooded being he had witnessed awaken the Thalor dragon. "Exchange the hearts. Bury the souls, for it is time for new life as I command you to wake…I command you to rise."

Aleron paused for a moment as he recalled the words that Brencis had spoken.

"Rise the Blackwing, rise the man-beast. Rise with the soul of another. Rise with new life, rise with new meaning as I…summon you from…death. Hear me, I command you. Hear me as you slumber in death no more…"

Lord Elowen paused abruptly, his eyes widening in disbelief as each wound of both man and beast began to glow. Just as before, silver rays of light shone from inside the chest of either body. The light shone blindingly bright, though the flesh of the wounds did not bind as the Thalor dragon's had. It did not vein together with silver gild nor gleam metallic, though each being began to stir.

The exchange was complete, but unlike the other. There was no bond, no gild; no metallic scar was shown, though behind the gaping holes of leather stitching were hearts that began to beat. The chest of the Blackwing rose and fell as air passed in and out of its lungs, the blood of beast now coursing through the heart of man. The Blackwing shifted, leaping to its feet in fear. The creature stared at Aleron, its eyes glaring into his, its nostrils flaring. It stood stiff and silent like a frightened hound. Lord Elowen stared into the soul of the creature before speaking the soldier's name.

"Tobius Ridley," said Aleron, and almost immediately the Blackwing crouched before him as if bowing to a command.

Lord Elowen let out a great roar of laughter, a smile of bitter joy spreading across his face. Though his wits soon changed as the loud, rasped breathing of the soldier filled his ears. Aleron froze, stiff with fear and despair as he felt the man-beast's eyes upon him. His heart pounded within his ears as he slowly turned his head. Tobius Ridley's body stood crouched; its back arched as its spine was disfigured. Aleron watched in silence as the beast continued to transform. Long, sharp talons pushed through its fingertips, sprouting from every finger and thumb on each hand. The doublet beneath the iron armour twisted and stretched as its blood thickened, pumping harder and faster through Tobius's veins as its flesh grew dense. Its neck thickened; muscles doubled as did bone. The creature growled, bearing its newly grown row of razor-sharp teeth, a forked tongue flickering.

Aleron's eyebrows raised independently, his eye twitching as the metallic sound of crumbling iron filled his ears. The beast scratched and grabbed at the iron cuirass around its torso, two lumps protruding from its shoulder-blade region as it turned its back on the madman. Aleron watched, expecting two scaled wings to pierce through the armour, but the creature was too disfigured. It roared in fury and frustration as it tried to leap from the ground, but its lack of wings forced it back down.

"They cannot sprout wings," said Aleron as he gazed at the beast in awe. "Why can they not sprout wings?" he snapped, grumbling to himself.

The creature turned toward him, fierce and full of rage. Saliva dripped from its mouth as it grew bloodthirsty, sniffing the air. It turned toward the body of another soldier, lunging at it with its teeth bared, its jaws open.

"Cease it!" shouted Aleron, the Blackwing taking the order and leaping toward the man-beast.

The hunger-crazed man-beast cowered from the Blackwing, retreating backward and bowing its head, frightened. A loud screeching bark came from the cliff's edge as Francis and Gordon emerged, a large elephant-sized Blackwing bull toed behind them, draped in chains. This beast was twice the size of Tobius Ridley's dragon, its muscle tone greater, its wingspan doubled. It was almost the size of Thalor. A grim, malice smile spread across Aleron's face, for he knew in that moment that he could build an army of the darkest possession. He knew he would go undefeated.

Allegiance

Crevark fell away beneath her as Sintra's dragon rose high into the air, the princess clutching the creature's neck with her knees and thighs. The crowd beneath her stirred, women and children of the village rushing out the Iron Gate of the citadel as they watched the dragon take to the sky and fly off into the distance. Sintra made for her first alliance as she neared Redbend, the citadel appearing on the horizon already. The princess was astounded at how fast she could cross the land. It would take a solid day's ride from Crevark to Redbend.

"Write to Golorah and write to Hallem," she had ordered her maid and bookkeeper before she left. "Inform King Brutess and Queen Martina of the news. Tell them war is coming, war will soon be here. Send for an army, as many as they are able to gather. Tell them that Lysandra of Thane has fallen and Lysandra of Crevark is falling. Tell King Edmund and King Batonn that the Queen of Crevark sends for them. Write to Dunlaw, ask aid from King Judah and Queen Jacinta, and send for an army. Wish them haste across the black sea and across the mountains of sand. Inform them of the coming war; tell them it does not stop at Crevark. Tell them it will soon come for Golorah, Dunlaw, and Hallem. Tell them no one is safe until Aleron Elowen is dead."

Elara put ink to parchment as Cornelius trained a new raven. They sent for alliance and allegiance just as the princess had ordered.

"I am Sintra Lysandra of Crevark, I wish to speak with your King," said the princess as she landed in the quad of the citadel Redbend.

King Bryce entered the quad of his citadel, Queen Rubella doubling backward as her eyes lay to rest upon the dragon on which Sintra remained seated.

"What is the meaning of this?" asked King Bryce Tead, his eyes widening in utter shock and disbelief. "Are you ill-minded to sit upon such a deadly creature?"

"Fear not, King Tead. This beast is tame," she replied.

"No such beast can be tamed!"

"Do your eyes lie, King of Redbend? Perhaps your Queen's expression will prove this real? That is if you believe your eyes fail you."

"Nonsense, my eyes fail me none," spat the King. "What is it you wish to say? Do you bring news?"

"Aye, King Tead, I bring grave news..."

"Grave news?"

"I'm afraid war is upon my kingdom. I assume you received the news of my father's death; King Alaric no longer reigns; he was slaughtered by Aleron Elowen."

"Lord Elowen, Knight of Knights?" gasped Rubella.

"Yes, Queen Tead, he has taken the throne but fled in search of me. He now forms an army of unspeakable darkness, an army of beasts that will come for my estate."

"Then defend your kingdom, Lady Lysandra," said Bryce.

"I'm afraid I cannot, King Tead, for my father's men were slaughtered as well. I have no army; thus, I send for aid."

"Why should we come to your aid, princess? You did not marry, so therefore you are no Queen to rule."

"I am the rightful heir to my father's throne, I am Queen. Dragon Queen of Crevark, and I send order for your alliance. I send for your army to join me as I defend my kingdom, for if Crevark falls…so will Redbend. As will every kingdom in the realm, as I fear this madman will not stop at one; he will not stop until he has them all."

King Bryce Tead was gobsmacked; he feared turmoil and defeat. But furthermore, he loathed disloyalty. A cold hatred spread across his face; he loathed the betrayal of a knight to his kingdom. A fire grew fierce within his belly. He swore to attack any man that would harm his kingdom or wife.

"We ride within the hour of dusk, Dragon Queen; we will come to Crevark's aid. You have yourself an army of two thousand, for only two thousand men I have," said Bryce. "Bear is with you and Bear will fight," he finished, referring to the sigil of his house.

"I thank you," said Sintra, bowing to King Tead. "Crevark thanks you."

"We are at your service, Queen Lysandra," said Rubella kindly.

The dragon flapped its wings and rose into the air, taking to the sky once more. It soared over mountains and open fields, over shorelines and lakes until the next two kingdoms came into sight, with Lake Gwathmey sitting between them.

Denton and Pentrone were only a few kilometres apart, so it was no marvel as to why they combined their sovereignties.

Lansing Bronn of Denton was, after all, a widowed man, having rolled the head of his late wife Queen Ellayda for her affairs. Queen Fleur Rithe of Pentrone was also widowed, as her husband King Corbett Rithe was no more. King Lansing and Queen Fleur's alliance had been years in the making. It was only a matter of time, though they still weren't wed. Sintra flew over Pentrone, which was as much alive as Thane had been for a decade, a complete disregard for the beings that currently dwelled there; so on to Denton she travelled.

The princess strode into the Citadel of Denton where two flags hung above the throne, one a stag and the other a stallion; the Sigils of their House which would soon be officially combined. Sintra knelt before King Lansing, keeping an ear out for any stir within the quad as she had left her dragon to feast upon a drum of fresh fish.

"Greetings, Sintra Lysandra, 'tis a relief to see you alive and well after the fall of your father and kingdom," said King Lansing. "But I'm afraid we haven't the room for your stay."

"It is not your accommodation I seek, King Bronn, for I still have accommodation of my own. And my kingdom has not yet fallen, though it's not far off."

"Then what is it?"

"Forgive me. I do not mean to intrude, but I must inform you of grave news."

"Grave news?" asked Fleur, waving Sintra to her feet.

"A great war is coming, Queen Rithe, for the madman still lives. I ask for your army to defend my kingdom; I send for aid."

"Why should I give you an army?" said Lansing, blankly.

"Amid my sleepy state upon the fall of my father, I happen to know you fled with no care in this world for other than your own. Did you not have honour for your kingdom brother then? Do you not have honour for your kingdom sister now?"

Queen Rithe looked to King Bronn with a saddened expression before saying a word.

"Forgive us, Sintra, for we fled in fear of the madman. Disrespecting our kingdom brother, your father King Alaric…may the lord rest his soul…was indeed not our intent. Nevertheless, our swift actions should not be ignored. You have our service."

King Lansing frowned toward his Queen, sighing in frustration.

"Very well," he said sharply.

"Many thanks, King Lansing," said Sintra, nodding toward Bronn and then Rithe. "Queen Fleur."

"One more thing, princess…"

"Please, I am a Queen now," she replied.

"Queen Lysandra," he corrected, nodding his head with a sharp, sarcastic grin. "Who and what exactly are we at war with?"

"If you both would kindly follow me, I would like to show you something. I'm afraid you will not believe it from my mouth."

King Lansing frowned; his brow furrowed as he stood to follow Sintra out of the great hall and into the quad. Fleur two steps behind him.

"Brace yourself, King Bronn. The age of dragon reign has been born," said the princess, walking out into the quad toward her dragon.

"Cast that thing back to hell," snapped Fleur, frightened.

"Fear not, Madam Rithe. This creature is tame."

"That creature took Thane, it ought to be banished, slaughtered," shouted Lansing, drawing his sword from its sheath.

The dragon stirred; its eyes fearful as it glared down at King Lansing and his sword.

"Put down your sword," said Sintra, swiftly holding her Thalor blade to King Bronn's throat as he passed.

"Oh Sintra, you wouldn't," gasped Fleur, her hands flying to her mouth.

"That dragon is legend, for it contains the Metallic Heart and the soul of my lover. The soul of a knight; noble blood runs through its veins."

"It is the Thalor dragon, the beast that ended Thane."

"And I hold the Thalor sword against your throat, Lansing Bronn, the very sword that ended this beast's life before I took its heart in my hand and replaced it with that of man. If you do not believe in legend, I suggest you send for your bookkeeper right away," growled Sintra.

With that, Fleur disappeared into the citadel in search of her bookkeeper.

"I haven't the time for argument," she spat, "Nor do you. When Aleron is done building his army of beasts, he will come for you once he is finished with me."

"What beasts do you speak of?"

"Blackwing. Black-scaled monsters that breathe toxic fumes and spray flesh-melting seethe. Beasts that are hunger-crazed for the blood and flesh of man. Among these are man-beasts, half man and half beast, and believe me, Lansing Bronn…they will stop at nothing until Aleron has felled every kingdom in the realm."

The doors of the citadel burst open as Fleur and her bookkeeper entered the quad. The old man looked much like Cornelius, if not a few years younger.

"Inform your King of the legend of the Metallic Heart," Sintra said to the bookkeeper.

"Oh, my lord, it is a great legend," started the old man, stuttering in fear as he eyed Sintra's sword. "Unknowingly, it has existed for thousands of decades. Dark Magic, witchcraft as some would say, where the heart of a beast is taken and replaced with that of man. Where the heart of man is taken and replaced with that of a dragon. A reincarnation used to save great men killed at war. But fatal in the wrong hands…"

Sintra silenced the old man with her free hand.

"Your King does not believe that such legend has been performed on this dragon."

The bookkeeper's eyes grew wide as his mouth fell open. His gaping mouth turned into a widespread grin as the old man approached the dragon with no fear at all.

"Felonius, are you mad? That creature will butcher you in an instant," said the King.

"Nonsense," he laughed. "This beast has the gentle, kind soul of man," said Felonius as he stood beneath the creature, pointing above his head toward the silver metallic scar that ran down the chest of the dragon. "Metallic Heart…the legend exists, my lord."

Felonius laughed like a small child as he touched the warm scales of the dragon, the beast eyeing him suspiciously. Lansing Bronn lowered his sword in disbelief, his expression awestruck as the dragon did not stir or growl in the company of Felonius. Fleur blinked rapidly as she could not believe her eyes. Sintra sheathed her sword.

"Fear not this dragon, my kingdom brother, but fear those that come for us," she said. "Does your army remain mine?"

Lansing Bronn clenched his jaw tight as he was deep in thought; he then turned to the princess.

"Aye! We ride at dusk, fifteen hundred men from Pentrone and another thousand from Denton. You have a growing army, no doubt?"

"Two thousand from Redbend. I am yet to seek allegiance from Glennock, Ironsmead, Dumbrell, Lennox, and Gabor."

"Not Westrose, Crone, or Scarsgard?"

"I haven't much time; perhaps you could send ravens to inform them of my coming visit?"

"As you wish, Sintra."

"Farewell, princess," said Fleur.

"You will have Stag and Stallion alongside Dragon, at dusk, Queen Lysandra," said King Lansing.

"Until then."

With that, the princess climbed atop her dragon and wished her farewell. The dragon then flapped its heavy wings and rose gradually into the sky. The sun beamed down upon the creature and the princess as the clouds separated above them, the dragon's black-silver scales gleaming in the sunlight. Sintra looked over the land in admiration, Lake Gwathmey fading into the distance as she soared west to Crone.

"Greetings, Dragon Queen of Crevark," welcomed King Burkiss Raegor of Crone.

Sintra was surprised to see that King Raegor and his Queen did not stir at the sight of the dragon, though the knights and guards did not seem the slightest bit comfortable with the presence of such a beast. The dragon lowered at the entrance of citadel Crone, the King and Queen standing on the drawbridge.

"We have received word from King Tead, Sintra; four thousand of my men will ride to Crevark by nightfall. You have my allegiance."

The dragon rose once more as King Raegor bowed his head and waved the princess on. As she soared through the air, astonishment had not yet left her, for it was but less than an hour since she left Redbend.

Word travels with haste, she thought to herself, *perhaps Lennox and Gabor have received word as well.*

And indeed, Sintra's thoughts were right; as the dragon landed at the Iron Gate of Lennox, knights and guards stirred within the citadel.

"Greetings, Princess Lysandra, we welcome you," said King Edmund Artec.

Sintra stared down at the King from her dragon, glaring at Edmund Artec who was accompanied by his Queen Lorenna. As far as the princess knew, Lennox was ruled by King Kent Eagleston, not King Edmund Artec of Golorah.

"Greetings, King Artec. Where is Kent Eagleston? He reigns here if I am not mistaken," said the princess, but as she looked for a flag with Lennox's House Sigils of a Horned Bull, it was nowhere to be seen.

"Neither here nor there, Madam Lysandra. Do you not see that the Sigils of my house now hang upon the flag of this reign?"

"King Edmund, I demand to know the whereabouts of King Eagleston."

"On what grounds?" he snapped.

"Edmund Artec, do you not see the dragon beneath me? I do not see a beast at your side or within your reign…fear the beast, for it answers to me."

"His head resides on a stake. I took his pathetic reign from under him, just as any desperate King would."

"Desperate?"

Sintra remembered the parchment she received from Edmund Artec stating that he would not attend the tournament or her wedding the following day. It then occurred to her why King Kent Eagleston was also absent from such events.

"For a reign of his own, Sintra. I could not sit alongside my Queen's father and my brother any longer. Forgive my betrayal, princess."

"It is not I you betrayed, King Edmund. Nevertheless, will you fight with me?"

"I have only five hundred men, princess. I lost over a thousand in battle."

"But you and your men were victorious, Edmund Artec, a swarm of Hawk against a mass of Horned Bull," said Sintra.

"And a swarm of Horned Hawk alongside your dragon, Sintra Lysandra. We ride before nightfall."

"Horned Hawk, King Artec?"

"Aye, Madam Lysandra, a part of King Eagleston's reign will still exist…with mine. I could not take Hawk from Golorah, for Hawk still resides there. So, what better thing to do than combine them?"

"Very well," she replied.

King Kent Eagleston of Lennox was no more; who ruled the citadel now and forevermore was King Edmund

Artec, formerly of Golorah. The reign of Horned Bull is no more, but to be replaced by the Horned Hawk.

It was still early in the day as Sintra flew to Gabor. King George granted her only five hundred men; he despised her kingdom due to an unresolved dispute between himself and King Alaric. A feud that nobody understood, not even Queen Caprice or Queen Kaylah. Sintra thought it had something to do with her marriage and the fact that George Muucav refused a son to wed her. He feared their lives would be ruined by Aleron's hand.

"Crevark," spat King Muucav. "Always needing from me, always begging for aid," he teased. "Fine, I give you five hundred men, five hundred Wolves."

The princess was grateful; he could have given her none. She flew on to Glennock and Ironsmead, gaining six thousand men between both sovereignties. Glennock granted two thousand soldiers, two thousand Snakes alongside her dragon. Ironsmead a neat and generous four thousand, Lions in iron armour. Come noon, Sintra flew east to Westrose, greeting King Cane Bayard as she landed within his quad.

"Greetings, I have been expecting you," said King Bayard.

"Word from Redbend, no doubt?" asked the princess as she climbed off her dragon.

"Nay, I received a parchment from your kingdom. Did you not send it?" asked Cane, frowning in confusion.

"Not my hand, King Bayard, but truly my words," she replied, following Cane into the citadel.

Sintra smiled as three young princesses followed close behind. Gisela, Evelyn, and Hope Bayard, the three princesses of Westrose, giggled and whispered to one another a few feet behind, stiffening in silence as Sintra occasionally looked over her shoulder toward them.

"Run along, run along," said Cane. "The princess of Crevark and I have much to discuss. Or should I say Queen?" he asked, turning to Sintra.

"Our deepest condolences, Sintra, for the loss of your father, King Alaric," said Lenore Bayard, who sat at the throne as slaves and villagers bargained for goods. She soon cast them away.

Sintra nodded her head in thanks, her mouth thinning into a straight line as she forced back the hurt and anger she felt. Her growing army wasn't enough to sanguine the princess's frustration; she knew there were more than double Blackwing and man-beasts coming for her. She felt sick to her stomach as again she ordered men to fight to their deaths for her own cause, her own safety. Sintra now realized how it felt to reign a kingdom, as her father always said, '*Blood must be spilled in battle for enemies come like rain and fight like storm. It is the only way a new reign can and must be born.'*

"What are your numbers?" asked Cane as he seated on the throne beside his Queen.

"Two thousand Bears from Redbend, fifteen hundred Stallions from Pentrone, one thousand Stags from Denton, and a generous four thousand Golden Thrush from Crone. Five hundred Horned Hawks from Lennox—"

"Hawks reside at Lennox? What is this nonsense?"

"Not nonsense, King Bayard, as King Edmund has taken the throne at Lennox. King Kent no longer reigns, for he is dead."

"King Edmund, the dirty thieving scoundrel," Cane laughed. "I never knew he had the guts. Carry on."

Sintra raised an eyebrow at the humour King Bayard found at the slaughter of Kent Muucav.

"Wolves from Gabor, Snakes from Glennock, and Lions from Ironsmead. I am yet to fly to Dumbrell."

"I do not doubt King Donn and Queen Althea will give you many men, for Donn Courtendaen loves a good fight."

There was truth in Cane's words. Sintra remembered cries and cheers she heard from Donn Courtendaen on the battlefield at Crevark. The King of Dumbrell cooed on the fight between Aleron and the many slaves.

"Never takes sides, that man," said Lenore.

"Forgive me, Queen Bayard, but King Courtendaen will have to do more than take sides if he wishes to be victorious in the fields tomorrow."

"Aye, it is soon then?"

"I'm afraid it is. Too soon for my liking," replied Sintra.

"Breathe easy, Madam. I give you two thousand growling Badgers. I'd grant you more, but 'tis all I have. I lost great soldiers to that madman already, defending your kingdom on the passing of the king. Took us all by surprise he did, that Aleron."

Sintra nodded her head in thanks, though a sense of regret stirred within her stomach as she glared at the flag hung above the throne. A black and white Badger sat intertwined within a bush of thorns and roses, the Sigils for the house of Bayard at Dumbrell. The princess sighed.

"I thank you," she said, climbing atop her dragon before taking to the sky.

"Let Boar be in your favour," Cane shouted from the drawbridge.

As the princess rose into the sky, the three young princesses of Westrose stopped to gawk at the winged beast flying off into the distance. From Sintra's height, Gisela, Evelyn, and Hope looked like tiny insects as they played in the quad with the young squire boys.

If only I were that young again, she thought as she flew to Dumbrell. I'd much rather play with the squire boys than prepare for battle.

"Ah, Sintra Lysandra, we have been expecting you," said Donn Courtendaen as Sintra leapt to the ground, cringing as the sudden bend in her knees tore at the charred flesh on the back of her legs.

I must get that looked at, she thought as she approached King Courtendaen, who was accompanied by the King of Scarsgard.

"King Donn, King Lumen Karn," she greeted, nodding toward them both.

"We have been informed of a great war approaching your kingdom, Princess Sintra," said Donn.

"Please, I am Queen now."

"With all due respect, Madam Lysandra, I will address you as Queen when you have been formally crowned."

The princess nodded without quarrel, for there was truth in King Donn's words. She was no Queen; Crevark had no reign, for Aleron was no King either.

"A kingdom without reign is a kingdom soon to be lost," added Lumen Karn.

Sintra frowned, feeling as though her mind had been invaded as the King of Scarsgard unknowingly answered her thoughts. She always thought there was something strange about Lumen Karn but couldn't quite put her finger on it.

Perhaps he was just an odd type, secretive and slow. Always listening to conversation and argument instead of being involved. A sentence rarely passed his lips. Neither did a meal, it seemed, for the man was but skin and bone.

"I hope both of you can hold oath to allegiance for your kingdom sister, for I need an army. My numbers are greater but not great enough," said the princess, getting to the point. "Will you accompany me at war and fight alongside me?"

"Twenty-five hundred," said King Courtendaen. "Two thousand five hundred soldiers will come to your aid, princess. Tis all I have to offer."

"Having a passion for bloodshed, I thought you would provide me with double that," Sintra replied in disappointment.

"Aye, tis but my passion for bloodshed that my numbers wane. I hold a tournament every month, Lady Lysandra, something you would be aware of if you had bothered to attend. After all, I did attend yours."

"Forgive me, but why not have your men battle with blunted swords?"

"Sintra, it is bloodshed I desire, not underrated infant play. Besides, my men and I would come late to battle having smiths sharpen and mend all rebated and blunted weaponry. We simply do not have the time."

"Very well," she replied. "I thank you for your army. When do you ride?"

"Before nightfall."

Sintra nodded toward Donn before looking to Lumen Karn, his face expressionless as always, hardened with boredom it seemed.

"If two thousand five hundred Boars ride to your aid, two thousand five hundred Tigers ride too. You have my allegiance, Sintra."

"Thank you, King Lumen Karn," she replied, nodding to the King of Scarsgard.

"What are your numbers, Sintra?"

"Twenty-three thousand, King Donn, but I expect a few thousand more from Dunlaw and Hallem."

"Aye, you need all you can."

"We, my lord, for this war will not stop if I cannot defeat Aleron Elowen. The entire realm faces peril, King Donn."

"Perhaps I could gather every man from the village Dumbrell. Suit them in armour, provide them with weapons."

"Do what you must," replied Sintra. "I must fly back to Crevark and prepare; it is late."

"Until nightfall, princess," said King Donn Courtendaen, nodding his head toward Sintra.

She looked toward Lumen Karn for a farewell, but all he managed was a slight nod. Sintra climbed back onto her dragon and waved farewell as the creature leapt into the air, its wings carrying it high in the sky. The princess was relieved to have such a growing army, though she knew Aleron's army was greater. His numbers doubled with the Blackwing. She felt a sense of guilt overwhelm her as she didn't have the heart to tell them; though going to war meant defending their own kingdom as well as hers.

Perhaps Lumen Karn would have offered more soldiers if Donn Courtendaen had more than twenty-five hundred to offer, she thought. *If Edmund Artec hadn't taken Lennox from Kent Eagleston, I'd have double what he has given me. Perhaps King Elmore Artec and son Judah are as generous as King Burkiss Raegor of Crone and King Tien Westergard of Ironsmead, for their numbers are great,* she thought. *I need Falcon and I need Eagle.*

And as my father always said, 'Gabor can go to hell,' for five hundred men. King George Muucav is a fool if I've ever known one. *Twenty-three thousand is a great number but still not enough for the darkness that is coming.*

As these thoughts passed through Sintra's mind, her kingdom appeared on the horizon. It was early afternoon, but soon the land would be teeming with men on steeds as they journeyed to Crevark to make camp for the night.

As she flew toward Wraithveil Glade, a flash of red caught her eye. The dragon soared toward the forest, descending onto the ground in a rush of air. Urgency spreading across the princess. She dismounted her dragon with a heavy heart. The air thick with an ominous silence, broken only by the whisper of wind through the trees. She stepped towards a ruined carriage, now a skeletal remnant of its former glory, overgrown with weeds and vines. Splintered wood and tattered banners are strewn across the forest floor.

Her breath caught as she saw a royal pendant, a spiralled horned goat etched into its surface. The sigil for house Athelstan. Sintra clutched the pendant, feeling the weight of loss and betrayal.

She glanced over a small wooden bench, perfectly preserved in the centre of the carriage. Parchment and ink bottles were meticulously placed. Memories flooded back: almost three years ago, a raven had arrived, summoning her to King and Queen Artiss in Athelstan. Upon arrival with her father on horseback, she had been sent away. The prince had sent a raven, relinquishing his title and bond to the throne to pursue a life of lustful reclusion.

Brencis, are you with me?

"You do not want to see this, princess."

"Show me," she whispered in protest.

A piercing pressure enveloped her mind. Her eyes burned like fire. The forest began to circle around her as her reality drifted away. This vision differed from the others. Suddenly, she stood in the centre of Wraithveil Glade.

The air grew colder as she approached, a shiver running down her spine. The glade was bathed in a ghostly light, casting long shadows that danced menacingly among the trees. In the centre of the glade stood a dozen tall stakes, each one sharpened to a deadly point. The stakes were arranged in an ominous circle, their tips glistening with a dark, sinister sheen. Sintra's heart pounded as she realized what hung from each stake—bodies, lifeless and pale, swaying gently in the breeze. The sight was both disturbing and sorrowful, a morbid display of cruelty.

The princess walked toward the bodies. Each of their faces were a chessboard of blood and flesh, having been sliced to the point of anonymity. She could not fathom why; but a brutal task to conceal each identity, as each sigil was also removed from their clothing.

The forest seemed to hold its breath, the silence oppressive and heavy. Sintra's eyes filled with tears as she took in the scene, the weight of the tragedy pressing down on her. Each body was a testament to the brutality of the assassin, a stark reminder of the lives lost. The glade was a haunting graveyard, echoing with the silent cries of the fallen.

The vision broke, casting Sintra back to her reality. The realization hit her like a wave—he left nothing behind but took everything that mattered. Her eyes fell upon the carriages interior, where the prince's belongings lay untouched, mocking her with their stillness.

She looked up to see a wisp of black smoke, spiralling in the air just inches from the forest floor. Instinctively, she followed it. Knowing no other creature had bared such a trademark. She followed the wisp into the clearing of the trees, into Wraithveil Glade. Before her, just as Brencis had shown in the vision, stood twelve spikes. Bones hung from crimson shards of cloth, rattling in the breeze. Atop each spoke rested a skull, the sharpened timbre protruding through the skull of each body. Tears pricked her eyes, giving way to her newly hardened resolve.

"We must bury them," she whispered to herself.

Brencis. Help me. Use your magic.

"I haven't enough energy," he protested, "I'd need a host."

Princess Sintra stood in the eerie silence of Wraithveil Glade, her heart heavy with sorrow. The gruesome sight of the bodies hanging from the stakes filled her with a deep sense of loss and anger. She whispered a silent prayer for the souls lost to this brutality.

"Brencis, help me," she murmured, her voice trembling.

The ground beneath the stakes started to tremble and shift. Sintra watched in awe as the earth seemed to respond to her plea, forming neat, deep graves for each of the fallen.

Her eyes filled with tears of gratitude as she whispered, "Thank you, Brencis."

The bodies gently lowered into the freshly hollowed graves, the stakes retracting into the ground as if guided by an unseen force. Sintra's heart ached, but she felt a strange sense of peace knowing the souls would finally rest. As the last body was laid to rest, she fell to her knees, exhausted and overwhelmed. The forest stands witness to her pain, it seemed to sigh in relief, the oppressive silence lifting slightly.

She mounted her dragon once more. In the darkness of her sorrow, a flame of determination ignited, and Sintra knew she must hunt down this monstrous adversary. The air around her grew colder as she took to the sky, her dragon's wings beating a solemn rhythm. Vengeance and sorrow fuse within her heart, forging a path she is destined to follow.

War is coming

A deep, menacing growl rose from the beast's throat as Aleron neared, sword unsheathed and ready. Pale white strings of saliva dribbled from between its razor-sharp teeth, its mouth flooding with toxic seethe that gave off a putrid stench. The air was tainted with the reek of rotted carcass and burnt flesh, filling the madman's nostrils and making his stomach heave. The chains tightened on either side of the black reptilian creature, with Francis gripping firmly to its right and Gordon to its left. Blackwing continued to emerge from the cliff face; the caves beneath them held an endless stock of beasts that kept coming.

"Hold your ground," ordered Aleron.

His eyes watered as he neared the beast, its breath fumy and heated. Francis and Gordon pulled on the chains that restricted its movement, overlapping its neck, wings, and four legs. Another chain was wound tightly around its snout, with a lengthy chain on either side that each soldier grasped firmly. The men pulled the Blackwing down so that it bowed toward Aleron, a cavernous growl rolling deeper within its throat.

"Lift its head. I want its heart in my hand, not its head," demanded the madman.

Another cavernous growl emerged from the beast as its head was raised, its fiery red eyes looking into Aleron's with warning. The Blackwing bull was furious yet fearful as it eyed the hook blade Gordon had prodding deep and hard against the flesh of its throat. One swift movement could sever its jugular in an instant.

"You will be mine," whispered Aleron.

The Blackwing stirred furiously at Aleron's words, as if it understood. Gordon pushed his hook blade further into the beast's flesh, calming it instantly as the blade dug deep, drawing blood. Aleron held out his sword, admiring the beast for a moment before swinging his weapon. In one swift movement, he dug his blade into its flesh and pulled out its heart. The Blackwing dropped to the ground, its steaming black blood pouring over the stone. Lord Elowen held his prize in his hand, the heart steaming and warm. Gordon and Francis dropped the chains and turned in astonishment as every Blackwing now bowed before Aleron.

"That's what I call a reign," he boasted, a sadistic grin spreading across his face as he imagined the possibilities. The nest of Blackwing was his to command. Aleron strode toward Francis and Gordon.

"That beast was quite difficult to capture, my lord," said Gordon.

"Indeed, it was," added Francis. "We should have let you fight it by your own hand...until death."

"Until death? That thing would have slain me easily," replied Aleron. "It is the bull. It has the most power and the most will to fight."

"What will you do if that beast becomes stronger than you…in your skin?" asked Francis. "It will fight you until it has its reign back."

Aleron thought for a moment, acknowledging the truth in Francis's words. "Perhaps you could roll my head and then place my heart in the bull's body," he replied. "We all know how you would love that, Sir Gregory."

Both hosts had to be reincarnated for the legend to work, just as before. Though the truth didn't stop Aleron from stirring the hot flame of hatred already roaring inside Francis. He looked to the one man-beast he had already created. Its fiery red eyes stared back at him, twitching. Its attention was provoked by a sound or movement as it gazed off into the distance and then back to Aleron. But as Lord Elowen stood before it, glaring into its crazed soul, the creature stood still, waiting for a command.

"Right then," started Aleron. "As soon as I wake with my soul in the body of the bull…roll my head. The head of my former body, that is. And do it swiftly; a man-beast made from that is unspeakable."

"What'll we do with the body?" asked Gordon.

"Throw it over the cliff or set it alight," Aleron replied. "Ensure you exchange every soldier's heart with every beast you can. These are my only orders. Disobey them, and I will rip your heads from your bodies. You follow me at dawn as we go to war."

As the madman finished, he looked out over the citadel ruins of Thane. Thirty thousand black-scaled creatures bowed their heads toward him, their wings outstretched and resting on the stone ground—a gesture of service toward their new King. Another forty lay slain alongside the forty soldiers dead on the cold stone ground of the ruins.

"We will pick off men, young and old, along the way," said Aleron. "Exchange their hearts. My army will grow."

"The Blackwing follow you nonetheless," started Franics, "We do not need to slaughter more innocence."

"They grow more crazed with the metallic heart. The man-beasts will be perceived as man. It will be the ultimate surprise."

These were the madman's last words before he took a slender silver dagger from his belt, held it a foot from his chest, and plunged it deep into his own heart.

†

"What news, my lady? What numbers?" asked Cornelius Thatcher as the princess entered the Citadel.

"They all ride within the hour," said Sintra. "Twenty-three thousand soldiers."

"Those are great numbers."

"Twenty-eight thousand, a greater number but not enough. We will need the gods above to help us become victorious in the fields tomorrow."

"If it satisfies your optimism, Lady Lysandra, I've done some reading. If we find the ringleader and slay it…the Blackwing should flee and return to their dwelling."

"That is only if the bull is among the army, Cornelius. If Aleron has taken the Blackwing bull, that tactic is useless."

Sintra's suspicions weighed toward Aleron. She knew how he thought. A madman crazed for her head wouldn't think twice before possessing the body of a Blackwing bull, a ringleader that controls all other Blackwing, so that he becomes stronger and more capable of slaughtering her. The princess didn't doubt for a second that Aleron would try his hand at dark magic. She knew he witnessed the exchange; she knew that Lord Elowen was aware of the legend. Metallic Heart was in the wrong hands.

"I am mistaken, Cornelius," she said as the bookkeeper began to walk toward the great door of the Citadel.

Cornelius blinked rapidly; his brow furrowed.

"You're right, old friend; Aleron will use the ringleader to control all other Blackwing. It is the only way he can build a strong army."

"Yes, but they are slaves of the heart. Their strength may wane, for there was no bond upon exchange. Any man may simply speak the words, but it takes a great wizard to match the bond. Great power, great magic is needed to create the Metallic Heart, Sintra. If Aleron builds an army as you say, as Lord Edith has said, the power of the Blackwing will not be as strong, for there was no magic to bind and gild the wounds forever."

"Without the bond of magic, the man-beast and Blackwing soldiers are weak?"

"Indeed, princess. Their strength will wane unless a great magic being matches each and every bond," said Cornelius.

"And if there is no bond?"

"The Blackwing that contain the heart of man will not survive for long; they will perish, as will the man-beasts. Aleron's numbers will weaken."

"Not as much as one would hope, Cornelius. Aleron took forty men; the souls of those men now reside in their new hosts, the Blackwing."

"So, he really only made forty exchanges?"

"One hundred abominations," replied Sintra, "and thirty thousand Blackwing that follow their leader."

"That's quite a number, princess."

"Indeed, Cornelius, indeed it is. Let us hope his numbers do not grow."

That night, after Sintra feasted, Elara dressed her wounds after the wash maid helped her bathe. She retired to her bedchamber with the comfort of Nyom by her side. She felt safe and pleased in her bedchamber, like nothing had ever happened; everything was just as she had left it the night her father was slain. For a few hours, she felt young again, finding comfort as she pretended King Alaric slept peacefully in his bedchamber a floor below her. It was too harsh a memory to think of her mother beside him, or her sisters down the hall from her, or even her baby brother down the hall from her parents. Her heart ached for her family, but what was worse was the feeling of longing and loneliness that overcame her. She could never be with Riven again; she could never truly love him the way she longed to, the way it was meant to be. But Sintra couldn't escape the feeling that it wasn't meant to be at all; it hurt too much. The loss of her father, her falling kingdom, her helpless village people. Wraithveil Glade. The war. It all overwhelmed her, weighed heavily in her heart. Tears streamed down her face as she sobbed into her pillow, but exhaustion crept up on her, and she was soon asleep.

Sintra woke, the dampness of her pillow suggesting that she hadn't slept long at all, though her exhaustion had vanished. As she sat up in bed, a flicker of light caught her eye, a faint flame dancing upon her wall. She rushed to her window and stepped out onto the balcony, the cold air greeting her, biting at her flesh. It was still dark, but very early in the morning, though closer to night than day. As the princess looked out over the wall of the citadel, a line of spotted flame stretching on the dark horizon caught her immediate attention.

"They're arriving," she breathed.

Sintra dressed in haste before turning and running out her bedchamber door, Nyom not far behind. The princess strode down the cold, dimly lit hallway and down each flight of stairs until she came to the first floor of the citadel. She heard murmured chatter coming from the quad, along with the sound of metal clashing and grinding. Out into the cold air she stepped as she entered the quad, the stone ground cold beneath her feet.

"Morning, miss," greeted a strapping young man who paused his practice to bow toward the princess.

"That isn't necessary, soldier," she replied. "Morning."

The young man's opponent paused as he bowed toward Sintra as well. He was a tall, thin young man, his face darkened with stubble. They both stopped and glared at the princess as if waiting for an order. The other forty men in the quad grew silent; the grinding of the metal against stone came to a stop as the smith paused his duty. Two other men practicing on the Pell also paused to gawk at the princess. Sintra frowned toward them, raising an eyebrow as they continued to stare.

"Carry on," she said.

"Ah, I see you've met my youngest and newest soldiers," said King Burkiss Raegor as he entered the quad from a side door. The very door Sintra had used to escape to the village one night.

"Greetings, King Raegor. I trust you and your men rode with ease. I welcome you with my hospitality. There are many beds in my citadel if you require a light slumber."

"Thank you, princess, but that won't be necessary. I brought my cabin-cart and napped along the way. But your kindness and generosity please me, especially when you have lost so much. How do you stay strong?"

"With great difficulty, King Raegor. But 'tis I who should thank you for your generosity. Four thousand soldiers is quite a number."

"'Tis nothing but great allegiance, Sintra. My men took an oath when they took their swords; they will defend any kingdom brother with great honour."

"Of that I am glad, Burkiss. You have made quite an army then, possibly one of the greatest."

"I do hope so, princess. We best not be failing this kingdom's new Queen."

"Oh King Raegor, you could not fail me. I am blessed to have such great allegiance from my kingdom brothers in a time I feared I'd be so alone. You come to avenge my father, no doubt."

"Aye, your father was a good man before he was poisoned by Aleron's lies and treachery. But it is you we honour now, princess."

"And I am grateful," she replied, smiling warmly. "Please help yourself to the kitchen. Prunella will kindly cook you up a warm meal if you desire. All you men need your strength."

"Thank you, princess, and may the gods bless you."

King Burkiss Raegor passed the princess with a warm smile as she headed out the side passage of the citadel. As she stepped out into the field, she strode through the grass wet with dew, her feet as cold and stiff as ever. As she turned the corner of the citadel's edge, a small village of tents and campfires came into view. Flags displaying house Sigils flicked in the breeze. Sintra saw Bears of Redbend, Stag and Stallion of Denton and Pentrone combined in one area. She saw Snakes of Glennock and Lions of Ironsmead. Boars of Dumbrell and

Tigers of Scarsgard—Donn Courtendaen and Lumen Karn had pitched their tents close by one another. As the princess looked on, she saw Horned Hawk, Eagle, and Falcon. King Edmund sat alongside his brother King Batonn Artec by a small campfire, their armoured suits of iron and mail gleaming in the firelight. Sintra looked over her shoulder to see flags of Badger in the distance; spots of flame, torches lit as Westrose entered the field. The very same line of spotted flame she saw from her bedchamber window. She turned and strode toward the lively village of tents to welcome her army.

"Greetings, princess," said King Elmore Artec of Golorah.

"Aye, welcome to my kingdom, King Elmore. I am pleased that you and your sons answered my letter, granting generous numbers between you. I am very happy to have Eagle and Falcon fight alongside me and my dragon."

"Aye, this dragon you speak of, Sintra, where may it be?"

"Feasting on fresh fish at Lake Gwathmey as we speak," she replied, curious about King Elmore's query.

"I see. And is there truth in what I hear of your changing house Sigils, princess? From Crow to Dragon, am I mistaken?"

"Most definitely not mistaken, King Artec, for this dragon is of great importance to me and my kingdom. The

Sigils of my House will change upon victory; I will honour the dragon once we have defeated Lord Elowen. My kingdom is changing, Elmore; why not give it a new face?"

"Indeed, princess, a far stronger face than Crow…"

"A far stronger face than any other, Sintra," said Queen Rachel as she walked up behind her husband. "And why should you not take that honour? You've fought and slain the dragon already, something many of these men combined could not succeed in. But you have strength and will like no other, princess, just like your mother when she was a young warrior."

"My mother was a warrior?" asked Sintra, awestruck.

"Aye, indeed, she was. And a great one at that," added King Elmore.

"Before she was Queen, Caprice could cast one hundred arrows within thirty ticks of the clock. The bow and arrow were her weapons, for speed was to her advantage…"

"Had the eye of a hawk, your mother," added King Elmore.

"She was taught by her father's arrow smith to make her bodkins. Made them sharp, slender, and light, she did. The more slender they were, the faster they would fly, cutting through the air like a newly sharpened blade," continued Rachel.

Sintra stood in astonishment as she imagined her mother casting arrows toward the enemy. She found it hard to believe, though she never knew much about her mother despite their shared love of books. She was disappointed that her father rarely spoke of her mother, though she understood the hurt King Alaric felt when he dared think of her. But Sintra felt blessed to know that it was indeed her mother who gave her the blood of a warrior when she was born.

The princess had always wondered why she had such courage and skill, such strength and will to fight. King Alaric never fought as hard as a King should when defending his kingdom. Always lingering on the sidelines while his men were taken down by the enemy. *A coward,* she thought to herself, *no dishonourable man is worthy of the throne.* Or perhaps it was his courage and honour that wooed Caprice all those years ago.

Perhaps it was Aleron who ruined a great King by taking away his one true love. Creating a hard, impatient man who used whores excessively and found pleasure in making slaves of small children. The bitter ways of her father became all she knew as the gentle, caring man she once knew disappeared. The real King Alaric had faded into the background, into nothing as cruelty was bequeathed on him by the madman. It was a comfort to know that her mother was her own woman, not as impressionable, something that reminded her much of herself.

"Queen Caprice was a great woman and as each day has passed and will pass without her, she will forever be missed. Deeply," said Rachel.

"Thank you, Madam Rachel."

The Queen of Hallem embraced Sintra with a hug before standing back to admire the princess's beauty, despite the absence of an elegant gown. Queen Rachel gasped in horror as she looked down at Sintra's feet.

"Someone get this poor child some slippers," ordered Rachel, glaring at Sintra's frozen feet, "or leather boots…something."

One of King Elmore's men came forward with a pair of leather lace-ups, another with a bear fur coat that he handed to Rachel. Queen Artec draped the coat over the princess and seated her on one of the many logs that surrounded Hallem's fire. Rachel then proceeded to wrap Sintra's feet in woollens before placing the leather boots overtop.

"I can lace them," said the princess.

"Nonsense, let me," replied the Queen.

Queen Rachel Artec had raised six children, two of them girls, Rubella and Brittanie, so lacing leather boots that weren't on her own feet was nothing new to her.

"Queen Rachel, I want to thank you for helping me the night my father was killed. Without your help, I would have most likely been butchered myself."

"You should be thanking your bookkeeper and your maid, Sintra, but I thank you for your acknowledgement," Rachel replied. "Your mother meant a great deal to me, and so do you."

The princess nodded her head in thanks, for she didn't know what to say. She found herself excused when Queen Rachel turned to her husband's conversation with his son-in-law Marteez Uman of Glennock, King of the Snake. Sintra stood to her feet and left the campsite of Hallem. She soon found herself wandering through the village of tents, nodding toward King Lansing Bronn and Queen Fleur Rithe as she walked past their campfire.

In every direction were knights, guards, and village men in silver armour that gleamed orange in the firelight of the many campfires that also lit up the village of tents. Steeds stirred, sensing the great danger that headed for the wide-open fields they rested upon. The tree line of the great wood was three kilometres from the citadel and another five hundred metres from the campsite. Soon that wide, open, empty space would be teeming with twenty-eight thousand soldiers, some on horseback while others would march honourably to war. It was hard to think such a great number would fit comfortably on such a field, a giant beast alongside them. Thousands of black winged creatures in the sky.

"Princess Lysandra," came a familiar voice.

As the princess turned, she was greeted by Cedric, who was accompanied by several men in violet shining armour.

"Sintra, you have done well. These numbers are great, but you must speak to your kingdom brothers; you must devise a plan of attack," said Lord Edith.

"I'm not sure all have arrived, Lord Edith."

"Indeed, they have, Sintra. My men greet them in the field."

"Your men?"

"Aye, come with me," said Cedric, taking her arm and leading her back the way she came.

As Sintra walked alongside Cedric, the several men that had stood behind him broke off from their small group. The princess watched as one of them engaged in conversation with Lansing Bronn and Queen Rithe, another with Elmore Artec and Marteez Uman, as Sintra walked briskly through the village of tents. She came to the edge of the open field, her eyes widening in shock as her numbers were now greater. A large mass of knights and guards in violet armour, built tents, tended to horses, and made fires. Westrose had settled to their left.

"As you left for Redbend to seek allegiance with your kingdom brothers, I left for Sidon to do just the same. A generous ten thousand soldiers, I give to you, Sintra."

"Thirty-eight thousand," she said under her breath. "That could almost make us evenly matched."

"Almost, Sintra, although Aleron's army grows."

"Yes, Lord Edith, I am well aware. I take it you spoke with Cornelius before you left."

"Aye, indeed. He insisted on telling me before I took my leave. He then sent a raven to Sidon as I saddled the steed, informing them of my coming visit. They sailed all day long. I met them at the docks east of Golorah, ten thousand soldiers sent and gathered by the King himself."

"Great numbers, great generosity. I must meet your King and thank him."

"He would be honoured to meet you, but not today, Sintra. He stayed in Sidon to attend to other duties."

"You say they sailed, Lord Edith. But I see steeds the many."

Sintra eyed the many horses that occupied large pens, a whole fifty acres of field fenced off for horses alone.

"Aye, princess. The wind was in their favour as they crossed the black sea. As for those steeds, Sintra," said Cedric, stifling a laugh, "those belong to Donn Courtendaen of Westrose."

"I see," she replied, feeling quite embarrassed.

"My men marched with haste as I led them upon the white steed, Sintra."

"Have they rested?"

"Not yet."

"Send them by twenties to my kitchen; Prunella will fix them hearty meals."

"You mean that Prunella?" asked Cedric, pointing to a woman who strolled through the village of tents.

Both Sintra and Cedric watched as the kitchen chef took a large steaming pot from a crate and handed it to an Ironsmead Knight. She then strode to the front of the crate where a stocky mule was reined and pulled its lead. Prunella stopped at the campsite of Gabor and reached for another large steaming pot. Two Knights took the pot from her and returned to the campfire as Prunella returned to lead the mule. As Sintra looked on, she noticed two familiar faces weaving in and out of the thousands of knights and guards that stood around in chatter. As the crowds parted, the faces grew bodies, large baskets strapped to their fronts and backs. Cornelius and Elara handed a roll of bread to each man, reaching inside the baskets and pulling roll after roll. Once the baskets were empty, the bookkeeper and the maid reached into potato sacks that hung by their sides, pulling out smaller rolls of bread.

"Someone has been busying themselves in the kitchen," said Lord Edith.

"Indeed, they have," replied the princess, smiling.

As Sintra and Cedric continued to watch as Cornelius, Elara, and Prunella nourished the soldiers, a large group of supremacy approached them. The princess snapped out of her daze as her kingdom brothers and sisters came forth for council. She nodded as they stopped before her.

"Do you have a spare tent?" Sintra asked Cedric.

"Is yours not worthy of this meeting?"

"Mine?"

Lord Edith pointed to a large crimson tent that sat empty and silent to the right of the makeshift village. As she turned and made for it, she was followed by the gathering of Kings and Queens that strode casually behind her. Once inside, Sintra's breath was taken away as it felt all too familiar; she remembered being in a similar tent many years ago as King Alaric had prepared to travel to war. She had sat by her pregnant mother in front of the warmth of the fire; she was just five at the time. With the array of furs and woollens sprawled across the ground along with the cushions and furs surrounding the small fire in the centre, the dimly lit candles, the smell of burning wood, and the strong bitter scent of parchment ink, it all came flooding back to her. King Alaric had been a great, honourable man. He had made great decisions within his tent, and Sintra promised herself she would do the same. As she approached a wooden desk, upon which lay a map of her kingdom, she turned to face over a dozen expressionless Kings and Queens, waiting for her to speak.

"Greetings, Kings and Queens, brothers and sisters of my estate. I welcome you all humbly and with great honour and gratitude," she started. "Please gather closer so that I may begin."

Sintra's nerves were jumpy. She had no clue what to say or where to start. She remembered the things her father had said to his army and his allegiance, as she sat at his counsel when she was five, even then she barely understood. She looked down upon her map, fondling the small wooden carved objects, animals that represented the Sigils of each house of sovereignty. She took the wolf in her left hand, the stag in her right, and set them on the front line, on the edge of the first field on the map.

"King George, I want you and your five hundred men to form a line of defence one hundred men wide. To the right, King Lansing, you and your one thousand men do the same. Defence line one hundred men wide."

"Aye," said King George Muucav.

"Aye, Madam," said Lansing Bronn.

Sintra took the bear and falcon in one hand and set them both alongside the stag.

"King Tead, beside Bronn's army, I want you…"

Sintra continued to plot each reign over the landscape that will be their battlefield.

"What is your plan of attack?" asked King George, once all Sigils were placed in position.

"I will lead the front line; we will attack on both feet and mount. As the second line attacks, I want every bowman casting arrows into the air. Once the shower of arrows hits the enemy, every man on foot from line three will charge. Lord Edith's men will then attack from the sides as I command, and the fourth line of defence will then charge, men on foot leading. I want every single man to carry a dagger on his belt. Any men that can cast an arrow, I want two full scabbards and a bow on their backs. Those that cannot cast arrows will carry axes. Every single King, Queen, knight, guard, or villager will carry a sword and shield. I trust all your men have armour. We form lines an hour before daybreak; we attack at first light. Are there any questions?"

"There are rumours that Lord Aleron Elowen is no longer man but beast. How do we look for him if these things all appear the same?" asked Prince Theodore Artec, who had crept inside the tent unseen.

"Nice of you to join us, Prince Artec," said Sintra before continuing. "The truth in this rumour is left unquestionable...I will attack the madman, for it is my family and my kingdom that I avenge. Go now and prepare yourselves for battle. Eat. Rest. Sleep if you must. Inform your troops of the plan of attack."

Sintra turned away from the group as they began to retreat out the door of the tent. She sighed. She knew she had a better chance of becoming victorious if every arrow, sword, and axe was pointed toward Aleron, but she had to slaughter him herself. It was a need she felt deep inside. A flutter in her stomach. A sign that she should be the one to slay him and put a stop to this madness. The tent was silent within a few minutes. Sintra turned to see that Cedric Edith still remained.

"Lord Edith?"

"It will be alright, Sintra, trust me."

She wiped her face as tears had wet her skin. Her cheeks grew scarlet as she flushed before Lord Edith, embarrassed for showing weakness in a time of strength.

"Come with me," he said, holding out his hand. "I want to show you something."

The Violet Cuirass

The princess took Lord Edith's hand and followed him out of her tent, the cold air biting at her skin. She strode through the wet grass as they made their way toward the tent of Sidon, a violet tent decorated with embroidered lines of lavender. Once inside, Sintra felt calm, the warmth of the fire greeting her fondly. The scent of burning pine filled her nostrils along with something else she couldn't quite place—

a mixture of lavender, cinnamon, sandalwood, rosewood, and honey.

"I see you've succumbed to the calming essences of Sidon's tent," said Lord Edith.

"Aye, but how is it I feel so calm when a great war approaches?"

"The mixtures of aromas you smell, Sintra, are calming essences. They fill this tent with peaceful tranquillity, a serenity to calm the mind and spirit of any man that enters. A war zone would be tense without calming spirits, princess, and why stress our soldiers before their great battle commences?"

"Indeed," she whispered, too calm to raise her voice any higher.

"Sit, princess," said Cedric, seating Sintra on one of the many cushions surrounding the small fire.

He then covered two small bowls that contained burning incense, minimizing the scents within the tent as they proved too powerful and overwhelming for the princess.

"What is it that you must show me, Lord Edith?" she queried.

"Ah, yes."

Lord Edith took two black velvet sacks in either hand before making his way toward Sintra. He seated himself to her left, handing her the first black velvet sack.

"What is this?"

"Gifts from my kingdom, Sintra, open it."

"I thought you wore crimson, Lord Edith."

"Aye. We do. Sidon's sister reign sent this."

She fumbled with the soft velvet sack, caressing its delicate cloth with her fingers. She pinched one end of the sack and tipped the contents into her lap. A silver scabbard full of arrows fell into her lap. Its metallic iron shimmered violet just like the Knight's armour of Sidon. Sintra held the scabbard against the firelight of the campfire, flowing lines and floral spirals glimmering in the orange light. Each arrow within the scabbard had a newly beaten silver bodkin, thin, slender, and etched with fine delicate lines.

"They're beautiful," she beamed. "But what good is a scabbard of arrows without a bow?"

"Such haste, princess," said Cedric as he handed her a silver bow, delicate flowing lines etched into it as well.

Awestruck, the princess took an arrow from her scabbard and loaded her bow. The image of her mother came to mind as she pictured herself as a great warrior casting arrows at the enemy. She lined the arrow with one of the wooden poles of the tent, a firm grip on the fletching as she pulled against it.

"Have you ever used a bow and arrow, Sintra?"

"No," she replied bluntly, closing an eye to better her aim.

"Then I suggest you put that down before you hurt somebody. You haven't the skill or decent aim to plunge an arrow into that pole; your arrow will fly straight through the tent and most likely plunge itself deep into someone's torso."

"Every man wears armour, Lord Edith, including the Kings and Queens. It wouldn't hurt to risk—"

"A fatality?" Cedric interrupted. "Sintra, those aren't ordinary arrows; they are of stronger fibre and creation than those arrows an ordinary bowman wields."

"How so?"

"They are of similar origin to your Thalor sword."

"They are of dragon bone? Or scale?" Sintra asked as she lowered the bow and arrow.

"Both, princess. The stem of each arrow is made from the bone of dragons; the bodkin is carved and beaten from scales."

The princess unsheathed her sword and held it alongside the arrow she still held within her hand. The etchings were similar, delicate lines that glimmered in light and appeared as though they were finely carved by man. Sintra's blade shone metallic blue and silver, similar to that of the armour she had seen on Cedric's men, similar to the scabbard of arrows Cedric had just given her.

"Is the armour on your men's backs made from the same substance? Taken from dragon?"

"Indeed, it was. But my men, the men of Sidon, do not hunt dragons for their scales or bone. My kingdom holds no pilferers or poachers. Our sisters in Bristlevale farm dragons by the name of Speartongue, but they are not as beastly as the Thalor dragon, nor are they tempered like the Blackwing."

"I've heard of the Speartongue, Cedric," Sintra said, baffled. "I just never knew they existed. Cornelius always told me Bristlevale was an enchanted place, a myth."

"Bristlevale truly exists, Sintra, as does the Speartongue."

The princess knew of the sacred kingdom Bristlevale from books and fairytales. She knew the Speartongue as giant, bristled beasts that were more elegant and delicate than and malicious. They were large, thin creatures with sharp spikes of bone that protruded from the flesh that covered their chests, legs, rump, and head like pointed armour, needle-like but strong. The stomach, back, and neck were free of the spindly pointed armour, growing only flat silver and violet scales that started white from birth.

The Speartongue dragon was introduced to the kingdom by a single egg laid in Bristlevale centuries ago. From it hatched a Speartongue that possessed both female and male characteristics. As their lives grew old, each Speartongue remained male until their day of eternal rest. Within a decade, this beast laid a thousand eggs, all of which hatched in time. The first Speartongue to roam the kingdom was dubbed the leader of the beasts for it was the eldest and the wisest. He was named Briargard. The men of Bristlevale saw the beast as a threat and tried to slaughter it, but each and every woman grew into mindless savages, wiping out the male population of the kingdom. From then on, Bristlevale was run entirely by women.

The Speartongue leader rewarded the women with a lengthened lifetime that they drew from the dragon's powers, but Queen Aerona stated that this was not enough, that this did not protect them from the enemy. That was the decade the first Speartongue was sacrificed, surrendered to the Queen so that she might harvest all she could from the beast. The scales, bones, and meat were taken from a Speartongue. Every bone and scale was tailored into weaponry and armour, for their strength was unlike any steel or iron. The meat was cooked to nourish the people of Bristlevale; it doubled their muscle strength and is even believed to have strengthened bone.

The women became immensely hard to defeat in battle, their bodies and steeds covered in armour crafted from Speartongue scales, their swords and arrows from the creatures' bone. The people of the surrounding kingdoms saw it as a heinous hunting act, but Briargard saw it as a willing sacrifice made to his people to protect them, to protect the moonlit liquid of the sacred pools of Bristlevale.

On every full moon, the water within the pools of Bristlevale would turn white beneath the moonlight. The water would grow into a sacred liquid that held an essence of immense strength and nobility; a magic powerful enough to defeat the greatest wizard or to unravel the greatest and darkest of dark magic. The sacred liquid was named Hazahriah, said to be the blood of a great moon beast that lived centuries ago. Hazahriah contained a magic that would consume the mind and soul of one who chose to drink it, giving them the immense power to destroy great things, including great legends that came to pass centuries ago. This white moonlit liquid was sought after by many and was the cause of every war that broke out against Bristlevale. Queen Aerona knew Briargard was sent to her kingdom to protect the Hazahriah, but she also knew he secretly desired its taste and power.

Sintra's thoughts were interrupted as Lord Edith unveiled a violet metallic cuirass tailored for a woman. Its delicate, flowing lines curling and spiralling from base to breast. He handed the violet cuirass to the princess.

"A gift from the Queen of Bristlevale, my lady, sent with my men as they sailed across the black sea. The Queen greeted them on the back of her Speartongue before they took their leave. She has great admiration for you, Sintra, for you are the only two women in all the lands that dare ride on the back of a beast."

"A violet cuirass…like the armour your men wear," said the princess, enthralled.

"Indeed, from the very same decade Speartongue," replied Lord Edith.

"If the Queen of Bristlevale has heard of the great war of darkness, why not send an army? I've read the legends, Cedric."

"Do not detest, princess, for the people of Bristlevale have their own importance."

"To protect the Hazahriah, I am aware. But why not let Briargard protect it for just one night?"

"You do not know how long this war will last, Sintra. And Queen Aerona has her reasons for not trusting Briargard."

"Which are?"

"They aren't any concern of yours," snapped Cedric.

Sintra was taken aback, receiving a scornful smirk from Lord Edith. *Why did he have such a strong connection to Queen Aerona and Bristlevale?* she thought. Lord Edith's manner this night was inexplicable, but Sintra decided not to push her query.

"Forgive me, Lord Edith, it is none of my business. Tell Queen Aerona I thank her greatly; this cuirass just might save my life," she said softly, feeling remorseful for pushing Cedric's patience.

"That's quite alright, princess. And indeed, it will, thus why my men wear it."

"If you don't mind me asking, Cedric," she started slowly, "how did your men come by the Speartongue armour?"

"It was a gift from Queen Aerona, just like yours."

Sintra grew suspicious as to why the Queen of Bristlevale was suddenly so generous. But she dared not speak her query.

"Try on the armour, princess," suggested Cedric.

Sintra raised an eyebrow toward Lord Edith, knowing he meant to change the subject. The steel knight helped the princess with the cuirass, lifting the armour over her head and buckling it shut on either side of her torso. She then took the bow and arrow in her grasp again.

"How do I look?"

"Like a great warrior, Madam," said Cedric Edith, smiling. "'Tis a perfect fit."

"'Tis a perfect colour."

Their moment of amusement was suddenly overshadowed by cries from outside the tent. The army stirred, steeds whinnying in distress. The princess and Lord Edith rushed to their feet and strode outside. Guards ran past, swords in their hands and shields on their arms.

"Soldier, what is the meaning of this?"

"A great black beast has entered the field, my lord," said a soldier as he rushed past them.

Riven. Sintra's heart sank as she thought of her Thalor dragon. She ran after the soldiers, running past them as her feet pounded the ground as hard as she could make them, leaving Lord Edith behind. She came to the clearing, her heart racing as her eyes rested upon her dragon.

"PUT DOWN YOUR WEAPONS," she cried. "I DEMAND THAT YOU STEP AWAY FROM THAT DRAGON AT ONCE."

The guards and knights surrendered their swords and arrows, stepping away from the Thalor dragon as the princess stormed toward King George, who had ordered his men to wrap the beast in chains. King Elmore Artec entered the field with King Donn Courtendaen, King Lumen Karn by his side as usual.

"Unhand that creature or so help me, King George, I will have your head," demanded Sintra, her temper rising as she approached him from across the field.

"It is a black beast, is it not? A beast that comes for your kingdom. Is this not what you wanted, princess?"

"George Muucav do not take me for a fool. That is not the beast we fight, that is not the enemy."

"It appears to me to be the enemy," King George replied.

"Unhand that creature before I take your head myself," growled Sintra.

She glared into George Muucav's eyes; her temper as mad as a raging bull. King George glared back, his face stern. Sintra looked to his guards and knights who had the beast in chains.

"Unhand that poor creature before I take all of your heads," she growled under her breath.

The guards and knights followed her order, dropping the chains immediately and stepping off the field. King George looked over to King Marteez Uman and King Lansing Bronn. Queen Rithe, King Cane, and King Tien were not far behind. Crevark's kingdom brothers and sisters stood by Sintra, glaring at King George, who now appeared to have made a fool of himself.

"Listen to Sintra," said King Elmore. "For that beast is not our enemy."

"That dragon is on our side, you moron," snapped Lansing Bronn.

But King George did not budge.

"Do you want a war of your own, King George?" asked Queen Fleur Rithe.

"I should have declared war against Crevark long ago," started George. "Though it seems Aleron Elowen did as I have dreamed for a decade."

"Take over Crevark? Kill innocent women and children? Make guards and knights of slaves?" queried Queen Rithe.

"Nay, you blasted idiot. Slaughter King Alaric Lysandra…"

The small crowd fell silent for a moment.

"Come now, you're making a fool of yourself," said King Lumen Karn.

Sintra was shocked to hear the man speak, let alone coax George away from the dragon. But King Muucav was stubborn and didn't move an inch.

"You are the fools," shouted George. "Not I. The man took my only true love, Caprice. She was to wed me, but the gods only know how she fell for that fool."

"My mother would never have wed such a traitor like you, George Muucav. Pack up your tents and leave at once. Take your five hundred men with you. You are a disgrace to your own kingdom," said Sintra.

"'Tis the truth, King George, you've betrayed us all," said King Elmore.

"You won't have my Faye, the wedding is off," barked King Tien before he turned and stormed away.

"You won't have my Gisela or Evelyn, neither" added King Cane, he too leaving the field in anger.

As Gabor's lifelong alliance with Westrose and Ironsmead fell, rage grew within King George. His blood boiled.

"I suggest you sheath your sword and walk away from this, King Muucav," said Lord Edith, who now stood to Sintra's left.

"You betrayed our trust; you dishonoured your oath. You must leave now or surrender to the consequences of treason," said King Elmore, stepping forward to stand beside Sintra.

"I am not going anywhere," spat King George, turning toward the dragon with his falchion. "But I will succeed in what I came forth to do."

"Riven, fly, fly now!" ordered Sintra.

The dragon lifted its head and looked toward the princess and then back to King George, who now raised his sword. The dragon did not move. Sintra's grip tightened on the bow and arrow that she still clutched in her hands. Before she knew it, she had lined the silver Speartongue arrow in the bow and aimed for King George's back. Sintra pulled on the fletching of the arrow before letting it slip between her fingers.

"Sintra, no!" said Cedric, but it was too late.

The metallic violet arrow plunged deep into George's back. He turned toward the princess, a hurt expression across his face along with anguish. Blood splattered from his mouth as he gasped, looking down to see a silver bodkin protruding from his chest plate armour. King George raised his head to look at the princess.

"Do you wish to plead guilty for your treason?" asked Sintra.

Strings of bright red saliva dribbled from his mouth as he growled in detest. Using all his energy, he took a dagger from his belt and threw it at the princess with such force. The blade hit the centre of the violet cuirass that the princess still wore and fell to the ground. Simultaneously, another arrow plunged deep into King George's chest, this time from Queen Rithe, who had a bow and scabbard of arrows of her own. George fell dead to the ground. The Wolf King of Gabor was no more.

"Treason is only punishable by death," said Sintra as she turned toward the growing crowd behind her. "All of you return to your camps."

"You did as any other would have done, princess," said King Courtendaen. "If you hadn't, I would have."

"If he had fled when he was ordered, war would have hunted him down anyway," said Queen Rithe.

"That cuirass you wear, princess, is some armour," said King Elmore, eyeing Cedric suspiciously.

"Nonsense," said Lumen Karn. "Luck was on her side; it was the hilt of the dagger that hit the cuirass. And no doubt…dinted it."

"Come…see for yourself, Lumen Karn," said Lord Edith. "For it is a violet cuirass, armour made from the scales of the great Speartongue beasts of Bristlevale."

"Dragon scale?" gasped Fleur Rithe.

"Aye, the very same. This armour was sent to the princess for her own protection."

"Sent by whom, Steel Knight?"

"Queen Aerona of Bristlevale."

King Lumen Karn raised his eyebrows in disbelief, and Queen Fleur Rithe gasped, for they had only heard of Bristlevale in myth.

"If this is true…no weapon is able to pierce that armour," said Lumen Karn, raising his dagger.

"Aye, but 'tis true. No weapon, not even a blade carved from the tooth of the very same beast, can puncture that armour," replied Cedric.

Lumen Karn approached Sintra with his dagger, hesitating as he took slow steps toward her. Donn Courtendaen tried to pull him back, fear in his eyes for he thought the King of Scarsgard had gone mad.

"'Tis alright," Lord Edith reassured Donn. "It will not puncture the cuirass."

"I do not wish you harm, princess, for I am no traitor. If this should wound you, take my head on a stake if you must," said Lumen Karn as he stood before the princess.

Sintra's heart pounded inside her ears; she had never been more frightened in her life. As Lumen Karn raised the dagger, the princess braced herself, closing her eyes and holding her breath. The King of Scarsgard hesitated before pounding the violet cuirass with the tip of his blade. The armour did not dint, buckle, or scratch. He tried again with a little more force, but the blade bounced right off the armour, no pierce whatsoever. Sintra opened her eyes and sighed, for she was not dead. No harm had come to her at all.

"Impossible," he gasped.

"Possible, King Lumen, for my eyes do not fail me...that blade did not leave a scratch."

"The weapon did not leave a scratch or a dint," said Fleur. "You're very lucky, princess. I had a great feeling that you will not die in the field on the morrow."

"At sunrise, Queen Rithe, for 'tis near."

"Yes," said Sintra. "Best prepare."

With that, the princess glanced at King George's dead body once more before she strode through the crowd and made for her tent. Once inside, she took the small wooden carved wolf from her desk and threw it into the fire with such force, with such anger and hatred. Despite the incredible discovery made of the violet cuirass, anger still dwelled within the princess. She valued her new piece of armour greatly, for without it she would have taken a dagger to the heart.

"Why didn't I see this coming?" she asked as Lord Edith and King Elmore entered her tent.

"You weren't to know, princess. No one knew of his duplicity," said Cedric.

"You have done me proud, Sintra. You make a fine warrior…just like your mother," said Elmore.

"What are we to do with the body, my lady?" asked a soldier as he poked his head inside the tent.

"Burn it!" said Sintra bluntly.

"Strip it of all armour and weapons and donate them to those that lack," said Cedric, ushering the soldier away from the tent.

"It could have well gotten out of hand. What if King George turned on me during battle?"

"That is not possible now, for he is dead," replied King Elmore. "And if he had, you have many soldiers to protect you."

"Yes, of that I am grateful. I must write to Gabor."

Sintra gathered a piece of parchment, a quill, and a small inkwell. She then sat at her wooden bench.

"Send for a raven; I need a parchment bird at once," said the princess.

"As you wish, Sintra, but first…what shall you do with King George's five hundred? They wait for your orders."

"See if any of them will speak treason, behead those that do. Send the others to your son; I know King Edmund Artec lacks in numbers."

King Elmore nodded once before leaving the tent. Sintra proceeded to write to Gabor.

Queen Kaylah Muucav of Gabor,

It is my solemn duty to inform you of your husband's death, for King George Muucav of Gabor attempted an act of treason against my kingdom, Crevark. As princess and rightful heir to the throne, I am soon to be crowned Queen; therefore, it is my duty to punish those that plot against me. As you know, treason is not taken lightly, thus he was punished by death. I have no regrets as I burn King George's body to ash, as no traitor deserves proper burial. I must also inform you that your lifelong alliances with Westrose and Ironsmead no longer stand, as King Cane and King Tien will not give their daughters' hands to a traitor's offspring. My deepest apologies.

Princess Sintra Lysandra of Crevark

"It is a harsh truth," Sintra said to Cedric as he read the letter before tying it to the raven.

"It is not your concern of Queen Muucav's feelings, Sintra. Her husband attempted treason; thus, King George is no more. You did what you had to do in order to protect your kingdom. It is done."

"I am aware, Cedric Edith, and I am grateful to have such great allegiance with my kingdom brothers and sisters. Truly grateful."

"Splendid. Now you really should rest. You need sufficient energy."

"I've rested enough, Lord Edith. Perhaps you could help me practice?"

"Practice?"

"My swordsmanship skills," she replied, "and perhaps my archery skills?"

"Ah, princess…I doubt you need the practice. You possess great strength and fighting skills. My own eyes saw you slay the dragon, and as for King George…a close target, but you plunged the arrow through his heart, Sintra."

"My arrow missed the traitor's heart; it was Queen Rithe's arrow that ended him. I would much like to improve my skills all the same, Lord Edith."

"Very well."

Sintra followed Lord Edith out of the tent and into the cold air of the morning. The horizon in the far distance was growing dim as the sun was only three hours from rise. As the princess followed the steel knight, the scrape and clash of metal on metal sounded from a field where several soldiers practiced on Pell and against each other. Swords clashed with armour and shield. Lord Edith handed the violet scabbard of arrows to the princess, her grip tightened on the bow she still clutched in her hand. Sitting fifty metres from where they stood was an archery target; red rings had been painted on a wooden target board. Sintra wondered why her father never taught her to cast an arrow, though he was always teaching Soren things from a very young age. *Most likely a man's thing,* she thought to herself, *but if my mother can be just as good as man, if not greater, then so can I.*

Sintra lined a single Speartongue arrow into her bow and aimed for the target. Cedric lifted her arms and straightened her back, improving her posture and stance.

"When you're ready, princess," he whispered.

The soldiers paused from their activity to watch the princess. Sintra closed one eye, aimed the bodkin of the arrow to the centre ring, and pulled on the fletching. As she released her arrow, it plunged deep within the centre of the wooden target.

"A direct hit!" cheered Cedric.

Lord Edith left her side to retrieve the arrow as Sintra loaded her bow once again. Just as before, she aimed for the centre of the target, pulling on the fletching and releasing the arrow. It shot from the bow, vibrating the bowstring as the fringe of the fletching brushed past it. Again, the arrow plunged into the target, travelling further into the deep hole that Sintra's first arrow had made in the wood.

"Another direct hit," said Cedric. "Sintra, I'm impressed."

"Distance the target further from me, Lord Edith," said Sintra, loading two arrows into her bow.

With the help of two soldiers, Lord Edith moved the wooden target another fifteen metres from the princess. As the three men moved from her firing range, Sintra set the arrows against her bowstring, one atop the other, and pulled back the fletching. The arrows shot from the bow and flew through the air toward the target, both bodkins cutting into the wooden target, plunging deeper than before.

"Remove the arrows, Lord Edith, and distance the target another fifteen metres."

Lord Edith did as he was ordered, moving the target so that it now sat one hundred metres from the princess. More soldiers in the field paused their practice to watch as the princess lined three arrows into her bow, one atop the other. Sintra pulled on the fletchings and released the three arrows, sending them through the air at such speed. A quick thud-thud-thud sounded as the three arrows hit the target in a quarter of a second of each other, plunging into the same hole the princess had aimed for from the beginning.

"Remove the arrows, Steel Knight of Sidon, and distance the target another one hundred metres," said Sintra.

Again, Cedric did as he was ordered. The princess closed an eye and aimed a single arrow at the target once more. She took a deep breath, and as she released it, the arrow shot from her bow and travelled through the air. The single thud was awaited by the princess, Lord Edith, and the many soldiers that stopped to watch, but there was no thud, for the arrow travelled right through the wooden target. The many arrows the princess had already cast at the target had weakened the wood. The arrow was lost beyond the target and beyond the field in which they stood.

"Your accuracy astounds me, princess; you've never shot an arrow before this day."

"Aye, Cedric Edith, but it is her mother's blood that runs through her veins," said Queen Rachel Artec as she approached them.

"Pardon?"

"Do not tell me you know nothing of Caprice Lysandra," said the Queen, taken aback. "She was once a great princess warrior. Princess Sintra possesses the same agility, aim, and strength as her mother did. It is no marvel the princess casts an arrow well, Cedric Edith."

"Ah, yes. That explains why the princess needs not practice her archery. Perhaps 'tis the same with a sword," said Lord Edith, taking the bow and arrow from the princess.

Sintra drew her Thalor sword as Lord Edith drew his. They both stood for a moment, armed and ready before Cedric led with his right foot and swung his sword. The iron blade clashed with the princess's again and again. Sintra lurched toward the steel knight; her sword collided with his. Cedric swung his sword hard and fast, the sound of metal on metal filling the field. Clashing and scraping.

"My, my, Sintra, you're better than I had hoped," said Cedric, trying to catch his breath.

"I have surprised myself, Lord Edith."

"You will do very well in battle, princess…I think you are ready," he finished.

The Steel Knight surrendered his sword and stepped away from Sintra. Cedric bowed his head once toward her and sheathed his sword.

"Aye, quite ready indeed."

Victory and Sacrifice

The Blackwing bull roared to life, twitching its head back and forth between Francis and Gordon, strings of saliva dripping from its mouth. An odour of rotting carcass and burnt flesh hung on the air, but the beast's red fiery eyes were drawn to something else—a newly born man-beast that stirred and slowly climbed to its feet. A deep growl escaped the man's throat as it turned toward Francis and Gordon. It shrieked loudly as sharp talon claws sprouted from its fingers. The sound of crumbling iron was heard as the man-beast tried to sprout wings, its body distorted and twisted beneath, restricted by the iron armour. Its breathing grew hoarse as anger and fear rose within. Gordon took a step toward the man he once followed as a leader. Looking into its eyes and deep into its soul, he saw that the man was gone from this body, all that was left was a shell. A host for a parasite to take over.

Sir Leoss raised his falchion above his head, the beast glaring at him inquisitively. The large heavy falchion came down on top of the man-beast's head, severing it in two as the blade travelled from its head to its torso, splitting it down the centre. Gordon swung the sword again, this time horizontally, severing the separated pieces of its head. Lord Aleron Elowen's distorted beast-like face fell to the ground, as did his misshapen body. The erroneous King Aleron Elowen of Crevark was no more, for what was reborn was far worse.

A dark, cold creature thirsty for the flesh and blood of the princess. A reptilian beast that grew scales over its body, thick and impenetrable, black as raven's wings. Two large sharp pointed horns protruded from each side of its skull, similar to those that lined its back and tail. Its scaled lips pulled back as it gave a snarl, presenting two rows of large razor-sharp teeth. A fang protruded on either side of its mouth. The Blackwing bull was much the same as any other, though larger, stronger, and more muscularly defined. It rose to its feet like a man as it turned to glance at the one hundred newly born Blackwing and man-beasts that stirred to life. Each man-beast grew confused and anxious inside their new bodies, growing sharp talon claws, razor-sharp teeth, and red fiery eyes. Their actions mimicked those of the first newborn, becoming frustrated as they realized they could no longer fly, for they could not sprout wings.

As the Blackwing bull now contained the heart of the madman Aleron Elowen, he was saluted as the new Blackwing King. He looked out over the citadel ruins of Thane. Thirty-one thousand dark, sadistic creatures bowed their bodies toward him, Blackwing wings outstretched and resting on the stone ground. The only two true humans among them were soldiers Francis and Gordon, who were without a doubt scared stiff and mindless.

The Blackwing bulled barked into the air, but the two men remained unmoving, unsure of what to do. The creature met their line of site, another barking growl escaping its throat.

Suddenly Francis stood rigid, his breath shallow as the Blackwing dragon's gaze bore into him. The creature's eyes, red and fathomless, seemed to pierce through his very soul. Francis felt an overwhelming force grip his mind, a cold, rigid presence that began to consume him from the inside.

Gordon watched in horror as Francis's eyes turned black, the whites vanishing completely. His face twisted in agony, but his body remained eerily still, as if held by invisible chains. The air around him crackled with dark energy, the presence of the Blackwing bull intensifying. When Francis finally spoke, his voice was no longer his own. It echoed with a deep, otherworldly timbre, resonating with the malevolent power of the bull.

"Much better," the voice boomed, sending shivers down Gordon's spine.

He wanted to flee. His hook blade trembling in his hands. But fear held his feet to the stone pave. The ruins seemed to darken around them, shadows lengthening as its influence spread like wildfire.

Francis's body moved with unnatural grace, his movements fluid and predatory. He raised a hand, and the ground beneath him trembled, responding to the Blackwing command. Gordon could only watch in helpless terror as Francis, now a puppet of the Blackwing dragon, advanced towards him, his eyes burning with a sinister light. Black and demonic, his soul lost to the creatures dark will. He was no longer human; but a vessel.

The bull barked to the colony of Blackwing and man-beast, every one of them raising their heads as they looked to their leader. The flock growled and hissed as Francis' tongue began to translate.

"For too long I have sat in squalor, slept on the ground, and begged for scraps. My family despised me; they hated all I was and all I gave them. I sought opportunity and was rewarded with greater things. It occurred to me then that I, Aleron Elowen, could do great things. I found noble blood within myself and became a gallant knight. The Knight of Knights, I was.

"I found myself a Queen, but the whore betrayed me, and now I must take what was granted to me. I must take what is rightfully mine. My kingdom, Crevark. But why stop there? I will rise, and you will rise with me. We shall raid every monarchy until no other reign exists but mine. We will rise until all bow to us. We will fly…and march into battle. We will fight them. We will destroy them. Crevark will be mine."

†

The air grew stiff and eerie as the princess' army stood silent and waiting. Three hundred acres held over thirty-eight thousand soldiers. Steeds stirred, digging at the ground with their hooves as they sensed the dangers approaching. The wind picked up, rustling the leaves and branches of the trees in the great wood. Carried through the trees and onto the fields was the overpowering stench of rot. An odd wave of heat greeted each and every man as it coursed through the field. A horse whinnied and reared.

"Hold your ground," demanded the princess who stood on the front line.

Sintra was just metres from the edge of the great wood as she felt thousands of eyes upon her. A glacial tremor ran up her spine as she felt the enemy approach. The wood had never seemed so dark and gloomy as she peered through the trees. Emptiness stirred inside her as every animal, bird, and insect had fled the great wood. She felt a flutter in her stomach. The enemy was coming fast.

Where is my dragon? I need my dragon, she thought to herself, summoning him. *He must have fled after that ordeal regarding my kingdom's newest traitor, that or he hunts for food again.* She turned her steed to face her army, progressing into a light canter as she made her way along the front line.

"Stand straight and stand tall," she yelled. "Find your courage and find your strength. Raise your spears and swords. Raise your axes and load your bows. If we do not become victorious in this field today, Aleron will come for your families. He will not stop until every reign is in his power. He will not stop until all of us are dead. He will take your children as slaves. He will have their heads if they protest or feed them to the warg of the Infinite Forest as their insides are expelled. We fight here today, and we fight to the death."

Whispers from the front line were carried throughout the army as the message made its way to the end line. Every man stiffened and retightened their grips on their weapons as the princess's words were heard by all. Sintra turned toward the great wood as she stood in the front line once again. The silence of the great wood was replaced with the rustling of leaves and twigs as the enemy drew close. A darkness filled the sky as thousands of Blackwing flew overhead, entering the field from above. Man-beasts emerged from the wood's edge, crouching and distorted, growling and barking. Soul stamped his feet, eager to charge.

"NO PRISONERS!" cried Sintra, raising her sword. Her cry echoed by the army that followed her to war.

As the princess charged with the front line, soldiers by her side, a shower of arrows sprayed the man-beasts. Some fell wounded, left to be trampled by the charging steeds and soldiers that flocked into the wood. Sintra swung her sword, the oscillating blade severing head after head as she made her way through the mass of abominations. They were filth, bloodthirsty and raging. They swung axes and held spears, yet none of them had the intelligence to cast an arrow. Of that, Sintra was grateful as she cantered toward one, closing in on the distance between them. The man-beast's eyes were fiery red; its mouth leaked saliva for it was hungry for blood.

Every abomination was ravenous for some kind of morsel of food; even the dead bloodied remains of their own kind seemed apt. *Cannibals.* The man-beast before her lunged its axe into the air. Its blade hit the princess's violet cuirass and fell to the ground, leaving no mark or scratch whatsoever. Sintra loaded her bow with a single arrow. Pulling on the fletching, she released her grip and plunged the arrow deep within its brain. It fell dead to the ground.

A Blackwing charged her, its wings spreadeagle, lifting the horse into the air and knocking the princess to the ground. Sintra climbed to her feet, swinging her sword as she turned. The Blackwing that knocked her to the ground grew ravenous as it started to rip into the flesh of the white steed.

Soul, she whimpered within her mind.

Sheathing her sword, the princess loaded two arrows into her bow and pulled on the fletching. Just as she had practiced, she plunged the arrows into the heart of the Blackwing. The beast paused, giving Sintra the perfect chance to draw her sword and roll its head. Men were down all around her, a single man-beast drinking the blood of one of her soldiers.

"Drink my blood, you filth," she growled, casting an arrow into the centre of the man-beast's brain.

Sintra ran from the wood and onto the fields, her heart racing as she saw more of her dead soldiers. A shower of arrows was cast into the air by the Knights of Sidon, their silver and violet Speartongue arrows dropping them like flies. Three soldiers swarmed a beast as it squirmed on the ground, having fallen from the sky. The three of them plunged their swords into the beast, one of them taking the creature's head. Soldiers from Gabor and Scarsgard cast their arrows into the air, but their arrows bounced off the flying beasts.

"Take cover!" one of them cried.

Shields were lifted above their heads as the arrows turned and fell from the sky. Arrows plunged into Sintra's shield as she held it above her head. Running toward the citadel, she saw the Blackwing bull descend from the air and into the quad. The sky was dark with black beasts, swooping to the ground as they picked up horses and soldiers, throwing them across the field. Sintra watched in horror as one Blackwing sprayed its toxic seethe over a group of Ironsmead soldiers. They screamed in agony as the seethe melted their armour, consuming their flesh, blood, and bone until each man dropped dead to the ground. The princess watched as the beast proceeded to rip the burnt, melting flesh off one of the soldiers.

The Thalor dragon loomed in from the distance, swooping toward the Blackwing with its body upright as its long sharp talons dug into the beast. The dragon soared high into the sky before throwing the Blackwing into three other ravenous beasts that crept their way toward Sintra.

The princess watched in awe as her dragon lifted two Blackwing within both of its giant clawed hands, throwing them hard against the ground. It hunted down a Blackwing that tried to flee; a beast was untouched by Aleron, its own heart still beating within its chest. The Thalor dragon clutched the creature, crushing it within its grasp. Its giant mouth engulfed the Blackwing's head before ripping it from its body and tossing it into the air. The dragon hunted another black-winged creature, stalking it like a lion as it pounced and took the beast in its mouth, its razor-sharp teeth clamping down hard. Black blood dripped and oozed from the monster's limp body. Sintra's dragon threw it away and hunted another that flew toward the citadel.

The princess's heart almost came to an abrupt halt as she watched a mass of Blackwing swarm King Donn Courtendaen and ten of his men. His soldiers cast arrows, but the iron bodkins did not penetrate the beasts' flesh. The princess loaded her bow and cast an arrow toward one Blackwing that approached the group of soldiers. The arrow travelled deep into the beast's brain, dropping it to the ground instantly. Sintra cast arrow after arrow, killing three more Blackwing that closed in on King Donn, but she wasn't quick enough with the fourth arrow as her scabbard was now empty.

A pure Blackwing swooped King Donn and his men, spraying them with its toxic flesh-melting seethe. As the men screamed in anguish, their armour crumbled, their flesh melted. Splintered blackened bones lay across the field, sprinkled like breadcrumbs. Sintra couldn't help but be reminded of an almost identical scene in the village of Thane.

She looked to her dragon, absorbing its behaviour. It didn't scatter charred bones. When it ate, it ate its prey whole. A profound realisation made her head spin.

It wasn't Thalor.

Raging with a newfound ferocity, the princess ran after a Blackwing, leaping at its legs before it could fly higher off the ground. Her weight was not enough to bring the creature down. It swung its legs and threw the princess to the ground, but it did not wound her. She rose to her feet as the beast turned and swooped for her. Sintra drew her Thalor sword and readied herself for the dragon. It screeched and hissed as it came for her, opening its mouth as it prepared to spray more toxic seethe. Sintra's dragon roared like thunder, turning in the air as it began to swoop the beast that now hunted the princess.

Sintra prepared herself with her arms outstretched, but she soon turned and ducked as a giant scorching fireball was cast toward her, engulfing the Blackwing in flame. As the princess crouched on the ground, she felt warmth against her back, though the violet cuirass stopped the fire from burning her flesh. She patted her singed hair, but as she turned and stood, she soon leapt to the ground as six Blackwing swooped her, flying after the dragon. Sintra rolled onto her back and sat up as she watched the Thalor dragon turn in flight. He breathed fire over every creature within reach. Beasts fell to the ground, engulfed by flame that grew worse as the air fed it oxygen.

"Run," said a familiar voice as if right beside her. Brencis was close.

Sintra made for the citadel, swinging her sword and leaping over dead bodies as she ran. She plunged her blade deep into man-beasts. Her oscillating blade severing heads from their bodies. She paused as a Blackwing stood fifty metres before her; its wings outstretched as it prepared to swoop. Before the beast could get off the ground, she cast her sword toward it. The blade plunged deep into the creature's heart, killing it instantly. Another Blackwing came up behind as the first dropped to the ground. She loaded her bow and cast three arrows toward it. One plunged deep into its brain, the other two cut into its heart. The princess's dragon shrieked for her as it turned in the sky, its wings outspread.

Sintra! She heard in her mind.

Sintra ran toward the Blackwing, pulled her sword free, and sheathed it. She pulled her three arrows from the black beast, wiped the blood against her leather trousers, and put them back in her scabbard.

Two metres from where she stood, she saw another dead beast with at least four silver, violet arrows plunged deep into its chest. She proceeded to take those too as her dragon screeched once more, looming toward her with haste. She clutched her bow with both hands and raised her arms above her head as the Thalor dragon swooped toward her, grasping the bow with its sharp claws and raising her off the ground.

Blackwing swarmed her as she hung beneath her dragon. She held on tight, kicking her legs as the beasts snapped at her. The princess looked above as four large black creatures now clung to her dragon, snapping and hissing. Tearing at its flesh.

Sintra looked down toward the war zone where at least twenty thousand soldiers lay dead or wounded. The only mass somewhat unscathed was Cedric's men. But where was

Cedric? The princess watched as a Blackwing hunted Queen Fleur Rithe. Sintra gasped in horror as the beast took Fleur's head in its mouth and tore it from her body. Lansing Bronn charged the beast, slicing open its chest with his sword, its heart and gizzard spilling from its body. King Bronn swung his sword furiously, beheading three more Blackwing before another charged him, knocking the sword from his grip. He fumbled at his bow, but each arrow bounced off the thick scales of the beast as he cast them. The princess cried out to King Lansing Bronn, but he could not hear her. Two Blackwing swarmed in on him, taking his life as they ripped him limb from limb, his iron armour tearing like parchment beneath their talons.

"I have to end this," Sintra cried to her dragon. "Take me to the leader."

Sintra's dragon hovered over the quad, still fifteen feet from the ground. The princess let go of the bow and fell through the air, landing on the straw roof of the stables. Her dragon dropped her bow into the quad with a loud clatter as it flew away, fighting off more Blackwing that swarmed him.

She rolled off the straw roof of the stable and landed on the ground. A loud thumping filled the quad along with an echoing thunder-like grumble. Her heart pounded inside her ears as she stepped out into the quad. There it was. The Blackwing bull pounded on the entrance to the citadel, scratching at the wooden door with its sharp talons, twitching its tail from side to side as anger stirred deep within its core. To Sintra's shock, the beast had a rider. One of which she never thought would turn on her.

"You really think I would cower away while I let my kingdom brother and sister fight for me?" asked Sintra.

The beast turned fast. A deep growl vibrated its jaw and teeth, its fiery red eyes twitchy.

"Sintra, the Whore Queen," spoke Francis.

"Francis Gregory, I never thought I'd see the day…"

As the princess glared into Francis' black, demonic eyes, she felt empty. She thought of his loving wife, and his three young daughters. Her heart sank.

"I am Aleron Elowen. Blackwing King of Crevark, and all the land the light touches."

"You are the scourge of Crevark!" she spat.

"Give up the throne, Sintra. Your kingdom is falling around you. Soon there will be nothing left of your pitiful reign," hissed Francis. "Not even you."

"I will fight for Crevark as long as I live," she growled. "You'll have to pry my reign from my cold, dead hands."

"Just like your father?" he laughed, "You make this too easy for me. In fact, your entire family made it too simple a feat."

Francis climbed off the black creature and proceeded to take a few slow steps toward her. Black, empty eyes bore into hers. He titled his head mechanically from side to side, sniffing the air around her. A dark, menacing laugh escaped his throat.

"Soren was the easiest," he started, "All I had to do was snare a poor defenceless rabbit and wait for the gentle soul to arrive."

"Don't you dare talk about my baby brother," Sintra's words came deathly quiet, she was too enraged for tears to prick at her eyes.

"He asked for you. He pleaded for his life. He didn't understand why you wouldn't come for him."

Francis continued to torment Sintra. His words painting a picture within her mind that sent bile straight to her mouth. It took every ounce of energy to push it back down. Her lips parted.

"I'm so sorry Francis," she whispered.

As the 'S' rolled off of her tongue she had nocked and flew an arrow straight through Francis' skull. His eyes rolled into the back of his head, the whites appearing briefly before his eyelids closed. His body falling to the stone floor in a lifeless heap. The Blackwing bull let out a core shattering shriek that vibrated through Sintra's chest. As it lunged for her, a figure emerged from the shadows.

"No harm will come to this lady," said Cornelius, appearing from the shadows with a sword of his own.

The old man approached the Blackwing, his body tense and shaking as the beast frightened him, growling and hissing.

"Cornelius, no!" ordered the princess.

"I see, I should have killed you when I had the chance," laughed Aleron inside Sintra's mind.

Why can I still hear you? The princess queried.

Cornelius neared the black creature and swung his sword, but the blade missed. A deep growl rolled from the bull's throat. Standing upright, it knocked Sintra to the ground in a deliberate forward lunge, splitting the old man's stomach open in one swift movement. Cornelius's gizzard spilled from his body, steaming blood spurting and spluttering from his mouth as he fell to his knees.

"Cornelius!" screamed Sintra.

She rushed toward the old man but was knocked to the ground by the beast again. As she lay on her back against the hard cold ground, she watched as Cornelius's life slipped away from him as he bled out in the centre of the quad. The Blackwing bull approached the princess. It ripped its large sharp talon claws along the front of her chest, but the violet cuirass was not pierced. The beast roared in anger, slamming its foot down on the princess's torso. The wind was knocked from her lungs, but the cuirass did not crumble.

"Your plan is not as you hoped, Aleron," she spat.

She took her sword from her side and sunk it deep into the flesh of the beast's armpit. The Blackwing roared in distress as it lifted its leg. As Sintra climbed to her feet, the beast cut the flesh on her arm as it struck her again, its claws piercing the iron armour. The princess cried in pain as blood dribbled down her arm. While the bull went for her again, three arrows were plunged into its back.

"Step away from her," demanded Lord Edith, loading another arrow into his bow as he stood metres behind the beast.

The Blackwing turned, grabbing and swiping at the arrows in its back. Cedric plunged another arrow into its lower leg as it charged him. The Steel Knight loaded his bow again but did not move quickly enough. The bull backhanded Cedric with such force he was sent through the air. He crashed into the stables, breaking the beams as his back hit them. He lay motionless and silent as the straw roofing of the stable caved in, burying him alive.

Sintra scuffled backward, wincing as she leaned on her wounded arm, as the Blackwing beast came for her again. Out of nowhere, Brencis appeared behind the bull, drawing a white bone sword and a wooden staff. The being clashed the two together, sending white lightning-like waves toward the bull. The creature wailed as its body tensed, the waves of white light charging through its body. Sintra watched nervously as the white light vanished. The beast turned toward Brencis, charging for it, but as the Blackwing raised his arm to strike it, he disappeared.

Roaring in frustration, the beast turned around again and again. Brencis reappeared behind it, sinking the white bone blade into its back. The bull shrieked in distress; its cry so ear-splitting that Sintra covered her ears. The Blackwing turned, its tail knocking the hooded being to the ground. A low rumble came from the beast's throat, its mouth flooded with white stringy saliva before spraying Brencis, but he disappeared once again.

The seethe ate away at the leathery cloak until it disintegrated into nothing. A wisp of black smoke whirled behind the Blackwing as Brencis appeared, without his cloak. Staff and white bone blade in his grasp, the green-scaled beast cast another beam of white lightning toward the bull. It retreated backward as Brencis blinded it, its body tense as charges of light coursed through it. Sintra glared at the glow. White lightning beams travelled directly from the staff and sword to the sun that sat highest in the sky.

As the Blackwing was stunned and stiff. Appearing out of thin air, the Thalor dragon swooped into the quad, clutching the Blacking in its grasp and soaring high into the sky. Sintra watched as the black creature snapped at the dragon's legs, but the mightier beast took a wing in it's mouth and tore it clean from the bull's body. The Blackwing screeched in protest and panic, thrashing its head and tail about in attempt to free itself. The dragon dropped the black wing from its mouth and proceeded to effortlessly tear off the other. Sintra watched from the ground, her eyes a silent query as she questioned the true soul of the dragon.

Thalor or Riven?

The dragon fly higher into the air before turning to soar back to the earth, gravity fuelling its speed. The Blackwing crashed into the quad, crumbling the stone pave as the dragon cast the creature from its talons.

Sintra seized the moment and climbed to her feet. Red blood dripped down her arm, her wound throbbing as it gaped open. With great effort, she loaded her bow and lifted her arm out straight as she lined the first arrow with the beast. Blood dripped to the ground, a small pool forming at her feet. She pulled on the fletching of her arrow and released it. The Blackwing roared in anger as the arrow plunged deep into its ribcage, inches from its heart. The princess loaded two more arrows into her bow, one atop the other. As she released the fletchings, the arrows sunk into the beast's ribcage once more, piercing its black heart.

Brencis disappeared as the Blackwing dropped to the ground, gasping for air as the wound in its side gaped open. It turned slowly, trying to grab at the arrows, but its strength waned. Its head hung to the ground, a deep growl rumbling within its throat. Its legs slipped on the hard stone ground, failing it as they buckled beneath. The Blackwing gasped for air and fought to stay alive. Sintra approached it. She drew her Thalor sword and stood several feet before the Blackwing.

"Any last words, Aleron Elowen, before I end you?" she spat.

The beast growled, moaning and sighing deeply. If this creature hadn't the heart of the madman, she so longed to destroy, the princess would almost feel sorry for the poor helpless beast.

"You have taken all I own, all that is near and dear to me. My mother, Queen Caprice. My sisters, Princess Serillah and Princess Serena. My baby brother, Prince Soren. You took my father, King Alaric, and his men that were dear friends of mine. You slaughtered my people or held them as slaves. The village men you condemned to their death, forcing weapons upon them before exchanging their hearts for that of beasts'. And now…now they lie dead on the fields of Crevark. Once innocent men. Once fathers, and once brothers. Once husbands, and once lovers. Condemned to their death by the seed of Lucifer," spat Sintra.

Another deep growl eluded the beast's throat, rumbling from its stomach and rising to its mouth.

"I know you hear me, and I know you understand every word I say."

She paused, lifting her sword and letting it sit on the beast's neck. It flinched slightly but gave in. Out of breath.

"You will not rise, for you are no King. You're an abomination. You have taken all I love, including my dear Riven who is damned to be a dragon for eternity. You have taken all from me, but you will not take my reign or this realm."

Sintra raised her Thalor sword and with all her strength and energy forced it down upon the Blackwing bull's neck, upon Aleron's neck. The blade sliced through flesh and bone with ease. The head tumbled to the ground, black blood spurting from its gaping wound as its head rolled to a stop at Sintra's feet.

"Crevark will not fall today."

The Blackwing bull was dead.

Aleron Elowen was dead.

The Reign of the Dragon is born

The princess fled from the cold, silent quad of the citadel, rushing out through the Iron Gate as four of Cedric's knights lifted it. The Blackwing retreated to their nest, leaving the sky empty and free of beasts. Thousands of bodies lay strewn across the fields as Sintra stepped onto the grass. Brave knights, guards, and slaves had fallen. Innocent men had fallen. Fathers and brothers had fallen, all to honour her kingdom, to defend Crevark and all the realms. The field was eerily silent, haunted by the death of those who fought in a great battle—a war of darkness. A tear slipped from the princess's eye as she wept for both victory and defeat. Her kingdom still stood, her reign secure, but so many she loved had been sacrificed. She wept silently for those who had fallen in her name, those who had fought to protect her.

Cornelius Thatcher's face appeared in her mind as he took his final breath. Her kind-hearted bookkeeper was no more. The devastation might kill Elara. Queen Fleur Rithe of Pentrone, King Lansing Bronn of Denton, King Donn Courtendaen of Dumbrell, and King Marteez Uman of Glennock had all fallen. Only a small remnant of their men remained.

Thick black smoke filled the air as the remaining soldiers piled the bodies and set them alight to farewell their spirits and souls. A hand rested on Sintra's shoulder as Lord Edith wept beside her.

"The bodies of the enemy are to be piled separately and burned to ash. The bodies of royalty will be burned with the soldiers; they fought as one, they will die as one. They will be honoured," said Sintra through her tears as she entered the field.

Her dragon landed a few metres away. The princess laid a hand on its neck.

"They have fled their nest. The nest is empty. They retreat over the oceans," said the voice within her mind, but it wasn't the familiar, loving voice she longed to hear.

In the midst of all that had happened, Sintra realized she must bid farewell to her Riven, for she could not love him as she wished. His soul might exist within a dragon, but it would never be the same. She turned toward Lord Edith, who busied himself with counting the survivors. She sighed. She was victorious, yet she was so terribly emotionally wounded.

I should be thrilled; she thought to herself. *I should be prancing around in utter joy, for I am victorious. I avenged my family. I avenged the King, and now I am to be Queen— Dragon Queen of Crevark. Yet I find myself miserable.*

"It will pass," said Brencis within her mind.

"Brencis, show yourself."

"I cannot, for I will be slaughtered, my lady. What is done is done. You were granted your love, for he has the metallic heart. And now you may rule alongside him as Queen. Aleron Elowen is no more, and the prophecy has been fulfilled."

"The prophecy was tainted, Brencis. I did not die."

"Aye, you live. But that is all that has changed."

"I beg to differ, for the Blackwing bull was defeated; the flock has fled over the oceans. There are no three dragons here, just one."

"Perhaps it was not Blackwing within the prophecy, Sintra, for I sense three dragons with you."

"Three dragons with me?" she asked, but her thoughts went unanswered as Brencis vanished once again.

The green-scaled beast frustrated her more than anything when he disappeared without notice. The princess wanted to summon him back, but she thought it useless as he would not return. Instead, she turned to Lord Edith.

"What are our numbers?"

"Due to the Speartongue armour and weaponry my men carried; I lost two thousand men. Sidon will be happy to have eight thousand men return. Perhaps we should have approached Queen Aerona of Bristlevale for another dragon sacrifice."

"I doubt she would have given easily, Lord Edith. Do continue."

The knight read aloud from his list of fallen. Reading the names of those that sacrificed their lives in her honour. But as the tally grew, as did her grief.

"Enough," said Sintra, raising a hand. "I've heard enough. It wounds me deeply. I want a wash maid and new clothes. I want to feast and rest. Oh, how I want to rest."

"That can be arranged, my Queen," said Lord Edith softly, taking her by the arm and leading her to her citadel.

†

A low murmur of chatter filled the great hall as crowds of guests entered through the great wooden doors of the citadel. Villagers and slaves mingled among the mass of royalty, knights, and guards. The chatter faded to whispers, then to silence. Upon the throne sat a princess, her lengthy crimson gown trimmed with gold flowing over her delicate body and slippered feet. She shuffled slightly in her seat, wincing as her bandaged legs, concealed by the gown, rested against the cold throne. Her long dark hair flowed past her shoulders, resting softly on her crimson breast. A small, intricate crown sat upon her head, the same crown she had worn since birth. Its dainty floral spear rim gild shimmered in the well-lit citadel, where large candles flickered on chandeliers hanging from the ceiling.

On either side, stretching from the throne to the grand wooden doors, were lines of guests. Among the crowds of royalty stood the remaining free people of Crevark and Thane. The slaves were freed, and the people were granted sufficient food and shelter by the princess. Elara stood to the right of the princess behind the throne, deep in mourning for Cornelius. To the princess's left was Lord Cedric Edith, Steel Knight of Sidon. Addressing the congregation was Priest William Pyst. His speech was long and drawn out, causing some villagers to yawn and sway. He held his hands in the air while speaking prayers, talking to the gods above, summoning their blessing.

Outside in the night, the Thalor dragon peered through the grand entrance of the citadel, listening to the ceremony within the great hall. He lay silent on the cold stone of the quad, resting his head on his giant paws. A few metres from the large, scaled creature were eight silver arrows lying in a pile of ash. The Blackwing bull had been burnt to ash the day before, its head now residing on a stake at the edge of the great wood—a warning to the Blackwing beasts and a trophy of Crevark's victory.

The fields before the citadel were a graveyard, the burnt ashes of kings and queens, guards and knights, left upon the wind that swept through the grass, carrying their spirits far away—the spirits of great warriors. The dragon in the quad raised its head as the priest came to the most vital part of his speech.

"It is with great honour that I present to you the Princess of Crevark, Sintra Lysandra."

Sintra rose from the throne and bowed her head toward Priest William Pyst before addressing the congregation herself.

"On the day before this, a great army went to war. An army that defended this kingdom from a great darkness that threatened to spread over the land. Today, I honour those who fought against the madman's army of darkness, the Blackwing beasts, for Aleron Elowen grew accustomed to dark magic and the misuse of great legends—mythical legends created for the good of mankind.   "Among other things, as the princess and the rightful heir to this throne, I comfort your minds by assuring you that the dragon accompanying me is not to be feared. The Thalor dragon within my quad is here to protect and defend this kingdom," the princess looked toward Queen Kaylah, suspicious of further treachery by her, as her husband was a traitor, "Though he will take orders bestowed upon him by none other than myself."

Queen Kaylah Muucav lowered her head, her facial expression screaming regret. She was embarrassed and saddened by the duplicity of King George as she admired the princess.

"Furthermore, war has proven us victorious. Let us honour those who have fallen, not only for this kingdom but for every realm across the land. We must honour the dead, our fallen soldiers, our fallen warriors, for without them we would not sit comfortably within the walls of this citadel today. As the only living Lysandra of both Thane and now Crevark, I grant you freedom. I grant you peace, and I grant you prosperity. The reign of the dragon is born."

Priest William Pyst stood by the princess and gently removed the crown from atop her head. He laid the delicate floral spear-gilded crown upon a silk cushion that Elara held above her head as she knelt before the princess and the priest. Priest Pyst then turned to Lord Cedric Edith, who held a similar cushion bearing another magnificent crown. This white gold, diamond-studded crown had previously belonged to Queen Caprice when she reigned. It was slightly taller, fit for no princess. Priest William Pyst lifted the delicate ring of white gold off the pillow and stood behind the princess. Sintra stood tall before her congregation with honour.

"In the name of all that is good and just in this land, I, Priest William Pyst of Thane, crown you Queen Sintra Lysandra of Crevark, and of Thane, and Queen of the Thalor Dragon," announced the priest, lowering the crown onto Sintra's head.

The congregation bowed their heads, as did the priest. Knights knelt to the polished floor of the great hall, and the villagers rested their fists upon their chests.

"Hail to the Dragon Queen," said one man, raising his fist into the air.

The congregation repeated the man's cheer without hesitation.

"Hail to the Dragon Queen, Hail to the Dragon Queen, Hail to the Dragon Queen."

A single tear rolled down Sintra's cheek as her kingdom cheered for her, honouring her, loving her. In that moment, she wished her family could see her. She wished so hard that they were among the congregation within the citadel. She felt a flutter in her stomach as a feeling of warmth spread throughout her body, for standing in the entrance of the great hall of the Citadel, were a king and queen she knew all too well.

King Alaric and Queen Caprice Lysandra smiled warmly at their daughter from a hundred metres away. Beside her parents stood her siblings, their warmth radiating in silent harmony. Serillah, Serena, and Soren smiled fondly, a golden beam of sunlight favouring them. Sintra's heart ached, for she knew this vision couldn't be—they were no more.

She smiled lovingly, kissing her hand before raising it towards them. The image began to fade, dissolving into the ethereal mist. The hurt that had once gripped her heart lifted; she knew her family were finally at peace. She had avenged them, reclaimed her kingdom from the clutches of Aleron Elowen, who was no more.

As the last remnants of the vision vanished, she felt a surge of strength. She was no longer just Princess Sintra. She was Queen—Dragon Queen. And she was rising.

"Cedric," she whispered to the knight who stood by her side.

"What is it, my Queen?"

"I feel faint. Take my hand before I collapse," she whispered so that only Lord Edith could hear.

"Do you fall ill, my Queen?"

"No, Lord Edith, I think I'm with child!"

"Oh," he replied, "What ever shall we do?"

Sintra seated slowly on her throne and turned to Cedric, "I must fly to Bristlevale at once."